"An intriguing mystery with an amora[...]
the world of paperback books cou[...] [...] [...]
Ben Aaronovitch

"Andrew Cartmel introduces a new kind of heroine, entirely
immoral, somewhat venal and slightly foxed." David Quantick,
Emmy award-winning producer of *VEEP*

PRAISE FOR THE VINYL DETECTIVE

"A surprising, refreshing story… this novel is a winner…
the series will be a hit." *New York Journal of Books*

"A quirky mystery of violent death and rare records."
The Sunday Times

"One of the most innovative concepts in crime fiction for
many years. Once you are hooked into the world of the Vinyl
Detective it is very difficult to leave." Nev Fountain

"This tale of crime, cats and rock & roll unfolds with an
authentic sense of the music scene then and now – and a
mystery that will keep you guessing." Stephen Gallagher

"Crime fiction as it should be, played loud through a valve amp
and Quad speakers. Witty, charming and filled with exciting
solos. Quite simply: groovy." Guy Adams, critically
acclaimed author of *The Clown Service*

"This charming mystery feels as companionable as a leisurely
afternoon trawling the vintage shops with a good friend."
Kirkus Reviews (Starred review)

"Marvelously inventive and endlessly fascinating."
Publishers Weekly

DEATH *in* FINE CONDITION

The Paperback Sleuth

Also by Andrew Cartmel and available from Titan Books

THE VINYL DETECTIVE
Written in Dead Wax
The Run-Out Groove
Victory Disc
Flip Back
Low Action
Attack and Decay

Sleuth

DEATH in FINE CONDITION

Andrew Cartmel

TITAN BOOKS

The Paperback Sleuth: Death in Fine Condition
Print edition ISBN: 9781789098945
E-book edition ISBN: 9781789098952

Published by Titan Books
A division of Titan Publishing Group Ltd
144 Southwark Street, London SE1 0UP
www.titanbooks.com

First edition: June 2023
10 9 8 7 6 5 4 3 2 1

This is a work of fiction. All of the characters, organisations, and events
portrayed in this novel are either products of the author's imagination
or are used fictitiously. Any resemblance to actual persons, living or
dead (except for satirical purposes), is entirely coincidental.

A CIP catalogue record for this title is available from
the British Library.

Printed and bound by CPI Group (UK) Ltd, Croydon, CR0 4YY

For Ann Karas

"We now anticipated a catastrophe,
and we were not disappointed."

—Edgar Allan Poe, *The Narrative of Arthur Gordon Pym*

PROLOGUE: A PERFECTLY NICE GIRL

He was dead all right.

The man was lying on the floor in front of Cordelia. She stared down at him as the wind screamed through the broken window in the storm-wracked night outside.

He was dead, beyond question.

He was dead and Cordelia was *glad* he was dead.

Also lying on the floor, some distance from the man, a reassuring distance although Cordelia supposed it didn't really matter anymore, since he was now dead, was the gun with which the man had so recently been trying to kill her.

Cordelia was breathing hard in a ragged rhythm and, hardly surprisingly, her eyes stung with tears. What perhaps was surprising was the reason she was crying.

It was the *unfairness*.

The sheer unfairness of it.

Cordelia was a perfectly nice girl—she really didn't think that it was being immodest or overstating the case to say this. She was a perfectly nice girl and it was entirely unfair that she should have ended up in a situation such as this.

It was like something out of the crime stories of James M. Cain, she reflected as she stood there listening to the wind screaming in the night and looking at the dead man lying at her feet and trying hard not to think about where she was, what had just happened, and what she had to do next...

Cain's classic novels—*Double Indemnity*, *The Postman Always Rings Twice*, *Serenade* (there was an edition of this with a particularly fine cover)—all dealt with perfectly nice people who ended up in hellish nightmares, inexorably propelled there by their passions.

And that was what had happened to Cordelia.

Admittedly, her passion was for acquiring rare vintage paperbacks... But nevertheless. Here she was.

As the intensity of the storm grew and the keening of the wind became ceaseless, she looked at the dead man.

She didn't want to get any nearer to him.

She didn't want to touch him.

But she was going to have to.

It really was quite unfair.

1: FORGERY

It had all begun some weeks earlier with Cordelia standing outside her house, thinking, rather tensely, that the first thing she had to do was get back inside unseen.

Cordelia should never have gone out, but she'd needed quite urgently to scoot down into the village to obtain, of all things, a fountain pen.

The local bookshop had turned out to have one in stock. Luckily. The pen was in her hand now, a Lamy 2000, cool and elegant. It hadn't been particularly cheap, but once she'd decided to buy one, Cordelia decided she had to have a good one.

Previously, whenever she'd needed a fountain pen—and she did occasionally need one for her work—she'd always borrowed Edwin's. Naturally, Edwin owned a fountain pen. It was all of a piece with his Rohan corduroy trousers, his bicycle clips and his unseemly addiction to the *Guardian* crossword puzzle.

Cordelia stood outside the house now, some distance away, at the corner.

The challenge was to get back inside without Edwin seeing her. The trouble was, he could be sitting or standing in direct line of sight of at any of the downstairs windows or, much worse, might actually be outdoors.

Cordelia's heart sank at the thought.

Edwin outdoors.

In the garden, or perhaps in the entranceway. He could be pretty much anywhere depending on the time of day and the available light. Working on his beloved bicycle.

Edwin had a special kind of steel frame device for working on his bike.

Of course he did.

The frame looked like a cruelly emaciated robot on which the bicycle could be mounted, the starving robot clutching it, making the bike easier to repair or maintain or pimp, or whatever stupid boring things stupid boring Edwin did with his stupid boring bicycle.

Cordelia eased forward on the pavement. She might be fretting for nothing. She couldn't actually see any sign of Edwin outside the house…

But at this distance and at this angle, Cordelia's view wasn't ideal and there were a number of places where Edwin and his reprehensible bicycle frame could be lurking in concealment.

She couldn't see enough of the front garden. And, to see more, she would need to get nearer and put herself in a position to be reciprocally spotted by the al fresco cycle mechanic. The *hypothetical* al fresco cycle mechanic. Cordelia hesitated. Get nearer and potentially expose her presence to Edwin, or wait?

But wait for what?

And she didn't have much time. Cordelia realised that she was fondling the pen like some kind of talisman. She put it away and checked the time again. If she got into the house now and set to work, everything would be fine. Wait any longer and things would begin to get problematical. Really quite problematical.

Cordelia hesitated. Should she make a dash for it? There was no sign of Rainbottle.

That was promising. There was no way Edwin would be outside except in the company of his dog.

And vice versa.

Rainbottle was a rather agreeable auburn mutt—perhaps in a bid for camouflage, he was approximately the same colour as his master's cherished corduroys (Ash Brown). The dog was certainly much preferable to the owner. But Rainbottle was disposed to lying quietly dormant, out of sight but vigilant, his tail occasionally swatting back and forth while, from concealment, he watched his master tenderly ministering to his cherished velocipede.

The dog worshipping the man, the man worshipping the bicycle.

So just because there was no sign of either of them, there was no guarantee they weren't there.

Shit.

Cordelia needed to make a decision and move. She had to move now.

But if Edwin spotted her—

And then Cordelia saw the cat.

It was next-door's ginger tom, somnolent and surly and much given to taking a dump in Edwin's rose beds. (Clever little cat.) It had just emerged from under the gate of next door, oozing its corpulent form beneath the wrought-iron structure with impressive ease and then making a beeline for Edwin's house and those very rose beds.

Cordelia moved forward with matching swiftness, jubilant, silently thanking the crafty little crapper. There was no way this providential puss would approach their house if Rainbottle was outside.

And if the dog was indoors, then so was Edwin. The two were inseparable, dog virtually invisible against those trousers.

Which just left the windows to worry about. Being spotted from the windows.

Cordelia darted forward, ducking into the concealment of the waist-high whitewashed wall at the front of the house. She was bent down because if she straightened up, she would be clearly visible to any potential Edwin in any downstairs room. But straighten up she must.

Cordelia raised herself with judicial caution to peer over the lip of the low wall.

Edwin wasn't in the front room, so the coast was clear. Cordelia got up and opened the gate, a pale green wooden thing with an art deco sunrise carved into it. The hinges of the gate tended to squeak but Cordelia periodically spritzed them with a fine lubricating oil purloined from Edwin's bicycle maintenance kit, in mind of just such occasions as this.

Congratulating herself on her foresight, she opened and closed the gate silently behind her, moving swiftly and noiselessly across the black-and-white-tiled garden path.

Her key went into the front door, also silently—more far-sighted lubricant spraying of a mechanism with the residue of dead dinosaur—and Cordelia eased it open, slipped inside, and closed it behind her without a sound.

There was no danger of Edwin hearing her footsteps in the front hall thanks to the sound-deadening qualities of the hateful red and yellow ethnic rug that extended like a very long and very diseased tongue from the landing upstairs all the way to the front door, its final unfurling presenting itself lapping at the feet of unwitting visitors. Cordelia stepped inside the red hallway.

Not only was the interior of the hallway painted red, so was the upstairs landing and the staircase itself. Edwin had eccentric ideas about interior design.

Up the stairs she went, moving slowly, despite the urgent need to get into her room and get to work, because there were a number of hazard areas on the ascent, where if you put your foot down, the wooden staircase complained.

Indeed, even the lightest pressure would create a loud, agonising creaking that would inevitably bring Edwin out of his lair at the back of the house, like a lamprey lunging on its prey. A lamprey in Rohan corduroys.

But luckily Cordelia knew these danger spots by heart. So, treading carefully, she moved up to the landing with the loo on it, and then up the remaining section of staircase to where she finally stood now, safely outside the door of her attic room. Cordelia opened the door, went in, and was mildly disgusted with herself to find that she'd broken out in a sweat.

Quite apart from everything else, it was undignified.

Having to hide from one's landlord.

But the fact was, Cordelia was late with this month's rent; and if Edwin pressed her for it, she simply didn't have it. Or rather, she *had* had it, but had spent it on other things. Better things.

She'd been *compelled* to spend it on other, better things.

Compelled by the fact that spending it that way was so much more fun than paying the rent.

But with a bit of luck, funds were about to be topped up. Topped up to such an extent that even Edwin might get paid.

Cordelia took out the fountain pen. It was black and silver and felt heavy and reassuringly well engineered, as it ought to, considering the price, an appreciable fraction of the rent she no longer had.

But Cordelia hoped the pen would soon pay for itself. And more besides.

Some years ago, Cordelia had been amused to discover an esoteric fact from the byzantine world of book dealing. Of course, she always known that any handwriting by a former owner in a book tended to lower the price of that book. So far, so obvious…

And, infuriatingly, it seemed there was always some abhorrent klutz who thought it acceptable to despoil a beautiful first edition with some repugnant personal message that permanently and significantly reduced its value.

Unless it was written in fountain pen.

That's right: if it was written in fusty old fountain pen and not a dreaded modern pen, be it ballpoint or fibre tip, so long as *those* abominations were avoided, then, thanks to some deep-rooted retro snobbery in the rare book trade, it was deemed to be okay.

An inscription in fountain pen was as good as no inscription at all.

Cordelia had had occasion to take advantage of this piece of arcane lore a number of times in the past when she'd come across a rare and valuable paperback, pristine but for the fact that some bastard had written in it. These memoranda were inevitably penned with some unacceptable modern writing implement.

So, Cordelia took a fountain pen—up until now she'd borrowed Edwin's—and painstakingly wrote *over* the price-lowering inscription, rewriting it, lovingly following its contours, saturating the old skeleton of the handwriting, until it looked like it had always been written in fountain pen.

And suddenly, *voila*, the book was back up to its full market value.

Fountain pen in hand, Cordelia moved to the large table where half a dozen neat stacks of paperbacks waited, competing for space with her dining area.

The paperbacks were all stuff she could sell, including some nice items—an immaculate Tom Wolfe Panther with a Philip Castle cover, to name one—but nothing to get particularly excited about.

Except for the Quiller.

Quiller was a monitonic secret agent who had been a rival of James Bond, George Smiley and Len Deighton's nameless operative from the 1960s. Vintage Quiller paperbacks in exemplary condition, which was the kind of condition Cordelia tried to deal exclusively in, would always fetch a few quid. Except for the last novel in the series, which had become dramatically rare.

And was now priced accordingly.

Over the years Cordelia had found a number of copies, often in quite dodgy condition, yet she had always flipped them at a considerable profit. Then just last week she had found one in a charity shop in Chiswick in spectacularly good shape. In top or, as the book trade put it, *fine* condition.

She would easily be able to sell it for fifty times what she'd paid for it.

But… hubris…

That hadn't been quite good enough for Cordelia.

She'd got to thinking how much more she might be able to sell the book for if it had also been signed by the author. Of course, it *hadn't* also been signed by the author. But that had never stopped her before.

So, she had borrowed Edwin's fountain pen. Because Cordelia had also now standardised on using that whenever she was going to create the one kind of handwriting in a book that could be guaranteed *not* to lower its value. Quite the opposite…

Which was to say, an inscription by a famous person.

Or more simply, the signature of the author.

Many was the time Cordelia had counterfeited an author's signature using a good old fountain pen. Edwin's good old fountain pen.

And so, when she got the Quiller book, it was inevitable she would jack the price up by making it another putatively signed copy. So, with Edwin's pen she had set to work painstakingly, sitting in the good daylight of the bay window seat that was her favourite thing about her attic room and, in brutal truth, its only redeeming feature.

Cordelia had been very proud of the job she'd done that day.

But the ink had hardly been dry when she'd gone back online to gloat over her accomplished penmanship and confirm what a splendid forgery she'd achieved…

And indeed her work *had* been perfect. The signature was utterly convincing. But while establishing this gratifying fact, she also made a horrible discovery.

The book she had just signed had been published *posthumously*. Oh fuck.

She'd just signed the author's name in a book that was printed some fair while after the author had departed this world.

Oh fuck.

Instead of meticulously increasing the value of her acquisition, she'd just saddled it with the most obvious of forgeries.

Now, if she went ahead and sold the damned thing, it could start people wondering about all the other rare, signed paperbacks she'd flogged. People might start thinking she was a shameless and systematic counterfeiter, underhanded upgrader and an all-around sharp operator.

All of which, of course, she was.

And if her reputation went south, so would the price Cordelia could command for the books she sold.

There was only one thing for it.

Turn the signature into an inscription.

And to do that seamlessly and convincingly required a fountain pen. She couldn't borrow Edwin's because with his landlord hat on, so to speak, he would be eager to talk to her about the small matter of her outstanding rent. Or not so small matter. Certainly not so small in Edwin's mind. What passed for his mind. Hence the Lamy.

Cordelia confirmed what she knew—that the colour of the ink in her new pen precisely matched Edwin's—and proceeded to write inside the book.

A few seconds later, what had been a lone, bogus signature—
Adam Hall—had become part of a respectful inscription. *The last
novel by the great Adam Hall*. Cordelia added the dates of the
author's life, inspected it, and set it aside, satisfied. What had once
been a blatant forgery was now a rather touching memorial. In
fountain pen.

And the book was saleable.

Again.

Thank fuck. Thank goodness. Thank fucking goodness.

2: BOOK HUNTING TERMS

It was considerably easier sneaking out of the house than sneaking in, because Cordelia had been able to formulate a pretty good idea of Edwin's whereabouts, having stood on the landing listening carefully for some five minutes.

She'd thereby established that her landlord was in his little sitting room at the back of the house. She'd concluded this from the occasional sound of movement—up from the armchair and across to the biscuit tin on the sideboard; Edwin deliberately kept this on the other side of the room to enforce a kind of rationing on himself—and back to the armchair again, biscuit craving temporarily abated.

Edwin was thus occupied, safely ensconced there in his bijou sitting room with Rainbottle, probably most of the time with his feet in his sensible woolly socks comfortably propped up on the back of the dog reading the cookery section of the *Observer*. Edwin, not the dog. If past form was anything to go by.

And anyway, even if he *did* hear Cordelia, so long as she moved briskly he wouldn't be able to get to the front door in time to engage her in any form of conversation; in particular, in any form of conversation that would lead them by a very circuitous route but with a maddening inevitability, like a labyrinth in a Borges story, towards the destination of having a discussion about her being late with the rent. Really quite late.

But Edwin didn't hear her, and Cordelia was out the door, down the steps and into the street.

Outside in the crisp fresh air and the autumnal chill, she paused to look back at the house.

Astonishingly, she had lived here for three years now, pretty much ever since she'd left university, with the degree in English literature which her mother had rather unkindly characterised as "About as much use as tits on a pterodactyl."

(As a leading palaeontologist and a recognised authority on the neurobiology of the reptile–avian transition, her mother was in a position to know.)

Cordelia's mother, and her passive, shiftless and ever-acquiescent father, had struck a deal with Cordelia whereby they'd pay off her student loan if she agreed to move out of the family home. And, it was strongly implied, never come back. This was just fine with Cordelia. She had then gone through a sequence of varyingly seedy flat shares before she'd had the good luck and good judgement to secure Edwin's attic.

It hadn't been easy finding a room to rent which could safely accommodate her collection.

Her beloved paperbacks.

It had been while at university that the paperback bug had bitten Cordelia. During one spring break she had gone to Amsterdam for the obvious reason but discovered to her astonishment that it had more to offer than dope cafés. And she didn't mean the picturesque canals or flower markets or brothels.

It transpired that Amsterdam was probably the world centre, certainly the European centre, for the vintage paperback trade. Cordelia had accidentally wandered into a street market where there was a stall selling what she would later realise to have been a really first-rate selection of rare and desirable items. The lurid covers had immediately attracted her, with their exotic aura of a lost and distant era that was at once more innocent and more depraved than her own.

The one that really did it for Cordelia was the Bantam edition of Hal Elson's *Tomboy* with the James Bama cover. She had always been a devotee of crime fiction, and this was a key text in the "JD" or "juvie" (juvenile delinquent) crime subgenre of the 1950s, which found its apotheosis, or its nadir if you were Cordelia, in *West Side Story*.

Hal Elson, who turned out *not* to be a pseudonym for Harlan Ellison, later to become another paperback favourite of Cordelia's, could tell a strong story.

But it was the cover art that hooked her…

A teenage tramp with dirty blonde hair very like Cordelia's was leaning against a wall with a cigarette negligently held in one hand, her entire posture a sexual challenge, leather jacket falling open to reveal the aggressive jut of her *belle poitrine* in a clinging brown sweater. Also on show were a pair of tight, rolled-up blue jeans displaying the artist's incredible mastery of the depiction of fabric texture. The masterstrokes, though, were the dirty sneakers on the girl's bare, sockless feet and the sardonic, knowing defiance on her feral babyface.

This little paperback book was absurdly expensive and not in perfect nick (she had subsequently long since upgraded to a treasured copy in fine condition), but Cordelia *had* to have it. She'd spent all the remaining money she had earmarked for binging in the hash cafés on buying *Tomboy* and then picking up from the same stall, for a modest additional increment, *The Book of Paperbacks*, a crucial reference work featuring some amazing colour reproductions of classic covers, written by Piet Schreuders, a local lad.

And once she started dipping into Schreuders's book, that had been that.

Cordelia had found her calling.

Now she hurried happily along, her jaunty newish red rucksack bouncing on her shoulder. A cool clean breeze flowed in from the direction of the river and the rucksack patted Cordelia on the back as she walked.

It was a light pat because it was mostly empty, the rucksack, since she was planning to shortly fill it with books. With a lavish find of rare paperbacks.

Corresponding to the happy patting on the outside, Cordelia felt a happy pulsing inside that was the pleasurable anticipatory excitement she always experienced when she was on her way to a book sale.

This one started in a few minutes and was at the local church, St Drogo's. It was to be a grand sale of old paperbacks with the proceeds going to repairing and maintaining St Drogo's early-twentieth-century Bauhaus roof, the perpendicular purity of which was said to evoke Gropius, but which was also acknowledged to let the rain in, and leak a lot. Really quite a lot.

Cordelia didn't give a shit about the church's early-twentieth-century Bauhaus roof, or indeed the entire school of Gropius. What she *was* interested in was the healthy torrent of books donated by the local churchgoing community, many of which would be of exactly the vintage, and hopefully the genre, in which she was most interested.

In other words, lurid crime paperbacks of the 1950s and '60s.

The more lurid the better. Visions danced in her mind. Immaculate copies of green-spined Corgis with John Richards covers, Carter Browns with Robert McGinnis art, preferably the original Signets, but some of the international editions were nice, too. Or, most especially, some British Sleuth Hound titles, with their fabulous Abe Prossont covers.

Cordelia was by now frankly addicted to collecting these, and their ilk.

But like many an addict-turned-dealer, she had found a way to support her habit. And, indeed, turn a profit. Which was how she came to make a living—of sorts—hustling vintage paperbacks.

Which was why she was now hotfooting it through Barnes towards the white and green blocks of that miniature Bauhaus masterpiece of ecclesiastical architecture, St Drogo's—those flat roofs really did let in the rain, though, and repairs weren't cheap. Someone—Cordelia's face twitched into a smile as she hurried along—*someone* had suggested that one way of raising funds for the church roof would be by holding a sale of *paperbacks*.

As Cordelia crossed the road by the Sun Inn, a sleek silver car, spilling sunlight, came swooping towards her, moving fast, from the direction of the rather complex traffic junction by the duck pond.

Cordelia was compelled to jump back out of the road, onto the pavement, out of the path of the vehicle.

True, she hadn't been looking where she was going, and she'd been in a considerable, some might say reckless, hurry. But, nevertheless, she turned to the car, looking to make eye contact with the driver and give him a good thorough cussing.

And she saw that the driver wasn't a him, but rather a her.

And not just any her. *Her*. The Woman.

Eye contact had been made and it was like someone had thrown the switch on the electric chair. But in a good way. An electrifyingly good way. At least, that's how it was for Cordelia…

With the Woman looking out at her from the silver car, window buzzed down, an expression of sincere concern and contrition on her face. Her face, her face.

Her lovely face.

The deep copper tone of her skin contrasted so wonderfully with the silver fuselage of the car that it took Cordelia's breath away.

"I'm so sorry," said the Woman. "I was going too fast. It was entirely my fault."

Cordelia stared at her, still rendered breathless, still unable to formulate a single syllable. And then, with a wrench of desperation, she recovered the power of speech. And uttered this deathless soliloquy: "That's okay. No problem!"

"Sorry," said the Woman again. And she smiled again. And then she drove off.

Cordelia stared after her, cursing herself.

That's okay. No problem!

How brilliant. How witty. And the rising, emphatic, cheery inflection on "no problem"…

What magnificent words for her to have used to sanctify the occasion. This sacred occasion – sacred wasn't too strong a word. It was the first time the Woman had ever spoken to her. The first time she'd spoken to the Woman.

Cordelia had always regarded herself as pretty damned good looking. But whenever she was in the vicinity of the Woman, she felt herself disclosed as a snaggle-toothed, wall-eyed frump. Probably with flies circling her. A stupid shallow grinning white girl with dishwater blonde hair which she hadn't even bothered to brush this morning.

The Woman, in contrast, loomed in Cordelia's mind as composure personified.

The Woman had been cool and beautiful and kind and amused and penitent. Of course she had.

And she had smiled, smiled, smiled that *smile*…

Cordelia stared after her. The Woman had completely vanished now, but Cordelia gazed in the direction the car had gone, the shiny silver car. Hoping that it might do a U-turn and come back. She tried to make this happen, to bring the situation about by sheer willpower. She tried to visualise the car coming back. They did say visualisation worked, didn't they?

Hurrying footsteps behind her on the pavement brought Cordelia back, at least partially, from this reverie. Someone was approaching her, gaining fast, then was beside her, then was abruptly brushing past her in a negligently rude and brusque fashion. Cordelia only glimpsed this person out of the corner of her eye as he shouldered her to one side, but an all-too-familiar aroma of body odour intruding on her nostrils was more than enough to convey his identity.

The Mole.

Well, there was a book sale, so of course the Mole was here.

Unlike Cordelia, the Mole didn't specialise. Whereas Cordelia was obsessed (not too strong a word) with paperbacks, the Mole was obsessed (not too strong a word) with books in general. Large lavishly illustrated glossy hardcovers about the history of steam engines were as likely to go into his rucksack as—may he never find them, or at least never find them before Cordelia—vintage Boardman Bloodhound crime paperbacks with Denis McLoughlin covers.

The Mole knew what had value, and if he found such before Cordelia, he would scoop it up.

Cordelia watched the Mole's stocky, bent back hurrying away, garbed in his traditional Mole garb of waxed cotton jacket and jeans.

Cordelia had known the Mole, or known of him, for as long as she'd been collecting books, which was as pretty much as long as she could remember.

Whenever she turned up at a jumble sale or boot fair or, as in this case, a church sale, there he would be hurrying to get in first, the

Mole. Obsessively searching through the books and snapping up bargains, greedily gobbling up the best titles and, as Cordelia later learned, reselling them at a smart, sometimes eyewatering, profit.

In short, a rival.

The thought of this rivalry brought Cordelia the rest of the way out of her fantasy of the Woman in the car.

The accursed Mole.

Cordelia scooted.

She hurried across the road, once again not bothering to look out for approaching cars. Once again displaying the sort of flagrant disregard for traffic safety that had already almost got her run over by the Woman.

Wait.

Of course.

Of course, she realised, *that was why the Woman was here*.

The book sale.

She had come in search of vintage paperbacks, too.

And if she'd found somewhere to park her sleek silver car close to St Drogo's, then the Woman was probably already at the front of the queue that had now begun to form. Whereas Cordelia, despite arriving on the scene well before the sale was officially due to start, nevertheless found herself near the back of that queue. She couldn't believe it…

Cordelia was still a long way from the church and yet there was already this line of people stretching in front of her, people in their droves, ready, eager and willing to buy books. Many of them people who could probably actually read. And all of them obviously loving the prospect of a bargain.

The riverside suburb where Cordelia lived was inhabited by some of the richest people in London, and indeed featured a sprinkling of some of the richest in the world. Yet a myriad of these locals had turned out on this bonny autumn afternoon in search of cheap books.

But then it had always been Cordelia's observation that no bastard likes a bargain better than a rich bastard.

It proved to be a long slow wait in the queue—in actuality it was less than five minutes, but it felt like an eternity, and indeed in book hunting terms it might as well have been. Because by the time Cordelia got inside, it was all over.

3: SAINTED NOT STAINED

The entire floorspace of the communal central area of the church of St Drogo's was given over to the book sale—ranks of paperbacks conveniently arrayed spine-up in shallow crates for easy perusal (at least, by the literate), on long trestle tables.

This big space packed with tables, all covered with books, was pretty much Cordelia's idea of heaven. So a church was certainly an appropriate setting.

Or at least it *would* have been her idea of heaven if it wasn't already writhing with a crowd of bibliophile bargain hunters who had arrived before her.

All presided over by an enormous stained-glass window occupying virtually an entire wall of the central atrium of this Bauhaus masterpiece, a rectangular shaft rising fully three floors through the hollow heart of the building, all the way to its famously problematical roof.

But by the time Cordelia had got in here, with that big window looming balefully over her, all the good stuff had gone.

Cordelia was too late, or rather not early enough, and consequently she was getting a look at the way a book sale would appear to your average punter, the customers who never knew what treasures, what bargains, what bargain-priced treasures, surfaced at such events.

Because such gems are all always snapped up in a few crucial seconds after the doors were opened.

And Cordelia hadn't been here for those few crucial seconds.

As a result, she was now getting what you might call the civilian's view of a book sale. A very average and lukewarm book sale indeed, except for the austere industrial elegance of the surrounding architectural detail and the big stained-glass window featuring imagery which reared upwards in angular, modernist graphic design decisions above them.

This window was indeed a sight. Cordelia found it at once as dreary as a long afternoon at school and strangely compelling in a nutty, idiosyncratic sort of way.

She looked away from the window and briefly watched the Mole snapping up science fiction paperbacks with fingers that seemed driven by steel springs. Even at this distance Cordelia could see that it was dross—all gaming titles—but from the way he was grabbing it he must have a definite buyer in mind for this stuff. Then, as soon as all of these had been gobbled up, he moved on to something else. Cookery and food books.

Again, the Mole started expertly searching through the titles and immediately adding any valuable item to his growing pile. He grabbed a vintage Len Deighton volume of cartoon cookery strips in a long horizontal-format Penguin edition from the 1960s that Cordelia would have happily had herself if she'd got there first.

Cordelia's eyes drifted in disgust from the Mole and back to the stained-glass window looming above him. This naturally featured the eponymous St Drogo, a nondescript fellow if ever there was one. But the possessor of radiant beauty in comparison to the array of grotesque faces that surrounded him in a baleful, gurning halo of floating heads.

Cordelia wasn't sure if this was because the stained-glass artist simply hadn't been very good at doing faces, or whether they were deliberately, intentionally ugly, or if, third possibility, they were supposed to be "primitive" in a stylised way like Picasso drawings having both eyes on one side of their face. In the manner of one Peppa Pig.

The other thing that set this stained-glass window apart from other, perhaps all other, stained-glass windows was that it consisted of grey stained glass. Yes, shades of grey.

What a bold idea – to do stained glass without the colours! It gave Cordelia a chuckle every time she thought about it.

All right, there *was* some colour, the odd austere hint of frosted green, but none of the radiant richness of hue that one associated with a stained-glass window. Or as Cordelia liked to think of it, in this case, a *sainted* glass window. Since it wasn't really stained—in the usual sense of bright colours—but at least it featured a saint.

Cordelia paused for a moment under this majestic explosion of restrained expressionism, a still figure among the hurrying, jostling throng. She decided there was no point plunging into the acquisition of paperbacks among this throng since there were none here to acquire; anyway, none *worth* acquiring.

Thus she concluded as she stood beneath the window, the autumn afternoon sunlight shining through it. Shining on her weakly through its minty-green glass, milky-white glass, a myriad of grey tones of glass, and an intense gleaming black for the pupils of the smiling saint's eyes that had the cast of obsidian—volcanic glass.

Sainted but not *stained*, she thought, pleased at her own wit, and that was when she saw the Woman and her heart leapt in her chest like a fish in a net.

Cordelia's heart, that is.

The Woman's heart was unlikely to be leaping with excitement for all sorts of reasons. Primarily because she seemed to have had a dull old time of it and was already in what Cordelia recognised as the closing stages of her paperback hunting adventure.

The Woman stood there in her skin-tight indigo jeans, into which was so loosely tucked a silk shirt in an exotic turmeric shade of orange. The Woman's skin was a subtle and spellbinding shade darker and richer than the colour of the silk, her lovely sleek shaven head gleaming as she bent over the books, giving them a swift roving final inspection.

To Cordelia, the Woman had the look of a connoisseur who had already combed through what was on offer, had found it wanting, but was nevertheless giving the stuff a valedictory once-over before leaving. And the way she was going through the books was entirely admirable. It gave Cordelia a thrill, both personal and professional, to see her thus winnowing these crates of paperbacks.

Only properly small-format pocket-sized books—known in the trade as "mass market paperbacks"—even received consideration from the Woman, and when she paused to select a title, it was always something exemplary. The Woman's choices kicked ass.

From having seen her in action in the past at other book sales, Cordelia knew that these choices included, but were by no means limited to, Coronet bullet-hole Richard Starks, original Raymond Hawkey-designed Pan James Bonds, and the cream of golden age crime—especially early green-and-white Penguins, the ones with the slightly off-looking, corrupt-looking, depraved-looking penguin depicted in silhouette on them. Preferably with the dust jackets.

Naturally the Woman disdained all detestable modern oversized trade paperbacks.

What a magnificent human being she was…

As Cordelia watched her, the Woman suddenly froze, then picked up a book in surprise. She looked at it for a long moment, a thoughtful frown on her sweet face. Finally, the frown faded and she put the book down again crisply and with great finality, as if it was radioactive or otherwise insufferably contaminated, and moved on.

Moving on entailed moving towards Cordelia, who quickly looked away, pretending to be closely examining the books in front of her. This would have been a waste of time if ever there was one. Because the books in front of her were all contemporary crime fiction of the shadowy-figure-in-a-bleak-urban-setting school of photographic cover art. Admittedly enriched by a sprinkling of the shadowy-figure-in-a-bleak-*rural*-setting school of photographic cover art. If you could call it art. Which, let's be frank, you couldn't.

It was junk.

Where were the books with covers consisting of bold silhouetted hand-drawn images against primary colours? Black on red, say, with a hint of yellow…

While Cordelia was pretending to look through the junk, the Woman had found one of the church volunteers who staffed the tables and was now paying for her books. The church volunteer took her money and offered change, which the Woman declined with a gracious, gorgeous smile as she departed with her purchases. Her negligible and not particularly interesting purchases.

As the Woman left the room, so did the light, fading through the stained glass as a cloud passed over the sun outside and a corresponding cloud passed over Cordelia's heart inside. Deep inside. She stared after the Woman…

"You're too late," someone said. "All the good stuff is gone."

Cordelia looked around. The Mole was standing beside her, looking at the feverish book-buying activity all around them.

He was incontestably right. Nevertheless, Cordelia was inclined to contradict him. Just on principle. She looked for some evidence to refute what he had just said. To refute the irrefutable. But all the good stuff *was* gone.

They were standing in front of the crime section—a gratifyingly large section—but Cordelia could see that there was, for example, nothing left of Agatha Christie but post-Fontana editions, the cover art of which represented a variety of aberrations. That was about the level of it. Unable to refute the Mole, Cordelia ignored him instead and went in search of the book that seemed to have to sparked such a reaction of fearful repugnance from the Woman.

It was at the far edge of the crime section and was something called *Cold Angel, Dead Angel*. Judging not least by its author's stoutly Nordic name, it was a slab of Scandi-noir. And one wrapped in a very poorly designed cover, mostly given over to that Nordic name and featuring the slogan: *Another terrifying adventure for Penumbra Snow*. For whom? On the back cover it declared, *Miss Snow is hot*. Miss Penumbra Snow—Jesus, what a name—was evidently the heroine of the novel.

It looked to Cordelia like a piece of self-published junk. So she set it aside again, quickly, feeling faintly tainted. She could easily understand why the Woman had put it down with such alacrity. But why had she picked it up in the first place? That was the question.

"That thing's turning up everywhere," said the Mole, in turn looking at the book and dismissing it even more quickly than Cordelia or the Woman had. Nothing of monetary value here, the Mole's tingling—or in this case *not* tingling—book-sense evidently told him.

Cordelia glanced towards the door, leading to the church vestibule and exit, through which the Woman had just disappeared. From Cordelia's life. Perhaps forever. She sighed inwardly and turned away from Mole.

"Are you off now, then?" he said, in the querulous tone of someone nerving himself up in a desperate attempt to prolong a conversation.

"I have an appointment. Business, things to do, people to meet…"

"But that's not for…" said the Mole glancing at his wristwatch. Yes, he sported a wristwatch. A pink Powerpuff Girls Swatch, worn apparently quite without irony.

"*What?*" said Cordelia.

"Nothing, nothing, nothing," said the Mole quickly, realising the magnitude of his error and also putting his arm behind his back to hide the wristwatch, as if that would help anything.

"You were about to say, 'But that's not for another half an hour'," said Cordelia, turning to face the Mole.

It was true, she was running about half an hour early for her appointment with the buyer for the book in her rucksack. But Cordelia liked to arrive early for such business meetings, especially when she had contrived to convene them at Sadie's, her favourite local restaurant-cum-café-cum-delicatessen. By arriving early, she could ransack the cum-delicatessen part for some tasty high-end treats—cave-aged cheddar and Poilane sourdough, for instance, all easily consumed later in her attic room and therefore not requiring a visit to the communal kitchen of her house, where she would be compelled to commune with the dread Edwin.

Such treats would cost a fair sum of money. Money which she didn't have yet, true, but she soon would have.

When she sold the Quiller book to the buyer who'd contacted her online...

The buyer who had contacted her online.

Cordelia stared at the Mole. He flinched under her unsparing gaze. "You're Bibliophile 88 aren't you?"

"Er, me?" said the Mole. "Um…"

"You are, you bastard."

"Um…"

"And you want to buy *this*," said Cordelia, unslinging her natty little red rucksack, delving into it, and taking out the recently amended copy of *Quiller Balalaika*. "You arranged anonymously online to buy it and asked me to meet you today to hand over the money. So—hand over the money."

As soon as the book had appeared, the Mole had ceased to prevaricate or be tongue-tied. Instead, he'd snapped into his full coldblooded book-selling sociopath mode. Or in this case, book-*buying* sociopath. Which meant a careful inspection was in order, before any money might change hands.

"Not bad," said the Mole coolly, giving as little reaction as a professional poker player while he inspected the cover.

"Not bad?" said Cordelia. "It's damned nearly perfect."

Now the Mole looked up at Cordelia, the cover of the book reflected as twins in the dense lenses of his glasses, professional suspicion colouring his question. "Then why are you selling it?

"Because I've just upgraded my personal copy, hence I've put my now second-best *old* personal copy on the market. Luckily for you," said Cordelia. "A unique chance to acquire at an advantageous price a vanishingly scarce copy of this rare and valuable title in fine condition." Then, subsequent to this boilerplate, adding with just a hint of threat, "Assuming I do decide to sell it to you."

"Why wouldn't you?" said the Mole.

"Because you approached me creepily pretending to be somebody else."

"I didn't pretend to be somebody else, I *am* Bibliophile 88," said the Mole. Then he became once more absorbed in his examination of the book.

Despite being a tiresome generalist, the Mole knew enough about paperbacks to handle this one with proper respect and care. Having thoroughly inspected the cover and satisfied himself that the spine didn't have a crack or a lean or a roll—the latter inspection involved the Mole holding the spine of the book up to his eye and sighting along it as though along the barrel of a gun—he opened the cover, also doing due diligence, which meant opening it very gently so as not to pull the cover stock away from the paper block at the hinges.

Crucially, when he opened the book itself and began to turn the pages, he did so again gently and with great care so as not to commit the cardinal sin of breaking that pristine, unbroken spine. On older paperbacks the glue that joined the paper block to the cover would grow quite brittle and could quite easily cause all sorts of problems if handled at all roughly. As it happened, the Quiller book was of a rather more recent vintage, but the Mole still handled it judiciously.

"There's some writing inside," said the Mole, like a prosecutor presenting a damning morsel of fact during a cross examination.

"That's why I'm letting go of it. And that's why I said 'nearly perfect' instead of 'perfect'."

Cordelia could see the Mole nerving himself up to try to beat her down on the price of the book. But in the end his desire to swindle her was overwhelmed by his desire to impress her with his erudition.

"Luckily for you it's been written with a fountain pen," he Mole-splained. "If the writing in a book is in *fountain* pen, you see…"

"Just get on with it," said Cordelia.

The Mole obediently fell silent and riffled through the pages of the book—riffling with care and hardly opening it, to protect that pristine spine. Cordelia knew what he was doing. He was checking the page numbering. But the Quiller was all there. As Cordelia had established before she'd shelled out a few quid on it in Hamster Rescue or whatever the name was of that charity shop in Chiswick.

The Mole inspected the back cover again. Or pretended to. He had run out of things to check but was still, for Mole-like reasons of his own, seeking to prolong the moment.

"The money," said Cordelia.

"Money?" Looking up at her now, the Mole's glasses reflected the grey-green panorama of good old St Drogo and friends.

"Pay me."

"How much did you want again?" As if he had forgotten. Cordelia repeated the price and the Mole began some preliminary price-reduction tooth sucking, but when Cordelia reached to take the book back from him he snatched it away and with his free hand took out a wad of cash—Cordelia was somewhat disappointed to see he didn't have it secured in a Powerpuff Girls money clip—and paid her the asking amount.

She put the money away and turned to go. Immediately the Mole's voice rose behind her. "We could still…" he said.

"Still?"

"Still go for a coffee."

"But I don't need to meet you for a coffee to hand the book over and get paid. Because I just handed the book over and got paid."

"I thought we could just… have coffee," said the Mole. "I thought we could still have a coffee."

Reflecting on all the times the Mole had ruthlessly shoved her aside to grab a rare paperback for himself, Cordelia said, "Sorry. Things to do. Bye."

She left him staring down at the Quiller, and then secreting it in his rucksack before returning to the books on the table in front of him. Back to business for the Mole.

And for Cordelia, too.

When she was sure that no one was looking, she moved to the wall of the hall opposite the big stained-glass window and opened an interior door that was for church staff only and was strictly forbidden to the public.

But then Cordelia had never thought of herself as a member of the public.

4: A CRATE OF CRIME

Cordelia clicked open the door and quickly slipped through it.

Shutting it behind her abruptly sealed off the hustle and bustle of the church hall as the door latched into place with another, reassuringly solid, click—the roof here might not be much cop, but whatever disciple of Corbusier had fashioned this edifice had at least known how to craft a good sturdy door. Cordelia let herself relax for a moment.

Seeing the Woman had quite thrown her. It had thrown her off her stride.

And on top of that, the revelation that her client for the Quiller book had turned out to be the Mole. Naturally that had thrown her a little further off her stride.

But business was business and Cordelia was here to get on with business.

She moved quickly and silently down the narrow corridor. The potentially claustrophobically narrow, yet stylish, art deco corridor. The matching long narrow white rug underfoot (it was called a runner) was a kind of oatmeal-coloured linen affair intermittently and discreetly figured with little grey crosses, presumably as a reminder to those walking on it that they were in a church—in case they were likely to forget—but it absorbed the sound of her footsteps in a reassuring way.

Cordelia would prefer that no one knew she was here. Backstage, so to speak.

While this building possessed areas and spaces that were notionally vestries, vestibules, offices, chancel, chapel, choir, nave, sacristy, stalls, transept and pulpit—all the usual boring church paraphernalia —here at St Drogo's they shared a distinctive sleek, uniform industrial look.

The colour scheme, as with the stained-glass window, was an austere pallet of white and grey with just a little green and a judicious use of black for highlights. So, sealed in here, under artificial light from pearly lozenge-shaped sconces in the ceiling, away from the church's main hall, the interior looked very like the compartments and corridors and staterooms plus tiny crew quarters lurking under the decks of a sober but elegant art deco ocean liner gliding out on the vast ocean of religion (of the 1920s, when it was built). Which, of course, was also the ocean of money if you wanted to get into it. (Then and now.)

St Drogo's had cost a pretty penny to build a hundred years ago when the Bloomsbury Set had applauded its uncompromising aesthetic purity and monochrome modernism, and now that they were all unfashionably dead it was still costing a pretty penny just to maintain.

"Maintain" being a euphemism for "stop the whole place falling down". Hence the almost stroboscopic reconstitution and revival of the various church roof committees with their many and varied fundraising strategies.

Well, if the frenzy of spending she just had left behind was anything to go by, the latest church roof committee had done all right with the book sale. Or rather, they had done all right with *her* book sale. But Cordelia's bitter chagrin at having arrived too late to effectively join the bibliophile commotion began to drain away as she padded down this art deco ocean liner corridor, on her clandestine errand.

She arrived at the vestry. A vestry is simply a room in a church used for storage. So, in non-ecclesiastical parlance, a storeroom.

A storeroom where her partner in crime was waiting for her.

Monika—with a 'k', as she very insisted on reminding everyone—was a volunteer at the church. All too often there was a powerful smell of booze wafting from her bulky figure. But fortunately not today.

Today Monika Dunkley—that had a 'k', too—was mercifully free of any such aroma. Although she did smell, oddly enough, of fear.

"What's wrong, Monika?" said Cordelia as she opened the vestry door, another good solid one, breathed the smell, and saw the sudden look of hunted-animal fear in Monika's eyes that was quickly replaced by relief as she recognised that it was just Cordelia standing looking in at her.

"Where have you been?" croaked Monika. "I've been waiting here for *ages*." She cleared her throat to shake off the croakiness. "What if someone came along?"

Cordelia shrugged. "So what? So what if someone came along? So what if they found you storing stuff in a storeroom? Storing church stuff in a church storeroom?"

"It's not the church's stuff anymore," said Monika succinctly, scoring a point for once and reinforcing the fact that this was one of the rare occasions when she might actually be sober.

"No," said Cordelia. "It's not the church's stuff anymore. It's mine. And here is my contribution to the church funds." She reached into the front pocket of her jeans—she had read somewhere that this was the most difficult pocket for a pickpocket to pick—and took out the wad of cash that the Mole had given her.

Monika stared at the money. Monika always needed cash. She didn't seem to have a job or any normal means of support. She was a sort of live-in companion and carer for a woman who owned one of those big flats by Hammersmith Bridge. Those amazing big flats. They cost a pretty penny, a very pretty penny, a stunningly beautiful penny, so to speak, those flats.

So the woman must be loaded.

Anyway, this loaded woman was apparently an invalid and she and Monika were old friends who had gone to school together, or been in a band together, or perhaps both, or something—clarity was not Monika's strong point.

And the invalid woman apparently maintained a strenuous effort to curtail Monika's drinking. This manifested itself in a policy of not giving Monika any cash.

Monika was a big woman, broad shouldered and stocky, with a bland, rather surprised-looking face under an impressively sculpted and tinted red mohawk haircut. Maybe that face was surprised by the haircut above it; it was certainly entitled to be. She was wearing a red-and-black tartan shirt and black jeans and a black leather biker jacket, although Cordelia was willing to wager a considerable sum that it was a quote-unquote "leather" jacket, i.e. plastic. The red badges studding the plastic jacket's lapel matched Monika's wacko hairdo and, come to think of it, key elements of Cordelia's own ensemble.

But Monika was not aware of that. Monika was not aware of much at all. At the moment, her entire attention was focused on the banknotes in Cordelia's hand. It looked like a lot of money, but it was negligible compared to what Cordelia would get for the contents of the blue plastic crate on the table.

Cordelia gave her the money. The deal was the Monika would donate half of it anonymously to the church, which would more than compensate them for any revenue lost by not selling these books in the book sale.

Whether Monika would actually do this was an interesting question. But just as Monika had been hypnotised by the cash,

Cordelia was hypnotised by the books, her entire attention now focused with—terrible cliché, but there you go—laser-like intensity on the crate of books on the table.

They were all crime fiction, these, all mass market paperbacks, all vintage, with painted cover art—not a single photograph of a shadowy figure in a bleak setting among them.

They were mostly British publications, but there was also a healthy helping of American editions that must have come from the collection of an expat, because they didn't have the specially printed price stickers that were the telltale sign of import copies brought over by a UK publisher for sale on this side of the Atlantic, and which could be painstakingly removed—the stickers—by patient and judicious application of the right kind of solvent.

(Using the wrong kind of solvent would also remove the cover art underneath the sticker, as Cordelia knew all too well. Oh well, live and learn…)

Among the American titles were a handful of John D. MacDonald novels that weren't published by Gold Medal—a rare thing. These were Dell First Editions—that was what it said on the cover—in a slightly smaller format than normal, pocket books for a smaller pocket, with blue-stained page edges and cover art by the likes of Mitchell Hooks.

There were also some earlier Dells, the fabled map-backs which featured a carefully drawn map of the scene of the crime in the story. What a great idea. Why didn't all murder mysteries come equipped with such a cartographical flourish?

There were also some of those Philip MacDonald Avon editions from the 1970s with eye-catching Magritte-like covers.

But the bulk of the bibliophile booty were British books. Fontana Agatha Christies with magnificent Tom Adams art, early editions with the variously coloured and illustrated, rather than plain white, back covers. Also Pan titles from the 1950s with the 'Great

Pan' designation, including a number of very rare titles written by the genuinely great Charles Williams, notably a copy of *Operator* with the hottie in slacks on the front.

And there were, joy of joys, over a dozen Sleuth Hound titles, all specimens with Abe Prossont cover art, lurid yet lyrical, displaying Prossont's amazing design sense and inventive hand lettering.

All in immaculate condition.

It was a tremendous treasure trove.

Cordelia knew all this already, before she even inspected the crate. Indeed, she only inspected it for purposes of confirmation. And gloating. Gloating at some length.

She knew the contents of the crate intimately. Indeed she'd been dreaming of it, literally dreaming, in considerable detail, for days now.

But now it was here in front of her. It was real and it was here, all here.

As the person who'd suggested the church book sale, and something of an expert on the subject of paperbacks, particularly paperbacks of this genre, Cordelia had been more than qualified to help sort the books, to triage the gratifyingly large assemblage of crime fiction the church had received in the form of donations from local folk.

But all the while, Cordelia had been carefully skimming off the best books into a separate crate, her own personal crate of crime. When all the really good stuff had been transferred into it, conveniently just about the right amount to fill the crate, with only a bit of filler—the Philip MacDonald Avon editions, for instance, weren't especially valuable but they were *nice*—she had put the crate on the floor under the table along with the other crates waiting to refill the gaps on the table as books were sold.

Cordelia had been required to do all this under the watchful eye of Vulture Face.

This personage was one of the old, or older, bags on the church roof committee and had been suspicious of Cordelia from the start. She had a narrow pale wedge of a face, sharp nose and considerable hair loss, all of which contributed to a striking resemblance, at least in Cordelia's mind, to everyone's favourite bald-headed corpse-eating scavenger bird.

Everyone else on the church roof committee had been falling over themselves to express their delight with, and gratitude to, Cordelia for contributing and making such a lovely, useful suggestion about the book sale, and indeed grateful to Cordelia just for being in her twenties instead of at least half a century older like everyone else on the committee, and for taking an interest in their superannuated selves and their disaster-prone Bauhaus roof.

But for some reason Vulture Face had thought that Cordelia was up to something. She had smelled a rat. Cordelia didn't know why. Perhaps vultures had a particularly keen sense of smell in that regard. They could certainly detect carrion at quite a distance.

Anyway, old Vulture Face had, rudely and offensively, seemed to suspect that Cordelia might try to pull a fast one and had therefore kept a close eye on her. This was all very insulting and quite uncalled-for, although of course one could argue that the elderly party was in fact absolutely right, indeed commendably perceptive, since Cordelia had, yes sir, been intending all along to pull a fast one and had actually, bravo, just succeeded in pulling it.

Cordelia gazed fondly at the crate of crime in front of her.

All this boring and enervating suspicion had meant that Cordelia couldn't insinuate herself any further into the book sale process. She didn't even bother volunteering to be one of the helpers out there selling books today. If she had, old Vulture Face would have no doubt watched her like a hawk—a mixed metaphor, or rather a mixed metaphor-cum-simile, but nonetheless that was what would have happened.

47

So, Cordelia didn't even bother trying to work behind the tables today. Besides, if she had done so, she would have been required to stay in the church hall, at the sale, for its entire boring duration. Instead of just dipping in at its thrilling commencement to skim the cream.

Admittedly, she had missed the thrill of that commencement today by arriving late, and had inevitably missed out on a few prizes (damn the Mole for grabbing those Deighton cook strips), but it didn't really matter because the cream had already been skimmed. Quite decisively skimmed.

She smiled at the crate of books and sighed a contented sigh. By an eerie and annoying piece of synchronicity, at exactly the same moment Monika also emitted her own contented sigh, as she counted for a third time the cash Cordelia had given her and then put it in the zipped pocket of her quote-unquote leather jacket and zipped it safely away.

Monika had been easy to enlist in Cordelia's little project. She was a bona fide regular church volunteer, something Cordelia suspected she did as atonement for her frequent boozing. So it had been simple enough to suborn her and get her involved with the book sale. Cordelia had pointed out the crate—*the* crate—to Monika, and had arranged for her to sneak it into this storeroom before the sale began.

Now Monika was anxious to get back to the sale where she was supposed to be working, so Cordelia told her she could go. Monika disappeared with alacrity, her jacket creaking—could it actually be leather? surely not—and closed the door of the vestry behind her, leaving Cordelia alone with the books. Her books. Soon to be other people's books. Collectors of rare and valuable crime paperbacks who were willing to pay a premium price to Cordelia for such top copies.

Although the toppest copies—that wasn't really a word, but never mind—were destined to end up in Cordelia's own collection.

She gazed happily at several of these for a moment and then forced herself to get to work. She opened her rucksack and began to pack the books.

There were far too many to be accommodated in the rucksack alone, of course. Which is why she had brought some plastic carrier bags. And some bubble wrap and sticky tape.

Cordelia began to meticulously wrap the books, in blocks of about a dozen each.

That was when she heard the voices.

She froze.

Voices in the corridor outside the vestry.

One was Monika's voice.

The other…

Cordelia quickly loaded the wrapped books back into the crate from which they'd come, threw her rucksack on top of them, swiftly looked around the room to memorise the position of everything, then firmly shut her eyes to get a head start, as much of a head start as she could, which wasn't much—

And then switched off the lights.

Willing her eyes to adjust to the darkness as quickly as possible, she moved promptly and confidently back to the table, banged her shin badly on one leg of it, picked up the book crate, and fumbled her way *under* the table with it, where she squirmed as far back as she could until she hit the cold stone wall at the back of the room.

There she hid like an animal at bay. Or actually, more accurately, like the nameless hero of Geoffrey Household's *Rogue Male* when he was being hunted by the Nazis. (They weren't actually identified as Nazis, but everybody knew what he was getting at. Geoffrey Household, that is.)

Because Cordelia had also identified the other voice in the hallway.

Old Vulture Face.

Those voices had stopped now but Cordelia drew no comfort from that. She trusted Vulture Face about as much as that personage trusted her. She strained to listen for footsteps, then realised that the stylish linen runner on the hallway floor made that a waste of time and instead took out her phone so she could check the time. She resolved to remain holed up here for at least fifteen minutes, perhaps half an hour, before making any kind of a move, and in the darkness and silence it would be easy to lose track of—

There was a sound outside the door. Cordelia immediately switched her phone to silent—how many conspiracies had been foiled by some wanker leaving their phone on?—and quickly put it away just as the handle of the door turned and it clicked open.

A yellow rectangle of light fell onto the darkened floor, the black shadowed outline of Vulture Face centred on it. Cordelia pressed her back against the wall behind her in a pointless and frankly rather humiliating attempt to retreat further under the table. Old Vulture Face, or rather her shadow, stood motionless for a long moment. Cordelia braced herself for the switching on of the light in the small room. Once that happened, she reckoned she was only safe so long as her vulture-faced nemesis didn't step into the room.

But Vulture Face did not switch on the light. And she did not step into the room.

She just stood there in the doorway. Stood there and *sniffed* loudly.

For a moment, Cordelia wondered if old Vulture Nose was actually able to sniff her out and was now making an effort to do so. But then she realised what the old bird was about. She had just encountered Monika in the corridor, hadn't she? And Monika had no doubt been looking sweaty and furtive because that was pretty much her resting state. So Vulture Face had put two and two together...

And concluded that Monika had been having a clandestine drink. Excellent supposition. Highly likely. Full marks for perspicacity, oh Vulture-Faced One, but sadly, on this particular occasion, no cigar.

Vulture Face stood in the doorway sniffing, trying to detect the smell of booze, and failing to do so. Then she stopped sniffing, made an odd and rather touching little sound of defeat, and closed the door again, without ever bothering to turn on the lights.

Monika remained under the table. She gave it a full quarter of an hour, sitting huddled there in the darkness, breathing in the comforting and somewhat intoxicating smell not of illicit booze but of old paperbacks, the dry, spicy smell of old paper.

It was so comforting and so familiar, so much a part of her life, of essentially what Cordelia was, that she very nearly fell asleep.

But when the quarter hour was up, she crawled out from under the table, stretched—stretched and yawned, rather luxuriantly—then switched on the light, retrieved the crate from the floor, and set it on the table again.

She finished wrapping the books in bubble wrap, distributing them between her rucksack and her plastic bags, and then switched out the light, stepped out of the vestry, closed the door behind her, and left the church by the back door that was never locked and gave onto a pretty little graveyard planted with flower beds among the ancient, weather-worn headstones dominated by a large oak tree. A very large oak tree.

Cordelia left the churchyard and headed off towards Castelnau, on a quick detour to the pet shop to pick up some doggie treats for Rainbottle. She was in a celebratory mood and felt like spreading the love.

The rucksack was pleasantly heavy on her back, the bags heavy in her hands as she strolled along, all packed with plunder. Cordelia smiled. What was it the Mole had said?

"All the good stuff is gone."

It was now.

5: GUILTY

The scam Cordelia had pulled at St Drogo's book sale gave her a warm glow of satisfaction that lasted for days. It also provided a very welcome contribution to her funds. She'd done such a superb job of creaming off all the most valuable titles, and then subsequently did such a magnificent job of selling them on at a stiff mark-up, that the profits veritably flooded in.

To the extent that even Edwin got paid.

Good old Edwin, with his exciting Rohan corduroy trousers (today he was wearing the Richmond Green pair), must have somehow sensed that she was flush because he had insisted on her not only paying last month's rent but also coughing up *this* month's rent too. In advance, or anyway more in advance than usual. (Or at least, less in arrears than usual.) Oh well. Cordelia looked on the bright side. She supposed it was a relief not to have to sneak around in full landlord-avoidance mode. For a while, anyway.

And even after paying a stinging double dose of rent, Cordelia still had some funds. And she'd had some fun.

Indeed, she'd had so much fun, skanking the book sale, that she even began to feel a certain pang of guilt.

This came about after hauling her illicit booty home from St Drogo's and listing it for sale on her website, working at her computer while Rainbottle, borrowed from Edwin for the afternoon, remained contentedly stationed under her chair strategically positioned for ease of intermittent patting by Cordelia, occasionally swatting the floor with his tail and periodically receiving rewards for being a good boy in the form of doggie treats.

Then Cordelia decided to give herself a reward for being a good girl (or, if you wanted to be nit-picking about it, being a bad girl) in the form of a dinner at her favourite restaurant.

Sadie's was her much-loved hangout in the village and a local institution. As she'd strolled towards it that evening, Cordelia had the happy anticipation of a fine meal in her tummy and the hot and happy anticipation of a number of large (250ml) glasses of wine— they did a very nice house red at Sadie's, a creamy Rioja. Maybe even preceded by a cocktail or two.

She had arrived at the restaurant at the luminous moment of an autumn evening when the darkness seemed suffused with late golden light, or maybe it was vice versa. Anyway, the staff in Sadie's were just switching their interior lights on, and this bright rich light spilled out onto the street and lit it all up like a showroom display.

Specifically a showroom display of a sleek silver car.

And there, like an absurdly beautiful model hired to show off this sleek silver machine to its best advantage, was the car's owner, the Woman herself.

She was accompanied by someone Cordelia had seen with her before. The one Cordelia thought of as her ferocious friend, who looked very much like another showroom model. This girl was white, about the same age as the Woman (which was to say just a few years older than Cordelia), and was a black-haired, blue-eyed knockout, like a femme fatale from a vintage Bob McGinnis cover painting.

But Cordelia only had eyes for the Woman.

In the warm wash of golden light from Sadie's high windows—the Woman and her friends had evidently just come out of the restaurant after dining; if only Cordelia had come earlier, she and the Woman would have been eating in Sadie's at the same time, their eyes might have met... Who was Cordelia kidding? Even if their eyes *had* met, Cordelia would never have taken advantage of the situation. She would never have the nerve do anything. Like go up to the Woman in front of her friends and speak to her—in that warm golden light, the Woman and her friends were about to unlock their car and get into it and leave, leave, leave.

Friends plural, because the black-haired, blue-eyed knockout was with some instantly forgettable guy.

Cordelia had paused outside Sadie's, pretending to study the menu in the window, but actually eavesdropping. And the forgettable guy was saying to the women, "Who the hell is St Drogo, anyway?"

"Patron saint of the physically unattractive," said the Woman promptly and casually and knowledgably, taking out her car keys. Cordelia's heart soared skyward. Patron saint of the physically unattractive! That explained the freakshow arrayed around good old Drogo on the stained, or rather sainted, glass window. Cordelia had never known that. And she'd been walking past that church, and hearing its name, for years.

But the Woman had known.

Was there anything the Woman *didn't* know?

So Cordelia's heart soared. But then it plunged. Because, inevitably, as she watched them, using their reflection in the restaurant window behind the menu so as not to give the game away, they began to unlock the car and open its doors.

They were going.

Cordelia wished there was something she could do about it, but there was nothing. They were going. They were about to get in the car and drive off. But not before Cordelia was able to catch a final snatch of conversation, one that made her heart plunge further still and would lead to those aforementioned feelings of guilt.

Because she heard the other girl say, "So how was the paperback sale?" And the Woman sighed—how Cordelia's heart was tugged downwards by the profound sadness of that sigh—and said, "Pretty much a complete bust."

There had been such a keen note of disappointment in the Woman's voice that Cordelia froze right there on the pavement, overcome by the first of many pangs of guilt, because the book sale had been pretty much a complete bust for the Woman only because Cordelia, cunning scamp that she was, had got there first, got there illicitly first, and skimmed the cream.

She couldn't stand it. In a hot flash of decision, Cordelia resolved to tell the Woman what had happened—to tell all. The crate of crime, the crate of cream, illicitly skimmed and vestry-concealed. To tell everything. To confess everything.

So she opened her mouth and drew breath to do just that, but of course by now the two supremely hot women and the forgettable guy were all in the car and closing the doors, sealing themselves inside, sealing themselves away from her as the Woman, who was driving as always, started the engine, and then they were gone, slipping neatly into the traffic flow and disappearing at startling speed.

They were gone, as the first stumbling belated words came out of her mouth—"Excuse me…"—drowned by the sound of the engine.

Cordelia closed her mouth again.

The moment was over. Even the extraordinary quality of the light changed to something mundane. The numinous moment of infinite possibilities—what if she had spoken to the Woman, what if she had confessed all, what if the Woman had forgiven her?—was at an end, and Cordelia was just a girl on her own on the pavement outside a restaurant.

A stupid girl.

Outside a very good, restaurant, though.

So Cordelia went into Sadie's and enjoyed her supper anyway. After all, she would have been a fool not to.

(And, although of course she couldn't know it then, it would be one of her last chances to relax. To really properly relax and enjoy her carefree little life. Before the shit started hitting the fan… And, not to put too fine a point on it, before people started getting killed.)

6: WEED

While she still had a few quid left in the kitty, there were certain things Cordelia had to do, certain things she had to spend her money on. Rent was, of course, not among these, was never among them, but she'd already been forced to pay that. Positively compelled against her will. By corduroy-clad Edwin.

Edwin was an odd sort. On the face of it he should have been a total loser. But he seemed to have hidden depths. For example, although Cordelia would have been tempted to dismiss him out of hand as a Rohan-attired, sandal-shod dud and all-around sexual non-starter, Edwin had a startlingly steady string of girlfriends. Admittedly they were all of the same sort, boring make-their-own-muesli, fresh-air-and-bicycling types. But there was a constant and apparently inexhaustible supply of them and, what's more, Edwin always seemed able to stay friends with them after their no doubt supremely dull affairs were over. A trick that Cordelia never seemed to manage to pull off with her own exes. Perhaps because her affairs weren't quite so dull.

Anyway, having been forced to pay Edwin the rent was all the more reason for Cordelia to prioritise the things that *really* mattered, and buy them while she still had the money. And at the top of that list was…

Weed.

Cordelia hadn't yet quite run out of weed, but the way to avoid running out—horror of horrors—was to always replenish her stash at this stage.

She commenced this process by making a carefully worded phone call, then, having confirmed with her dealer that supplies were available and having made an appointment, Cordelia walked along the river to Barnes Bridge station and there caught a train to Putney, from where she hopped on a bus that carried her across Putney Bridge.

Sitting on the top deck of the double-decker, Cordelia felt a familiar rising thrill while the sullen green Thames passed sluggishly below her and she rumbled towards her destination. Soon she would be heading home with a healthy consignment of Class B drugs to beef up her stockpile.

Then she could get high. So high that her little overpriced attic room would seem to extend its boundaries endlessly and become a realm of wonder.

Cordelia hopped off the bus and hurried into the labyrinth of side streets near the cemetery in Fulham (named, with great originality, Fulham Cemetery). She walked past a Middle Eastern grocer with an array of mysterious vegetables outside his shop, past a disgraceful number of estate agents, past an antiques shop—no books—another antiques shop—just hardbacks—and then turned a corner and headed towards her dealer's.

The house, a tall angular white box with roughhewn stucco walls and an entrance concealed through a gate and up some steps, was like something out of North Africa. It made her think of Paul Bowles and William Burroughs. And, of course, their books.

Bowles's 1950s Signets with Avati cover art were vaguely collectable, but they weren't really Cordelia's cup of tea. On the other hand, William Burroughs…

Sudden greed washed over Cordelia as she fantasised about finding a first edition of Burroughs's *Junkie*. This had been published pseudonymously as by William Lee and had actually been an Ace Double (that fabulous imprint which offered two separate books with two different and invariably lurid covers, bound back-to-back).

Indeed, *Junkie* had been one of the first Ace Doubles, D-15, backed with *Narcotic Agent* by some nonentity chump called Maurice Helbrant. Published in 1953.

These days, a prime example of one of these babies could change hands for upwards of three grand, assuming it was signed. By Burroughs, of course—not Helbrant, Christ on a bicycle…

And, of course, signed was never a problem for Cordelia.

Dreaming paperback dreams, Cordelia went through the narrow arched opening in the white stucco wall and up a narrow blue-and-white-tiled staircase—more Moorish influence. Just as she reached it, the ground floor door, all black iron and milky glass, suddenly popped open and the well-dressed dude looked out at her.

The well-dressed dude was tall, black—well, to be pedantic, very dark brown—powerfully built, handsome, suave. Cordelia was invariably speechless in his presence. He was cool, imperturbable, vaguely threatening. Cordelia was merely speechless.

They stared at each other for a moment. The well-dressed dude—he was currently wearing pink jeans which on someone else, the Mole would be a good example, would have been ridiculous, but on his long muscular legs were simply magnificent, and a chunky dark green sweater with brass buttons and an odd collar, all of which were ineffably hip in an offbeat and intoxicating way—this glorious apparition regarded Cordelia with thinly veiled scorn.

Then he shut the door in her face. Apparently whatever he'd opened it for could wait until she was safely gone, contemptible creature that she was. Feeling suitably chastened, just for the fact of her existence, Cordelia continued on her way. On her way up the stairs to do a drug deal.

Cordelia had the distinct impression that the well-dressed dude knew exactly what his upstairs neighbour was up to, and did not approve. Of the neighbour or her customers. Particularly Cordelia, among those customers.

She sighed and went on upwards, towards her destination, the door on the second floor. She heard the sound of this also popping open before she reached it, but this didn't surprise Cordelia. Because her dealer not only knew she was coming, she would have seen her arrive.

Mrs Chichester had wireless cameras all over the place and could see any potential callers ascending the stairs on one or more of her computer screens long before they reached her entranceway, with its gleaming black door, novelty doormat and sentinel potted yucca.

But Cordelia saw that it wasn't Mrs Chichester who'd opened her front door. As the figure emerged from behind the screening greenery of the large and thriving yucca, it was revealed as a man.

A young man whom Cordelia knew. Although she couldn't immediately remember his name, remembering it was somewhat inevitable because Cordelia had inadvertently coined a vivid mnemonic for it.

Once upon a time, back in the distant days of her childhood, Cordelia and her odious brother had been dragged by their parents to visit some friends of their parents, and the friends' dreadful children. Nothing, mercifully, remained of that visit in her memory except the discovery that these children had an entirely different euphemistic terminology for bodily functions than Cordelia's own family.

To wit, "tinkles and grunties".

Cordelia's brother had become utterly obsessed with this phrase for a good decade afterwards, and in their teenage years had even insisted that one day he and Cordelia should form a singing duo called Tinkles and Grunties. They were hampered in this enterprise, thankfully, by the fact that neither of them could sing a note.

Though, of course, her brother had, against all odds, later carved out a vaguely related career for himself as a DJ. And, appallingly and astonishingly, he had managed to achieve some—it stuck in her craw to use the word—*fame* in this area.

Anyway, that was this buffoon's name. Not Tinkles, but close enough.

Tinkler. First name Gordon. Or something like that.

Tinkler was chubby, somewhat bulge-eyed, with beseeching brown spaniel eyes. He was evidently a few years older than Cordelia but in no way seemed more mature. Continuing this theme of mild paradox, he consistently came across as lustful yet sexless. At least to Cordelia. And now his face lit up at seeing her.

Cordelia reflected woefully… Why did she always attract people such as Tinkler and never, never, never the likes of the well-dressed dude or, above all, the Woman?

This Tinkler person was beaming, jubilantly descending the stairs, narrowing the gap between them, coming to join her. "So, ah, you've come to see Mrs Chichester?" was his vivacious and insightful opening salvo.

Cordelia nodded and slipped past him towards Mrs Chichester's door. She had no time to waste. She needed to score and then get home and then get on with her busy and jam-packed evening of having a good time.

Tinkler called up after her, "I could wait for you."

"What?" Cordelia swivelled to look at him.

"We could, ah, we could leave together."

"Leave together?"

"Ah, I could wait for you until you've finished seeing Mrs Chichester. And then I could give you a ride." Gazing at her, he added, "I've got kind of red."

He'd what? Was the idiot confessing to some kind of *inflammation*? Possibly sexually transmitted? That was certainly what it sounded like. It must have been what it sounded like to Tinkler, too, because he hastily corrected himself. "I mean I've got my car. I've got it with me. I drove here today. In Kind of Red."

"Wait… your car has a name?" *Kind of Red?* What sort of wanker had a name for his car?

"I actually used to have a blue model and it was called Kind of Blue. But something happened to that car. It's quite an interesting story…"

"Save it," said Cordelia. "For another time."

"It involved me nearly dying," said Tinkler, hopefully.

Not nearly enough, thought Cordelia. Rather unkindly.

Mrs Chichester opened the door and smiled at her. She ushered Cordelia in then shut the door very firmly behind them, and set about locking it with equal firmness and great finality, using no less than three different locks.

Normally this kind of behaviour might make a young woman in someone else's house a mite nervous, but at your drug dealer's it was downright reassuring.

Mrs Chichester was about the same height as Cordelia, so on the tall side for an old bat. She was wearing a pink and green tweed jacket (from Maje by Judith Milgrom, if Cordelia was not mistaken, and if so, not cheap), bright pink Nike Essentials (all right, these *were* cheap) tracksuit top and bottoms, and bright green suede ballet pumps with tiny purely decorative laces tied in a dainty bow at the tip of each toe.

And, good lord, a pearl necklace.

Mrs Chichester had a thin, pale face, the paleness and thinness of which were emphasised by a pair of round steel-rimmed spectacles with black enamelled frames. The eyes behind those spectacles were of such a cold, arresting intelligence that they firmly discouraged any notion of laughing into her face—that thin, pale face—perhaps in response to all those fashion faux pas to the south of it.

Mrs Chichester led Cordelia out of the small entrance hall into the somewhat larger but still small room where she always did business.

This room was square and windowless with a frosted glass door to the left that, Cordelia knew from glimpses during past visits, led to a tiny but very well and expensively equipped kitchen. On the right was another doorway, this one hung with a red-and-white beaded curtain, which led to some kind of parlour.

The room they were now in, the business room, so to speak, had a bare wooden floor, a bare wooden dining table and bare wooden chairs. On the table was a sealable plastic bag of the kind that might contain a sandwich. This one did not contain a sandwich. Instead it was full—well, half full—of densely packed brownish-green vegetable matter.

Cordelia tried to keep her eyes off it, or at least not forthrightly stare at it while she and Mrs Chichester concluded their small talk about whether or not Cordelia had found it difficult to get here today, what with the traffic being what it was, especially on the bridge, Putney Bridge that is, thanks to the other bridge, Hammersmith Bridge that is, being closed.

As soon as the small talk was over, Mrs Chichester stepped smartly to the table, picked up the bag, and turned to Cordelia with it. The drugs were always ready and waiting on the table whenever she came on a buying mission. This meant that Mrs Chichester never had to go and fetch them, and therefore never had to give any clues about where she might store her merchandise.

A very sensible precaution, though Cordelia was willing to bet she could have located Mrs Chichester's stash easily enough and in pretty short order. It was, after all, a small flat and there were only so many places you could hide a large supply of potentially very smelly resinous contraband.

But right now she was only concerned with one small portion of that contraband, in the plastic bag that Mrs Chichester was holding.

"Oh, by the way," said Mrs Chichester. "You use a *sous vide* cooker, don't you? To decarb the weed?"

"Yes—in fact, one that you recommended," said Cordelia politely. "Thank you for that," she added, even more politely. "It's really very good."

"Oh yes, the Russell Hobbs 25630," said Mrs Chichester. "It was a *Which?* magazine Best Buy." The last statement seemed to arouse a certain unwholesome excitement in her.

"Well, anyway, it's certainly very good," said Cordelia, handing Mrs Chichester the previously agreed amount in cash, and beginning the delicate process of disentangling herself from this conversation while not seeming to be grabbing her drugs and getting the hell out of here as fast as she possibly could, while actually grabbing her drugs and getting the hell out of here as fast as she possibly could. Because one did not wish to appear rude.

But Cordelia wanted to get home, and get cooking, so to speak.

"Anyway, thank you for this." Cordelia held up the bag with its wonderful weight of weed in it. "Good to see you."

"And good to see you," said Mrs Chichester with a kind of glazed and hasty formulaic vagueness, such that Cordelia realised, with a rush of gratitude, that her hostess was as eager to get rid of her as Cordelia was to be gone. "I hope the traffic is kinder for you going back," she said as she escorted Cordelia to the front door.

"Oh, I'm sure it will be fine," said Cordelia. And she *was* sure it would be fine. Because even if she did end up stuck in traffic hell, she had this lovely little plastic bag with its agreeable payload to keep her company, to provide a tight and promising bulge in her pocket and guarantee the prospect of a pleasurable evening ahead. An evening of sybaritic activities which could be profitably contemplated on the sunny top deck of a becalmed double-decker bus with an idling engine and a firm seat cushion vibrating under some cherished portions of her anatomy.

Cordelia opened her mouth to say goodbye, but before she could do so the doorbell rang and both of them jumped, nearly out of their skins, because the sound was so close at hand, and so unexpected. Although there shouldn't really be anything unexpected about hearing a doorbell when you were standing beside the front door.

But drug deals do tend to put people's nerves on edge.

Certainly, Mrs Chichester didn't look pleased. She looked angry in the way someone looks when they are tense to begin with and then on top of that suddenly startled. Clearly she hadn't been expecting anyone. She reached into the pocket of her pink and green tweed jacket and took out her phone.

For a moment Cordelia thought she was going to call for reinforcements or something, but then she realised Mrs Chichester was looking at the output of one of her spy cameras. And she relaxed, although making a disgusted-sounding sigh.

"Would you mind just stepping back in here for a moment? This won't take long." She led Cordelia back into the business room and then shooed her on through the beaded curtain and into the parlour. "I'm sorry about this," she said, as the beads swung shut again, sealing her off from Cordelia. She didn't sound sorry, though. She just sounded annoyed.

The doorbell rang again, somehow managing to seem more impatient this time, and Cordelia could hear Mrs Chichester hurrying towards it, while making a small vocalisation which could easily have been of a profane nature. There was then a fairly lengthy pause, enlivened by a final bad-tempered ringing of the bell while Mrs Chichester unfastened her intricate triumvirate of locks.

Meanwhile, Cordelia looked around the room where she had been—only briefly, she hoped—warehoused. She understood why Mrs Chichester had done this. A dealer's was like an old-fashioned doctor's office or bordello: it was bad form to have the customers run into each other. Nevertheless, she wondered how long she'd have to cool her heels in here.

She looked around her. The parlour was slightly larger than the business room next door and, unlike that spartan cubicle, actually boasted a window. This looked out onto a street below which was, like most residential London streets, thickly crowded with cars, parked both legally and illegally. A more boring assortment of motor vehicles you'd be hard pressed to find, all unexcitingly grey, white or silver grey…

Except for a single striking vintage convertible of some kind, painted a pale green and open at the top to reveal dark blue leather seats.

Cordelia realised that she'd been hoping, quite irrationally, to see a certain sleek silver sports model.

Now that particular dream had been thwarted, her hope moved on to the possibility—remote, true—that the Woman was now driving this vintage open-top job which Cordelia could see more or less directly below her.

The Woman did, after all, change cars frequently, and was always at the wheel of something stylish and often drove just such an old classic model. This fantasy suddenly ramped up as Cordelia thought, *Perhaps the caller at the door…?* But then when she darted to the beaded curtain and began to illicitly listen, she immediately heard that whoever Mrs Chichester was now talking to was a man.

As Cordelia attended to the low buzz of their conversation, Mrs Chichester and the man moved closer, coming from the entrance hall into the business room, and Cordelia stepped smartly back from the beaded curtain, although detection of her eavesdropping seemed a pretty remote possibility.

But before she retreated, she did catch a few key words, such as "drains", "lease" and "ground rent". Enough to surmise that Mrs Chichester was talking to her landlord. Poor Mrs Chichester.

Cordelia started pacing the room, a caged animal. The path of her pacing snaked around the red brocade sofa, a slightly paler shade and a different pattern than the wallpaper, and the two matching armchairs, all with stubby little polished wooden legs that looked faintly deformed, and the long oval antique coffee table of varnished walnut that might well have been handsome. It was hard to tell because of all the magazines piled on it. (Some monstrosity called *Your Home* was very much in evidence.)

She looked around the room, increasingly desperate for entertainment or simply diversion. The only other feature of interest in here—though "interest" was overstating it—was a small, framed photograph on the wall. It was the only decoration anywhere on the walls, which seemed to suggest it was of some significance. But, as if to immediately contradict this, it was situated behind the sofa and crammed into a corner at such an awkward height that it compelled anyone, in this case Cordelia, to perform a certain number of contortions while kneeling on an adjacent armchair to get a good look at it.

In a very simple and cheap modern chrome frame, that was very much at odds with the whole aesthetic of the room, was a photograph, a somewhat bleached image of two people, both with such garish red eyes as a result of the photographic flash that they looked like a pair of mad albino cannibals.

The pair were a stocky middle-aged man and an old woman so tiny she might have been a dwarf. They were both smiling toothy smiles that displayed matching dreadful dentition so similar it clearly identified them as members of the same family (and, thought Cordelia, the same very limited gene pool).

The woman had white hair and was wearing a shapeless pink frock that made her look like she'd come costumed as a raspberry blancmange for a fancy dress party (her white hair could be the whipped cream on top, or something). The man was wearing baggy blue jeans and a black T-shirt with a red photographic close-up of a dog's head on it. The dog looked like a Rottweiler, which went with the general beefy and thuggish look of the man, with his bullet head, freckles and thinning ginger hair. One beefy arm, pale and freckled, with a rudimentary blue tattoo of some unidentifiable shape on it, was draped lovingly around the shoulders of the tiny woman.

The photograph had been taken indoors and this happy couple—mother and son, she inferred—were standing against a background of...

Cordelia literally jerked back in shock.

Then she instantly bobbed towards the photo again to confirm, against all unbelievable odds, that she'd actually seen what she thought she'd seen.

Yes, my god, yes...

7: THE PHOTO

Cordelia stared at the photo.

The background of the image consisted, at its right-hand edge, of a thin vertical strip of wallpaper decorated with particularly large and gruesome yellow roses against a white backdrop. But that was just one thin strip. The entire remainder of the background was filled by a *bookcase*. A bookcase jam-packed full of books. And all the books were paperbacks with matching lavender spines featuring bold black lettering in sans-serif capitals and, at the base of each spine, a small trademark symbol consisting of a vertical yellow rectangle with a black shape in it. This shape was too small to see clearly, but Cordelia didn't need to see it clearly.

It was the Sleuth Hound emblem.

She was looking at a bookcase full of literally dozens of original Sleuth Hound paperbacks. And it was clear from the way the light was falling on them, and the smooth regularity of the lettering, that the spines of the books were all flat, uncurled and unbroken. In fact, they appeared to be pretty much immaculate.

What Cordelia saw in this photograph was the finest horde of these rarities she'd ever encountered. The finest and most extensive and most gorgeously preserved. Someone had taken loving care of these beauties—they all dated from the 1950s, but the photo depicting them was of a vastly more recent vintage. Cordelia was able to surmise this not least from the rather over-emphatic Hugo Boss logo on the sleeve of Ginger Thug's T-shirt.

If Cordelia was not mistaken, and she was pretty damned sure she wasn't, she was looking at a magnificent collection of Sleuth Hounds that someone had lovingly maintained and cared for, for close to seven decades. Right up to the present day.

And Cordelia had to get her hands on them.

There was no way on earth that such a stupendous prize of paperbacks could be allowed to remain in the possession of these people. People who obviously didn't adequately appreciate what they had. "Obviously" because only Cordelia could adequately appreciate this trove.

And they certainly weren't Cordelia.

Cordelia, who certainly *was* Cordelia, immediately began to scheme about how to make them her own.

First, she'd need to convince Mrs Chichester to reveal the identity of the chumps in the photograph. Then she would need to make contact with the chumps, gently open their minds to the possibility of letting go of these worthless old paperbacks, and then come up with an offer that would convince them to sell these without alerting them to the fact that they were being duped and in reality the "worthless" old paperbacks were worth a small fortune...

Cordelia sat on the red armchair beside the framed photo, hotly contemplating negotiating strategies, as though this scenario was an immediate and pressing reality rather than a fervid and remote fantasy. She quickly decided that trying to pretend the books were worthless was a bum idea. It brought to mind all too clearly that classic Roald Dahl story about the idiot who made such a song and dance about how worthless a priceless collector's item was, that the people selling it decided to... Well, suffice to say it didn't end up well for the idiot, or the priceless collector's item, and it served him right.

No, Cordelia would take a completely different tack. She would launch a full charm offensive, presenting herself as a lovely well-mannered, well-educated, sympathetic girl—it should be particularly easy to pull this one on the Blancmange Dwarf. Cordelia had a knack of winning over female oldsters (Vulture Face at St Drogo's was a notable but rare, and therefore unworrying, exception)—but importantly a lovely well-mannered, etc. girl who was also very impecunious, and madly devoted to collecting rare and valuable—No, Christ, strike that, eccentrically dedicated to collecting charmingly peculiar but *definitely not* rare or valuable old paperbacks.

Maybe this could be dressed up as Cordelia writing a thesis or a book or something about charmingly peculiar old paperbacks. Yes, a book. There was certainly room for another book on the subject to supplement the foundational texts by Piet Schreuders (her beloved *The Book of Paperbacks*), Thomas L. Bonn (*Under Cover*) and Geoffrey O'Brien (*Hardboiled America*).

And Cordelia desperately needed these paperbacks of theirs, of Dwarf and Thug, to allow her to do a proper job on her book. Therefore she was willing to shell out a generous sum, far more than she could afford, what with being so very impecunious and so forth, to secure them.

Usefully, large swathes of this cover story would actually be true. Cordelia had seriously contemplated writing such a book on collecting collectable paperbacks, though she'd never framed it in quite such tautological terms. The main thing that had stopped her so far was her imperative desire to get hold of all the really good titles for her own collection before alerting the world at large to their existence. Which could take some time. Getting hold of them, that is.

How much money should she offer for the books in the photo? Cordelia realised that she was getting way ahead of herself, but she couldn't help it. She hadn't been so excited since... Well, since the Woman had almost run her over by Barnes Pond.

She moved restlessly back to the photograph again. How frustrating it was that she couldn't quite read the titles on the spines of the books. The resolution of the photo was almost, but not quite good enough. However, Cordelia could infer some of the titles simply on the basis of relative word length.

For instance, hovering just by the Blancmange Dwarf's right ear was what was almost certainly a copy, a preposterously immaculate copy, of *Kiss Me Deadly* (four letters, two letters, six letters) by Mickey Spillane (first name and last name of much the same length). Cordelia's heart began to hammer at the sight of this. It was the most sought-after Sleuth Hound of them all.

Like the Tolkien editions of the 1960s from Ace Books (the three volumes of *The Lord of the Rings*, with Jack Gaughan covers that gave the legit Ballantine editions with their Pauline Bayne art a run for their money...) it had been unauthorised, effectively a pirated edition, and had not surprisingly become the subject of a lawsuit and was subsequently suppressed, and was therefore now vanishingly rare.

It also had a stonking Abe Prossont cover.

Staring at the framed photograph, Cordelia began to puzzle out what some of the other books might be, on the assumption that they were in alphabetical order.

As Cordelia did this, she abruptly realised that there were sections of the bookshelf that weren't even in the picture. In other words—*there were more books*. She began to simultaneously calculate, as though adding up two parallel columns in a ledger, how much she should offer to buy the books from Blancmange Dwarf and Ginger Thug, and how much she would then be able to sell them on for.

Even though the exact sums at the bottom of each column were hazy, it was instantly clear that the difference between the two would be vast.

And it would all be pure profit for her. But beyond the profit motive, there was the irrefutable fact that these shelves contained many books that Cordelia didn't have in her own personal collection, that she'd never even seen in the flesh, or in the pulp. And still more titles that she already owned but in battered or second-rate shape, not like the fine condition copies on display here…

As she was preoccupied with these speculations, something triggered a warning in Cordelia's consciousness.

The conversation between Mrs Chichester and her landlord, which up until now had been an indistinct but constant background buzz, had suddenly ceased. Suddenly and apparently definitively.

Cordelia felt a flare of alarm. Now, far from wanting Mrs Chichester to complete her business with the landlord and get back in here as fast as possible, so that Cordelia could skedaddle, she was fervently praying that they would continue to have a very long and very detailed conversation to give her time to plot a strategy.

All at once the voices started up again, dispelling the silence, but before Cordelia could fully enjoy her feeling of relief, she recognised that those voices were now falling into the unmistakable cadences of conclusion and farewell. Followed by the sounds of the front door closing and then of Mrs Chichester relocking the assorted locks.

And as a sardonic fate would have it, it was at just this moment that Cordelia had an idea. A really good idea.

She wanted to see the titles of the books in that bookcase, yes? The photograph wasn't sufficiently high resolution to allow that, correct? Well, there must be some software out there in the wonderful world of the web that would increase the sharpness of the picture and allow the titles to be brought clearly into legibility.

But to do that she would need a *copy* of the picture…

And the really good idea that had arrived was that she should take a picture of the picture with her phone.

As staggeringly obvious as it was, this notion had only just occurred to her. And, disobligingly, it had chosen to occur at pretty much the moment when, judging by the sounds from the entrance hall, Mrs Chichester had finished relocking the locks and starting walking back towards the room where Cordelia was sitting.

Sitting and desperately trying to drag her phone out of her pocket, and then switch the fucking thing on—why did the fingerprint reader *never* work? It *never* worked. Cordelia pressed her finger to it again and again and again, the idiot phone responding with an obstinate buzzing vibration on each attempt, and each time the phone told her that the fingerprint wasn't recognised. Now it was telling her that she had made *too many attempts* and was therefore asking for a password, and Cordelia was frantically typing the password, mistyping the password as it happened, then typing the password again, correctly this time, and was now at last allowed access to her phone, her own fucking phone, thank you very much, and hitting the camera icon and scrambling to aim the phone at the picture and on the wall and take a photo of it and another—a series of photos, just to be on the safe side—and then sticking the phone back in her pocket and then scrambling off the chair and moving away from the photo on the wall…

Just as Mrs Chichester came in through the beaded curtain, the curtain parting around her in a somehow sinister fashion as if she was a demonic entity rippling through from another dimension, albeit a demonic entity uttering the words, "Sorry about that. Problems with the drains, all very tedious."

And then falling silent and looking at Cordelia who was standing there and, despite doing her level best to look entirely innocent, no doubt looking as if she had been up to something, because of course she had been very much up to something.

Mrs Chichester regarded her with suspicion. "Anyway, that was my landlord," she said. "But he's gone now, and if you give it just a moment for him to clear off, you can be gone too. Sorry to keep you."

"No problem at all," said Cordelia, perhaps a little too brightly. Judging by the increasingly suspicious frown on Mrs Chichester's face, much too brightly. Behind her wireframe spectacles Mrs Chichester's eyes, those very intimidating eyes, began to gaze past Cordelia and move around, apparently roving the room and doing an inventory, checking to see if everything was okay or if, perhaps, Cordelia had stolen selected issues from her collection of *My House* magazines.

Cordelia took a deep breath—doing so, she hoped, merely metaphorically and utterly silently—and decided to take the plunge. "I was just looking at that photograph."

"Photograph?" Mrs Chichester's gaze snapped back to lock onto Cordelia, and then shifted swiftly to the framed picture on the wall which, after all, was the only thing Cordelia could be talking about, and then looked back at Cordelia who, if the old bat had only waited a moment, was pointing at the photo.

"Yes," said Cordelia, trying not to wither under Mrs Chichester's gaze, which wasn't easy. "I was just wondering who it was in that photograph. Who it was a photograph of…"

Far from the response that Cordelia was hoping for, perhaps a relaxed nostalgic chuckle followed by a lengthy and affectionate anecdote—Cordelia would have happily sat through any amount of prolix maundering if there was a chance of find out where those books resided—an anecdote concerning old so-and-so, preferably complete with their current location, (please god don't let it be, for example, New Zealand), instead Mrs Chichester just repeated the question, or rather paraphrased it. "Who is it?" she said.

"Yes," said Cordelia

"Someone you don't want to know," said Mrs Chichester.

This was uttered with such clipped finality that it killed the conversation quite dead and a lengthy silence ensued. Not quite willing to surrender so easily, and also partly just to fill that silence, Cordelia said, "Well, they have some very nice books."

Mrs Chichester said nothing to this. She just looked at Cordelia, and then looked at her watch.

Cordelia got the message.

Outside the door, listening to Mrs Chichester triple-lock it behind her, Cordelia tasted the richly bitter flavour of defeat. Half an hour ago she would have been pleased as Punch just to be standing here, poised to begin her journey home, with a bulging bag of newly bought weed in her pocket and an evening of frenzied fun ahead of her. But all that seemed empty now, hollowed out, without savour. Because she knew about another possibility, a fabulous, alluring, golden possibility. A possibility of paperbacks. But one that was adamantly shut off from her.

Maybe next time she came here…

Cordelia stood on Mrs Chichester's doorstep, lost in a brooding and scheming reverie. Then there was the sound from the steps below her of the well-dressed dude's door opening. Cordelia immediately moved behind the large potted yucca whose intricate contorted branches and dense spiky foliage provided a pretty fair place to hide, especially if you stood sideways.

She just couldn't stand the thought of the well-dressed dude spotting her and giving her another one of his looks of scorn. Right now, feeling defeated as she did, on top of everything else, that would have been just too much.

Cordelia saw that the well-dressed dude had changed his clothes. She felt a little tinge of regret that the pink jeans were gone. He had changed into a suit, a dark blue double-breasted chalk-stripe suit that fitted him like a dream, and over it he wore, perhaps in response to the hint of rain in the clouds above and no doubt in a sartorial echo of the chalk stripes underneath, a white coat, a ravishing white trench coat with its buttons neatly concealed under a thin elegant flap.

Cordelia surmised that he was on his way to church, not least because of the suit and coat, but also because in his hand the well-dressed dude held a book that was evidently a bible. He held it in a certain way, fingers curled around it, spine of the book resting gently cradled in them, which Cordelia had once read was the approved way of carrying this holy book. God alone knows why. Perhaps quite literally.

Cordelia reflected that this was actually a pretty good way to carry paperbacks safely and respectfully and without harming them. But the bible the well-dressed dude held wasn't a paperback. One of many reasons to take no interest in it.

Oddly, instead of closing the door behind him, the well-dressed dude just stood there, more well-dressed than ever, staring back through the open doorway. Then another man emerged and joined him. And at the sight of this person Cordelia experienced a minor cardiac convulsion, but of a very different sort than the dude in the trench coat had engendered in her breast.

For here, unmistakeable despite not wearing a T-shirt with a Rottweiler or any sort of dog on it, was the Ginger Thug. The extraordinary, almost supernatural nature of this coincidence was instantly vitiated by the words drifting up towards Cordelia as the two men closed the door and descended the steps, talking.

Talking about drains.

He was the landlord.

The Ginger Thug was the landlord of this property. This begged the question of why Mrs Chichester, or in fact anyone, would have a photograph of her landlord in her parlour, but one mystery at a time... *Solve one mystery at a time*, thought Cordelia, waiting a cautious interval and then following the men down the stairs. By the time she emerged from the Moorish arched doorway in the white stucco wall and out onto the street, they had gone their separate ways, the dude to the left on foot, doubtless heading towards a church with implausibly high sartorial standards, and the Ginger Thug to the right to climb into a car parked outside the house.

Literally climb into it, because it was the open-topped vintage sports model Cordelia had seen from the window above.

The sports car had a bulbous, old-fashioned look to it. Smooth and streamlined, but in the somewhat laughable manner of a bygone age—think *Flash Gordon* and phallic rocket ships. It was a sort of off-mint green colour. The sort of colour a mint would achieve if you had partially sucked it then dropped it on the floor where it ended up kicked under the sofa and was only discovered again a considerable length of time afterwards.

Cordelia was able to make all these observations because she saw the car again later, just a few minutes later, when she had walked back to the bus stop where she was standing waiting for the bus to take her home again.

The bus, another double-decker, had just pulled in when the Ginger Thug drove past her, his car making a thunderous racket with its vintage and no doubt turbo-charged, or super-charged or whatever the terminology was, engine. Cordelia watched it go by as she was getting on the bus and reflected on the cruel nature of fate, giving her one last glimpse of the possessor of that stunning and utterly undeserved collection of Sleuth Hound paperbacks, accelerating away from the bus and along the A219 towards the Putney Bridge Approach, before he vanished forever.

But maybe not...

Because, in a gratifying example of natural justice, once Cordelia took her seat at the front of the top deck and the bus trundled laboriously forward, it ran almost instantly into thickly congested traffic. And there stuck in the traffic, like a fly in jam, a green fly in predominantly grey, white and silver jam, was the car. Cordelia realised, jubilantly, that the good old reliably appalling London traffic was such that the thunderously speedy sports car could make progress no more quickly than her lumbering red bus.

She wasn't sure what good this did her, or indeed anyone, but at least it postponed the dismal moment when the car, and therefore any hope—though what kind of hope was it?—of getting hold of her Sleuth Hounds (she'd already begun to think of them as hers) disappeared finally and altogether.

Despite herself, Cordelia began to formulate a faint idea, a tentative fantasy… or, more brutally, a forlorn hope, that despite her every attempt to squash it or put it from her mind, grew all the while the car remained in sight. An idea, fantasy and hope that the books might be hers.

Plus, she took a picture of the car with her phone. A picture which very definitely included the licence plate. (Who was she kidding?)

Then Cordelia began to brace herself for the inevitable disappointment she knew was to be hers. She knew all too well the tricks fate liked to play on her, such as having the Woman turn up at the book sale at St Drogo's, only to promptly vanish from her life again, leaving Cordelia not only heartbroken but also guilty (because of the scam she'd pulled and the effect it had had on the Woman— paperback sale disappointment. Cordelia could *empathise*.)

Nevertheless, she couldn't take her eyes off the car as it crawled across Putney Bridge, just a few vehicles ahead of the bus. Near enough for her to get a very good look at the Ginger Thug's bald spot in the middle of his head of thinning ginger hair. Cordelia took a certain amount of vicious satisfaction in that bald spot. It was the least he deserved for being the possessor of those wonderful books that rightly belonged, if you thought about it—or at least thought about it in a very distorted and partisan, not to mention delusional, way—to Cordelia.

But the bridge was the final bottleneck, and as they rolled south across it into Putney, things began to loosen up and the traffic started flowing more swiftly. And, in a doomful preview of the inevitable finish, the Ginger Thug began to signal a right turn, the little red lozenge of a light above his rear right bumper flashing with sardonic cheerfulness, as if maliciously winking at Cordelia.

It was very clear to Cordelia what would happen now. Her bus would continue straight ahead up the High Street, while the Thug's car turned right along the Lower Richmond Road, paralleling the river and disappearing off towards Putney Common and points west. That was the end of it, then.

Or maybe not.

Because from her vantage on the top deck of the double-decker, Cordelia could see the car taking a left turn almost immediately after it turned right. In other words, it turned into a local street that Cordelia knew.

She leapt from her seat as if impelled by an electric shock, then hurried downstairs and elbowed her way off the bus, just before the doors closed again, at the last bus stop on the bridge. Then she crossed the High Street by the old church tower with the blue clock, navigating the lethally complicated intersection in a fury of impatience, but forcing herself to be vigilant because it certainly wouldn't do to get run over now.

Then she was on the Lower Richmond Road, walking fast, walking past the big and rather lovely old red-brick mansion flats on the side of the street opposite the river, heading towards the execrable modern (also red-brick) "luxury" flats. Cordelia felt light-headed and her heart was lurching in her suddenly hollow chest.

Because just along here on her left was the street the car had pulled into. It was a street that Cordelia knew.

More specifically, it was a street that Cordelia knew to be a cul-de-sac.

Cordelia turned into the cul-de-sac. On one side, to her left, was the solid continuous brick wall of a block of flats, formerly a warehouse, interrupted by numerous windows and extending upwards for four floors. To her right was a row of proper old-fashioned little houses with tiny front gardens, some of which had been planted densely with flowers, others which had been paved over and turned, horridly, into parking areas.

On one of those that had been turned into a parking area was parked the green sports car.

Cordelia stood on the opposite side of the road, staring at it. She had been right. A surge of triumph hit her like a wave smashing against a wader in the shallows. She almost keeled over with the combined feeling of victory and relief, as the adrenaline ebbed out of her system, like that same wave withdrawing.

She had been right. She had run her quarry to his den. This was where the Ginger Thug lived. She didn't know what her next move would be, how she would initiate contact, how she could ingratiate herself, how she could *get her hands on those books*.

But she knew where he lived.

And that was the crucial first step.

As she stood there, still shaky with the aftermath of the chase, the front door of the house opened and the Ginger Thug came hurrying out, slamming it behind him. He jumped into the car again, gunned the engine, and drove off, roaring past Cordelia, leaving her in a cloud of intoxicatingly toxic exhaust fumes as he disappeared in the direction of the river.

Cordelia stared after him, like a proud parent watching her child score a goal at football.

It didn't matter if she didn't know what the next move was. She would figure it out. She would make contact somehow. She would get those books now. All of this was possible, because she knew where he lived.

And then a terrible thought hit her.

What if he *didn't* live here?

What if it was just a place he had visited?

He was a landlord, wasn't he? What if this was just another one of his rental properties? The stunning likelihood of this thesis hit Cordelia with a sickening force. Her skin prickled with a hot, sticky feeling of defeat.

She almost sat down right there on the pavement and cried.

If this was just another of his rental properties, then her goose was well and truly cooked. She could approach the tenants and try to get the Ginger Thug's contact details, but how likely were they to give them to her? To someone they didn't even know. After all, Mrs Chichester *did* know Cordelia, and she wasn't about to give her those details.

Cordelia walked, on feeble unsteady legs, across the road towards the little house. She had no idea why or what she was going to do, but she had to do something. She stood in the little paved parking area beside a patch of oil. Somehow, she took comfort from that patch of oil. It meant a car was regularly parked there. Perhaps the Ginger Thug's car. Maybe she was right after all. Maybe he did live here. She looked at the front door, fake mahogany with a fake brass knocker on it.

She stared at it, but stare as she might, she knew there was no way she was ever going to knock on that knocker. Or ring the bell set into the wall beside the door. The house had a decisive feeling of emptiness, anyway. No one was at home. She was willing to bet money on that. So she just stood there.

Then she drifted to the bay window to the left of the front door that jutted out over a few small terracotta pots containing dead plants that stood at the edge of the parking area. There were curtains drawn inside the window, but they hadn't been drawn all the way across and there was a thin gap she could peer through.

Cordelia peered through it. If asked what she was looking for, and if she'd replied honestly, she would have said she was hoping to see a bookshelf packed with the lavender spines of a glorious collection of Sleuth Hound paperbacks in fine condition.

But in all truth, she didn't expect to see that.

And she didn't see it.

But what she did see was almost as good.

For there in the shadows of a poky little front room she saw wallpaper of a very familiar design, a design that had been seared into her memory just an hour or so earlier, featuring some particularly obnoxious big yellow roses on a white background.

When she saw this wallpaper Cordelia laughed out loud, a laugh of sheer relaxation and relief. She felt tension draining from every muscle in her body.

It was the same room as in the photograph.

She stepped away from the window, giddy and elated, and now moved to the front door.

Standing before it, she took out her phone.

For the sake of anyone who might be watching—you couldn't be too careful—she pretended to be making a call. *Hey, I'm standing at your front door but nobody's at home, did I miss you?* was what she imagined herself to be saying, or rather imagined was what anyone watching her would imagine her to be saying.

But instead of saying anything at all, Cordelia was using her phone to surreptitiously take photos of the front door.

Specifically, to take photos of the lock on the door.

8: GREEN BUTTER

A week later, Cordelia was sitting in the window alcove of her attic room in the shifting silver light of a chill, rainy autumn afternoon.

She had often reflected that this window seat was the only good thing about her poky little sanctuary at the top of dreary Edwin's dreary house. And she was thinking much the same right now as she sat here cross-legged; in the lotus position, in fact.

Cordelia could do a pretty good lotus position. As it happened, she had been pretty good at yoga generally. Which had made it all the more piquant—all right, bloody annoying—that she'd been banned outright from the local yoga joint or, more pretentiously, "ashram" (the Silverlight Yoga Centre, nothing ostentatious about *that* name) she had once attended so regularly.

Cordelia had enjoyed her sojourn there. She'd been a novelty among the women who did yoga at the (*gag*) ashram. The other regulars consisted mostly of spry crones, architectural students, thin pale vegans, trust fund kids trying to pretend they had a soul, and yummy mummies attempting to restore their pelvic floors for the benefit of their chump husbands.

Cordelia had attended regularly and for a long time.

She'd finally been booted out last year, for dealing weed. But she'd only been dealing it on the side. In fact, if you thought about it, she'd been providing a valuable service. Making a quick and easy exchange of cannabis for cash with the yummy mummies et al, all of whom were badly in need of a little drug-induced sunshine in their lives.

Her ouster had been all the more annoying because Cordelia had developed quite a thriving and efficient little business, taking orders in the women's changing room after the morning class while people were getting out of their yoga gear and back into their street clothes.

Cordelia had been very low key and discreet when taking the orders. And she always arranged to meet her customers later in the "peace garden" in the "ashram" beside the *gift shop*, the last being the only bit of that sequence which didn't require heavy quotation marks; it was where the yoga mats and ancillary merchandise was flogged. Adjacent to it, in the peace garden she would pass over the Class B goodies (purchased from Mrs Chichester and sold on at a healthy mark-up) and collect her cash.

It had been a very good system. But someone had ratted her out and she'd had to sit through a detailed scolding by the people who ran the yoga centre, an assortment of bores in loose-fitting saffron garments, the precise shade of which indicated their position in the hierarchy (they never would have used the word *hierarchy*) of the yoga racket.

The main thrust of this scolding was that it wasn't so much that she had been dealing weed, what with the use of psychoactive substances having a long and honourable pedigree out in the mystic East, etc. etc. What had really brought opprobrium on Cordelia's head was that she had dared to sully the pure tranquil sanctity of the (puke) ashram with her filthy hustling commercial activity.

Cordelia had, with considerable effort, managed to keep her cool (maybe the yoga was working after all) and resisted the urge to point out that they were holding this scolding—sorry, discussion— in the room above the *fucking gift shop*.

But then the saffron-clad scolds had gone on and begun to shake their heads, more in sorrow than anger naturally, and explain, as though to an idiot infant, that Cordelia was spiritually undeveloped, stunted, altogether and incurably an inferior being.

At which point all restraint had fled and Cordelia had briskly walked them through a summary of the recent history of the yoga centre, how they'd trebled the price of their lessons and then, when people, naturally, complained, had explained that this wasn't some species of greed, oh no, it was solely a one-off initiative to pay for the (admittedly quite nice) peace garden that they'd been constructing.

But Cordelia had remarked that once the construction of the peace garden had been completed in all its meditative glory—whispering fountain, pebbles arranged in an inscrutable zen pattern, beds of scented herbs planted in wooden tubs—the price of lessons hadn't dropped back to its original reasonable level but had remained, surprise, surprise, permanently pegged at its new stratospheric height.

When she pointed this out to her accusers it had shut them up good and proper for a long, gratifying moment. And then things had got heated. Really rather heated. The phrase "capitalists in orange pyjamas" might possibly have been uttered at one point, possibly by Cordelia, in relation to the staff of the yoga centre, and that hadn't gone down very well, either.

So she had received the boot. The old saffron boot.

Which was perhaps a good thing. The weed selling had never been anything except the most sidelong of side hustles and dropping it had had the beneficial effect of focusing Cordelia fully and completely on dealing in paperbacks. So it had actually been a good thing. Silver lining time. Everything happens for a reason and all that. Cordelia didn't even miss the extra cash.

What she did miss was the yoga lessons. Not because of the yoga workout itself, which she could easily replicate here on her own in her little attic room using the worn blue mat (purchased in the, ahem, ashram gift shop) that waited, rolled up and ever ready, in her wardrobe. No, what she missed was being able to check out the other practitioners. The fit ones. With the bracing ever-present possibility of a hook-up. A yoga-based hook-up.

Still, the experience had left her able to do a pretty good lotus position and she was sitting in one now, looking at the photographs she'd taken of the Ginger Thug's front door on her cheap shitty phone. Sitting, in her rather good lotus position, on the thin pale blue cushion on the built-in wooden bench under the window. Cordelia had been going through pictures looking for ones she could delete. This was a periodic campaign she had to run because the shitty memory on her shitty phone was so shitty that it was always running out.

And while she was grudgingly spending a wet afternoon doing this, culling the photos, she had eventually come to the one of the door. The more-than-one of the door. The many photos of the door. The front door of the house where an idiot with an incredible book collection resided.

Cordelia studied the meticulous close-up photos she'd taken of the lock on his door.

Taken on that day, driven by a hot and sincere intention to commit larceny. Wait, was burglary larceny? Or was it a felony? Anyway, with the intention to commit burglary. To overcome the lock, to penetrate it, to violate it and break into that shadowy, silent little house with its big collection of books, books, books. And liberate them. Bring them back here where they would be loved and appreciated and cared for and treasured.

And, admittedly, some of them sold.

But who was she kidding?

Despite firmly resolving to do so, to do the break-in, and telling herself she would set a plan in motion at any moment, over the last week or so it had gradually become evident that she was never going to set any plan in motion or do any break-in.

Because Cordelia wasn't a burglar.

This wasn't how she rolled. Or, to put it differently, she didn't have the nerve.

Simply didn't have the nerve.

Now she sat here, the truth inexorably dawning on her, on this miserable grey rainy afternoon, finally being forced to confront it and accept it. So she sat here staring at her phone, a phone choked with photos of a front door and its lock that would never yield to her attempts at burglary. Or anything.

Cordelia lifted her finger to begin deleting the photos...

And then did nothing.

Instead she scrolled through to the earlier photos, the ones that had begun all this, the ones she'd taken at Mrs Chichester's of the picture hanging on the wall: Ginger Thug, Blancmange Dwarf, paperback cornucopia backdrop.

Cordelia stared at these images feeling a painful combination of lust and loss.

She had been right about the picture. She'd transferred it to her laptop and she'd been able to use image enhancement software to bring the titles on the spines of the books into full legibility. And it had been better than she'd imagined. Or worse, if you wanted to look at it that way. She now had a complete list on her computer of all the Sleuth Hounds visible in that photograph (and of course there were *more* that *weren't* visible).

And what a list it was. So, the lust she felt was a deep carnal craving to get her hands on those titles. *List lust*.

And the loss she felt was the bruised and tender knowledge that she didn't have the balls to burgle the house. So there they would remain, these lovely books, out of her reach and unappreciated by their owner. Lost to Cordelia forever. *List loss*.

She took one last look at that wall of lost treasures then switched the phone off and set it aside. She hugged her knees and tried to get cosy in the window seat. In the pale light coming through the rain-smeared windows Cordelia sat, knees to chin, rocking a little, humming a tune and trying to remember what the name of the song was but not really caring one way or another.

Grey day outside.

Grey day inside.

But something was fighting that grey mood. Bucking the trend.

Cordelia tried to identify what she was feeling good about. I mean, what was there to feel good about? Then she identified it. She had felt a distinct little warm pang of relief at not having deleted those pictures.

The pictures of the lock on the door. She still had them. She could still make use of them.

Cordelia shook her head, disgusted at herself. Make use of them? Who was she kidding? Why perpetuate this delusion? She wasn't going to break into some stranger's house and steal *paperbacks*. Although admittedly that was the only thing it was worth breaking into a house, anyone's house, to steal.

But she didn't have the nerve. Just didn't have it. When you came right down to it, she didn't even have the nerve to strike up a conversation with the Woman. Let alone sweep the Woman off her feet.

Let alone have the nerve to break into a house like this and rob it. To plunder it. To burgle. To steal. To break and enter.

Steal. Rob. Plunder. Loot. Break in.

Breaking and entering… Penetrating and violating.

The words were really quite arousing. Cordelia began to cheer up. She resumed humming. Maybe she couldn't burgle that house, but there *was* something she could do. Right here and right now.

She got up from the window seat, and in a rising mood of excitement bustled around the room and began to carefully choose a selection of paperbacks.

She started with some strict criteria, picking the books for relevance—notable among these was *Lady Burglar* by John Creasey, an original Sleuth Hound with an immaculate Abe Prossont cover.

The painting featured the eponymous light-fingered lass and Prossont's command of light on human flesh was never more ravishingly on display than here. The saucy blonde was dressed in a striking emerald-green top hat and precious little else.

She set about searching impatiently through her library for other burglary-related titles with really good—for which read *stimulating*—cover art.

The British Banner Books edition of *The Burglar* by David Goodis wasn't bad, with its temptress in a red nightie in a painting by Julian Paul that had been recycled from *Justice* magazine ("Amazing Detective Mysteries"). So she added that to the pile. But shortly thereafter she was compelled to broaden her terms of reference and choose some other titles which had nothing to do with house breaking or burglary, notably *The Voodoo Murders* by Michael Avallone (Gold Medal 703, "Death danced beside her") with its stunning Mitchell Hooks cover art of a sensual sinuous dancer.

The slender, scantily clad dancer's skin tone reminded Cordelia hotly of the Woman. And perhaps her face even a little?

Following a new theme now, she selected her original US Dell paperback of *Cotton Comes to Harlem* by Chester Himes, the movie edition with its staggeringly beautiful Robert McGinnis cover, almost psychedelic in the intensity of its colours, featuring two African American women of such upfront and defiantly in-your-face sexuality that in many ways it remained unsurpassed. Onto the pile it went.

Outside the house, the increasing tempo of the rain matched the rising rhythm of excitement inside Cordelia. It tapped on the window as, humming—humming with excitement—she made her preparations.

Cordelia would fantasise away the rest of this rainy autumn afternoon (and a good portion of the evening and night) with a romantic daydream of breaking into a stranger's house. A beautiful stranger's house. Or maybe she would be the beautiful stranger and someone would be breaking into *her* house. That would be the basic scenario, the setup, so to speak.

The rising mood of excitement reminded her that there was something she urgently needed to attend to now. If she wanted to be high in time to take full advantage of the overlapping Venn diagrams of *sex* and *drugs*, she really needed to get cracking.

Mrs Chichester had been right about Cordelia partaking of edibles.

There were a number of advantages to ingesting your weed this way instead of smoking it. For a start, if you smoked it and you had a dreary *Guardian*-reading eunuch of a landlord called Edwin, he could *smell* it, setting his dreary nose a-twitch. And, of course, drawing smoke into your lungs, any kind of smoke, was a bad idea. The capitalist in orange pyjamas at the (projectile vomit) ashram had certainly been right about that. Everything began with the breath, and you couldn't breathe without your lungs.

The most compelling argument for edibles, though, was *strength*. The amount of weed that might get you mildly high in a joint would, when taken internally through the digestive system, blow your head off.

Which was exactly what Cordelia wanted to happen to her head.

Hence the good old Russell Hobbs 25630 sous vide. "Sous vide" meant under a vacuum. Essentially it was a method of slow cooking, in this case slow cooking some ground-up weed—at a constant temperature of 115 degrees centigrade for two hours. This process was known as decarbing. It activated the THC by burning off the acid side-molecule attached to it.

Once the weed was activated, Cordelia added butter to it—the finest organic sweet butter, Cordelia used Isigny Sainte-Mére Beurre Doux Bio, purchased at the local farmers' market—then returned it to the sous vide for four hours to get the THC out of the leaf fragments. Then she'd pour the resulting mess into a cheesecloth and force it through a sieve and put the sieved butter into the fridge.

And now, on this rainy afternoon, it was time for it to *come out* of the fridge.

Come out to play.

Cordelia went to her refrigerator, her elegant black, silent Barcool 40 mini-bar refrigerator, and looked proudly at her handiwork. The discs of butter had acquired a classy olive-green tinge thanks to their close encounter in the slow cooker with the decarbed weed.

Now she took out one of the discs and opened the cellophane-wrapped loaf of Poilane sourdough that rested on her table, and put a slice in her toaster. She didn't toast the bread, exactly, she just warmed it and then spread it thickly with the green butter, waited for the butter to melt a little on the warm bread, then sank her teeth into it, leaving crescent toothmarks in the greenish butter and savouring the contraband cannabis flavour.

As soon as she had eaten her slice of buttered toast (all right, warm bread) Cordelia began to feel somewhat stoned. This was an anticipatory placebo effect. But soon, pretty darned soon, it was going to be replaced by a genuine drug effect.

Cordelia resumed choosing books for the long, pleasant afternoon ahead. The very long and very pleasant afternoon.

Outside the day was greyer than ever and rain was lashing the window, but Cordelia's attic room began to assume the trappings of a realm of wonder.

Cordelia had been here before and was very glad to be back again.

She wouldn't have been so glad if she'd known what was about to happen.

9: SELF CARE

Cordelia undressed.

She took her time about it, as if someone else was undressing her, or as if she was undressing someone else.

When she was done, she padded barefoot across the dusty floorboards of her room and stood looking at herself in the full-length mirror in the corner, the one opposite the window, so positioned that there was always an odd little slice of sky in the top right-hand corner of the mirror, like something in a Magritte painting.

She looked at herself, pretending it wasn't Cordelia looking at Cordelia in the nude, but rather *the Woman* looking at Cordelia in the nude.

Then she resumed being Cordelia again and turned away from the mirror and put on her robe, her pale green silk robe, the light electric feel of it on her skin being exactly what she wanted just now, smooth and soft and weightless on her skin as she moved around the attic room.

Cordelia took out a selection of oils and ointments and accessories and put on some music. Janelle Monáe. Then she lit a candle for atmospheric illumination. She thought about lighting another one, a scented candle. But instead she opened the window, the one over the big back garden, just a little gap, about a paperback thick, and let in the sad smell of the rain.

The final green autumnal scents of the year.

A cool breeze blew in stealthily behind her as she turned away from the window, flowing around her and reaching mischievously inside the loose front of her robe, like a cool invisible hand sliding in over her breasts, caressing, dug-hardening, sensitising. The silk sliding over her skin compounding the sensation.

Cordelia was suddenly well and truly stoned, the blood surging in her, her heartbeat heavy and hollow with excitement, her ribcage like an echo chamber. She felt her pulse moving against every centimetre of her skin. Cordelia looked around and quickly assessed the room. Yes, everything was ready. She was good to go.

She was like a bird, ready to spread her wings and take flight on the swelling updrafts of lust. It was going to be a wild, tumultuous flight, it was going to be very good indeed. And by the time she landed, crash-landed, some hours from now, she would be good for nothing except a long, long night of deep, deep sleep.

She moved towards the bed, her big double bed, the bed that one day she would share with… that in a *few minutes*, in her mind at least, she would share with…

There was a knocking at the door.

Cordelia froze. She told herself that she hadn't heard a knocking at the door. She told herself it was something in the music, something she hadn't noticed before, some percussion sound she hadn't noticed, amazingly lifelike, so realistic that it sounded like—

There was more knocking at the door

It had to be Edwin, but why was it Edwin? Edwin never came up here. Edwin had many, many flaws, innumerable flaws, but at least he never came up to her room uninvited. So why was he doing so now?

The handle of the door rattled and rotated.

Thank god she'd locked it, because—

She hadn't locked it. She'd forgotten to lock it.

The door opened

Oh fuck.

It wasn't Edwin.

It was much worse than Edwin.

Standing in the open door, wet through with rain and in no way improved by that, was Cordelia's brother Stuart. Better known by his nom de guerre, an unerringly accurate one for all sorts of reasons, of *Stinky*.

Stinky stood in the doorway, blinking, for a moment, getting his bearings. And then he saw Cordelia and smiled and came into the room—came into *her* room, uninvited, but that was Stinky all over—and closed the door behind him.

"How did you get in?" said Cordelia.

"You landlord, what's-his-face, was out walking the dog. I ask you, walking the dog in this weather? Is he out of his mind? Poor bloody dog, it was soaking. Anyway, I bumped into him and his poor bloody dog and we came back to the house together and he let me in."

"Edwin just let you in?"

"Sure. But he made my bodyguards wait outside. Have I told you about my new bodyguards? They're Swedish. I got them cheap because they're on the run from Sweden. Anyway, what's-his-face, your landlord, said you were up in your room. And you are." He looked more closely at Cordelia. "I haven't interrupted anything, have I?"

"I was just about to have a bath," lied Cordelia.

But she could tell Stinky wasn't buying the lie. He grinned at her and, despite herself, Cordelia could feel her face growing hot.

"No kiss for your big brother, then?" said Stinky.

"Look at yourself."

Stinky looked at himself. He was wearing a hoodie decorated in what would have been a winter camouflage pattern, except it was rendered in shades of pink and purple, accompanied with tight black jeans and pointy black shoes. He was soaked through, but apparently unconcerned about that. Or about his shambolically disarrayed, wet hair, which was exactly the same mousy not-quite-entirely-blonde shade as Cordelia's. (Thankfully, though, she'd been spared his potato nose and bulbous lips. Genetic roulette.)

"Sorry if I'm wet," said Stinky. "Looks like you're pretty wet yourself. Or about to be."

With a mortifying thrill, Cordelia realised that, with unerring Stanmer-sibling accuracy, Stinky had worked out exactly what she was up to, or was about to be up to.

He began to wander around the room and then moved, as if magnetically drawn, to the cache of carefully selected paperbacks she had stashed on the nightstand (Joycean pun) beside her bed.

"Is this the pile of books you're going to wank over?" he enquired, with studious, indeed solicitous, interest.

"*Don't touch those.*"

But Stinky had moved on and was now examining her accessories. "Oh my days. Is this what I think it is? Does it even *fit*? I mean, really. Oh, my word."

"Put it down, Stinky." This time spoken more calmly, with a cold detached deadly calm, because Cordelia was angry at herself for letting him get to her.

"And what about this one? Which way up does it go?"

"Don't. Touch. Anything."

Stinky wheeled around and grinned at her. "You hadn't started yet then? No, if you had I imagine I would have been able to smell it. I mean, the dog *downstairs* would be able to smell it. I mean, with his nose, with the sensitivity, do you know they're millions of times more sensitive? You know. The dogs. Their noses. Than ours. Than our human noses. It's amazing. It's literally amazing. Anyway, if you'd started flicking the bean that poor dog, the smell, with its sensitive nose, it would find itself rolling on its back in horror. The poor dog, all the way downstairs in your landlord's flat. All the way down there the poor dog is sniffing and its sensitive nose is twitching and thinking, my god, what's that? Has someone dumped a cargo of sardines? Has there been some kind of trawler collision?"

Cordelia had remained impressively and impassively silent throughout this with perhaps just the slightest quizzical suggestion of a young woman, a fashionable and attractive young woman, in an otherwise empty and quite silent room listening for the recurrence of an annoying, occasional and possibly entirely imaginary buzzing or humming noise, perhaps electrical in origin, that spoiled the otherwise perfect and utter tranquil silence.

Meanwhile Stinky, to his credit, or something, didn't falter.

"With the stink," he added, in case she hadn't got it. "Of your fishy fanny," he added. In case she still hadn't got it.

"You don't want to buy any weed, then, Stinky?" said Cordelia, moving smartly towards the door and opening it, holding it open in clear invitation for him to clear out.

The resulting transformation of Stinky's demeanour was instant and rather heart-warming. He was suddenly speechless, open mouthed and bug eyed, because that was of course exactly why he'd come around. Her brother had a sixth sense about when Cordelia had scored drugs and always came scuttling over to make a purchase. Indeed, it was the only reason he ever did come over.

"Bye-bye then, Stinky," said Cordelia, holding the door open wide.

"Oh now, hang on, wait a minute, Cordy," said Stinky hastily, eyes shuttling as he tried to remember the details of how to appear congenial, or simply behave like something resembling a human being.

"Bye-bye."

"Cordy!" An agreeable note of unadulterated whining was now evident in Stinky's voice, as he began to cajole, then apologise, then beg and then grovel.

Somewhere between the begging and the grovelling, Cordelia closed the door again because it was getting draughty standing there half in her room and half on the landing just wearing her robe. She let Stinky whine and beg a little longer before relenting and getting out a portion of her latest purchase of weed which she hadn't yet transformed into edibles.

She sold this to Stinky at a price that was an order of magnitude higher than what she'd originally paid Mrs Chichester for it. But, disappointingly, Stinky didn't even wince. That was how wealthy he was. How undeservedly wealthy.

As soon as he'd handed over the money and pocketed the weed, Stinky reverted to type. Like a life-size inflatable novelty being suddenly refilled with air, he refilled with rudeness. Cocksure rudeness.

He strutted back to the nightstand and, before Cordelia could stop him, he had picked up the paperback on top, inspecting it with contempt. "*Lady Burglar*!" Stinky laughed, and as he laughed, a gob of spittle shot from his mouth onto the cover of this immaculate, rare, Sleuth Hound.

Cordelia seized the book from him and hastily rubbed it against her silk robe, to remove the Stinky saliva. She rubbed it thoroughly and with great care and then set it aside, livid with rage and looking for something heavy and painful to hit her brother with.

But she heard the door close. Stinky had accurately read her mood and wisely decided to flee.

Cordelia carried the book to the window and inspected it carefully in rainy daylight, turning it at various angles. She couldn't see any trace of Stinky spittle on it. The book was undamaged. Luckily for him. Below, Stinky himself could be seen leaving, without closing the gate behind him, and hurrying off down the street, a certain jauntiness in his stride, now that he had drugs which he would no doubt smoke with one of his undeserved gorgeous girlfriends before having undeserved sex with her.

For her part, Cordelia no longer felt the slightest bit inclined to any form of sexual activity. That mood was well and truly gone. That ship had sailed. That bird had flown.

She put away the money Stinky had given her, richer but also richly humiliated.

Humiliation gave way to cold fury. And something else. An iron certainty.

Cordelia discovered to her surprise that she had made a decision. She picked up her phone and shuffled back through the photos, and then turned her laptop on.

Whatever else happened, one thing was beyond question.

She was going ahead with the break-in.

10: BREAK-IN

Cordelia had given some thought to how best to guarantee that the Ginger Thug was away from his house when she broke in. Because if the owner of the house *wasn't* away when you broke in, that could quite easily lead to embarrassing complications. Burglary 101.

Having decided that the break-in was actually going to happen, Cordelia had been pleased to discover how calm she was about the whole affair. She resolved to take her time and not hurry things. And yet somehow, at the same time, she remained absolutely sure that this wasn't some kind of self-deceiving delaying tactic, a way for her to save face with herself while she went about gradually dropping the project...

No, the burglary was going ahead, she was quietly and decisively certain about that. (Thank you, Stinky; the first time Cordelia had thanked her brother for something in recent memory.)

But she had to get it right.

So, she decided to do a number of dry runs and reconnaissance forays.

These proved to be fun, not only because they provided an exciting tingle of anticipation thanks to the illicit conclusion they were working towards, but also because they offered the subsidiary entertainment of altering her appearance each time.

Cordelia didn't want to be frequently seen, or recognised, in the vicinity of the crime scene. What was to be the crime scene. The crime-scene-to-be.

(Just the words "crime scene" were exciting. Not least because they brought to mind the Woman's fab blog about paperbacks, *Clean Head's Crime Scene*.)

Cordelia especially didn't want to be seen, or recognised, by the Ginger Thug himself. But it wouldn't do for her presence to be clocked by anyone, really. No one must suspect that she was scoping out the neighbourhood. So, each reconnaissance foray involved Cordelia making herself look as different as possible.

It had been like dressing up when she was a kid, and she'd had a lot of fun hunting through charity shops for clothing to wear on these missions. The sort of clothing she would never normally wear, and would never wear again, after it had served its purpose of concealing her identity.

Disposable fashion, indeed.

So, dolled up in various sets of what amounted to fancy dress, Cordelia had checked out the Ginger Thug's residence. This surveillance had been complicated by the fact that his little house was situated in a cul-de-sac. There were only a limited number of times you could walk down this street and pretend that you hadn't known it was a dead end—*Oh, drat*—and then walk back out again, while carefully scrutinising the Ginger Thug's place in passing without seeming to do so.

Luckily, the block of flats across the road from his house turned out to have an exit in this street. More fortunate yet was the fact that you could access this block of flats from the main road, which was to say the Lower Richmond Road. You could just walk in through large and fancy glass doors that no doubt contributed to the ludicrously elevated price of a flat in this dump, and into a similarly large and fancy foyer.

From the overpriced foyer you could either try to access the flats themselves, which required passcodes, or go through an unguarded fire exit that led along one of the world's most boring grey concrete corridors to a far-from-boring side exit door.

Far from boring because it opened almost literally directly across the street from the Ginger Thug's house.

Although the main entrance to the block of flats was never locked, Cordelia was concerned that it might be equipped, Mrs Chichester-style, with security cameras.

In fact, there were two such cameras in the foyer.

Cordelia carefully mapped out the position of these cameras, and determined that they were aimed at the two keypad entry points, for lift and stairwell.

But there was no camera on the fire exit, so it was possible to come in through the front door and leave the building through the side door via the fire exit without your presence ever being recorded by the cameras.

Not that it would necessarily be a problem if her presence was recorded; who would go through hours of video footage in a building that had nothing to do with the one she was breaking into? Even if they did, what would they see but a well-dressed—in fact, *well-disguised*—young woman passing through on a number of random occasions. For all anybody would know, this woman, or rather this series of women (because she really did think her disguises were that good), were simply taking a shortcut through the building on their way to a perfectly legitimate destination. A number of perfectly legitimate destinations.

But you couldn't be too careful. Especially when it was your first break-in.

Her first break-in… Cordelia wondered whether there were greeting cards to commemorate such occasions. There certainly ought to be. *Wishing you joy on your first break-in.*

So, on several occasions, she entered the block of flats, exited by the fire exit, crossed the street to the immediate vicinity of the Ginger Thug's house, and strolled leisurely back out of the cul-de-sac, all in a completely non-suspicion-arousing manner.

The facts that she gleaned from these strolls past the Ginger Thug's house were scanty but useful. Firstly, the Thug seemed to live alone. In particular, there was no sign of the Blancmange Dwarf. Cordelia somehow wasn't surprised. Surely anyone that old must be bunged up in some kind of a home? She'd probably only been wheeled out of such a home for the duration of the photograph and then hastily wheeled back.

Secondly, the presence or absence of the Thug's car seemed a fairly accurate indicator of whether he was at home or not. This seemed glaringly obvious—if his car was gone, how could he be at home? But it didn't allow for scenarios such as him leaving his car at a garage for repair and getting a ride back to his house. Or getting stinking drunk somewhere and ditto.

Either of which represented circumstances where it would be very disconcerting for Cordelia after entering his premises by illegal means. *Hi there! I seem to have wandered into your house by accident. Don't mind me...*

The third useful fact, which began to emerge after a number of visits, and was fine-tuned by stationing herself at a river embankment café, at an outdoor table where she could watch the entrance to the Thug's road, was that he tended to leave his house between ten and eleven in the morning, driving off in his car in either of the two directions immediately available along the Lower Richmond Road, up-river or down-river, with no particular pattern as to which way he went.

Cordelia had no idea what time he returned. Because she never stayed long enough to witness this event.

What she did know, from a further half dozen such café-based stakeouts (the caramel frappuccino wasn't bad at this place) was that he had never, so far, returned within the two hours that she spent at her table on each occasion, becoming overly caffeinated and catching up on her reading (mostly John Dickson Carr novels in the Bantam 'spooky' editions—cartoon bats fluttering on the back cover—with the author's name run stylishly sideways down the front).

And two hours should be ample time for what Cordelia had in mind.

So it was that on a Tuesday morning in early October, with weather indecisively shifting from blazing sunshine to moody cloud (Cordelia favoured the moody cloud; irrational, she knew, but it somehow seemed to better shroud the nefarious goings-on that she had planned…) that Cordelia set off for her final and climactic visit to the Ginger Thug's cul-de-sac.

She caught the train to Barnes and then walked from there, a not-negligible walk of about half an hour, but it had seemed preferable to continuing on any form of public transport, with their irritatingly omnipresent surveillance cameras and recordings, which would drop her off closer to her final destination.

Because Cordelia was, unavoidably, fairly memorable in appearance today.

This was occasioned by the large, but almost entirely empty, rucksack she was wearing on her back. This was not her treasured red 'Emma' by Sevda London rucksack—although it *was* red. It was her new and considerably larger Eurohike Nepal 65 rucksack, bought at a gratifyingly reduced price. It was a proper camping-and-trekking-type rucksack with padded shoulder straps and a belt to keep it firmly and comfortably on the camping-and-trekking-type wearer. Or indeed on Cordelia. Comfort mattered.

More to the point, she had calculated that it would accommodate perhaps as many as three hundred purloined paperbacks and allow her to carry them away with the maximum amount of concealment and ease.

When the big package had arrived, of course, with annoying inevitability Edwin had been on hand to see it and ask what it was. Cordelia had fessed up to it being a rucksack and immediately explained it away by saying that she had snapped up a bargain, which she had, and that (otherwise devout non-camper that she was) she was getting ready for festival season.

Indeed, things really had begun to feel festive…

Cordelia whistled as she walked away from the railway station, striding along briskly down a curving road lined with trees, the breeze cool on her bare legs.

She had chosen her costume for today to go with this rucksack —in other words, to look like the sort of person who would be clumping around London lashed to such a thing, while also offering the maximum disguise value.

To that end she was wearing cut-off denim shorts—her legs actually looked pretty good in these, especially after she applied the fake tan that made her look like someone who habitually wore such shorts rather than someone who was trying them on for the first time, for reasons of pure criminality—plus a Lonely Planet T-shirt, a fashionably frayed denim jacket (quite a number of useful pockets in this), an undeniably fetching batik silk scarf knotted debonairly around her neck (this was a backpacker with *class*, folks), another matching scarf tied around her head, to conceal her hair colour, and a large, some might say absurdly large, pair of sunglasses.

Oh, and hiking boots.

Altogether she looked, Cordelia believed, the very picture of a young European trekker. Or perhaps a government-sanctioned Israeli assassin under deep cover.

And, happily, the hiking boots were proving usefully comfortable on the long walk from the station to her target.

Cordelia strode smartly past Putney Common, past the abandoned hospital—who needed hospitals? Clearly shutting them up and allowing them to fall derelict was the sensible thing to do— and, as soon as practicable, cut away down Festing Road and then proceeding to walk along Putney Embankment beside the river. This was a much less populous area and consequently she was far less likely to be observed.

What's more, the sun came out from behind a mass of clouds and lit up the water of the Thames, turning it a golden shade tinged with olive green that wasn't a million miles from the colour of the diverting discs of dope-infested butter that nestled foil-wrapped in Cordelia's fridge. Waiting for her to come home and celebrate a successful burglary.

The river flowing so slowly and majestically and beautifully beside Cordelia gave rise to a tranquil mood as she contemplated such a success.

Or it would have done if her system wasn't so thoroughly awash with anticipatory adrenaline.

Finally it was time, and she cut back to her right and marched onto the main road again. She was gratified to see that she had calculated accurately and had emerged virtually opposite the cul-de-sac.

Cordelia paused and waited patiently for the traffic to thin enough for her to cross the road safely, and then hurried over to the other side and entered the Ginger Thug's street.

Cordelia had considered getting a coffee at her favourite stakeout café and sitting there waiting until she saw the Thug leave in his mint-green sports car. But there were a number of things wrong with this scenario. Being the memorable girl with the big red backpack was prominent among them, but there was also the possibility that the Thug might have left *before* she got there, so she would have a long and fruitless vigil and then would have to cross the road and go into the cul-de-sac anyway, to check what the hell was happening.

So instead, she had contrived her arrival for approximately a quarter after eleven in the morning, which was about fifteen minutes later than the Thug's latest habitual departure time. Hence he should be gone, gone, gone.

And he was.

As soon as Cordelia entered the cul-de-sac, she saw that the green sports car was absent from the parking area outside the little house. An escalating sense of excitement caused her to stop whistling and start humming instead, a happy little work song, as she hurried towards the house. *Here we go...*

Cordelia was unavoidably exposed as she now walked along this street, but it was a short street, and on the near side what few houses there were tended to have the curtains drawn over their windows. And on the other side, the site of the big block of flats with the very useful side exit, there were admittedly numerous windows almost all without the benefit of curtains drawn or blinds pulled down, but they would invariably belong to young urban professionals who were at this time of day out at their offices, slaving every hour god sent to pay for those self-same flats.

So, Cordelia doubted there was even anyone around to see her as she reached her destination and left the pavement and stood at the front door of the little house.

The first thing she did was ring the doorbell—pressing it with her knuckle (no fingerprints, please). She had considered this point very carefully—ringing the doorbell—and had decided that it was absolutely essential. If there was anyone in the house, she had to find out now, before she commenced any frolicsome felony. (Burglary was indeed a felony. Cordelia had looked it up. At least, in America it was. The term wasn't used here in Britain. "Felony", that is; "burglary" was used quite a lot.)

She rang the bell. If there was someone at home, as heart-breaking as that was, it would be much, much better to find out now. And she'd cooked up a cock-and-bull story, all ready, in case someone did answer the door.

Cordelia smiled the smile of a friendly backpacker girl in readiness, a friendly backpacker girl who had got lost and had a highly implausible but nonetheless better-than-nothing story about looking for a house of the same number but on a parallel street. If asked, with justification, why she hadn't just looked at the fucking name on this street to check it, she would explain that, friendly, smiling empty-headed backpacker girl that she was, she was just following the directions her phone had given her.

Plus, who hadn't, at one time or another, been screwed over by their GPS?

In fact, actually an all-too-plausible scenario, Cordelia thought, on reflection.

But one which she would not need to set in motion.

Because, under her knuckle, the bell rang and rang and then rang some more, with that distinctive echoing sound of a bell ringing in an empty house.

And, more to the point, no one came to answer it.

Now Cordelia took her knuckle away from the bell and began to unbuckle the rucksack and ease it carefully off her back, quite carefully, not because it was heavy but because she didn't want its contents—its sparse contents—to hit the concrete underfoot with any great force.

She didn't want to damage her burglary tools.

These were precision items purchased online and at considerable expense, considerably more expense than the big red rucksack she was carrying them in.

Before accessing these tools in the handy rucksack side pocket where she'd secreted them, Cordelia paused to study the lock on the door of the Ginger Thug's house.

The photograph she had taken on her first visit here—how long ago it seemed, a visit now cast in a golden glow of nostalgia—had allowed Cordelia to identify the lock as an example of what was called a pin-and-tumbler system.

Having swiftly researched these online, Cordelia felt that she was now in the position of being an expert on the subject.

Basically, the idea was to get a cylinder inside the lock to turn and thus open the door.

But the cylinder had five holes in it and was prevented from turning by a series of five pins held in place by springs. The lower parts of each pin were of a variable length and the correct key for the lock would have notches in it that matched these varying lengths. So, when you turned the key, these lower parts of the pins were rotated to one side, riding comfortably in the corresponding notches of the key, and hence rendering the cylinder free to turn.

Cordelia would achieve the same effect. But instead of using a key, she would use her exciting new set of lock picks and something called a torsion or tension wrench, also new but frankly not quite as exciting.

These items were all of the highest quality and, like her new fountain pen, hadn't come cheap. For some reason, burglary tools were niche market items.

She began to dig them out of the side pocket of her rucksack and transfer them to the breast pockets of her denim jacket, where they jingled festively and began to very much get her in the mood for a spot of lock picking and house breaking.

Then Cordelia picked up the backpack and put it back on, carefully settling the shoulder straps so they wouldn't chafe, but also positioning them so that she had easy access to the pockets of her jacket, and finally cinching the belt snugly around her waist again.

Besides being capacious and comfortable enough for making off with the loot, her jumbo rucksack would also serve the very useful function of concealing her from anyone watching. Certainly they would be able to see a girl with a big red rucksack standing here at the door of the Ginger Thug's house, but they would not be able to see what that girl was doing.

Which was commencing her break-in using the tension wrench, a small L-shaped metal bar, to test the torque of the lock.

Cordelia loved the word *torque*. When she had looked up the definition online, she began to nod off at the words "rate of change" and was pretty much fast asleep by the time she reached "angular momentum". So instead, she had resorted to the good old *Oxford English Dictionary*. Not a paperback but a real, physical book nonetheless. And a big one. And a good one. Its wonderfully pithy definition of torque was: "A force that tends to cause rotation."

Beautifully clearly and simply put, and capable of being grasped by an intelligent adult human being.

And a further clear reminder that, apart from pornography and shopping, the internet was good for nothing.

Well, possibly burglary tutorial videos.

Testing the torque of the lock, Cordelia should be able determine by the slight yielding if it turned clockwise. She would then gently hold the lock in that position while she inserted the pick and used it to 'tickle' the pins, as she thought of the process, feeling them as they shifted upwards, and then pressing back down under the force of the spring.

The trick was then to push the upper component of each pin upwards until it cleared the cylinder. As soon as it did so, that all-important lower part of the pin would drop back into the cylinder.

But because of the torque she would hopefully be expertly exerting, and the slight misalignment of the cylinder, the upper section of the pin would come to rest harmlessly on the outer surface with an audible *click*. According to the video she had scrupulously studied, this was called "setting the pin".

She would vary the amount of torque for each pin, increasing it for some but easing it off for others. But at all times she must take great care not to ease it off completely. If she did, the cylinder would slip back, the holes would align with the upper pins on their springs, and they would shoot back inside the cylinder, locking it again and ruining all her good work.

Just the thought of this was enough to make Cordelia sweat. *Sweat*, she thought, *like a whore at Mass*, as the saying went.

Once all the pins were set, she would use the wrench to turn the cylinder and open the lock. At this point, if she had misjudged which way the cylinder turned—if it was anti-clockwise rather than clockwise—she would also have to start all over again.

Like a whore at Mass.

Cordelia took a deep breath and took out her tension, or torsion, wrench.

And then she hesitated.

Before she got started, some instinct made Cordelia try the doorknob.

It twisted, clunked, and sagged inwards…

The door was unlocked.

Cordelia swung the door open and went into the house, moving so quickly it was almost like falling inside. Into the shadow and gloom and the unfamiliar smell of the place.

The door had been unlocked.

Why had the door been unlocked?

Was someone at home after all (despite the lack of car outside, despite the unanswered doorbell)?

Cordelia screwed her courage to the sticking place and forced herself to call out.

"Hello?"

In spite of the screwed courage, her voice was thin and feeble and taut with nerves. What if someone answered? Well, then the increasingly implausible lost-backpacker-girl story would still have to serve.

Silence. Maybe she hadn't called loudly enough. She considered yelling again. Perhaps she should shout "Cooee", as she understood people to shout as a form of greeting, in Australia. She could be an Australian backpacker girl.

Or she could shout "Yoohoo!" and be American.

On the whole, though, she'd prefer herself to be a rather chic and hot Euro backpacker chick, so perhaps she should shout "Bonjour!" Or what did they say in Italy?

Cordelia realised that, frankly, she was starting to lose it. So, before she began gibbering hysterically, she took a deep breath and simply hollered, again, "Hello!"

This time the word came out louder. Much louder. Very much louder.

Give or take, it was like the sound a spotted hyena might make if someone stepped on its tail.

And it echoed in the house.

In the empty house. The now clearly and obviously empty house.

So Cordelia closed the door behind her. She debated briefly over whether to lock it or not, decided not, then took proper stock of her surroundings. Not much to see in the shadows. The place evidently belonged to a miser who didn't even believe in leaving a few token anti-burglar lights on when he went out.

Served him right if he got robbed.

She debated even more briefly whether to put a light on, again decided not, and waited patiently for her eyes to adapt to the half-light, dazzled as they were after coming in from the bright day outside. As her eyes gradually adjusted, she looked down at the little table that stood just inside the front door.

It had three black metal legs arranged in a tripod configuration and its top was a removable circular brass tray. On the brass tray was a heap of unopened junk mail, all addressed to one Colin Cutterham.

So that was the Ginger Thug's real name.

Hello, Colin.

Cordelia looked around at Colin Cutterham's little house. The place was cool with perhaps a bite of damp in the air. Cordelia hoped the house wasn't seriously damp. Damp wasn't good for books. But she couldn't smell serious damp, or the telltale scent of mouldering paperbacks.

What she *could* smell was a lingering fragrance of cooking. Unexpectedly, curry. And apparently rather a good one.

Cordelia knew her curries and this didn't smell like one of the cheap, crappy store-bought ones, or a dodgy takeaway. It smelled like it had been a good one, cooked from scratch. She heard her stomach gurgle in response to the spicy aroma and she discovered that she was hungry. In fact, she realised now, she had been hungry for hours, ever since she'd woken up this morning, but the stress and excitement of the imminent break-in had supressed her awareness of it.

Now that she was inside the house, though, now that she had simply opened the door and strolled right in, she felt entirely relaxed.

So, instead of turning to her left and going into the front room of the house, her ultimate destination, she started forward down the short corridor and walked through the open doorway—it didn't even have a door attached to it—into the kitchen.

It was like she'd stepped through a time warp into the late 1950s. Or possibly the early 1960s.

The cooker was of that vintage, a gas-burning monolith fashioned of curved cream enamel with black fittings. As was the white enamel—not metallic—sink with its old-fashioned taps and a brown plastic washing-up bowl resting, inverted, in it. The refrigerator was a grumbling behemoth of the same era, all white with a brand name in cursive script on it and a recessed chrome handle, both of which looked like they more properly belonged on a big Cadillac automobile. The kind with fins.

The only things here that decisively said twenty-first century were the microwave oven and a digital radio, stationed on the counter and refrigerator respectively. Cordelia tried not to notice these, since they spoiled the time travel illusion. The whole place was spotlessly clean, which surprised her.

It seemed the Ginger Thug was houseproud. Sorry, *Colin Cutterham* was.

On the counter beside the sink, a Formica counter with a black-and-white marbled pattern, were a number of plastic containers, or rather glass containers with plastic lids lying beside them (more anachronistic twenty-first-century intrusions into the time warp). The containers contained the curry she had smelled from the hallway. Cordelia surmised they had been left out to cool before going into the fridge or freezer.

Her stomach growled.

Cordelia found herself seriously considering sticking some of this curry in the microwave or even a frying pan and having a quick snack before she continued.

Continued with the break-in.

But that was a mad idea, cooking herself a meal in the house she was robbing. What next? Would she be taking a shit here? Would she turn into a shitting burglar? There actually was such a phenomenon.

Cordelia knew about it from reading George V. Higgins's *The Digger's Game*. (Or was it *The Friends of Eddie Coyle*?)

Some people believed such behaviour was a deliberate act of desecration, of further desecration, inflicted by the burglar on the property owner. Cordelia suspected it was more likely just nerves, plain and simple.

Nerves? Cordelia performed a quick survey of herself. Sphincter tight, bowels all in good order.

She would neither take a shit, voluntary or involuntary, nor warm up a curried treat. She would get down to business.

Cordelia made herself turn away from the kitchen.

She was all too aware why she had been standing in here. It wasn't the smell of the curry, as attractive as that was. Or, rather, that was just the excuse for coming in here, instead of going into the front room of the house.

What she was doing was displacement activity.

Stalling for time. Here she was, finally here at the scene of the crime, and she was reluctant to get down to it. What she had contemplated for so long in prospect, what she had fantasised about in such detail, was about to become concrete reality.

Cordelia was reluctant for that to happen. Because of the doubt that had always been hovering in the background, like a constant buzzing sound (not as loud as that immense fifties fridge, though).

Doubt.

Not doubt about whether she would go through with the robbery…

…but whether there was anything here to rob.

Her heart began to slam heavily in her chest, the first really overt sign of stress since she had got up this morning. Cordelia made herself turn and march out of the kitchen and back down the corridor towards the front room and the moment of truth.

Because this entire operation, this whole burglary thing, had been based on a glimpse through the gap in the curtains of the window in the front room of this house. A gap that had never varied or widened, and which had permitted her a peep at the wonderful wallpaper with the big yellow roses on it.

The same wallpaper she'd seen in the photograph, beside the bookcase full of Sleuth Hound paperbacks.

She'd seen the wallpaper, all right. This was the same house, she had no doubt of that. She had seen the wallpaper.

But she hadn't seen the *bookcase*.

Now she forced herself to walk down the corridor and turn right, to meet her fate.

She marched into the front room, her potentially-pointless rucksack brushing against the doorframe and the door, which was wedged open with a small brass figure of a spaniel, and she braced herself. Braced herself to see the room where the bookcase had once stood, but was now gone.

Perhaps there would be a faded patch on the wall, perhaps there would be a new piece of furniture, perhaps there would be a widescreen television (enemy of literacy, enemy of books)…

There was no faded patch. There was no new furniture. There was no television on the wall.

The bookcase was there. Just like in the photograph.

And, just like in the photograph, it was full.

11: JACKPOT

Cordelia stood there for a moment, just taking it in. Just drinking it in. A whole wall full of Sleuth Hound paperbacks.

Admittedly, it was a small wall, in a small room, but...

Jackpot.

She moved quickly and selected half a dozen books, pulling them off the shelf. She set them down on a table. In the tranche she'd just selected was the pirated edition of *Kiss Me Deadly*. This incredibly rare (and therefore valuable) specimen on its own justified breaking in and robbing the place.

At least, it did to Cordelia.

She started pulling random bunches of books off the shelves. She was so excited that her hands were shaking wildly. She forced herself to stop, to calm down. To work methodically. She would start at the top...

The top shelf was the most difficult to get at. So, on the premise that it was always good to get the hardest part of a task out of the way first, Cordelia decided to clear this shelf now. To reach it she needed to stand on something. The easiest option was to use the floral armchair which was already situated, more or less, in front of the bookcase, in an ideal position to access the shelf. She was about to stand on the arms of the chair when she realised that the soles of her boots were dirty, and she might leave boot prints on the ugly floral arms of the chair.

Not only did that seem unnecessarily churlish, Cordelia also felt it was unprofessional to leave any evidence—she experienced a tiny apprehensive fantasy flash of being in the dock in court and the boot prints being offered as evidence.

That wouldn't do.

She had a quick look around for something to put on the arms of the chair to stand on, some rags or bits of cloth. Nothing in here…

She went back down the hallway towards the kitchen. But then she found herself irresistibly tempted to explore further. Instead of going into the kitchen, she moved along a side corridor, past a tiny spartan loo, past a bathroom with a bathtub and shower (yellow cartoon ducks on the shower curtain), and finally to a gloomy bedroom.

What Cordelia saw on the wall of this bedroom not only obliterated any awareness of anything else in the room, it nearly stopped her heart in her chest.

There, hanging high on the wall opposite the bed, was a framed piece of art. Of *cover* art. Paperback cover art. The Abe Prossont painting for *Night Walker* by Donald Hamilton, with the sensuous silhouette of an implausibly nubile woman rendered in neon red bisecting a ghostly blue floating outlined image of a giant face, a man's bandaged face.

For one heart-stopping moment Cordelia thought it was an original. An original piece of art by Abe Prossont—and in that moment she began calculating just how the hell she could steal it. It was *huge*. It wouldn't fit into her rucksack, even if she removed the frame. How would she wrap it? How would she conceal it from casual scrutiny as she carried it away with her?

But then mundane reality made itself felt and Cordelia realised it wasn't a piece of original artwork at all. It was far too large, for a start. It was just a scan of a cover, blown up to a vast beautiful size, and framed.

She turned from the painting, dismissing it. Not without a pang of real regret.

As she did so, she found herself looking at a small brown wooden dresser. On top it was an oval mirror in which Cordelia could see herself—more specifically, see herself looking down at what else was on the top of the dresser.

What else was on the top of the dresser was money.

Cash.

Rolls of banknotes. At least half a dozen of them, thick rolls.

Later, and indeed sooner, it would occur to Cordelia that it was very much to her credit that it never even crossed her mind to take this cash.

She was here to steal *paperbacks*.

Cordelia made her way back down the hall, fetched two sheets of paper towel from the kitchen and took them back into the front room, put them on the arms of the armchair, stood carefully with her boots on the paper squares, and swiftly and efficiently looted the top shelf of the bookcase, transferring the Sleuth Hounds carefully onto the table in neat stacks.

She quickly glanced at each book as she prepared the stacks.

Almost all of them had Abe Prossont cover art, of course. But occasionally, on very rare occasions, there cropped up one of the dud non-Prossont covers. These had been done by an artist, the word barely applied, using an airbrush. An incompetent hack who managed to make the airbrush an instrument of visual torture rather than a valuable addition to the illustrators' arsenal (cf., for instance, the fab Alex Schomburg). The Sleuth Hound airbrush-wielder's clumsiness in depicting the human face and form was matched by a complete inability to convincingly portray plants, animals, places, buildings, clothing, weapons, machinery or household objects.

Cordelia considered leaving the books with these covers behind. But in the end, she decided to take them too. There were only five or six of these all told among the hundreds of titles, so they wouldn't take up much room in her rucksack, and leaving them behind seemed like it might provide some sort of clue to anyone investigating the crime…

Plus, in an odd way, it seemed like bad manners.

Once Cordelia had cleared the shelf, she methodically transferred the books into her big red rucksack, first wrapping them prudently in bubble wrap, the thin kind of bubble wrap, which would protect the books while not taking up too much space in its own right. Which was important because it looked as if the rucksack would be just big enough to accommodate all the books from the bookcase. Nice.

It was very satisfying to see a plan come together.

Once the top shelf's books were safely packed away, she moved to the next shelf down. Cordelia could reach this without standing on anything, although she had to stretch a bit.

She was halfway through clearing this shelf when she heard the sound of a motor in the road outside.

In fact, right outside. It seemed to be coming directly towards this house…

Cordelia wasn't unduly worried, though.

Never in her experience had the Ginger Thug—sorry, *Colin Cutterham*—come back this soon after his departure in the morning.

So surely it wouldn't be him?

Surely it *couldn't* be him.

In fact—and Cordelia relaxed emphatically and totally as soon as she realised this—the engine sound was all wrong. It wasn't the thunderous throbbing roar of the little green sports car. That sound was actually unmistakeable and she couldn't fail to recognise its approach.

And this was not that sound.

Nevertheless, Cordelia went to the window and looked out, peering very carefully through that familiar gap in the curtains from a low crouch so that no one on the street outside would see a face at the window.

Peering cautiously thus, she was able to see that the vehicle was a van, indeed the red and white van of a familiar well-known courier outfit.

And it had pulled up outside not this house but the house next door.

The engine of the van went off and the driver got out. He was wearing the red and white uniform of the courier firm which consisted of a hideous tunic, a baseball cap, and truly humiliating and very short shorts, kind of a fetishist's spin on vintage Boy Scouts shorts. Altogether it was an ensemble that Cordelia thought, not for the first time, had been designed by a sadistic paederast to provide amusement through the degradation of his employees.

The poor wretch in baseball cap, tunic and very short shorts opened the rear doors of his van, rummaged, emerged with an extremely boring-looking brown cardboard box, delivered it to the house next door and then departed again.

Cordelia waited until he was safely gone, and then wondered why. She was just wasting valuable time. She turned back to the bookcase and resumed taking the books off the second shelf from the top.

She had just finished clearing this when she heard another vehicle outside.

Cordelia ignored it. The only engine sound she had to be alert for was the distinctive thundering sound of Colin Cutterham's sports car. She set the final books from the second shelf onto the table, neatly squared off the pile, took the roll of bubble wrap out of her rucksack and then—

And then she froze.

Because, from the street outside the house, echoing off the big wall of the block of flats opposite, came the distinctive thundering sound of Colin Cutterham's sports car.

It couldn't be.

Cordelia hurried to the window—it couldn't be him.

It was him.

The bulbous little mint-green sports car was approaching from the direction of the main road, slowing as it neared the house. Cordelia spun around and looked at the room, with her giant red rucksack propped up in one of the armchairs like an impertinent and uninvited visitor staring insolently up at the bookcase with its top two shelves stripped clean of books, gaps as obvious to Cordelia's eye as missing teeth in someone's smile.

She spun the other way and looked out the window again.

The car was directly outside the house now.

In fact, it had pulled a little past the house. *Maybe he wasn't stopping here. Maybe he was going somewhere else.*

No.

The car had stopped but the engine was still running. Colin Cutterham was looking back over his shoulder, arm casually draped over the back of the blue leather driver's seat the way she'd once seen it draped over the shoulders of the old woman in the photo—

He began to reverse the car into the parking space outside the house.

Cordelia stared frantically around the room, feeling a horrid flash of déjà vu. Someone was coming and she had to hide herself, and she had to hide the books, too. It was Vulture Face in the vestry all over again.

But with this nasty little complication: not only did she have to hide herself and the books, she somehow had to also conceal the fact that she'd already cleared two shelves. *Missing teeth in someone's smile.*

She flashed a look through the window again. Outside—just outside—Colin Cutterham was painstakingly reversing into his parking space. Cordelia turned back to the room.

The contents of the room, besides the all-important bookcase, consisted of two armchairs decorated in a despicable floral pattern, a two-seater sofa decorated in a different but no less despicable floral pattern, a hulking old cathode ray television set and a small table with a square of lace on it.

A square of lace and now dozens of paperbacks, in the process of being stolen.

There was a space between one of the armchairs and the wall where she could hide her backpack. And there was another space between the other armchair and the sofa where she could hide herself. But those were the least of Cordelia's worries.

The *most* of Cordelia's worries, to put it that way, was the bookcase with its two shelves stripped clean…

Outside, the car was reversing into the parking space.

There was no way she could get the books she'd already packed away into her rucksack back out again, unwrap them, and restore them to the top shelf, so Cordelia made an instant decision. She grabbed the remaining roll of bubble wrap and the two squares of anti-boot-print kitchen towel and stuffed them out of sight in the rucksack, then hauled the rucksack itself up and stuck it into the space behind the armchair.

Yes, it was now effectively concealed from view by the old-fashioned high back of the chair.

Which just left the small matter of the dozens of paperbacks on the table…

Outside, the car had finished reversing into the parking space.

There was no time to hide those books anywhere, especially in the rucksack, especially now she'd put the fucking rucksack behind the fucking armchair.

And there was still the matter of the empty shelves in the bookcase, which would be instantly visible to anyone coming into the room. No, wait, that wasn't strictly true. Any empty shelves at eye level or lower would be visible.

But not necessarily the *top* shelf.

The fact that the top shelf had been stripped bare was entirely likely to escape notice in any casual survey of the room.

But the shelf under it—

Outside, the car was now parked and stationary but the engine was still running.

That lower shelf had to be refilled. *Now.*

As Cordelia came to this conclusion, she was already scooping the books off the table. She had to return them to their shelf not in small careful bunches the way she'd removed them, but in massive slabs, the most massive slabs she could manage. There were nine piles of about a dozen books each on the table. She now combined three of them into one tall stack, compressed between her hands, held so tightly that her forearms ached. Held tightly because she didn't dare drop them, not only because she mustn't damage the books—

The engine of the car was still running.

—but because if she dropped them there was no way in heaven, Earth or hell she could pick all the spilled books up again in time to get them back onto the shelf.

Cordelia shoved the big stack of books she was clutching successfully back onto the shelf. Then she returned to the table and combined three more piles into a big stack—

The engine of the car was still running. In fact, instead of being switched off, it abruptly revved furiously. Was he leaving again? Could her salvation have come so easily?

No, it was just some sort of sports-car-owner's affectation, revving the engine before you switched it off.

And, yes, as Cordelia returned the second big stack of books, held horizontally with some painful strain, to the shelf, he switched the engine off.

Cordelia spun back to the table and combined the last three piles of books into one big stack.

In the sudden silence of the street outside, there was the sound of the car door clicking open.

Cordelia rotated the final stack of books until it was horizontal and shoved back it onto the shelf…

It didn't fit.

It wouldn't go.

It was jammed.

Cordelia's arms were aching with the effort of holding the stack of books together, but if one slipped out, they would all go, tumbling to the floor. Like the loss of a keystone causing an arch of bricks to collapse.

Why wouldn't they fit on the shelf? Cordelia frantically tried again.

The handle of the front door could be heard turning in the hall.

Then Cordelia saw what was wrong. The book under her right hand had come out of alignment, and its cover was caught on the vertical upright at the far end of the shelf. If she just shoved the books forward with all her strength, she could force them onto the shelf.

The handle of the front door rattled.

But if she did that, the cover of the book would be bent in half.

In the hallway, the front door snapped open.

The beautiful, pristine, fine-condition Abe Prossont cover would be bent in half.

Cordelia wasn't going to do that. Cordelia *couldn't* do that.

She heard the front door swing open fully and hard, bad-temperedly striking and bouncing off the hallway wall as it did so.

Cordelia backed away from the bookshelf again, adjusted her hand position, corrected the angle of the book on the far right, and then moved forward once more and successfully slid all the books onto the shelf, filling it, filling the gap.

Outside in the hallway the front door *didn't* close again.

Cordelia stepped hastily away from the now-full shelf and moved between the sofa and the armchair and sank down on her haunches, out of sight. She sank down so low her chin was on her knees. She could smell the dusty carpet under her and the dusty furniture hemming her in.

Outside in the hallway was an ominous silence.

The loudest sound in this small sitting room was the pounding of Cordelia's heart.

She held her breath.

And then the front door slammed shut again with a sound that made her body jerk fearfully.

And in the hallway, Colin Cutterham began to curse.

He knew she was here.

How did he know she was here?

Colin Cutterham's voice was an angry snarl. "Fuck me," he said. Cordelia felt a spurt of mortal terror. What had she forgotten? What had she neglected? What had given her away?

"Fucking idiot," snarled Colin Cutterham. Then he added, "Fucking losing it. Fucking door. Fucking unlocked."

Crouching there between armchair and sofa, chin on her knees, Cordelia was overcome with an exquisite sensation of relief. (Also, she couldn't help agreeing with the fellow that he'd been a fucking idiot to leave the door unlocked.)

Colin Cutterham (it seemed somehow disrespectful to think of him as just Colin) now moved down the corridor towards the kitchen. He didn't even glance into the room where Cordelia was hiding. After a moment's silence she heard the refrigerator door open and close. Then Colin Cutterham (Mr Cutterham, on the other hand, seemed *too* respectful) came out of the kitchen and went into the loo.

Cordelia knew this by the loud splashing of urination, followed by a tight wrench of a fart, and then the sound of the toilet flushing. After that, Farting Colin moved further down the corridor, presumably to the bedroom, where he remained in silence for a moment or two, and then came back down the corridor, whistling cheerfully.

Again, he didn't even glance into the room where Cordelia hid.

What he did do was go back out the front door, closing it loudly and this time, judging by the rattling of keys, locking it very thoroughly.

Bolting the stable door, thought Cordelia... *No, wait,* locking *the stable door after the horse has* bolted. *Get your proverbs right, girl.*

Outside, the powerful booming engine of the sports car started up. The noise diminished rapidly as it pulled away. Cordelia rose from her crouch in her hiding place and hurried to the window. This wasn't easy because her legs were trembling under her, shaking actually, and not just because they'd been locked in an uncomfortable crouching position. Nevertheless, Cordelia managed to wobble to the window just in time to see the car reach the mouth of the cul-de-sac and turn right, disappearing in the direction of Putney Bridge.

Cordelia stood up straight—she'd had to crouch down again to peer out the window through the gap in the curtains—and now her legs really let her know how they felt. She just about managed to stagger to an armchair and collapse into it before they gave way completely.

Once in the armchair, she leaned forward so that her back wouldn't make contact with the back of the chair. Because her shirt was soaked, literally soaked through, with sweat. She didn't want to get the armchair damp because that would have been tasteless, not to mention unhygienic. Not to mention leaving DNA evidence.

After a while her shirt dried off and her legs felt a bit steadier, so she stood up and finished taking the books off the shelves and packing them carefully into the rucksack. After a while longer her hands stopped shaking.

When she was done, she decided not to tempt fate or waste time, and just get the hell out of there. She slipped the rucksack on—the back of her shirt was still clammy against it, but there was nothing she could do about that. She strapped the big red rucksack tightly to her and stepped out of the little sitting room and headed for the front door.

On this side of the door there was no keyhole, just a standard Yale latch with a turn-handle on it. You simultaneously turned the doorknob and released the latch to open the door.

Cordelia simultaneously turned the doorknob and released the…

The latch wouldn't release.

The door remained shut.

Of course, she thought, Colin Cutterham had double-locked it. Hardly surprising after leaving it unlocked before. And once it was double-locked, you could only unlock it with a key.

Or, of course, thought Cordelia merrily, with a set of lockpicks. She was going to have a chance to use her burglary tools after all. She began to loosen the belt on the rucksack so she could take it off and get at the tools…

And then Cordelia experienced a dizzying instant of vertigo, as the realisation hit her.

There was no keyhole on this side of the door.

She couldn't insinuate her locking-picking tools into the keyhole because there wasn't one.

The only way you could unlock this door, with a key or with a lockpick, was from *outside*.

And if she was outside, she wouldn't need to.

Catch-22.

Or, to put it differently, Cordelia was now locked inside the house.

Cordelia backed away from the door as though it was suddenly a source of contagion.

Her stomach was churning. She felt such an intense emotion that for a moment she couldn't identify it. She expected it to be fear, but it wasn't.

It was anger.

Sheer rage.

This was simply *not acceptable*. First Colin Fucking Cutterham coming back early—he never came back early—and now he had left her locked inside the house. How much more of this crap was she expected to endure? It wasn't fair. It simply wasn't fair.

And Cordelia wasn't going to put up with it.

If necessary, she would simply smash a window and—

A window.

Cordelia hurried back into the little sitting room and to the bay window, which consisted of three separate sections: left, right and central. They weren't double glazed, which was why she'd been able to hear all the sounds outside so clearly. Instead, all three were the old-fashioned design known as sash windows, glass panels in wooden frames that slid upwards. There were twin curved brass fittings at the base of each wooden frame where you could grab them and…

Cordelia moved to the one on the left and grabbed the brass fittings and hauled on it, hard.

Nothing. The window wouldn't budge.

Cordelia's heart was pounding and her whole body was shaking now. What was she going to do? She tried the other windows. They were the same. She forced herself to calm down and try again. She went back to the first window and heaved on it.

Nothing. Had it been painted over, sealed with old paint?

Deep breath. Try again—

And the window shot open so suddenly that Cordelia nearly fell out.

Fresh air and birdsong flowed in, the air cooling the sweat on Cordelia, the birdsong soothing her.

She leaned on the windowsill for a moment, feeling the exhaustion that came at the end of great tension.

She sighed, and as if in response, her stomach grumbled.

Cordelia thought for a moment and then closed the window again. She looked at the brass fittings she'd touched and then rubbed them carefully with the waist of her T-shirt to remove any fingerprints. At this point she belatedly remembered the gloves she had brought with her. The green latex gloves—the shade of green as close as she could get to the green of the gloves on the *Lady Burglar* cover.

She got these out of her rucksack and put them on with a businesslike *snap*, feeling very professional. Like a very professional lady burglar.

Then she went into the kitchen, to check on something. As she'd suspected, the containers of curry were no longer on the counter. She opened the refrigerator and, yes, that's where they were residing now.

Theory confirmed.

Then she went into the bedroom to confirm a second theory.

The rolls of money were now gone from the top of the dresser. Right again. Plus, how lucky that she hadn't taken that money (which would have instantly alerted Colin Cutterham to the fact that he'd been burgled; in fact, was *in the process* of being burgled). Indeed, Cordelia hadn't even considered taking the money.

Virtue rewarded, thought Cordelia. Not without smugness.

Then she went back into the kitchen and opened the behemoth refrigerator again, inspecting the containers of curry. There were three of them.

She took two, leaving one for Colin Cutterham.

She would have left two for him, but he'd pissed her off by coming back early and double-locking the door. One could hardly expect generosity after behaviour like that.

Cordelia wrapped the containers in paper towel and then bubble wrap and then put them in the outermost pockets of the rucksack with her burglary tools, all precautions designed to make damned sure that in case the containers came open or leaked, their payload of flavoursome golden oil wouldn't be able to stain all those lovely, lovely paperbacks.

Once that was done, she took the rucksack back into the little sitting room, carrying it but not wearing it. She opened the window and manoeuvred the rucksack carefully out, lowering it to the ground. And then she climbed out of the window after it.

If anybody saw her, the lost backpacker girl story would have worn very thin.

But by now Cordelia frankly didn't give a fuck.

She stood there outside the house strapping the rucksack on, taking her time.

Then she turned back and closed the window behind her.

It seemed rude not to.

12: CURRY AND LOOT

"My god, that curry smells good," said Edwin. "Did you cook it yourself?"

"Nope," said Cordelia. She was stirring Colin Cutterham's purloined and rapidly warming curry around in one of Edwin's big shiny frying pans with one of Edwin's big wooden spoons. (Edwin had very strict rules about which wooden spoons should be used with which kind of food, rules that Cordelia had blithely ignored until one day she found she'd cooked herself an otherwise perfect rice pudding which savoured strongly of onions; since then she abided obediently by the wooden spoon rules. Edwin was not always stupid or wrong; just mostly.)

Cordelia stirred the stolen curry carefully, warming it through but taking care not to let it burn. She was by now at last getting the hang of Edwin's cooker, which worked by means of the induction method, also known, as far as Cordelia was concerned, as black magic.

She could have prepared this meal using the microwave in her little attic room—after all, her burglary victim had thoughtfully packed the leftovers in microwaveable containers. But Cordelia hadn't felt like stinking up her room, even with such a fragrant stink as this fine curry.

Not least because the smell might get into the books she had stored there. A stockpile which included, now, the genuinely fabulous horde of freshly nicked Sleuth Hounds.

Plus, she had actually felt like a bit of company this evening. This post-burglary evening. This post-spectacularly-successful-burglary evening. Even if that company only consisted of her landlord and his dog.

So here she was in his kitchen—the landlord's, not the dog's—situated between the bathroom and his living quarters on the ground floor of the house, at the back. A far more modern and trendy and lavishly equipped kitchen than Colin Cutterham's, thought Cordelia. But somehow less interesting.

"You ordered it on one of your apps?" said Edwin, peering over her shoulder at the aromatic golden curry slowly warming in the frying pan. Edwin liked to think he was keeping abreast of developments in the world and the behaviour of today's youth by using words like "app".

"Yup," said Cordelia, immediately and mendaciously.

"I didn't hear them deliver it," remarked Edwin, a salutary reminder (along with the strictly segregated wooden spoons) that he was a lot less thick than he appeared and, indeed, could even be quite sharp. The sort of sharpness that one had to be careful not to cut oneself on, to coin a phrase.

"I picked it up," said Cordelia briefly, and come to think of it, truthfully. "In Putney."

"Well, it smells amazing," said Edwin, as if forgiving the curry for its Putney-based origins. At their feet Rainbottle whined, as if seconding this emotion.

"Shall I give him some?" said Cordelia, looking at the dog, or rather exchanging a look with him, Rainbottle's luminous imploring amber eyes reminding her of something, or someone, that she couldn't quite place at the moment.

"Best not," said Edwin. "As much as the old boy loves a curry, it doesn't do him any favours in the wind department. No favours at all." This was said with the decisive emphasis of bitter experience.

Rainbottle whined, as if in a canine flatulence mea culpa.

"How about you?" said Cordelia, pausing in her stirring for a moment and indicating the curry with the spoon.

"Me?" Edwin's face lit up. "Good lord, yes please. If I may. Thank you very much. Would you like some naan bread with it? I've got some Peshwari naan knocking around somewhere…"

Edwin warmed up the naan bread in another frying pan and then they sat down to dine together at the rectangular red-topped table with the yellow legs and folding sides that was a doppelganger of the one in Cordelia's room. Rainbottle joined them on the chair reserved for him with the tatty old cushion on it, obediently not making any attempt to grab the food and clearly—more evidence of canine intelligence—understanding the compact by which he was allowed to share their company but not their meal. Though he did indulge in a fair amount of heartrending whining and more of those soulful looks, with just a hint of reprimand to them.

Edwin was full of praise for the food. So full of praise that Cordelia began to wonder if she'd made the wrong decision, cutting him in on the loot, as it were.

But, she thought, if Edwin should insist on pursuing the matter later, for instance, asking for the exact location of the entirely imaginary business from which she'd, entirely imaginarily, purchased this delicious curry, so that he could purchase one for himself, for instance, Cordelia would simply lie smoothly, or continue lying smoothly and tell him that it had been a bijou pop-up concern that had now disappeared again.

Popped back down, so to speak.

* * *

Cordelia enjoyed a happy, in fact ecstatic, few days getting acquainted with the motherlode of stolen paperbacks that towered over all the other books stacked on her table. (Unlike its replica in the kitchen downstairs, Cordelia's table was always fully open because she always required full use of its surface area.)

A lot of these beautiful Sleuth Hounds, indeed the majority of them, were soon transferred from her tabletop to the bookshelves that lined every inch of wall space in Cordelia's attic room that wasn't occupied by the windows, the door, or—grudgingly allowed to exist—a wardrobe where she kept her clothes.

Those bookshelves contained the volumes of Cordelia's personal library, whereas the table held books destined for sale. There was some back and forth between the two, as now when the newly arrived Sleuth Hounds left the table to fill gaps on her bookshelf—it wasn't just *Kiss Me Deadly* that Cordelia had never found a copy of before, although none of the other missing titles matched it for rarity or value—or were used to replace inferior copies which she'd previously been quite pleased to have on her shelves but which, now, seemed almost shamefully substandard compared to the gorgeous stolen specimens of the corresponding titles.

Thus, books which she had contentedly tolerated for years in very good plus or very good or even good condition (which was to say, bad condition, pretty damned bad condition) were now unceremoniously booted out of her library, substituted with the Colin Cutterham collection copies (although she'd have to make bloody sure she never referred to them as such, at least not out loud, at least not in public, and not just because of excessive alliteration) all of which were, without exception, in fine condition.

Upgrading the books was, thought Cordelia with candid malice, like dumping your ex when you had a chance to go out with someone better looking. Far, far better looking.

On those rare occasions where her existing copies were as good or better than the Colin Cutterham ones, she listed the Cutterham copies (gotta love that alliteration) for sale on her website, along with a welter of her own, now upgraded and surplus to requirement, copies. The jilted exes, to continue the simile.

Over the next days and weeks these Sleuth Hounds, not surprisingly, proceeded to sell, and Cordelia's depleted funds began to look healthy again.

But one should always repair the roof while the sun is shining, thought Cordelia virtuously.

By which, of course, she meant buy drugs.

The recent, and reprehensible, visit by her brother had left Cordelia dope-depleted, so she set about repairing that deficit. Phone call to Fulham. Bus across Putney Bridge. And, next thing you knew, she was making her way up the steps at Mrs Chichester's faux-Moorish dwelling.

And coming down the steps was, oh Christ, that Tinkler personage.

Again.

Suddenly Cordelia realised what, or rather who, Rainbottle had reminded her of when he'd been gazing up at her so soulfully in Edwin's kitchen on the night of the curry. The fragrant, flavourful, filched curry.

Big doggy eyes.

Gazing at her now out of Tinkler's face.

The resemblance didn't make Cordelia think any more favourably of Tinkler. On the other hand, though, it didn't make her think any less favourably of Rainbottle. The poor mutt couldn't help whom he happened to resemble.

So Cordelia ignored Tinkler's big brown pleading eyes and his background buzz of conversation as he tried to engage her in a chat. Having issued a polite but formulaic brushoff, Cordelia had to virtually wriggle past him on the narrow staircase, which she was all too aware that he enjoyed—the wriggling past—but his enjoyment seemed a small price to pay for getting away from him.

She went on up the stairs and joined the potted yucca tree outside Mrs Chichester's door, rang the bell and, unlike the yucca tree, was invited into the house and darted smartly within.

As they went through the usual routine, Cordelia thought that Mrs Chichester seemed oddly subdued. But then drug dealers have their private lives and private moods, too. So Cordelia didn't give it overmuch thought.

However, as their transaction concluded in the business room, Mrs Chichester handed the bag to Cordelia, looking at her in rather an odd way, and said, "Do you have a moment?"

Cordelia's paranoia hit Defcon Five. Or was it Defcon One? Anyway, maximum Defcon.

But she played it cool. Mrs Chichester led her through the beaded curtain into the lounge, where they were greeted by the red furniture, red wallpaper and red carpet. On the coffee table was a similar, but not quite the same, pile of magazines, with some issues of *Country Life* now prominently displayed on top.

Cordelia suddenly had the horrible thought that Mrs Chichester might have finally decided to leave the city and move to the country and was gently breaking the news to her clients one by one. The bad news. The very bad news. Where would Cordelia score her dope now? She'd been coming here for years. All her other connections had long since dropped away. Cordelia began to calculate how much weed she had left, including the bag in hand, and how long she could make it last as she set about looking for a new connection.

She was concentrating so hard on this computation that she hardly registered what Mrs Chichester was actually saying. "…just wanted to apologise. When you asked about that photograph…"

Cordelia's gaze immediately swept to the photo on the wall, featuring the Ginger Thug, or rather Colin Cutterham (always nice to put a name to a face), and the Blancmange Dwarf and that fabulous array of books which were now in Cordelia's possession. Or rather, hers and her customers' possession—and back to Mrs Chichester.

Cordelia repressed any signs of the caught-red-handed guilt she felt and instead gave Mrs Chichester a bland look of careless, wide-eyed virtue.

"I wanted to apologise," said Mrs Chichester, "because I was a bit short with you."

A welcome, warm sense of relief spread over Cordelia. She concealed it with the same adroitness with which she'd hidden the guilt. Was *that* all this was about?

"I told you that it was someone you didn't want to know, in the photo. I should have been a little more forthcoming. It's actually a picture of my landlord."

After the roller coaster of emotions she'd experience in the last few moments, Cordelia very much welcomed the feeling of boredom that began to steal over her. The boredom of someone being told something she already knew.

"In fact," said Mrs Chichester, "this used to be *his* flat. I mean, he used to actually live here. He lived in this flat himself until he moved out when I rented the place. Some years ago."

Cordelia did a very good impersonation of someone who wasn't in danger of drifting off to sleep, polite attentive smile fixed on her face as she listened, or half-listened. She even made an encouraging noise, so Mrs Chichester would continue.

Mrs Chichester continued.

"And when I moved in, that picture was on the wall in here. He'd left it on the wall. It's a picture of him and his mother." Cordelia found this mildly interesting and quite gratifying in so far as it confirmed a theory of her own. "Anyway, I took the picture down and put it away safely, thinking I'd give it back to him next time he came over. But the next time he came over, before I could give it to him, he spotted that it was missing from the wall. And he told me to put it back up."

Mrs Chichester looked at Cordelia, her cool intelligent eyes unreadable behind her spectacles. "And I did. I put it back up immediately, and I have kept it on the wall in here ever since, carefully putting it back up after I redecorated. Do you know why I did that?"

"It's very sweet of you," said Cordelia.

"No it isn't. I did it because my landlord is the sort of man you don't want to cross. Not even in the smallest of particulars. And he is very attached to that picture because it shows him with his poor dead mother who passed away some while back."

Cordelia tried to make a sympathetic noise about the poor dead mother. But she couldn't insert a word—or noise—into Mrs Chichester's now flowing and unbroken monologue. "She was a big fan of crime stories. His mother. Which was ironic."

Mrs Chichester didn't volunteer why this was ironic, and Cordelia didn't attempt to ask.

"The point is, you do not want, you *definitely* do not want to come between a man like that and his beloved deceased mother. His memory of his beloved deceased mother."

Cordelia nodded eagerly as though this was a universally recognised truism.

"He is a man with a very bad temper. He can get *very* angry. And he was very angry when he visited me recently."

"Not with you?" said Cordelia. "Not angry with you?"

"No, not with me. But he was very angry, and I can't stress just how angry he was, as the result of someone having broken into his house and having *stolen* those books you can see there in the photograph. His mother's books, in fact."

This revelation actually had the effect of Cordelia feeling still less inclined than before to suffer any guilt for stealing the books. They hadn't even belonged to Colin Cutterham himself. They weren't his Sleuth Hounds. They belonged to someone who wasn't even here anymore.

"Those books that you said were very nice," said Mrs Chichester, her unwavering gaze on Cordelia. "Do you remember? When you asked me about that picture?"

Okay. Now Cordelia actually was on dangerous ground. She wished to hell she hadn't said that about the books, but she *had* said it and there was no way of taking it back, so instead she had to lean into it. So to speak.

"That's right," said Cordelia. Bright-eyed, innocent, cheerful, nothing-to-hide Cordelia. "They're some really great vintage paperbacks," she added, as if interpreting Mrs Chichester's query as a request for more information—why should anyone want to steal some old books? And here was Cordelia helpfully explaining, clarifying matters. "They're part of a series called the Sleuth Hounds—"

As Cordelia had hoped, a patently bored Mrs Chichester broke in on this. "We are talking about a very dangerous man," she said. "I would not want to be the person who stole those books."

"No, my god, no," agreed Cordelia, continuing her theme of nothing but wide-eyed innocence.

Mrs Chichester gave her a look of disgusted resignation and defeat. Then she sighed and showed Cordelia out.

As the front door closed behind her, followed by the sound of it being meticulously triple-locked, as required by tradition, Cordelia paused on the steps beside the big potted yucca and waited for her pulse and her respiration to return to something resembling normal.

Mrs Chichester couldn't prove anything.

She might suspect, but she couldn't *prove* anything.

More than that, she couldn't be certain that Cordelia actually had anything to do with the theft. Amiable and experienced liar that she was, Cordelia was certain that she'd given nothing away and stonewalled Mrs Chichester at every turn.

Mrs Chichester obviously *thought* she'd done it, but she didn't *know* and she couldn't be *sure*.

Nevertheless, Cordelia felt like she'd been through the wringer and various parts of her body were now well lubricated with perspiration.

As she stood there, her relief at getting through the ordeal was gradually replaced by a kind of offhand anger at Colin Cutterham. A very dangerous man? Fuck him and his thinning ginger hair and his noisy green sports car and his sadly deceased old mum.

Cordelia started down the steps and suddenly, as a sort of companion piece to the sinking feeling she'd experienced when Mrs Chichester invited her into the parlour, she now felt a sinking feeling of a quite different nature when she saw that, sitting on the steps just below her, was Tinkler.

He had waited for her.

He had been waiting all this time.

The hopeful happy look of welcome he gave her when he saw her only made that sinking feeling more profound. Cordelia shot a look of her own skyward, towards a deity she didn't believe in. I mean, hadn't she been through enough for one day?

And now Tinkler was saying, "I don't have Kind of Red with me this time, but a friend gave me a lift and they're picking me up in a minute and we could give you a lift, too…"

"No. Thank. You."

Tinkler shrugged. "Okay." He descended the stairs, a forlorn figure who nevertheless somehow failed to tug at her heart strings. At the bottom of the stairs, Tinkler paused and waved and then stepped across the pavement to the edge of the road and there was a smooth roar of a well-tuned engine and a car pulled in beside him. A sleek silver sports car.

At the wheel a stunning and stunningly familiar figure leaned over and opened the door, allowing Tinkler to hop smartly in and close the door swiftly, just in time, as she pulled away, smoothly and composedly, at considerable, calm, collected speed.

Standing there, filled with dawning mortal horror, Cordelia realised that she had just turned down a lift with the Woman.

13: BATH NIGHT

Cordelia was determined to count her blessings.

Yes, she had experienced the most terrible bad luck. The sort of seriously bad luck which you might expect to befall some poor chump of a character in Chapter 13 of a novel—a character who was superstitious about such things. (And knew which chapter she was in.)

Or if you wanted to be rigorous about it, not bad luck—in fact, not luck at all—but the natural and logical consequences of her own earlier behaviour. Chickens coming home to roost, would be one way to put it.

But in any case, yes, she had turned down a lift with the Woman, a chance to ride in the car with the Woman, to be driven by the Woman in her silver sports car.

In fact, it would have literally been a dream come true, a fantasy come true—although, of course, Tinkler would not have featured in that fantasy. Oh well.

She had missed an opportunity to sit beside the Woman, or at any rate in the same small automotive space as her, to breathe the same air, to talk to her, to get to know her, to see her at close quarters, make eye contact, feast her eyes on her, all in the most natural way, the way two people do when they're together.

Two new acquaintances who might become friends.

Who might become more than friends.

But she'd blown it.

She'd blown all that…

It served Cordelia right, she supposed, for being so unpleasant to Tinkler. But, in fairness, it was hard to know what other policy to take with such a person. Still, if she was being punished for it, punished by the cosmos, then fair enough.

Cordelia resolved to be nicer to him in the future. For obvious reasons. For bloody obvious, blindingly obvious, reasons. (But how could she have known that he knew the Woman? Even now, borne out by the evidence of her own eyes, it seemed a wildly implausible association.) But Cordelia resolved to take a more civil tone with him going forward. Obviously.

And she resolved to count her blessings.

For a start (first blessing), knowing that Tinkler was a friend of the Woman gave Cordelia a foothold in establishing the Woman's identity.

Up to now she'd known almost nothing about her.

Yes, she'd *seen* the Woman, on a number of occasions, not enough occasions, not nearly enough, in the flesh (flesh, flesh, flesh); had even met her if you wanted to stretch a point, although they certainly hadn't been formally introduced—ironically, painfully ironically, it turned out that Tinkler was in a position to have effected that miracle.

Yes, the Woman had exchanged words with her, a few paltry words. And almost run her over that time, the little darling…

But beyond that, Cordelia only knew the Woman through her blog, her masterful but pseudonymous blog about paperback crime fiction, *Clean Head's Crime Scene*.

Thanks to the blog being pseudonymous, she didn't even know the Woman's real name.

All that was set to change now.

As soon as she'd returned home, perfunctorily offering a greeting to Edwin as she passed him in the front garden where he was performing ritualistic bicycle maintenance, and was clearly disappointed that she hadn't come bearing curry, and offering a somewhat less perfunctory greeting, including some patting on the head and scratching behind the ears, the long, floppy ears, for Rainbottle, who nevertheless seemed equally disappointed—everyone was disappointed about something today—she had hurried up to her attic room.

She had closed the door behind her and scrupulously locked it. Recent previous experience with Stinky, not to mention the case of Colin Cutterham's front door, had taught her the value of conscientiousness in this area.

Then, immediately after she'd put the new batch of weed away—Mrs Chichester had told her it was a superbly strong new strain, but Cordelia hadn't even bothered to sniff it; she had other fish to fry—she opened up her laptop. Her beloved, somewhat battered, MacBook Air.

She had work to do.

Cordelia had never known the Woman's name.

She had first seen her at a book sale, one of the big ones in Bloomsbury, where she had knocked Cordelia's socks off—the way she went through the paperbacks, making splendid choices, especially of the vintage crime, winnowing, selecting.

Thereafter Cordelia would occasionally get a glimpse of her at similar events. And then the Woman would promptly disappear without a trace. Leaving Cordelia bereft. Her only solace—her sole solace—had come about as the result of Cordelia surfing the internet, as was her wont, in search of vintage crime fiction in paperback.

And that was how she had come across a blog entitled, somewhat mysteriously, *Clean Head's Crime Scene*. With no inkling of the person responsible for creating it, Cordelia had read, with increasing admiration and approbation, a number of the excellent posts (on Charles Williams, Mickey Spillane and Carter Dickson, née John Dickson Carr)—what sound judgement, what wit, what great cover scans—before finally scrolling to the top of the page where the title of the blog was accompanied by a *photograph* of the blogger.

Cordelia recalled fondly the enduring and highly pleasurable shock as she scrolled up and saw *the Woman's* face beside the logo at the top of the blog. No real name, no further identification, just that unforgettable face.

Cordelia had printed out that image of the Woman's face and lovingly framed it in a little circular silver frame.

The effect of that smiling face filling the tiny frame was positively iconic and delightfully decorative. Also, it appraised with an admirably non-judgemental gaze the antics it observed from the strategic position where Cordelia had stationed it on her bedside table.

But she still didn't even know the Woman's name.

But she did know someone else's name…

It turned out to be not Gordon but *Jordon* Tinkler, and a swift search of his socials revealed, hallelujah, yes, a treasure trove of photos of the Woman, including one fabulous shot of her in a two-piece swimsuit. A minimal two-piece bathing suit.

All right, let's be frank, a bikini. Bikini, bikini, bikini. A black-and-white domino affair.

More importantly—could anything be more important? Yes, miraculously, it could—the tags on the photos allowed her to learn the Woman's name.

Her gorgeous exotic name.

It was Agatha, highly appropriate for a crime fiction devotee—and sure enough, there was a photograph of her beside the statue of Agatha Christie near Leicester Square.

Full name, Agatha DuBois-Kanes. Good god. What a name! Exotic, posh, weird, hyphenated. There were lots and lots of pictures of her with cars. Cordelia had already known that the Wo—that *Agatha* was a skilful driver who frequently changed vehicles. But she hadn't guessed that she had such a veritable passion for them.

Cordelia decided that she would have to learn more about cars. For instance, which ones had the most comfortable back seats. Back seats that you could lie down on.

That two people could lie down on.

These and other thoughts swiftly led Cordelia to conclude that tonight was very definitely bath night.

Of course, every night was bath night, in a sense. Who but a deplorable stinking lazy reprobate went to bed without washing first? The idea of lying between clean sheets, and Cordelia insisted on clean sheets, washed twice a week (the laundry facilities in Edwin's house were another grudging plus for this place), the thought of desecrating such clean sheets with a dirty body was anathema to Cordelia.

But most bath nights consisted of no more than a swift and utilitarian shower in the utilitarian shower stall in Edwin's big bathroom downstairs.

But tonight would be *bath night*, in italics, with Cordelia immersed in the luxurious tub which was also in Edwin's bathroom and which, along with the spacious attic room with its nice bay window and the laundry facilities (and also, to be truthful, the winning poochy presence of Rainbottle) had decided her to become a tenant in this place in the first place.

With *bath night*, in italics, in prospect, Cordelia quickly and efficiently selected a clip for tub-time viewing.

Then she got some of her dope-infested—the correct word, of course, was "infused", but Cordelia liked "infested", with its sinister implications, much better—butter out of the fridge.

She then made some toast (okay, warmed a slice of bread in her toaster), spread the butter on it, and enjoyed it, checking the clock all the while, to make sure bath time would synchronise with drug time.

When the appropriate synchronous moment arrived, as indicated not just by the clock but by certain unmistakeable psychedelic sensations, she changed into her silk robe, took a big fluffy bath towel from her wardrobe, and added bath essentials to her crimson Szududu wash bag. Then, bag balanced on her laptop and towel over her shoulder, Cordelia padded barefoot down the stairs in her robe, past the front door and along the corridor towards the back of the house.

The first door on the left along here, painted red like the rest of the hallway but with tall thin panels of rippled opaque glass in it, led to the bathroom. Cordelia opened this and went in, cheerfully singing a little bath-night song to herself as she securely locked the door and set the water thundering into the tub.

Then she hung her robe on a projection at the top of the heated towel rail. This appliance was not the only useful bathroom accessory Edwin owned (one had to reluctantly concede that there *were* useful things about Edwin). There was also this splendid kind of shelf unit thing that could be hung across the bathtub, spanning its width. It was designed to hold soaps, sponges, mirrors or other accessories.

But in a kind of crucial bonus, a gift of the gods, Cordelia's laptop could also sit on it, quite stably and safely, with its screen open, and she could station it so it was in an ideal viewing position for a young woman who was up to her neck in warm sudsy water.

Of course, computers and water did not mix. But Cordelia had not knocked the MacBook Air into the tub yet, and she was confident she wasn't going to do so, no matter how exciting things might get.

Once the computer was in position, all she had to do was hit the start button, then lie back in the tub full of warm fragrant water.

Cordelia lay back in the tub full of warm fragrant water. The surprisingly good speakers on the computer started playing the music (by St Vincent) that Cordelia had added to this clip, and she relaxed and began to watch the narrative—admittedly, that was rather too grand a word for it—unfold.

On the screen a matched pair of scorching blonde porn-goddesses were drinking tequila and biting into limes. They were wearing clothes but not for much longer.

Cordelia set about enjoying herself.

Since the laptop was now out of bounds unless she dried her hands first, which would decisively spoil the mood, there was no pausing or stopping or restarting or rewinding the intoxicating stream of images on the screen.

Cordelia had to abandon herself to these visuals and be carried along by them and her response to them, carried at an accelerating rate, as though rushing along on rapids in wild dangerous waters, shooting towards the inevitable terminal waterfall where the rush of images would send her over the edge.

It was only as she was surging towards this nirvanic Niagara that Cordelia became aware of a poignantly overlooked porno opportunity. Why, oh why, hadn't she edited the shot of Agatha in her bikini (*Agatha* in her *bikini*) into this diverting travelogue?

Admittedly, that would have been perverted and transgressive and reprehensible and some might even argue borderline illegal—just to embark on a long list of reasons why it would have been so much *fun* to do…

She cursed herself for not thinking of it.

But it hardly mattered.

She had that shot in her mind.

Agatha. Bikini.

Cordelia had no need of technology.

She could rely on her sweet little imagination.

And the fixed on that image in her mind's eye.

Agatha…

Bikini…

Here we go…

Cordelia and her body and the brightly coloured imagery in her brazen little brain were all in shattering synchronisation.

Flowing together and flowering now at the perfect moment.

Perfect.

Now.

Now, now, *now*—

Tap-tap-tap.

Circumspect knocking on the rippled glass of the bathroom door. Knocking with knuckles, somehow you could tell they were knuckles, more specifically Edwin's bony, bicycle-repairing knuckles.

"Cordelia?"

From the steaming, stirring bathwater: "Yeah?" A single, strangled syllable.

Her mind came back from the image of Agatha in the bikini, pulled rudely back to other things, other matters, lesser matters, that exquisite instant now irretrievably gone.

"Will you be much longer?" a courteous enquiry from the landlord.

On that far side of the door, Rainbottle gave an engaging little whine, as though adding his own polite enquiry to his master's.

"No," snarled Cordelia through clenched teeth. "Not much longer."

The moment swirling away and draining into oblivion, just as the bathwater was swirling away and draining as Cordelia wrapped the chain around her toe and pulled the plug with her foot.

No point carrying on now. The moment had well and truly passed.

14: PAPERBACK SLEUTH

Cordelia's exploration of Tinkler's and Agatha's social media had, as a sort of side effect, acquainted her with their other friends. For instance, she had encountered plenty of photos and posts of the black-haired, blue-eyed bombshell (as seen recently outside Sadie's), and the bombshell's loser boyfriend (ditto).

And it turned out the loser boyfriend operated a vintage record hustle. Specifically, he advertised his ability to track down rare records for people. In fact, he actually styled himself the "Vinyl Detective".

After an appropriate amount of snorting and chortling at this ludicrous designation, Cordelia had got to thinking... She could offer similar services in her own sphere of expertise—not just selling vintage paperbacks, but actually tracking down valuable titles at the request of discerning customers. *Want lists welcome.* The more she thought about it, the more sense this made.

Also, if some fool could call himself the Vinyl Detective, she could call herself something equally outrageous.

So, she rebuilt her website—Cordelia had acquired pretty good image manipulation, editing and design skills; all developed, shamefully enough, through fashioning custom-made pornography for her own consumption, but what the heck, an acquired skill was an acquired skill—and rebranded herself and her business.

For her front page she created a simple but memorable small logo and then added a lavish illustration—a spread fan of great paperback covers, like a winning poker hand on a card table. She used an Abe Prossont cover, a Denis McLoughlin, a Robert Bonfils and a Jim Steranko.

Then, emulating that Vinyl Detective tosser, she added some immodest text about how she could find any book for any customer, any time. Providing it was a precious paperback. (No hideous hardcovers, please.)

Finally, in the wee small hours of the night, with her leafy, pricey riverside suburb spread out peacefully asleep all around her in her lonely attic room and utterly silent except for the occasional ghoulish scream of a copulating fox, Cordelia finished working on the website and went to bed, her feeling of satisfaction at a job well done somewhat tempered by the sheepish realisation that all this new-image relaunch nonsense was unlikely to make the slightest bit of difference...

But she was wrong.

When she woke up, groggy and sleep-sotted around noon, and logged in, there was a message waiting for her.

A prospective customer had found her revamped website and got in touch. *Already*.

The customer had left quite a long, friendly and chatty message praising the logo Cordelia had designed.

And Cordelia was indeed quite proud of that logo. She'd adapted it from the Sleuth Hound trademark, the yellow-and-black rectangle to be found at the base of the lavender spine of every book they'd published. The Sleuth Hound emblem featured a bloodhound in silhouette (a "sleuth hound" was an archaic name for a bloodhound) along with the capital letters—you'd never guess—S and H.

Cordelia had fashioned much the same for herself, except with the letters P and S.

The customer's message was downright heart-warming. It was rife with the informed kind of praise that seemed to emanate from someone who appeared to both know what they were talking about, and to appreciate what Cordelia was doing.

In other words, praise worth having.

Cordelia responded with an equally long and chatty reply in which she mentioned how the Sleuth Hound original, as cool as it was, had actually been a rip-off derived from two sources: the Boardman Bloodhound logo, designed by the great Denis McLoughlin, combined with the Pan "piper" emblem created by none other than, no kidding, Mervyn Peake.

Cordelia sent this message then went out to treat herself to a recklessly lavish brunch at Sadie's—foolishly expensive, but she felt that she should celebrate launching her reborn enterprise, and celebrate in style. Plus she already had a customer! Well, a prospective customer.

Then she picked up some high-end doggie treats at the pet shop next to the restaurant, returned home, and fed a few to Rainbottle and entrusted the rest to Edwin's keeping to be rationed out sensibly. Edwin was good at sensible.

Both dog and landlord were grateful enough, but both still looked like they would have preferred some stolen curry.

Then Cordelia went up to her room and logged back in, confident that there would be an equally garrulous and affable response waiting for her, from the prospective customer.

Nothing.

Total silence.

Cordelia realised that she'd come on as too much of a nerd and had scared them off. It rather hurt her feelings.

Oh well, fuck them.

Cordelia told herself to forget about it and threw herself into the long overdue task of listing some not very exciting but bread-and-butter titles which she knew would eventually sell and generate a small but steady income. She'd actually managed to forget the snub and the customer who wasn't going to reply when, as the sun went down outside her attic window, sinking in a smoky orange blaze towards the river beyond Barnes Bridge, the customer did reply.

Cordelia began to glow with pride as she hungrily perused the message. The sender professed to be seriously impressed by Cordelia's erudition—*The similarity of the Sleuth Hound logo to the Boardman one is fairly obvious*, read their reply. *But to my knowledge no one before has pointed out the resemblance to the Pan one. And on top of that, virtually no one is aware that Peake was the designer of the piper emblem. Full points for knowing that.*

The sender went on to say that they could see Cordelia was obviously a knowledgeable professional in this area and that therefore they wanted to hire her to find some books. A want list was duly attached. Perhaps Cordelia could send through prospective prices and a notification as and when she found copies. Although, within reason, price would be no object.

Well, naturally that made Cordelia even happier (*price would be no object*), and she hastily opened the attached document.

But as she read it, the pleasure and happiness she'd been feeling began swiftly to melt and drain away.

Replaced by a cold flow of fear.

Because the want list was exclusively Sleuth Hound titles, perhaps natural enough in the light of their earlier discussions. But, and here was the thing…

They were all titles she had stolen from Colin Cutterham.

Warning bells began to ring steadily and ceaselessly in Cordelia's head.

* * *

What better way, thought Cordelia, to flush out the person who had robbed you than by offering to pay top prices for the stolen merchandise? This realisation was so powerful, so shocking in its simple logical clarity, that Cordelia slammed her laptop closed, shutting it as if to prevent a malevolent pursuer emerging from it.

Not only that, but now she was sitting on the opposite side of her room, as far from it as possible, as though she still expected something to climb out of the computer and come after her, like the black-haired ghost-girl emerging from the TV screen in that Japanese horror film.

Get a grip, Cordelia told herself. Wasn't this all just delayed-reaction guilt at having robbed that poor slob? Cordelia wouldn't have thought she was capable of such an emotion, but you never knew. And maybe it was an aftershock from the tremendous tremor of guilt she'd suffered about being rude to Tinkler, behaviour that had cost her a ride with, and introduction to, the Woman herself. (Agatha, Agatha, Agatha.)

Maybe this all signalled the advent of a new and penitential law-abiding, respectful, sensitive and considerate Cordelia.

She certainly hoped not.

But the cold hard fact remained…

If Colin Cutterham wanted to find out who'd stolen his books, this was a damned good way to go about doing just that. Even if he didn't suspect Cordelia herself of the crime, perhaps he wanted to hire her. Both to help retrieve the stolen merchandise and to locate the person or persons who had stolen it in the first place.

And then he'd deal with them.

What had Mrs Chichester said? "We are talking about a very dangerous man. I would not want to be the person who stole those books."

Wait a minute.

Wasn't she getting way ahead of herself here?

Cordelia decided that the first thing to do was to find out if her customer actually was Colin Cutterham. Of course, if he was, and if he suspected Cordelia, he wouldn't be about to reveal his identity. But that would in itself be a clue: if this person was in any way cagey about revealing their identity.

With an action plan in place, Cordelia went back to her computer and opened it up again. The direct approach, she decided, was best. So she replied to the message saying she'd be delighted to follow up on the want list—giving nothing away there—and asking, as if it was the most natural thing in the world, for her new customer's name and address.

The response was so swift and upfront, *nothing to hide here*, that in itself it made Cordelia suspicious.

The customer's name was, purportedly, Toba Possner. Well, if you were going to make up a name you couldn't ask for an odder one than that, and the address was, allegedly, in Crouch End.

Cordelia immediately went online to see if there was such a person at such an address—not that this would definitely rule out Colin Cutterham lurking vengefully in the background, he might just have hired a dupe or intermediary to contact Cordelia.

Yes, someone called Toba Possner was indeed linked to an address in Crouch End; in fact, a rather nice large house with a low stone wall, impressive hedge and lots of trees, near Priory Park.

Next Cordelia searched "Toba Possner", intrigued whether this would prove to be a man or a woman. Woman, as it happened, although when you googled the name what you saw first was not a photograph of the woman herself but rather dozens and dozens of *paintings* by her. Brightly coloured abstracts, mostly, though there was some figurative work, too. And it was surprisingly good stuff.

Cordelia found that she was reluctantly impressed.

So, Toba Possner was a painter. She was also, when photos of the person herself began to appear further down the page, an elderly but rather regal and sharp-looking woman with a nice line in bohemian garb. Digging a little deeper, Cordelia discovered that Toba Possner had been at the periphery of a scandal a few years ago, when the writer of a children's book she'd illustrated way back in the 1950s was outed as a virulent antisemite.

Mind you, thought Cordelia, much the same could be said about Roald Dahl, if you dug deep enough, and there was no way she, or anyone, should stop reading Roald Dahl, genius that he was. So perhaps the take-home message here was that you shouldn't dig too deep into someone's background.

Nevertheless, she kept excavating Toba Possner, and found that no opprobrium whatsoever had attached itself to her from this scandal. Not only had she merely been the *illustrator* of the book and not the *writer*, she was herself Jewish.

In fact, the publicity had been beneficial to her, giving her a substantial midlife career boost. Or late life. She was in her eighties now, and looking remarkably well.

Was it possible that such a person could be Colin Cutterham's catspaw or—equal time for canines—dogsbody?

It seemed vanishingly unlikely.

But still possible.

Cordelia decided to meet her in person.

Cordelia had already developed an informal pattern of meeting customers for coffee at Sadie's; for example, when handing over books and receiving cash payments. She decided that with her rebooted business this would now become standard practice, whenever possible meeting clients face to face.

To add that personal, classy touch. Like a personal shopper.

And push the price of her services to her clients up into a new bracket.

Now the first such client was Toba Possner.

Who turned out to be a striking woman. Her eyes were a lambent amber. Her hair, cut short in a stylish curving contour that made a shapely setting for her face, was dyed a rich inky black. That face, like her hands, was intricately wrinkled but pale, almost transparent and remarkably unmarked by any kind of age spots or blemish.

She was petite and slender but still shapely, and evidently limber and unbowed by her years. Her ludicrous number of years. Cordelia hoped, as she approached her own century, she would look half this good.

Toba Possner's clothes consisted of black leggings under a black miniskirt, a black turtleneck sweater and black blazer with big black buttons, cut short so it fell well above her waist.

Okay, so a black theme. The only three splashes of colour were the leopard-skin pumps she wore on her feet, a leopard-skin-print silk scarf that she wore loosely knotted around her throat and a leopard-skin band on her black beret. It was an ensemble that could easily have gone badly wrong, but in this case had gone absolutely right.

This woman was old, but *chic*.

She settled into the chair opposite Cordelia and watched her, silently, unsmiling but somehow not unfriendly, as Cordelia ordered coffee for them both.

"I think I may be able to help you out with some of the titles on your want list," said Cordelia, aiming for a tone that was affable but all business, and lying through her teeth in the sense that she actually had no doubt whatsoever that she could source virtually every book the woman was after, without searching any further afield than the table in her attic room.

"That's very good of you," said Toba Possner. Her voice was low, slightly rough in an appealing way, educated but classless. It was as though she was so old that all the social-identification tell-tales which Cordelia was accustomed to assessing had simply been worn off her, leaving her as smooth as a stone on a beach, with her origins equally impossible to place.

"It will be a pleasure," said Cordelia. "Those Sleuth Hounds are gorgeous books." She watched Toba Possner closely, waiting for a reaction. A reaction that might include, for instance, a query as to whether they were sufficiently gorgeous to burgle a house for them.

"Really, you think so?" said Toba Possner, her eyes automatically moving to take in the waiter as he brought their coffee, and then back to Cordelia.

"Absolutely. I think the cover art is breathtaking. Magnificent."

"Hmm." Toba Possner had lifted her cup of coffee to breathe the aroma, and it was open to interpretation as to whether this was a comment about the quality of an americano at Sadie's or about what Cordelia had just said.

"Don't you think so?" continued Cordelia. "I mean, you're an artist yourself."

Toba Possner shrugged. "I suppose it's fair to say I wouldn't be looking for the books if it wasn't for the covers." It seemed a reluctant confession, extracted at cost. For some reason.

Cordelia decided to cut to the chase. "Why *are* you looking for these books?"

The woman shrugged again. "I used to own a set."

Alarm bells started ringing in Cordelia's head…

And were silenced again, or at least muffled, as Toba Possner went on to say, "A long, long time ago. And then, over the years, with one thing and another, I lost them. I lost track of them, and I lost *them*. Somewhere down the line."

"You had a complete set?" Cordelia couldn't help asking. She had done the maths and Toba Possner was old enough to have picked up these books when they were brand new. They would have been fresh off the presses. The thought of that, of buying these books when the colours on them were bright and crisp and the paper smelled inebriating with that new-book smell, was intoxicating. Intoxicating by proxy. Cordelia found vicarious excitement just in the thought of someone doing that.

"A complete set?" said Toba Possner thoughtfully. "Yes." Then she hesitated. "Well, not a *complete* set. There were a few titles missing. Ones I didn't want. That I never wanted."

Cordelia had a sudden flash of insight. "The ones with the airbrushed cover art?" These were the non-Abe Prossont ones, the misfit minority she had hesitated over even stealing at Colin Cutterham's. Though in the end she'd pilfered them with the others.

Toba Possner gave her a sudden surprised look. Then she smiled, revealing the perfect teeth of someone sixty years younger. And with a lot of money.

"That's right," she said. "That's exactly right. How did you know?"

"Because they're bloody awful," said Cordelia bluntly. "And you're an artist, so there's no way you wouldn't know they're bloody awful."

Toba Possner was nodding with approval. "True. It was terrible work. It didn't even have the power of crudity, or the integrity of the naïve."

"They were like Grandma Moses running amok with an airbrush," suggested Cordelia.

Toba Possner laughed. "Like Grandma Moses with an airbrush and a serious gin-and-tonic addiction to finance," she said. And Cordelia was surprised to discover that it was her turn to laugh.

When it came time to pay for the coffees, Cordelia, as always, sprang for them. This had invariably been her policy when meeting customers at Sadie's. And now that she was launching her new brand, she firmly intended to make it standard procedure. It singled her out as a classy operator.

Plus, she would more than make up for it by subsequently fleecing her clients.

But in this case she had quite a fight on her hands; as resolutely as she insisted on picking up the tab, Toba Possner insisted that, on the contrary, she would pay. This was a first.

In the end they fought to a draw, and finally agreed to split the bill.

Another first.

Cordelia decided there was no way Toba Possner could be a front for the comprehensively-looted Colin Cutterham. The giveaway was the fact that she had no interest in acquiring the books with covers by the Airbrush Ass-hat.

Anyone trying to track down those stolen Sleuth Hounds would want *all* of them, including the Airbrush Ass-hat's aberrations. So, Toba Possner was in the clear.

Which was good news, not least because it paved the way to having no hesitation about selling her new client a shitload of books.

Cordelia had almost every Sleuth Hound that Toba wanted right here on her table—the fact that Toba didn't care too much about them being in exemplary condition made her requests all the easier to fulfil.

In fact, Cordelia could pretty much complete her "investigation" and send Toba an invoice right now.

But it wouldn't do to make things look too easy.

She'd give it a few days before getting in touch with a cheery message of success.

Meanwhile, Cordelia set about knocking up a knockout design for a business card for her newly branded business.

On one side the card featured a vintage example of paperback cover art—she chose half a dozen variants, so she actually had six different business cards, at least different on *that* side—printed in colour, of course.

And on the other side it read:

> *Cordelia Stanmer*
> *Paperback Sleuth*

If she'd known what was coming, though, she would have been less concerned about business card design and more concerned about staying alive.

15: BOOK FAIR

The business cards looked *great*, and they came in stylish little boxes. Worth every penny.

Along with her name and the Paperback Sleuth title, she had included her phone number, website and email address, plus a QR code for those who were too damnably lazy or illiterate to use the other means of getting in touch with her.

Cordelia had had a substantial number of the cards printed up on high quality paper, glossy on the image side, naturally, but matte on the other side with her contact details. Not cheap, but there was no point cutting corners (should she have gone for the rounded corners? No; then they would not have echoed the rectangular shape of a vintage paperback book) and besides, she still had a decent amount of funds slopping around her account as a result of what she had begun to think of, fondly, as the Great Paperback Heist.

It actually *had* been rather great. Great fun. At least in retrospect. (To feel this way it was necessary to discount certain memories, such as collapsing into an armchair in Colin Cutterham's sitting room because her legs were not working; the aftermath of terror.) She was actually kind of sad it was all over. But the money it had brought was still with her, or at least a chunk of it.

And even if her money *had* all been gone, she still would have splashed out on the business cards.

Because the big Paperback Fair at Bloomsbury was coming up this Sunday.

And the Woman—Agatha—might be there. She attended these book fairs. She often attended. In fact, that was where Cordelia had first seen her…

And if she was there—*please, please, please, let her come*—Cordelia would boldly and smilingly hand a card to her.

Then she'd strike up a conversation.

Hello, I'm the Paperback Sleuth.

Cordelia had no doubt that she had the guts to strike up a conversation with Agatha now. After all, she was the girl who had robbed a stranger's house. (Why more virtue accrued through it being a *stranger's* house, she wasn't sure, but it did…)

Finally the day arrived, a sunny, wind-blown Sunday with tiny cyclones of dried leaves whirling up from lawns and pavements and the smell of autumn in the air, a few weeks before Halloween, when Cordelia caught the train to Waterloo, then the tube to Russell Square, and emerged blinking into daylight and made her way among the annoying tourist crowds flowing towards Woburn Place and Russell Square—the actual square itself—and her destination, the ranks of big hotels (the source, in fact, of all those annoying tourist crowds).

She walked up the side entrance of a hotel, a curving stretch of private road where taxis and big rumbling coaches pulled in, and went through the revolving doors into a hushed, softly furnished main reception area, tracing a familiar route, no need to read the event-announcing placards that had been strategically placed there today, and heading straight for the function rooms.

These rooms, big empty carpeted spaces that could be subdivided by drawing across tall folding floor-to-ceiling panels in a fetching shade of hearing-aid beige (a thrilling match for the carpets), usually hosted a host of stultifying conventions—self-help scams, plastic straw manufacturers, animal feed publicists, take your pick—but today one of them was hosting something much more exciting.

For what could be more exciting than a room full of vintage paperbacks for sale?

Well, a room full of vintage paperbacks for sale that also contained the Woman.

But a quick scan by Cordelia revealed that Agatha Sexy Double-Barrelled Name was nowhere in sight. At least, not yet.

Instead, very much in sight—a rather spirit-lowering sight, it had to be said—was the Mole.

He was doing his Mole thing, moving quickly along the tables, and snapping up…

Holy shit.

Cordelia realised what he was snapping up copies of.

She would have rubbed her eyes, if people in fact did such a thing. But she did actually blink, a swift involuntary series of blinks, which in no way altered what she was seeing.

The Mole was making his way among the tables, grabbing every copy he could find of…

Without even thinking about it, Cordelia launched herself into the fray, moving swiftly and sinuously through the mass of customers circulating among the tables that lined the walls, and occupied the centre of this big room, arranged in a rectangle that echoed the overall shape of the room, a sort of defensive formation to keep the customers at bay while the dealers milled about safely but rather uneasily, sheep surrounded by wolves, in the central space created by these tables, clutching paper cups of coffee and unpacking their stock to put it out on the tables.

Among that stock were numerous copies of an all-too-familiar crime novel…

And the Mole was snapping up every copy he could find.

It was the ludicrous self-published Scandi-noir abomination, *Cold Angel, Dead Angel*.

Cordelia didn't hesitate. She began picking up copies, too. There was only one reason the Mole would be interested in anything. Money. So if there was a profit to be turned—as mystifyingly unlikely as this seemed, given the quality of the book—then Cordelia wanted to be in on it, too. Of course she did.

The Mole saw what she was doing and made his way over to her, smiling. "So you heard?" he said.

"Of course," lied Cordelia.

Fortunately, the Mole was the sort of person who insisted on telling people things that they already knew. He was exactly that sort of person. "It seems the author was murdered," he said, excited to be divulging this information, even to someone he believed already knew it. "He was murdered in exactly the way that someone is murdered in his own novel."

"And how is that?" said Cordelia, intrigued despite herself. "I mean, how *exactly*? I heard," she lied, "but I didn't get all the details." She looked at the book, at the copy on top of the large and growing pile she was now holding in the crook of her arm. The dealer behind the table was giving her a doubtful look, as well he might. Why was she buying this crap? Cordelia took out some cash and waved it at him and he came over and she paid him quickly, before he realised that he'd catastrophically under-priced his stock.

She was basing this assumption, as it happened, entirely on the Mole's behaviour.

But Cordelia had no qualms about so doing. If there was one thing you could take to the bank, to use a certain figure of speech, it was the Mole's ability to nose out a profitable item.

"I don't know," said the Mole, in answer to her question about the murder method. "I haven't read it yet."

Of course. And the "yet" was a fig leaf. To Cordelia's knowledge, the Mole had never read a book in his life. Unless it was a price guide to collectable tomes. "But it's supposed to be very gory and very weird and very elaborate," he said. "And it's a limited edition." It took Cordelia a moment to realise that the Mole was now talking about the book, rather than the murder method.

"A limited edition?" said Cordelia sardonically.

"Well, a limited print run. It was self-published and it had a small print run."

Suddenly Cordelia was even more interested. She looked with malevolent envy at the pile of copies the Mole had acquired, considerably larger than Cordelia's own pile. The bastard was way ahead of her, she thought with rising anger—all this concerning a book which, five minutes ago, she would passed over without another glance.

"It's very sought after," added the Mole.

Then the Mole and Cordelia looked at each other, with those trigger words hanging in the air: *small print run, sought after*. And, abruptly, realising they were wasting time, and by extension money, they turned away from each other and without another word, without another trigger word, began to dart swiftly around the big, crowded, carpeted room, scanning the tables, grabbing every copy they could of *Cold Angel, Dead Angel*.

Soon, between them, they had cleaned out every dealer in the place. Those dealers were looking at them both with bemusement. Clearly the news hadn't reached them yet, thought Cordelia. Though, in another part of her mind, there was a distant warning signal.

What if the Mole had got it wrong this time?

What if she'd just saddled herself with an uncomfortable amount (red Emma rucksack full, and a couple of plastic carrier bags full) of an unsaleable book?

What if—and this was a genuinely horrific thought—the Mole had cooked up this whole thing as a revenge stratagem for her being mean to him? (Refusing to have coffee with him would be one recent example.) Cordelia felt the hot and unaccustomed sweat of a swindler potentially swindled, and her heart began to hammer in an annoying fashion.

She told herself to calm down.

The Mole wasn't trying to punish her. This was no revenge stratagem.

For a start, the Mole was far too boring for any such subterfuge. Plus, look at all the copies of this perfidious book that the Mole himself had bought.

No, if he was capable of plotting a scheme of retribution it would be a much less expensive scheme. The Mole was nothing if not a major cheapskate.

Cordelia was just being paranoid. This was all just residual guilt based on being mean to Tinkler in a similar fashion to the Mole (well, for heaven's sake, they were both well-qualified losers who insisted, in their well-qualified loser ways, on hitting on her).

Cordelia was just still feeling a bit bruised about being punished for that. Being mean to Tinkler. Punished by the cosmos by having to watch Tinkler and the Woman drive off together in the silver sports car, leaving her in the dust, figuratively speaking.

Anyway, in the worst-case scenario here, in which the unimaginable had happened—that there was a glitch in the Matrix, that a yawning void had actually opened in the space-time continuum and Cordelia had in fact been successfully scammed (*by the Mole?*) into wasting money—at least it was at a moment when, unusually, she had a bit of money to waste, was still in the black.

Nevertheless, just in case, Cordelia set about making a careful search of the other wares on offer at the book fair and picking up a few other choice items of interest which she knew she could resell at a significant profit, as a hedge, so to speak, against having been duped by the Mole (vanishingly unlikely) or against the Mole having wrongly identified *Cold Angel, Dead Angel* as a valuable resale item (also pretty damned unlikely, given the Mole's remorseless cash-register mind).

Most notable among these money-spinning hedge items purchased by Cordelia that morning were *Devil's Kisses* and *More Devil's Kisses*, published by Corgi (effectively the British affiliate of America's Bantam Books) back in the early 1970s. They were nominally edited by "Linda Lovecraft"—an hilarious and rather witty conflation of H.P. Lovecraft, towering weirdo horror maestro, and Linda Lovelace, then prominent porn star and leading, ahem, actress in *Deep Throat*. In reality, behind the pseudonym was the Englishman Michel Parry, who'd edited many a solid (and fairly staid) horror paperback anthology.

But *Devil's Kisses* and its sequel consisted of supernatural tales of terror with an erotic slant, sometimes a heavily erotic slant. Though not all highly explicit, they were, at their outer limits, essentially horror smut. Or at least horror sleaze, British style.

Devil's Kisses had proved something of a hit with the reading public and a sequel had been commissioned in short order, and it was this second volume which was the more collectable of the two. Because it contained a story by Chris Miller, frequent *National Lampoon* contributor and American humourist…

But someone in England hadn't found Miller's story so humorous, and had lodged a formal complaint. Scotland Yard duly warned Corgi that they might be in line for prosecution for obscenity, and the publishers, or their lawyers, had responded with spectacular spinelessness. Despite the story in question already having seen publication in the UK, in magazine form, in the *Lampoon*, with no problems whatsoever, they caved in and the book had been pulled from sale and the entire print run pulped.

Well, not the *entire* print run…

Of course, the dozy dullard dealer who had these books—nuggets of real gold—among the dross on his book-fair table today knew none of this, and Cordelia had smartly scooped them up. They were both in fine condition and she had picked them up for a song—a rather bawdy song, in this case—and she would soon resell them at many healthy multiples of the purchase price.

This little find would normally have put Cordelia in a positively jubilant frame of mind, and would have done so now if it weren't for two things… The nagging worry that the Mole might have led her down a blind alley, or up the garden path if you prefer, with this *Cold Angel, Dead Angel* thing, which she would now be lugging home so many copies of.

That and the fact that Agatha was a no-show.

Cordelia waited. And waited. Then, just to be on the safe side, waited some more.

When it became obvious she wasn't going to turn up, Cordelia gave the Mole one of her business cards—it seemed like too total a defeat not to hand out any of them; he was gratifying impressed by the quality of the card, by her marketing strategy and, above all, by her meretricious new moniker—and then she high-tailed it back home.

Once securely locked in her room—she was never going to make that mistake again—Cordelia fired up her laptop and began to feverishly check if the Mole had totally lost it or even, absurd thought, had got the better of her.

Looking on, in a manner of speaking, as she did this were the tall looming stacks of *Cold Angel, Dead Angel* which she had unpacked and placed on her table. Cordelia had a terrible feeling these tall stacks would soon be looking on *mockingly* when she'd confirmed that she had been, after all, well and truly skanked.

And by the Mole of all people.

But Cordelia hadn't been skanked.

Even a hasty and superficial survey of the lively digital hinterland revealed copies of this book selling for outrageous sums. Everywhere she went…

Except for one book remainder warehouse in the wilds of Cornwall where they still had copies at a rock bottom price. Cordelia immediately ordered every single one they had, paid for them (she'd qualified for free delivery!) and closed her laptop again with a great sense of satisfaction at having fleeced the carrot-crunching clowns of Cornwall.

Then she thoughtfully studied the stacks of the book in question and selected a copy for closer examination.

What was it the Mole had said? "The author was murdered in exactly the way that someone is murdered in his novel. It's supposed to be very gory and very weird and very elaborate."

Supposed to be… The Mole was flying blind because he hadn't read the book. But in this instance, Cordelia couldn't blame him. She couldn't imagine being able to bring herself to read this thing. It looked like such a piece of junk…

Then she discovered that she didn't need to read it.

She turned the book over and, for the first time, gave the text on the back cover some close scrutiny. Only to discover that it featured a virtual excerpt of the murder scene. Basically it was a wintery evisceration of some token victim—female and good looking, of course—with the disembowelment designed to evoke the angel-shapes kids made in the snow. Not a bad idea.

But talk about spoilers…

Cordelia turned the book over again, to look at the front cover, the abjectly lousy front cover, and found herself thinking, rather uncharitably, that the person responsible for this abomination *deserved* to be murdered in a horrible fashion. She set the book aside, her mood having been decisively lowered; she felt faintly soiled to even have these things on her table...

But she didn't feel soiled by the prices they commanded when she began selling them.

Which is what she began to do now.

Cordelia fired up her MacBook Air and went back on eBay again. If anything, the prices were higher than when she'd looked before. Was that possible? Yes, decided Cordelia, it was. Because dozens of paperback dealers and collectors would, like her, be returning from the book fair about now and switching their computers on. And many if not most of them would be checking on *Cold Angel, Dead Angel* to see what the fuss was about, to see why Cordelia and the Mole had been mopping up every copy in sight.

Cordelia realised that this made her a trendsetter and influencer (she discounted the Mole's involvement out of hand).

She did a quick search of the other mass sale sites—ABE, Amazon—and the specialist paperback dealers, Zardoz and PS Publishing. And she was impressed. There wasn't a copy of *Cold Angel, Dead Angel* listed anywhere for less than a hundred pounds.

Well, she could fix that.

Cordelia put a copy up for sale on eBay. She agonised briefly over what starting price to list it at. One pound or one pound fifty? In the end she settled on one pound. It seemed cleaner...

Three days later the book closed out at a hundred and fifty-seven pounds. Cordelia was jubilant. She wondered how the buyer felt —the idiot could have bought the same book at a saving of over fifty quid from any number of other places. But it was starting the listing at a low price that had done it. People became so hypnotised with the notion of a bargain that they locked onto the idea of buying the book and didn't drop out of the bidding even when it became a major loss-making proposition.

Target fixation, you might say. It apparently caused fighter pilots to fly into the ground.

It had certainly caused this bumpkin to crash and burn, financially speaking.

But he paid up fair and square and Cordelia printed out an address label, paid for postage online, packed the book and took it down to the local post office by Castelnau, dropped it off and walked home again, taking a leisurely stroll past the pond and thinking, not for the first time, how much she loved the rare paperback hustle.

Over the next little while Cordelia happily fielded enquiries from customers who were looking to hire the Paperback Sleuth to find copies of this book, and even more happily observed the shrinking of the stacks on her table. Not to mention the gratifyingly increased funds in her PayPal account. And in the same way that someone else might invest a windfall in government bonds or blue-chip stocks, it would normally have been a matter of standard Cordelia policy in a situation such as this to top up her weed supply.

But Cordelia currently had more than enough weed. Even if her vile brother paid another visit and bought a load from her, she would still have more than enough.

Nonetheless, she rang up Mrs Chichester. She hoped that her dealer, annoyingly perceptive as she was, wouldn't sense that Cordelia had an ulterior motive. An ulterior motive for buying drugs.

This was a first.

She obediently noted the day and time Mrs Chichester gave her.

Fingers crossed.

When Cordelia arrived at the familiar address in Fulham and started up the steps towards Mrs Chichester's house, she was humiliated to discover that her chest was tense with suspense. Would he be here? Yes, sure enough, coming down the stairs was none other than Tinkler. Hurray. Mrs Chichester tended to always block-book her customers into the same time slots, so the odds were that Tinkler would be here, but you never knew…

Cordelia gave him a smile and said, "Hello."

"Ah…" Tinkler was so taken aback that for a vertiginous moment it looked as if he might experience total brain freeze. But he saved the day by recovering rudimentary language skills, or at least the ability to imitate the last sound he'd heard, and he too said, "Hello."

"How is Sort of Red?"

"What?" Tinkler's head looked like it might be about to commence a three-sixty-degree spin.

"Your car," said Cordelia patiently.

"Yes," said Tinkler eagerly. "I thought that was what you meant. *Kind* of Red."

"Oh, Kind of Red, sorry."

"No need to apologise. It's a silly name, really, but you know. It sort of has a story attached to it."

To prevent him telling this story, or at least forestall it, Cordelia said, "Do you have it here today, your car?"

"Ah… yes."

"I don't suppose I could cadge a ride home?" Cordelia gave him her most winning smile.

Tinkler looked like a man struck by lightning.

16: BLUE NOTE PAPER

After she'd purchased her weed from Mrs Chichester, surplus to requirements at the moment but always useful to have on hand, and a necessary piece of window dressing for this scenario—Tinkler must never know she'd come here specifically to engineer a meeting with him—Cordelia bade farewell to her dealer and went out to meet Tinkler at the foot of the steps outside the Moorish house.

Then he drove them both back over the bridge in his old-fashioned little red car. Cordelia told him, truthfully, that it would be fine to drop her anywhere here on the south side of the river—Tinkler's own house was in the other direction to where she was headed, along the high street and up Putney Hill—but Tinkler insisted on driving her home and Cordelia didn't put up too much of a fight.

When he dropped her off, they exchanged phone numbers and Cordelia got out of the car and Tinkler drove off. Both of them jubilant, though for rather different reasons.

She went inside and up to her room, to switch her computer on and find a message from Toba Possner politely enquiring if she'd made any progress—if the Paperback Sleuth had made any progress—in her search for the titles on Toba's want list.

Cordelia glanced at the stack of Sleuth Hounds on her table

that she'd already prepared and, indeed, was already accustomed to thinking of as Toba's books.

She'd simply culled these from the general stock of Sleuth Hounds she'd been left with since the Great Paperback Heist. They were ready to go and just needed to be paid for, packed and posted.

All this could have been done some time ago, but it wouldn't do to make her "finding" of these titles look too easy. That would spoil the effect.

But she felt sufficient time had now elapsed, so she emailed Toba a reply, saying that she'd found a number of books on her want list (Cordelia decided to "find" the books in two instalments, thus bolstering the illusion of the Paperback Sleuth's tireless search for these rare titles) and accompanied it with an invoice—she considered giving Toba a discount; she liked the old woman, but that would have set a dangerous precedent—and asked whether she wanted the books sent by Royal Mail or a courier.

Toba Possner replied promptly. And paid immediately, which endeared her even more to Cordelia's heart. But she said not to send the books either by post or courier.

She asked Cordelia to deliver them in person.

Cordelia agreed readily enough to bring the books to Toba Possner, although the prospect of a visit to Crouch End did not exactly cause her soul to surge with joy. However, it turned out Toba didn't want her to bring the books there. Her house was in Crouch End but, she explained, her studio was in Chelsea.

The thought of visiting an artist's studio was genuinely exciting to Cordelia, at least when it was an artist she admired (some joker with half a shark in formaldehyde would have been a very different proposition), and when Toba offered to pay Cordelia's travelling expenses, she stoutly declined. Truth be told, she still felt a bit bad about not giving the old gal a discount. Maybe she would on the next, and final, batch of Sleuth Hounds which were perched on her table, all ready to go as soon as sufficient additional time had passed to sustain the illusion of hard work and industry in their finding.

Cordelia wrote the Chelsea address on a sheet of writing paper, using her fountain pen. She had bought the paper, luxurious pale blue laid vellum, in case she ever needed to write to someone important whom she wanted to impress. (Who could that be?)

But in the meantime, the paper was too beautiful to resist so she'd cracked open the packet and taken out a sheet and been waiting for an excuse to use it. And here was one. It would add a touch of class to the transaction. Below Toba's name and address she'd written a list of the Sleuth Hound titles to be delivered in this batch. Underneath the list she wrote, *All with cover art by Abe Prossont*.

Then, with a flourish, she underlined Abe Prossont's name.

And then, out of a sense of symmetry, she also underlined Toba Possner's name.

Having done that, with a feeling of a job well done, or at least on the verge of being well done, Cordelia decided to get on with some outstanding admin. Administration was, by its nature, inevitably less than riveting, so to enliven the work she helped herself to some green butter on toast.

With the help of the onrush of the dope, Cordelia set about dealing with the various tedious tasks that running a small business entailed. She started with the most boring and worked towards the least. The most boring was doing her accounts. The least, when she finally got to it, was book searching online.

Cordelia maintained a number of searches on eBay and ABE which notified her when any choice items turned up. But she'd learned that if she relied just on these automatic alerts, all kinds of treasures would slip through her fingers. As dull as it was, she also had to do manual keyword searches on Google at regular intervals. So she dutifully typed in "Sleuth Hound paperback".

Along with all the usual suspects—cover galleries on Pinterest, reviews on Goodreads, dead links of books that had been sold long ago at auction sites—Cordelia was intrigued to see a new listing.

It was on a free classified-ad site, originally set up by Australian emigrees but now used by cheapskates of every stripe. Just the place to find a potential jackpot, rare books being sold after a death or house clearance or estate sale, and going for a bargain price.

Intrigue turned to excitement as she saw a list of prime Sleuth Hound titles, accompanied by an illustration of the cover of *Night Walker* by Donald Hamilton.

The excitement curdled into disappointment as she realised that this wasn't a list of books being offered for sale. It was a list of books someone was looking to *buy*.

And then disappointment turned into wary fear when she read the advertisement all the way to the end. *Contact C. Cutterham.*

Followed by an email address, a phone number and a very familiar street address of a little house in a cul-de-sac in Putney.

Cordelia hastily got the hell away from this webpage, cleared her cache and closed her browser. None of which made any sense. There was no way Colin Cutterham could ever know she'd come across his clumsy little attempt to set a trap.

But the weed-infested butter was roaring through her system now and paranoia was in full flow. Paranoia and, oddly, regret.

The poor bastard, she thought, feeling ambushed by sudden and unexpected contrition. No wonder he'd illustrated his ad with the cover of *Night Walker*. It was no doubt taken from the enlarged scan he had framed on his bedroom wall…

Because that was all she'd left him after she'd picked his bookshelves clean.

Cordelia forced all thought of Colin Cutterham, looted chump and Ginger Thug, from her mind. She had no intention of letting him spoil her high. So she made herself concentrate on more cheerful things. Like her impending visit to Toba Possner's to deliver the books. And the funds that had already flowed from that.

Plus, going into that part of town provided a chance to check out the charity shops on the Kings Road—who knew what treasures those rich fools might had discarded? Maybe a boxed set of Penguin Somerset Maugham titles with the Harri Peccinotti/ Derek Birdsall covers, in fine condition, of course.

As her last onerous task of the evening, she set about wrapping Toba's Sleuth Hounds in bubble wrap—she seemed to spend a large portion of her life doing this, or similar—and caching them in her rucksack ready for delivery. Once this chore was complete, business would be concluded for today.

When the last of the books went into the bag, she added her handwritten note (Cordelia supposed it was an invoice of sorts, though a very classy one), setting it on top of the bubble-wrapped bundles.

She was now thoroughly stoned and her sinuous, serpentine handwriting, in dark blue ink, seemed to be floating slightly *above* the pale blue note paper. Cordelia reflected with satisfaction that if this was the kind of result she was getting out of turning the standard weed into olive green butter, then the new turbo-charged stuff would be frankly amazing.

Among the dark blue writing on the pale blue paper the two underlined names stood out emphatically.

Toba Possner and *Abe Prossont*.

They seemed embossed on the air, or at least on Cordelia's corneas, after she closed the rucksack and hid the paper from view.

Toba Possner and Abe Prossont…

A strange and disquieting thought flitted through Cordelia's head, like one of the cartoon bats on the back cover of a Bantam John Dickson Carr thriller.

She dismissed it, banishing that particular bat from her belfry.

But it came fluttering promptly back in and took up residence there. Permanent residence. Roosted, in fact, hanging upside down from a beam in her belfry and started a family, to extend the metaphor to breaking point.

Sighing, somewhat disgusted with herself, Cordelia decided to let this stoned notion play itself out to the end. So she reopened her laptop, opened a Word document and typed the two names.

Abe Prossont.

Toba Possner.

Was it?

Could it be?

At first glance it looked impossible, and she dismissed the idea out of hand. But it just wouldn't let go of her. The bat, with its entire family, was now flying around en masse inside her belfry in agitated excitement. To try to quiet them down, she retyped the names all in capital letters.

ABE PROSSONT.

TOBA POSSNER.

It still seemed impossible, but the bats showed no signs of simmering down. So Cordelia went through the names letter by letter, meticulously deleting each in turn and also the corresponding letter in the other name.

She did so with a growing sense of disbelief, and then triumphant excitement. And the bats in her belfry were going nuts.

Because it was true.

The names were anagrams.

They looked so different—there was something about the position of the 'e' and 'r' in each that made it difficult, if not impossible, to equate them on any kind of casual inspection, but it transpired they were essentially identical—merely variations on a theme.

Cordelia kicked herself for not having seen this sooner.

Not least because the clue was there, quite strikingly and obviously there, in Toba Possner's paintings. The bold use of colour, the striking compositions, the command of space.

These were all shared in abundance by the "Abe Prossont" cover art of over half a century earlier. The abstract forms of her non-representational work were even reminiscent of the brilliantly imaginative hand lettering on the Sleuth Hound paperbacks, the understanding of how to juxtapose contrasting shapes for maximum effect.

There was no doubt about it.

Toba Possner was Abe Prossont.

17: A COMMISSION

Cordelia went to her rendezvous with Toba Possner, taking with her the red rucksack full of Sleuth Hounds and her newfound knowledge. The paperbacks weren't a burden, but the knowledge was. Her client for these books was the very woman who'd created the artwork that made them so valuable.

But Toba would have no reason to suspect her own cover was blown. Nor, necessarily, any reason to welcome the fact.

How to handle this? Cordelia mulled as she got off the bus that had brought her from Clapham Junction, across Battersea Bridge, and into the teeth of the seething traffic in London's most fashionable neighbourhood.

Toba's studio was in a large handsome Edwardian courtyard of flats constructed out of rose-coloured brick just around the corner from Chelsea Town Hall. Cordelia was buzzed in via an intercom beside a set of tall black iron gates set in a stone archway. At the peak of the archway was an engraved inscription that declared the dwellings in the courtyard were part of something called the Sherman Trust and had been built in the early twentieth century.

Toba's flat was on the top floor, at the far end of an open walkway, with a memorably bright yellow door that opened as Cordelia approached, with its inhabitant cued and ready for her arrival Mrs

Chichester-style, but rather more welcoming. In fact, Toba was leaning out and waving to her.

As she served them mint tea—not really Cordelia's thing, but what the hell—Toba Possner's eyes moved to the stacks of paperbacks on the table and Cordelia felt the thrill of secret knowledge. Was she going to tell Toba what she knew? Was she going to out her, as it were? Or would Cordelia chicken out? Chicken out on the outing? She stalled for time by asking Toba what she was doing these days, as an artist.

"I will tell you what I *should* be doing. Taking commissions. But I'm terrible about that, about commissioned work. About getting around to it. Anything except my own stuff. It just takes a lower priority. It goes to the bottom of the list and somehow never quite makes it to the top. I even owe this nice young couple a painting of their *cats*. They paid me for it years ago, and they're such nice people. And the cats are very nice visually. The most amazing eyes on one of them. Most extraordinary turquoise eyes."

Toba Possner paused for a moment in contemplation of feline beauty. Cordelia scotched the urge to tell her that she herself was a dog person.

"I really must get that painting finished. I really am terrible. And, as I say, I must take on some more commissions. I need to beef up my cash flow because I have my eye on a little farmhouse in Provence. It's a gem of a place, and it's a long-held dream of mine to have a place in France."

Cordelia was seriously impressed. Here was a woman in her eighties who was not only still alive, but still fully alert mentally, blazing with creativity and thinking of buying a freaking farmhouse in freaking Provence.

She clearly had no intention of dropping dead, or slowing down, any time soon.

Talk about a role model.

Cordelia, not by and large a people person, rather liked Toba Possner. And she suddenly saw not only an opening for her to reveal her secret knowledge but also a chance to help Toba out. To do a good deed.

"Actually, I might be able to help you with that."

"With what?"

"With a commission."

"Oh, I wouldn't charge you full price. I could swap you for the books you're finding for me. A little sketch or something."

"No, not for me. For someone you *could* charge full price. Definitely charge full price. He has lots of money." Cordelia thought of how much money someone must make from owning rental properties all over London. "Plenty of money. And he would love to have a painting by you."

"He knows my work?" said Toba, a question poised between pleased and quizzical, as if she couldn't quite believe that anyone was aware of her art.

Cordelia took the plunge. "Sure, he's got some of it on his wall. Not an original, though."

"One of my prints?" Toba's emphatic black eyebrows were arched with introspection as she apparently reviewed the possibilities, mentally going through the catalogue of her prints.

"No, just a scan."

"A what?"

"A framed scan of one of your covers." Cordelia leaned forward and tapped one of the stacks of paperbacks with the tip of her finger. "One of the Sleuth Hound covers. I bet he'd jump at the chance to own an original. You could recreate one of your vintage cover paintings. And he could certainly afford to pay top dollar for it."

Cordelia still had her finger on the cover of the paperback—*Ride the Nightmare* by Richard Matheson, a cracking piece of artwork and some terrific lettering, the word "nightmare" was itself tangibly nightmarish—and Toba Possner was staring at it, and then she looked up at Cordelia.

"You know," she said.

"Yes," said Cordelia. After all her fretting it seemed this would be a discussion consisting of simple words. Meeting Toba's gaze was a little too much for her, though, so she looked away, at the paintings that hung on the walls in here, powerful colours blazing against the white paint of the walls. The inner rooms of the flat were painted a uniform, brilliant white, but the outer rooms and hallway were in gradients of yellow, growing more intense until they culminated in the dazzling canary shade of the front door. Rather a lovely aesthetic conceit, Cordelia thought.

She gestured at the paintings on the walls, mostly abstracts but also some landscapes, and then at the paperbacks. "I should have seen it immediately. The similarity in style. It's obvious. I don't know why I didn't spot it right away."

Toba shook her head. "On the contrary, it is amazingly perceptive of you. In all these years no one else has put two and two together despite the evidence being out there, in plain sight, so to speak."

"The anagram."

"Precisely."

"It's a really good anagram," said Cordelia. "Somehow the two names just don't *look* the same."

"Yes, it's something to do with the 'e' and the 'r'," said Toba Possner, and Cordelia felt a stirring tingle of connection, of two minds meshing.

"You know," said Toba, "it really is quite odd to have my cover blown after all these years. I invented good old Abe Prossant just after I left art school, when I took my portfolio around to various publishers and discovered that they were willing enough to hire me—at about half the going rate they would pay a bloke."

This information made Cordelia so furious that she swallowed half her cup of mint tea before she realised what she was doing.

"So I decided I would *become* a bloke," said Toba. "And command full price for my work. Thus Abe Prossont was born. Abe would do the artwork and sign it, and I would sell it for him, on his behalf. I became his agent, working mostly over the phone." Toba Possner smiled. "Anyway, well done for working out my secret identity. The Paperback Sleuth indeed."

Cordelia glowed with pride.

"Now," said Toba, "what is this about a commission?"

Cordelia gave her Colin Cutterham's details, the phone number and email gleaned from his online advertisement. The address of his little house was burned into her brain, post-burglary. She borrowed Toba's phone, and found the ad for her. "Please tell him you found this online and say it was what gave you the idea to approach him. Please don't mention my name, or my involvement at all."

"A bit of shadowy intrigue," said Toba. "I like it."

Once she returned home, still tingling with the excitement of the day's shared revelations, Cordelia decided that she'd earned the privilege of getting high. What's more, she would get high using the new and allegedly super-strong weed she'd bought from Mrs Chichester on her previous visit.

So Cordelia did the sous vide thing, happily throwing herself into the intricate and lengthy preparation process for the rest of the afternoon, and finally straining the butter into the waiting ramekins as the shadows of a moody autumn evening gathered in her attic room, and chilling the olive green treasure in the fridge just in time to render it spreadable on a piece of Poilane toast and be consumed at a suitable interval before she went down for tonight's bath.

Cordelia's first inkling of just how strong the weed actually was came as she tried walking down the stairs to the bathroom. She got as far as the landing immediately below her attic room before her mind wandered off the task at hand.

Here on the middle floor of Edwin's house were a series of uninhabited, and largely uninhabitable, rooms awaiting renovation and, eventually, theoretically, renting out. They had been in this state ever since Cordelia had moved in, and the fact that they'd never advanced beyond it were evidence both of Edwin's inability to see a project through and an obvious, complacent prosperity that enabled him to forego the revenue that renting these rooms would have provided.

Cordelia found herself wandering around the ghostly empty rooms—bare wooden floors, mysterious shapes of furniture bulging under dust sheets, half-demolished walls exposing the wooden skeletons beneath the plaster—until she wondered why she was carrying her wash bag and her towel on such an excursion.

Oh yes, *bath* time…

As she descended the stairs, each carpeted wooden step seemed to rise reciprocally under the pressure of her foot so that it felt, in a sort of M.C. Escher way, that she was going up as much as she was coming down. When she eventually reached the ground floor and found herself standing by the front door, she felt that several decades had elapsed.

This really was good dope.

It was at this point that she realised she'd left her laptop upstairs, but there was about as much chance of her going back up there to retrieve it as there was, just at the moment, of scaling the north face of the Eiger, using a toothbrush as an ice axe. Had she remembered her toothbrush? Yes, she had.

Never mind about the laptop. Although it could beneficially supplement her imagination for any frolicsome activities she chose to undergo in the warm scented bathwater (which she would soon be submerged in, up to her pretty little neck) her imagination on its own was more than up to the task.

Especially rocket-assisted as it was right now by the super-strong weed-infested butter.

The fun really began when Cordelia was safely locked in the bathroom—she'd managed to locate it, eventually—and the water plunging from the taps into the big bathtub started making a noise that seemed to be a deep and richly reverberant yet distorted voice offering a commentary that was simultaneously diabolical and salacious, just at the periphery of comprehension.

Like, say, Paul Robeson on amphetamines reading selections from *Devil's Kisses* and *More Devil's Kisses* on a badly tuned-in analogue radio.

Far from finding this frightening, Cordelia began to giggle with delight. This was clearly going to be a hoot. She must remember to thank Mrs Chichester for the high-octane goodies.

Carefully checking the temperature of the water—she didn't want to be a poster child for stoned disasters or have to explain third-degree burns to the nice people in Accident and Emergency, or was it first-degree burns? Anyway, maximum burns—but the temperature of the water was perfect, and Cordelia even remembered to take off her robe before climbing into the tub and immersing herself. Full marks, Cordelia.

However, just because she'd turned the taps off, didn't mean that the satanic soundtrack of the plumbing had ceased. There was nothing particularly unusual about this. The pipes in Edwin's house had always been given to eccentric and inexplicable noises, though nothing like the hellish hoe-down hootenanny that was resonating both inside and outside Cordelia's—very stoned—head tonight.

That in turn was nothing compared to the odd behaviour of the water, which seemed to be moving over her body and flowing and rippling like a semi-solid substance. Warm jelly, perhaps. Or liquid ectoplasm. Liquid ectoplasm with a technicolour Lush bath bomb fizzing in it.

This in further turn was nothing compared to the intensely vivid, virtually real, holodeck-solidity of the fantasies that she began to conjure in a mind-blowing fiesta of frenzied self-abuse. Fantasies involving ex-boyfriends, ex-girlfriends, near misses, porn stars, purely conjectural constructs and, finally and climactically...

Agatha Agatha Agatha Agatha Agatha.

That so smooth, so shaven head held between Cordelia's hands as she kissed it, warm and infinitely smooth under her lips.

Agatha Agatha Agatha Agatha Agatha.

In her black-and-white bikini, gleaming with oil, oil being applied with tender dexterity by Cordelia—*Here, let me help you with that, ma'am*—a gleaming droplet like a transparent, priceless gemstone caught shining in the perfect dimpled concavity of Agatha's navel.

Cordelia was now hooking her thumbs inside the black-and-white bikini bottoms—*Shall we just slip these off and apply a little oil here too?*—pulling them down, pulling them off to reveal...

And just at that moment, at that exact moment, the most revolting thought came to her, intruding into Cordelia's mind.

It came to her in a kind of inexorable behavioural algebra...

Tinkler... (Why was she thinking of Tinkler?)

Tinkler was friends with Agatha. (She'd seen as much.)

Tinkler was not shagging Agatha. (Obviously.)

Tinkler would *want* to shag Agatha. (Doubly obviously.)

So Tinkler would fantasise about shagging Agatha. (Duh.)

So what if (Oh, no), what if he was fantasising about shagging Agatha... *right now*?

At exactly the same moment that Cordelia was?

What if she and Tinkler were both thinking about Agatha at the same time?

Both *fantasising* about Agatha at the same time?

Cordelia couldn't help this terrible thought blossoming, emerging full-blown like a sinister time lapse flower fully opening its menacing petals just as she began to tip over the edge into uncontrolled ecstasy: Tinkler in his own grimy bathtub (of course it would be grimy) bludgeoning away at his porky schlong.

Both of them in the bath at the same time. Both fantasising at the same time. Both thrashing away in the water, the water, the water. And both reaching their immersed, Agatha-fuelled crescendos at the same time, at the exact same instant of synaptic overload.

For Cordelia this turned a surge of extravagant enflamed ecstasy into a flood of vast and horrid disgust, which somehow only deepened that ecstasy, while also making it feel thoroughly vile and made *her* feel thoroughly vile both during and, more especially, afterwards.

Vile and angry.

Not to mention very stoned indeed.

Which would explain why, as soon as she was out of the bath and dry, she got on the phone to Tinkler to give him hell. Yes, to give him hell for intruding on her fantasy.

And, what's more, Tinkler *apologised*.

Yes, he apologised for intruding on her fantasy. Like it really was his fault.

Which mollified Cordelia. To the extent that she heard herself inviting him around. Yes. Inviting Tinkler around. Right now. For a booty call.

This really was strong weed.

18: THE PAPERBACK SLEUTH'S
FIRST STAKEOUT

Thus began what was not a relationship—Cordelia made that very clear.

It didn't even qualify as a *situationship*, according to Cordelia. It was merely a sleazy series of booty calls and hook-ups, culminating in squalid, squelching third-rate sex—although, to be fair, after a certain step change this did develop into squalid, squelching second-rate sex.

The step change came about one day when Tinkler picked her up in his little red car—Cordelia declined to use its stupid name—to take her back to his house in Putney (a surprisingly nice little house, though of course sordidly disorderly and unclean), where she would spend the night.

Or the better part of it.

Or, it being Tinkler, the worse part of it.

But on their way to his house, Tinkler had asked if she would mind if he detoured on an errand for a friend. A friend who, it turned out, lived in a large and handsome mansion flat on Richmond Hill. The errand was dropping off some weed, so Cordelia could get behind that.

Plus, she had a funny feeling about who this friend might turn out to be…

Tinkler parked outside the house, which was just off Friars Stile Road on Terrace Lane.

The front door of the building, a narrow, elegant, art nouveau masterpiece worthy of Gaudí, was unlocked, giving access to a parquet-floored entrance hall and a narrow ornate gilt lift door and an ebony and glass stairway door, both of which, Cordelia noted, were locked with keypads. Access for residents only.

On the wall to the right as you came in were a bank of individual post boxes with brushed-aluminium fronts and brass locks, and also each with a slot allowing for delivery of items up to about the thickness of (hurray) a paperback book. Tinkler carefully posted a bag of dope through the slot into one such box, marked *Top Flat*, and then they left.

As they got back into Tinkler's shabby red vehicle and pulled away, he said, "My friend's called Agatha. She's really cool."

This came as no surprise to Cordelia, who had recognised the silver sports car parked outside the mansion flats. Her heart had been racing ever since. "I know," she said, and Tinkler gave her a startled look.

Cordelia, who saw no point in lying or dissembling, then went on to give a full and accurate account (well, fairly full and fairly accurate; she didn't mention this was the reason she'd struck up an acquaintance with Tinkler in the first place) of what she thought of Ms Dubois-Kanes. The phrase "the most ravishing human being I've ever beheld" was used at one point and caused Tinkler, at the wheel of the car, to start nodding like the sort of novelty nodding dog you occasionally saw on a dashboard.

"So you know her?" he asked, utterly redundantly.

"I know *of* her."

"And you want to sleep with her?"

"Of course."

"If you do," said Tinkler, "can I join in?"

This occasioned such loud and unrestrained laughter from Cordelia that Tinkler would have been within his rights to be offended, since it was so clearly intended to give offence. Instead, he joined in.

As if realising that this was all he *could* join in with.

"Of course not," said Cordelia, finally, wiping her eyes.

"Can I watch?"

"No. But it's not like it's ever going to happen," said Cordelia. Though in her secret heart of hearts she knew she was only saying this in the hope that it would somehow, magically, make it *more* likely to happen.

Tinkler was silent as they drove back slowly along a narrow, winding road through Richmond Park. Deer watched them with suspicion, as well they might.

Then Cordelia said, "Why was her car parked outside?"

"What?"

"Why was Agatha's car parked outside, if she wasn't at home? Or was she really at home and you just didn't want to ring her bell?" This last was said with a certain burning anger and contempt. Had she just missed out on a chance to see Agatha, not only see her but *meet* her, because of Tinkler's timidity?

"Oh, no," said Tinkler. "I want to ring her bell, all right."

And they both laughed.

"She's out working," he said. "Driving another car. Driving a taxi, in fact." He went on to explain, to Cordelia's fascination, that Agatha was a black cab driver, or had been. Since Uber and other ride apps had begun to erode that business, she had started to phase it out. "But she still owns a share in a black cab and works some shifts."

Tinkler then proceeded on a rambling account of random facts about Agatha. But Cordelia found everything fascinating, and hung on every word. "She's only recently moved into that place in Richmond. She finds it handy because we all live around here. Her friends." Tinkler proudly accorded himself this designation. "And also this guy she's dating."

"And who's that?" said Cordelia, casually, after a moment's silence. It was ridiculous. Of course Agatha was seeing someone. Of course she had a lover. But, nevertheless, the news was like a dagger in her breast.

"His name is Albert. He runs a gastropub."

A gastropub, thought Cordelia. Just when it seemed it couldn't be any worse.

Tinkler shot her a look. An oddly perceptive look, as it turned out. "It's okay," he said gently. "I want to kill him, too."

"So what does *Albert* have that makes him so special?"

Cordelia had uttered the name with such venom that Tinkler began laughing again. When he finished laughing, he replied, by way of explanation, "Fleet of vintage cars."

"Ah."

Cordelia's stock of the misbegotten *Cold Angel, Dead Angel* continued to sell strongly. She was making so much money out of the thing she decided to find out some more about it. She sort of felt she owed it to the dead (murdered) author, one Christer Vingqvist.

So she did a bit of research, and it transpired that Vingqvist's gruesome demise had taken place in a Swedish town called Trollesko.* As she dug into the detail, Cordelia suddenly found herself plunged into horror.

Not horror engendered by any aspects of the murder, but by the discovery that her *brother* was involved.

* see *Attack and Decay*, Vinyl Detective Book 6 by Andrew Cartmel

Not involved in the killing, of course, but in the publicity circus that had sprung up around it.

This was because the carnage was somehow connected with a heavy metal band, and Stinky had been making a documentary about them. (As appalling as it was to admit, Stinky had quite cannily parlayed his "fame"—Cordelia would go to her own grave before she removed the quotes from around that word—into making TV shows about music.)

At that point, Cordelia stopped digging and decided to ignore the whole heavy metal side of things. Not least because it involved her odious brother.

But not before she solved the mystery of how all these copies of *Cold Angel, Dead Angel*—a self-published aberration by an optimistic, under-talented and very dead Swede—had ended up in the UK. It seemed the heavy metal band caught up in the case had a connection with a London-based firm called (choke) Whyte Ravyn Records. One Jonathon "Jaunty" Pogson, the financial comptroller of the company, had apparently sensed a killing—no pun intended—and, for a very low price, he had bought up the few hundred copies of the book in existence (self-published novels naturally tend to have low print runs) and shipped them to England.

Being a financial wizard, Jaunty had been counting on their notoriety and the connection with the murder translating into brisk sales and high prices for these previously unsellable (and unreadable) books.

And, of course, he'd been absolutely right…

He just hadn't waited long enough.

Cordelia discovered—you could still find the dead website he'd set up in a failed attempt to flog the things—that Jaunty had tried to sell the books, grown impatient and had given up, dumping them on the market for whatever he could get.

In short, he'd cut his losses.

But, if only he'd kept his nerve, he would have made a fortune.

Now other people would make a fortune.

And a small slice of that would be Cordelia's…

Meanwhile, the Paperback Sleuth website continued to attract custom. People were sending her their want lists, and it was amazing what some people wanted. For instance, just this morning another chump had got in touch asking her to find a copy of none other than *Cold Angel, Dead Angel*.

Well, that was easily sorted.

Indeed, if they'd bothered to look, the chump would have seen that she still had copies listed for sale. But no need to rub the chump's—sorry, the *revered customer's*—nose in that, and disillusion them. So, Cordelia responded exactly as if she'd gone out and hunted down the book for them especially, and they duly paid the outrageous price she asked without hesitation or complaint.

It was only when she processed payment that Cordelia began to sense that something wasn't quite right…

She was on high alert (for which read full-blown paranoia) because of recent hijinks and the possibility of Cutterham trying to track her down. So when Cordelia recognised the PayPal handle on this transaction, recognised it as that of a previous customer, alarm bells began to sound.

You might well ask, so what? It was a return customer, now shopping with the Paperback Sleuth website. Surely grounds for celebration—hurrah. Customer loyalty.

But this time the order was going to a different name at a different address. Cordelia checked her records and confirmed this.

And both of the addresses—old and new—were local: in Barnes.

There was nothing inherently suspicious about this, or the change of location, or even the different name of the recipient. It could have been a gift—as preposterous as that seemed. (Who would give anyone a copy of *Cold Angel, Dead Angel*?) But Cordelia nevertheless felt a distinct pang of disquiet. Because, come to think of it, there was something vaguely familiar about this new customer's name.

In fact, there was something familiar about *both* the customers' names. New and old.

Then she realised why they were familiar.

And that was when Cordelia really went down the rabbit hole…

Cordelia acknowledged the payment for the copy of *Cold Angel, Dead Angel*, and then packed it for posting. She always sent her books well protected and professionally packaged, preferably using a Lil C-1 cardboard mailer. And that is what she did in this case. However, this time she also especially purchased a Jiffy bag and put the cardboard mailer inside it. Overkill, you might say, and you'd be right.

But she was using the Jiffy bag not for extra protection, but for extra visibility. It was a bright, not to say fluorescent, shade of hazard-warning yellow, and would be easy to spot from quite a distance away.

So she purchased a pair of binoculars—Nikon Aculon 10x21 in a fetching shade of red that would go nicely with her rucksacks—and waited for the binocs to arrive before posting the book to its buyer. She sent it specially tracked, which was well worth the extra expense because it provided the sender (Cordelia) with an estimated delivery window.

This was only accurate within four hours, so she had to be prepared for a fairly tedious wait. Thus, when she got the delivery alert, she wrapped up warmly and packed some energy bars and her new binoculars, and set off. Indeed, set off with a remarkable lightness of heart and keen sense of occasion.

The Paperback Sleuth's first stakeout.

The destination address of the book was less than a ten-minute walk away, just across the village green from Edwin's house. It was at the corner of a street running off Station Road. And, Cordelia had determined through a careful inspection beforehand (thank you, Google Maps), it was adjacent to Beverley Brook, the picturesque little waterway which wound its way through Barnes.

This location had, in fact, been pivotal in Cordelia's decision to purchase the binoculars. Because, after a brief but vigorous and invigorating autumnal walk, it meant she could station herself beside the brook and keep an eye on the target house (terraced, red brick, front garden approximately the size of a pocket handkerchief, but still no doubt worth a cool million—this *was* Barnes) with her Nikons while apparently scrutinising waterfowl gliding below on the glittering water —a trifle eccentric perhaps, but not overly suspicious.

Consequently she was able to clearly see the arrival of the postman and the delivery of the book, a distinctive and unmistakable flash of bright yellow, posted through the front door. Within seconds her phone buzzed to let her know the package had been delivered.

Thank you, efficient postie.

And it was only five minutes later that her theory was confirmed—oh, warm sense of triumph—with the arrival of *Edwin*.

Because those customers whose names had been familiar, the two customers who so oddly and improbably seemed to share the same PayPal account, had been two of Edwin's boring girlfriends. Two of his supremely boring, *Observer* knitwear-offer knitwear wearing girlfriends.

Now Edwin himself turned up, walking briskly, with a transparent plastic carrier bag in one hand, flapping against his Rohan corduroys. Inside the bag, easily revealed by the binoculars, were several containers of (of all things) *cat* food. Edwin went up to the front door of the house and, instead of ringing the bell, took out a key and let himself in.

Curiouser and curiouser.

He was back out again remarkably few minutes later, still with the transparent plastic bag. But now the cat food was gone and instead it contained the yellow Jiffy bag.

Edwin turned homewards. Cordelia followed him at a discreet distance. She had already worked out why Edwin had been carrying cat food, now left behind, and was in possession of a set of keys. From casual conversations in the past, she knew that more than once he'd been landed with the task of looking after one of his stultifying paramours' pets while the stultifying paramour was away somewhere.

It was just the sort of task that good old, agreeable old, reliable old Edwin was ideally suited for.

And he'd combined his visit today with the collection of the book that he'd ordered from Cordelia. The book that he clearly, for some reason, didn't want her to know that he'd ordered and that he didn't want coming to his own (and her own) address.

Staying well back and out of sight, Cordelia watched Edwin reach their house and go inside. She decided to wait for a decent interval to elapse before following him in. Otherwise it would look like she'd been shadowing him; which, of course, was exactly what she'd been doing.

And it was because she was waiting thus that she now glimpsed Edwin walking past the window on the landing halfway up the house. He'd gone straight up there once he'd gone indoors. Was he on his way up to Cordelia's room? If so, he was out of luck, because her door was locked.

Nonetheless, the thought of Edwin hovering outside her room propelled Cordelia into the house. She hurried up the front path, noiselessly unlocked the front door and stealthily entered. Standing there on the hateful ethnic rug, she could hear him moving around above. Edwin was not up by her room after all. Instead, he was on the unoccupied and half-demolished middle floor.

Whatever he was up to, he was up to it there.

Cordelia backed silently out and closed the door behind her and resumed her watch from across the street.

And so she was able to see Edwin come back down past the landing window, on his way downstairs again. Cordelia gave it another minute or so before she came in through the front door, bustling and making plenty of noise. Edwin called a jovial greeting from the kitchen and Rainbottle barked a jovial bark.

Cordelia called an equally cheerful hello and resolved to wait until next time Edwin was safely out of the house and do some exploring…

She didn't have to wait long—two days—for Edwin to go off on one of his marathon cycle rides. As soon he was out of sight, Cordelia was down from her room and reconnoitring the deserted floor below. She'd never noticed anything unusual about this area before, but then she'd never been looking for anything unusual.

It took her the best part of an hour to find it, and when she did, she kicked herself because she should have spotted it right away. It was one of the empty—i.e. doorless—doorways that led from one uninhabited room to another. And if you compared the vertical sections of doorway—the jambs—one was thicker than the other. By a good couple of inches (say the thickness of four or five paperbacks).

The whole wall on this side of the door, running a short distance to a chimney breast, was too thick. On the other side of the chimney breast the wall dropped back to its normal depth, running all the way to the window. The section of wall between chimney breast and door was a fake. A false wall.

It apparently consisted of bare lathe and chipped plasterboard with the wallpaper stripped away from it. But close inspection revealed that this was actually a rather beautifully contrived and wholly convincing counterfeit which hinged open. The hinges were on the side by the chimney breast and you opened the section, effectively a kind of door, by hooking your finger into what was apparently a random hole in the plasterboard at about shoulder level beside the door jamb.

You just put your finger in there, pulled, and the false wall swung smoothly open.

To reveal, wait for it…

A bookcase.

Disappointingly, not a bookcase stuffed with paperbacks. Yes, there were a few dotted here and there (both proper mass market specimens and shameful large format ones), but essentially it was a heterogeneous mix of hardcover books and paperbacks, with no attempt at uniformity.

What was uniform, though, was the subject matter.

Crime.

Again, disappointingly, not crime fiction but mostly non-fiction. The occasional novel did feature, including a classic by Colin Wilson, containing the debut of Chief Inspector Gregory Saltfleet. It was a quite lovely Panther original with the author's name printed in a stylish block of Gil Sans Display Extra Bold at the top of the cover. Cordelia recognised it as the one that had been purchased from her.

There were a lot of other Colin Wilson titles, but they were all non-fiction, true crime. Indeed, among them were *Illustrated True Crime* and *The Mammoth Book of True Crime*. And also *A Casebook of Murder*, *A Criminal History of Mankind*, *The Encyclopaedia of Crime*, *The Mammoth Book of Unsolved Mysteries* and *Order of Assassins*. Plus plenty of books not by Colin Wilson. All crime-based and mostly factual.

Strangely, Cordelia immediately understood why Edwin kept this mini-library so carefully concealed. Because it was a shameful secret. Downstairs, out in the open, Edwin had his matching Faber editions of the poems of Seamus Heaney and Penguin editions of the plays of Bernard Shaw, plus a large selection of volumes on green and environmental matters, a stupefying and soporific shelf of Booker Award winners and shortlisted volumes—these suckers could put you to sleep faster than a tranquiliser dart—and other worthy titles.

Downstairs, those were the books Edwin could be proud of, that he could advertise to the world, that he could own up to owning.

Up here were his guilty secrets, his guilty pleasures, lurid and prurient and reprehensible and not the sort of thing you wanted anyone to know were lurking around the place while you were steaming your quinoa and listening to Radio 3.

Effectively, this was his porn stash.

Especially, Cordelia suspected, Edwin didn't want his girlfriends knowing that he read this sort of stuff, instead of, say, *The Girl with a Pearl Earring* or *The Hare with Amber Eyes*. (Or possibly *The Hare with a Pearl Earring*.) But why, then, did he have the books sent to his girlfriends' addresses? Of course, he did that when they were away and he was dutifully feeding the cat or whatever. They were his poste-restante addresses. He could get books safely sent to them and no one need ever know about his sordid penny-dreadful leanings.

The books were neatly and properly arranged in alphabetical order, full marks Edwin, so Cordelia stooped down low and, sure enough, cosily nestled on the bottom shelf between *The Run of His Life* by Jeffrey Toobin (the O.J. case) and *American Sherlock* by Kate Winkler Dawson (the birth of crime scene investigation)— shouldn't this have been under 'D' not 'W'?—she found the copy of *Cold Angel, Dead Angel* which she'd so recently posted in the yellow Jiffy bag.

Presumably it had aroused Edwin's interest because of the connection with the real-life crime (there had been a piece in the *Observer* book section about it which had been instrumental in letting the cat out of the bag). Anyway, she hoped he hadn't purchased it for its literary merits.

Cordelia felt a fleeting regret that she'd charged poor old Edwin such an inflated price for the book. Then she reflected on his annoying and ruthless pursuit of the rent every month and felt a lot less bad.

She closed the false wall again, checked that everything was exactly as she had found it, and then went back up to her room, where she regarded her dwindling stack of *Cold Angel, Dead Angel* with a new affection. Without this dumb book she would never have discovered this other side to Edwin.

19: BENCHED

Cordelia soon found herself just happening to decide to go to Richmond to scour the charity shops there for second-hand paperbacks. And it was true that Richmond represented fairly rich pickings from a charity shop point of view.

And she did dutifully comb the charity shops, all the ones in the town centre and then working her way across the bridge. Richmond Bridge was reliably rather lovely and, indeed, today a family of swans sailed sedately under it while Cordelia watched them, brilliant white shapes floating above their white reflections in the murky green water. Cordelia wished she was gliding through her own life with such cool grace.

She was still standing on the bridge when the call came through. It was Toba Possner. "I'll keep this brief," she said, "because I'm calling from France and I'm not sure what the roaming charges are."

"France?" said Cordelia. "Provence, by any chance?"

"Yes," said Toba. She sounded odd.

"Have you been to see the farmhouse you're interested in buying?"

"Yes, but unfortunately all that has fallen through."

"Oh," said Cordelia.

"Something has happened," said Toba. "And I need to see you as soon as I'm back in London."

"Do you want to talk about it now?" said Cordelia, anxiety beginning to coil coldly in her stomach.

"No, when I get back will be fine. I just wanted to make sure that you're around. You will be around?"

"Yes."

"Excellent. Well, take care until I see you." Then she hung up, rather abruptly, and leaving Cordelia with the distinct feeling that something was wrong. *Something has happened.* But what?

Oh well. There was no point speculating until she had more information.

Cordelia walked across the bridge and worked her way through the charity shops on the other side—there was a rich seam of them here, although they petered out as you started to head in the direction of Twickenham. Twickenham itself was loaded with such places. But Cordelia had no intention of venturing out that far, even though it was only a short bus ride away.

Because she'd had enough, she had done enough. The formalities had been observed, so to speak. She'd made a deal with herself that she could only head up Richmond Hill, towards a certain handsome mansion flat, if she'd actually managed to find something on her mission of paperback plunder.

And it had looked for a while as if she might be heading home both empty-handed and empty-hearted. But then, in the last charity shop, furthest from the bridge, with poignant pictures of homeless dogs on the walls, she found an immaculate set of Michael Moorcock science fantasy extravaganzas in the early Mayflower editions with the wild psychedelic cover art. Not her cup of tea reading-wise, but eminently saleable, once she had painstaking removed the annoying price stickers.

She happily parted with the five quid that was all the books cost, collectively, and even made an additional donation to the charity—how could your heart not be wrung by the photos of the poor orphaned mutts? Then she set forth back across the bridge and up the hill...

On the street where Agatha Dubois-Kanes lived (Cordelia felt a song coming on) there was a rather handsome ornate Victorian black wrought-iron bench, conveniently situated directly opposite her place. It was at the rear of a wide band of pavement, set well back from a somewhat sad looking roadside tree, an urban tree decorated with windblown rubbish.

Cordelia sat there on the bench (surprisingly comfortable) and gloated over the Moorcock Mayflowers in a businesslike way, resisting the urge to start removing the price stickers from them; sliding a dexterous fingernail underneath, say, and levering the stickers up at one corner, just enough to peel them off. Such an action was all too likely to tear the precious flawless covers or leave a mark.

No, she would resist temptation and wait until she got back home, where there was a spray bottle of just the right kind of solvent for this job, a sticker-glue loosening solvent. Orange-scented, oddly enough.

All these thoughts kept Cordelia from being too furiously aware that she was sitting just across the street from Agatha's flat.

It wasn't like she was *watching* Agatha's flat. Cordelia was simply sitting on this rather handsome old bench, across the street from her place, studying today's purchases.

But she could only look at those paperbacks for so long and then, inevitably, Cordelia's eyes strayed to the building across the road and the row of windows at the top—like her, Agatha lived at the top of a house. Surely such a coincidence must mean something?

Surely only a crazy person would think that such a coincidence must mean something?

And then there was a flash of movement. Just a swift blur of shadow, but enough to tell Cordelia that Agatha was at home. She was in her flat. Right now. Right there, across the street. A stone's throw away.

If she threw a stone at the window and Agatha heard her, she would look out the window and see Cordelia on the bench.

Sitting on that bench, Cordelia felt her heart quite literally begin to throb. She had heard the expression, of course. She'd understood what it meant. Or she'd thought she did. Until she actually felt her heart begin to throb with despair because she was just a stupid girl sitting on a bench. Agatha had no idea she existed. Cared nothing for her, and knew less. Or was it the other way around?

Then Cordelia looked up.

Her heart stopped for a moment—a hot molten stoppage, a volcanic fleeting instant—and then began again.

Because Agatha was waving to her.

Cordelia stared upwards through the branches of the tree by the bench and she saw that…

Agatha was waving at her.

Agatha had opened her window at the top of the building and she was leaning out and she was waving to Cordelia, gesturing to her with a small billowing white cloth. A scarf? A silk handkerchief? Some *more intimate item of apparel*?

The supple white scrap of cloth billowed and twisted and flowed in Agatha's hand as she waved it. Waved it towards Cordelia. The meaning was clear.

Come to me.

The gesture was clear.

For a thrilling endless second Cordelia sat there, knowing that this was real and it was really going to happen…

All she had to do was stand up and walk across the road. She would walk across the road and press the bell on the elegant art nouveau brass plate beside the slender art nouveau doors, all writhing blond wood and green glass and black iron. She would push those doors open and Agatha would be waiting, and lead her up to her flat.

Then she would close the door behind them, and the white shape would be revealed to be, for instance, the skimpiest hand towel imaginable, just large enough when being stretched coyly by Agatha to cover her now naked body, just this teasing scrap of white cloth being held up to conceal that body from Cordelia for the last time.

Because as Cordelia moved towards her, it would be swept aside and discarded at last, revealing all as they embraced, first Agatha's hot skin on Cordelia's clothed body and then her hot skin on Cordelia's hot skin as she tore off her (Cordelia's) clothes and they were both naked.

All she had to do was stand up and walk across the road.

Cordelia realised, her heart slamming with the finality which signalled the end of one phase of her life and the beginning of another, a new and unimaginably richer phase, that this was all she had to do. For a moment she savoured the realisation.

How often do you know the exact moment when your life is going to change?

All she had to do was stand up, leave the bench, walk across the road...

Cordelia stood up.

She stood up from the bench, her eyes never leaving Agatha, partially screened by the branches of a dirty urban tree, leaning out the window at the top of the building on the other side of the road, waving the white signal to her.

And as Cordelia stood, instantly the billowing piece of white went soaring upwards.

Agatha had released it, fed it to the wind, let it go soaring free up into the heavens. Just as their love would go soaring free.

But even as Cordelia interpreted this metaphor—what a fabulous, subtle, erotic mind Agatha DuBois-Kanes *possessed*. This would be not only the beginning of the sexual adventure of a lifetime but also the intellectual adventure of a lifetime—she realised that the white shape had not gone soaring free.

It had not been released from Agatha's hand.

It had never been in Agatha's hand.

The billowing white shape was actually a scrap of rubbish— perhaps the remnant of a torn white plastic carrier bag—that had become trapped in the twigs on a branch of the tree and was twisting in the breeze. It had only *looked* like it was in Agatha's hand because of the angle of where Cordelia had been sitting.

And as soon as she'd stood up, all the visual relationships had changed.

Agatha was on the other side of the road, up in her flat.

The white scrap of rubbish was up in the tree, on this side of the road.

They had been two different planes of space squeezed together, an optical illusion, a visual trick.

The crappy white scrap of plastic bag continued to billow and wave on the branch where it was caught. And, beyond it, in a completely different plane, in so many senses, across the road and two storeys up, Agatha was indeed leaning out the window of her flat but not looking at Cordelia, she had never been looking at Cordelia, she was looking at somewhere and something else altogether.

She was looking at her phone that she was holding extended in her hand in what Cordelia immediately recognised as a frustrated attempt to get a signal.

And then Agatha abandoned the attempt, withdrawing inside again and closing the window.

Without ever having looked at Cordelia.

Cordelia sat back down on the bench again, too drained to do anything, too drained to move.

Finally she rose to her feet once more, almost forgetting her bag of books, absent-mindedly picking them up and then walking back down the hill, through Richmond to the station, feeling numb and empty and heartsick. And guilty. As though she was on some kind of penitential pilgrimage for a terrible sin.

But then, on the train home, she came up with a plan.

20: DOUBLE-DECKER KARMA

The idea came to her, with a warm painful rush, while she watched the scenery passing in a green blur outside the scratched and steamy train window, as they rattled and clattered though North Sheen and Mortlake, en route to Barnes. And once she got off the train there and walked across the wide stretch of grass behind the station with some fools playing cricket on it, and through the wild tangled patch of woods beyond, Cordelia weighed up the idea and became absolutely determined that this was the right course of action.

She would return to Agatha's tomorrow.

But this time not as a passive observer with no plan and no reason to be there—she would come bearing gifts.

Or rather, one gift. One particular, precious, and perfectly chosen gift.

When she got back to her attic room, cool and quiet and smelling reassuringly of vintage paperbacks, and locked the door behind her, Cordelia went straight to the bookshelf and, before she could lose her nerve, took the book down off it.

The Sleuth Hound edition of *Kiss Me Deadly* by Mickey Spillane, the incredibly rare pirated edition with the gorgeous, gorgeous cover art by Abe Prossont (her friend, Toba Possner!). The only copy she'd ever seen. Just about the only copy *anyone* had ever seen. The immaculate, fine condition copy that Cordelia had burgled with such painstaking and dissolute determination from the little house in the cul-de-sac in Putney which she now regarded with fond nostalgia, the way you might remember a place where you'd met your true love.

And maybe, in a roundabout way, that house would end up serving just such a function for Cordelia.

Because it had provided her with the perfect present for her beloved.

It was the most treasured, rarest and most valuable paperback in Cordelia's entire collection. It was her most prized possession. And she would give it away.

Sacrifice it for love.

Heart aching with that love and also, frankly, with the pain of losing the book, Cordelia set about gift-wrapping it. Then, after an eternity of agonised indecision, she untied the ribbon and reopened the box and added a very brief and enigmatic handwritten note on her special pale blue notepaper, written with her fountain pen.

From an admirer.

Endless hesitation ensued as she tried to decide whether to sign it then, with abrupt reckless decisiveness, she did indeed sign it. At least Agatha would know that the book came from someone called Cordelia, even if she had no idea who that was. Then she hesitated again, wondering whether to add an 'x' to her signature, to add a kiss…

Finally she realised the obvious—that this would lower the tone of the whole enterprise. So she just rested the note lovingly atop the tissue-wrapped book and closed the box and tied it up with the ribbon again.

Then, after another agonised eternity of indecision, she untied the ribbon, opened the box again and also included her business card. Then she closed the box again, threw the length of ribbon away (it was hopelessly frayed by now) and replaced it with a new one.

That night Cordelia slept fitfully and finally woke up at four in the morning. The first faint daylight had crept into her attic room. She slipped out of bed, skin prickling in the chill early air, naked in the cold room, and padded across the floor to the door.

She picked up the beautiful gift box, ripped off the ribbon, tore off the wrapping paper and took out the book.

Then she went back to her bookshelf and there, under 'S' for Spillane, restored it to its proper place.

Cordelia had not lost her nerve. It wasn't that. Not that at all.

It was something much worse than that.

She had simply realised that she couldn't do it. She couldn't let go of the book. She just couldn't do it. She wasn't good enough to do it. She wasn't pure enough to do it. She wanted to keep the book for herself. She *had* to keep the book for herself. It had to be hers.

The book, the possession of it, was more important to her than the greatest passion of her life. As it turned out.

So this was who she was.

She went back to bed and cried herself to sleep. Then she slept soundly until nearly noon.

Later that day something happened which led Cordelia to a peculiar speculation about Colin Cutterham.

Here was the speculation: she was moved to wonder if perhaps in a past life, or possibly even in this one, Cutterham had behaved appallingly to a double-decker London bus.

This was because, evidently, double-decker London buses seemed to have it in for him.

Double-decked karmic payback.

Cordelia concluded this as a result of what happened as she was riding from Barnes Common to East Sheen on just such a double-decker.

Yesterday's visit to Richmond had reawakened her appetite for shaking down the local charity shops in search of rare paperbacks. And there was a goodly number of those in Sheen—charity shops. (But also, hopefully, rare paperbacks.)

So there she was on a big friendly, throbbing and rumbling red bus, sitting on the top deck as she always did. As she had done that fateful day coming back from Mrs Chichester's, across Putney Bridge, trailing Colin Cutterham's sports car and witnessing him pulling into a cul-de-sac.

And as a direct consequence of that, the Great Paperback Heist had ensued.

Great for her, not so great for Colin Cutterham.

Of course, that was just one occasion. One data point, as the scientists might say. Certainly not enough to justify anyone in the rather odd surmise that double-decker buses had something against Colin Cutterham.

That came today.

Cordelia was staring happily out the window in the October sunshine as they rolled along. The bus had just reached the rugby club—hard to believe that people actually spent time (and *money*) going to rugby games, but there you were; it took all types— when she saw Cutterham motoring along in his reprehensible green roadster.

She watched his bald spot with satisfied malice as he jockeyed past the bus, impatient to overtake. Beside him in the front seat was a large yellow Sainsbury's shopping bag with a cartoon elephant on it. It was completely empty. Maybe he was impatient to fill it with something. He shot past the bus and disappeared and Cordelia forgot about him.

Until he appeared again some minutes later.

The bus was becalmed in traffic and had yet to reach Sheen. The fact that Cutterham was passing them *again* indicated that he had stopped somewhere along the way and was only now resuming his journey.

The reason this was important was because of what Cordelia now saw.

The shopping bag was still beside Cutterham in the front seat. But this time it was full.

Full of books.

Full of *Sleuth Hounds*.

Cordelia only caught a glimpse, her neck moving with whiplash swiftness as she followed the car, accelerating as the lights changed, the traffic started moving, and it shot ahead of the bus and disappeared.

But she knew what she had seen. There was no mistaking those covers.

As Colin Cutterham and his big bag o' paperbacks vanished ahead of her, Cordelia was left surprised, a little puzzled, and deep in thought.

The surprise faded rapidly, and the puzzlement swiftly yielded to that deep thinking.

When Cordelia had first got home with her rucksack of stolen goodies after the Great Paperback Heist, she had taken the books out and stacked them on her table and realised that arrayed before her she had the *entire* catalogue of Sleuth Hound titles, from the first in 1953 to the last (oh, sad day) in 1957.

So, a really impressive, indeed perfect, score.

But, sitting now on the top deck of the bus in the wan autumn sunlight, Cordelia realised that it was even more significant than that...

Because Cutterham, or rather his mother, had owned a complete collection of Sleuth Hounds. And Cordelia had stolen them, every one of them, even the ones with the dodgy covers by the Airbrush Ass-hat.

Yet Colin Cutterham had just driven past her with a bag full of Sleuth Hound paperbacks.

So these couldn't be different titles to the ones Cordelia had looted, because there *were* no more Sleuth Hounds.

The collection in the house had been exhaustive and she'd got them all.

So, quod erat demonstrandum, the books Cutterham had in his car were *duplicate copies*.

Which meant, oh sweet ineluctable logic, that he had a secondary stash of Sleuth Hounds somewhere.

And—more ineluctable logic—since he hadn't had them in his car when she'd seen him back at the rugby club and he *did* have them now, a big bag full of them, he must have picked them up somewhere en route.

Somewhere between here and the rugby club.

But where, exactly?

Cordelia sensed that her new binoculars were going to have another outing.

Colin Cutterham was a creature of habit, and that was helpful. Indeed, Cordelia was counting on it. She had made a note of the time when she'd seen him drive past the bus the second time that day and extrapolated backwards to when she had first seen him...

Then she subtracted fifteen minutes just to be on the safe side, and the following afternoon she stationed herself on the corner of Vine Road and the Upper Richmond Road, just past the rugby club and on the other side, at exactly this time. With her binoculars.

Nothing.

She remained there for two long, gruelling hours. Whenever

someone seemed to be taking too much interest in her and her red binoculars, she turned and directed them at Barnes Common, conveniently right beside her and chock full of birds and other exciting wildlife.

That threw the fuckers off.

After two fruitless hours she went home.

She returned the next day and followed the same routine.

Nothing.

The day after that, the same thing again. And again nothing.

On the fourth day she saw Cutterham, in his car.

He drove past the rugby club, past the turning onto Abbey Avenue (which led both to the eponymous abbey and the Silverlight Yoga Centre, her former haunt and scene of saffron-pyjamaed confrontation) and kept going.

Cordelia followed his progress with her binoculars.

The Nikons were approaching the limits of their resolution when she saw the red signal light flash on the back of the car, and then it turned left and disappeared down a side street.

Cordelia put her binoculars away and scooted across the road to the bus stop. She caught the next bus and hurried up onto the top deck, grabbing a seat at the front just before a pair of obnoxious teenagers could seize it.

As the bus approached the side street where the car had turned, she had her binoculars ready and craned her head to the left, ready to stare along it in search of Cutterham's car.

But she didn't need to.

Instead, she saw Cutterham on foot, approaching the junction of the side street and the main road. He was carrying his elephant shopping bag. She could see from the way he was carrying it that it was empty.

As the bus rolled past him, Cordelia rose from her seat, moved swiftly down the length of the bus, past the obnoxious teenagers who got up and hurried to occupy her now-vacant seat at the front. Cordelia reached the back of the bus and kneeled on the bench seat there and stared out the wide rear window.

She saw Cutterham, a shrinking, distant figure, standing at a wooden door in a long brick wall, holding his empty shopping bag in one hand. In the other hand he had a set of keys and was unlocking the door.

Cordelia got off the bus at the next stop, crossed the road, and caught another bus back, going the other way.

This had always been Cordelia's favourite part of the bus ride on this particular route. It preceded the parade of shops where the charity shops lived. And it came after a built-up residential area.

In refreshing contrast, it consisted of allotments. A communal garden expanse where residents could obtain a plot of land for growing things by the simple expedient of applying to the local council and going onto a waiting list and waiting forever.

The allotments were always a delight to Cordelia, the sudden sight of green growing things—and, in spring and summer, the eruptions of other colours in the forms of blossoms and fruit and vegetables—all this was a relief to the eye after the endless stream of urban architecture, be it residential or commercial.

Hence Cordelia was in the habit of taking a good, long, restful look at the allotments.

This time, it was anything but restful.

Cordelia swept her binoculars over her best-loved patch of garden—a mixture of ornamental cabbages and seriously impressive roses—and then her most hated patch, the one with the gnomes cavorting among the hydrangeas in postures of frozen, contrived commercial cuteness. Then she focused on one of the allotments she'd never really noticed before.

It consisted of a pair of not especially impressive and rather weed-crowded beds of what were apparently rhubarb, beside a large shed. What caught her eye was not the beds, or the shed, but the figure moving between them.

Cutterham.

He had just emerged from the shed. Actually, "shed" was not a sufficiently grand word for the building. Though there were a few other structures among the allotments that matched it for size, none were as well built or, for want of a better word, as serious as this shed.

It was constructed of concrete with a peaked roof, not a flat one which would have tended to let in the rain (never let it be said that Cordelia hadn't absorbed the lesson of St Drogo's). And the windows were proper glass ones. Double glazed by the look of them—i.e. better and more serious windows than he had in his own (recently plundered) house in Putney.

There was also a very solid-looking door on the shed, which Colin Cutterham had just closed behind him. He was carrying the elephant shopping bag, and it looked full.

Cordelia got off the bus at the next stop, almost opposite the wooden door in the long brick wall. She sat among a crowd of people at the bus stop, confident she was invisible. She watched the door (she didn't need the binoculars at this distance). It was only a minute or two before Cutterham emerged, carrying his heavy bag, and locked the door behind him.

Cordelia remained sitting at the bus stop, although she didn't really need to, and waited for Cutterham to drive past, having retrieved his car, which had evidently been parked down the side street. The bag was beside him in the front seat.

She hardly paid attention, lost in thought.

Cordelia had no doubt what was in the bag. More Sleuth Hounds, from some kind of secondary stash.

And, having just emerged from his shed in the allotment with said bag, Cordelia had a pretty good idea of exactly where that stash was stashed.

Which led to the inevitable question…
What kind of lock did that shed have on its door?

21: ALLOTMENT

Cordelia was not greedy. Nor was she crazy.

She had got away with one burglary, a flagrant, fragrant, flawless, textbook piece of breaking and entering plus, the icing on the cake, theft glorious theft. (Although she *had* come perilously close to being discovered—what if Colin Cutterham had happened to glance into that little sitting room?)

So, having got away with this perfect crime (she modestly felt that it was worthy of such a label), having arguably got away with it by the skin of her teeth, Cordelia wasn't in a hurry to chance her arm again. Or her teeth.

Her pretty little arm, or her pretty little teeth.

So she wasn't crazy…

She'd made a lot of money out of that score, not to mention (and more importantly) filling all the gaps in her own Sleuth Hound collection.

So she didn't *need* to rob Colin Cutterham, or his garden shed, again, just to make a bit more money, or to get duplicates of books she already had. Already had in immaculate, or fine, condition.

There was no need for any of that.

Because she wasn't greedy.

But…

What if, among the duplicate Sleuth Hounds in that shed in the allotment, was another copy of *Kiss Me Deadly*?

The rarest of all the Sleuth Hound titles. The Mount Everest, so to speak, of Sleuth Hounds. This book was worth a lot of money. But Cordelia had never even considered selling the copy she'd already stolen. She'd had to possess it for herself. To add it to her own collection.

Nor would she consider selling a second copy, if indeed there was one in the allotment shed.

She would gift it to Agatha, of course.

A gift of love.

So…

Where *had* she put those burglary tools?

Time was of the essence because, as Cordelia had seen, Colin Cutterham was already removing the books from the shed and taking them somewhere else. Presumably to his little house in Putney. Perhaps—horrible thought—he'd already finished transferring the books and what Cordelia had witnessed today was the last consignment.

Could fate be so cruel?

If it was, that was that.

Cordelia had considered, for only a split second, the possibility of re-burgling the Putney house. For a split second only, before decisively discarding the idea. Because she had little doubt that Cutterham would have upped the security at his home after being robbed. Who wouldn't? There might now be alarms, cameras, special security locks, all the paraphernalia which had been so refreshingly absent when she'd recently looted the place.

No, Cutterham would have dreamed up some serious countermeasures to deal with another break-in. Cordelia was sure of that. And she had absolutely no desire to discover what those countermeasures might be.

So, if all the books had already been transferred from the Sheen shed to the Putney parlour, then that was that. Case closed. Regrettable, but that was the way it was.

On the other hand, if there were still some Sleuth Hounds in the shed, she had to act quickly, before they *were* all taken away.

Act quickly.

Act immediately.

Act *tonight*.

The first thing Cordelia did when she came to this decision, while still trawling through the charity shops in Sheen (she'd picked up a couple of nice Penguin Raymond Chandlers with the tinted stills from the Bogart movies on the covers) was to schedule a pause in her journey home. For reconnaissance.

Thus, instead of riding the bus all the way back to Rocks Lane, she'd hopped off at the stop opposite the allotments, crossed the road and checked the door in the brick wall which gave access to those allotments, snapped a couple of photos with her phone, concealing this behaviour by using the usual ruse of pretending to make a call, then crossed the road again and caught the next bus to Rocks Lane. There, instead of continuing back to Barnes, she hopped on a train and headed off to do some shopping. Some highly specialised shopping.

Finally, back home at last, she waited until nightfall, making sure she ate a hearty meal just like Jack Aubrey always made sure his crew did before they went into battle (Cordelia didn't just read crime fiction). Then, once it was dark, she set off.

She was once more wearing the big rucksack she'd purchased for her premiere looting expedition and was carrying, or wearing, pretty much the rest of the same paraphernalia as before, except this time with a black sweater and black jeans instead of the T-shirt and cut-off denim shorts, and with the addition of an LED head torch with cushioned straps (for comfort) and a heavy duty pair of workman's gloves, both bought at the same shop in Clapham Junction, for cash, that afternoon, and both currently nestling in her rucksack along with, optimistically, bubble wrap and tape.

Going as far as Clapham Junction and paying cash might have been unnecessary precautions concerning the gloves and head torch, but Cordelia had decided to approach this project in a thoroughly professional manner.

If you're going to do it, do it right.

In the same spirit, she set off into the night—a crisp autumn night—and walked all the way to her destination. This transformed an approximately twenty-minute journey by public transport into one of an hour or so on foot. But it was far safer this way in terms of being spotted. And it made quite a pleasant nocturnal stroll if you avoided the main roads and cut through the leafy dark wild environs of the Common.

Eventually, though, it culminated in the very urban reaches of the Upper Richmond Road as Cordelia approached the allotments. She'd already scouted this area for CCTV cameras and the immediate vicinity was thankfully clear of any such nuisances, so she approached with confidence.

The entrance to the allotments was a battered wooden door, rather like the door of a house, set into a long section of brick wall. It possessed what was called a Chubb lock, which used bigger, fatter keys than the Yale locks Cordelia had so painstakingly trained herself to pick. Presumably this type of lock was pickable, too, but she didn't have time to learn how to do so, or to obtain any specialist tools which might be required.

But the door was in plain sight on the street anyway, so in any case standing there for a prolonged interval working on the lock in the middle of the night, fully visible to anyone driving past, wasn't really an option.

Instead Cordelia had figured out another way of getting in, cruder and more direct.

The brick wall on either side of the door was topped with broken glass and barbed wire, which frankly was overkill and downright inexplicable—did they really think anyone was going to break into their stupid allotment? Well, of course, Cordelia was about to do exactly that. But her venture was an *exception*.

In any event, Cordelia's plan for getting in was to climb directly over the door itself, where helpfully there was no barbed wire or broken glass.

She had donned her heavy-duty work gloves as she'd approached, keeping an eye on the traffic, which wasn't particularly heavy at this time of night. Nonetheless, she'd had to initially walk past the door, to avoid being observed by an annoying string of passing cars, and then double quickly back, but that was no problem.

Now was the moment. No traffic. No one who could see her…

All this time she'd been rehearsing in her mind what she would have to do, so when she reached the door, she set about her task without hesitation.

She raised her right foot as high as she could, well above her waist (years of yoga paying off here) and placed it firmly on top of the doorknob and then, again without hesitation, *stood up* on it, throwing her body upwards and putting all her weight on the knob, using it as a miniature step or ledge.

As Cordelia sailed smoothly upwards, the top of the door came into view and she grabbed it with her gloved hands and, feeling like an Olympic gymnast, though seriously overdressed for that role, she pushed firmly down on the top of the door, bringing her legs up after her, left leg first and then the right one, her foot coming off the doorknob.

Now she was half kneeling, half crouching precariously on the narrow wooden top of the door, which creaked rather insultingly under her weight. She wasn't *that* heavy.

Squirming in an undignified fashion, Cordelia got both her knees on top of the door, then wrestled herself rather clumsily over it and dropped into the deep silent darkness on the other side.

She landed, luckily on grass, with what might otherwise have been an injuriously jarring impact.

Not graceful, but quick.

It was very unlikely anyone had seen her.

The brick wall behind her now cut off the streetlights and, standing in its shadow, Cordelia's vision only gradually adjusted to the dark hushed spread of the allotment before her. Luckily there was a huge moon tonight, almost full, just emerging conveniently from a turbulent bank of creamy clouds which were like something in a Steranko cover painting. The moon itself was a big white eye opening above her, alert and ready to observe her activities with interest.

Cordelia oriented herself and made her way towards Cutterham's shed.

The long brick wall which screened the allotments from the road reduced the sound of the occasionally passing traffic to a distant, oceanic susurration. Other than that, Cordelia was surrounded by an eerie silence. This, along with the smell of green growing things all around her, made her feel like she was not in London anymore, but deep in the countryside somewhere.

She strode quickly among the allotments.

As she passed the one with all the gnomes, their frozen frolics no less ghastly by moonlight, Cordelia resisted the urge to smash up a few of the fuckers. A cool nocturnal breeze eased around her, stirring sour, aromatic smells of weeds and herbs and grass. There was a whirring, whispering clattering sound to her left which proved to be a miniature windmill spinning in the breeze, apparently purely decorative, crouching among a bed of squashes.

Maybe it scared the birds away, she decided.

Once Cordelia had left the windmill behind, the loudest sound was her feet padding rhythmically on the ground—until the silence was torn by a hellish screaming close at hand.

Cordelia paused and let the shock and adrenaline pass through her system, her heartbeat slowing as she forced herself to relax again. Because she'd recognised this terrifying sound as merely the unearthly exclamation of a couple of foxes fighting (or possibly fornicating, the lovable scamps) out there in the dark perimeter of the night.

When Cordelia reached Cutterham's allotment, she fitted her head torch and switched it on. The light was bright, intense and clean, and very tightly contained, with little worrying spill-over. Not that there was anyone who was likely to see it anyway. On this side of the wall the deserted allotments stretched all the way back to Richmond Park.

Almost immediately her big question was answered—the lock on the shed door was a Yale. If it hadn't been, Cordelia wasn't exactly sure what she would have done, although she'd mentally sketched a plan to look for something big and heavy enough to smash in one of the windows.

Quite possibly a gnome.

But, thankfully, none of that was necessary now.

Picking the lock in the dark wasn't much more difficult than doing so by daylight, since, if you thought about it, once Cordelia had glimpsed the lock clearly enough to insert her tools, all the subsequent action happened unseen inside the mechanism anyway. By feel.

Still, it took longer than she expected. Well over half an hour, including a couple of frustrating false starts. So, with hindsight, it was just as well that Cutterham had left his house in Putney unlocked that day when she'd pulled off the Great Paperback Heist.

Of course, before picking *this* lock Cordelia had checked the shed door to see if it, too, was helpfully unlocked. But no such luck. Perhaps just as well, really.

If it had been left open, she would have suspected a trap.

Speaking of which, Cordelia was on high alert tonight. She had resolved to be ready for anything—Colin Cutterham turning up to pick rhubarb by moonlight, collect a nocturnal consignment of books (please let there still be some left inside the shed) or perhaps conduct an occult midnight ritual to bring his poor dead mum back to life.

In short, Cordelia was prepared for his sudden appearance from any direction and by any means, including silent descent via hang glider or parachute from the high dark sky above.

With this in mind, once she'd exultantly defeated the lock and entered, she left the door wide open behind her and made it her first order of business to open a window in each of the other three walls of the shed, so that she had a clear escape route in every direction.

Safety first.

Only then did she begin to make a careful search of the shed's contents, revealed in tantalising segments via the tight cone of light projected from her head torch. These contents consisted of a depressing amount of standard, or what she assumed to be standard, allotment-shed paraphernalia, mostly arrayed on a long wooden workbench: plastic and terracotta plant pots of many different sizes, trowels and forks ditto, bags of compost, watering cans (not used in living memory judging by the spiderwebs inside them), bottles of weed killer and other pesticides (did they still allow this stuff to be sold? It all ought to be banned), heavy duty gloves (not as nice as hers) and a gleaming green hose coiled up on the bench like a sleeping snake.

There was also a metal shelf unit full of books.

Full of paperbacks.

Full of Sleuth Hounds.

When these finally swept into her cone of light, Cordelia's heart abruptly punched in her chest like a fist doing a victory fist bump. She stepped forward, breathlessly eager to examine them up close, only to discover that, thanks to the nature of her headlamp, this made the books more difficult to see as a whole. So she forced herself to take a couple of steps back from the shelf and make a careful examination, swinging the light across the shelves before finally moving in for a close-up. So to speak.

There were far fewer than there had been in the house in Putney. It was a fraction of that great collection. But—glass half full, Cordelia—there must still be close to a hundred titles here. And, a frantic and finally joyful search revealed, *Kiss Me Deadly* was among them.

Oh, sweet taste of victory.

With the doors and windows open all around her and a continual and somehow reassuring cool breeze circulating constantly past her, Cordelia set about dividing the books into roughly equal stacks and swathing each of these in bubble wrap.

By now she was getting pretty good at this.

Once wrapped, into the rucksack they went.

When this process was complete and the rucksack, reassuringly and gloriously much heavier now, was comfortably hung on her back, Cordelia tried to identify the pang of emotion which she suddenly felt so intensely.

Sadness.

Sadness that it was all over.

She took one last look around the small shed to make sure that she hadn't missed anything. She hadn't missed any paperbacks, that was for sure. There wasn't even any place where any might be hidden. Except perhaps…

Under the workbench, in the shadows, there was a large wooden box.

On the one hand, Cordelia was in a hurry to be gone, now that her mission was complete (and so successful). Why tempt fate? On the other hand, having come this far, would it not be foolish if she didn't completely explore the shed and make sure she'd got full value out of her break-in?

So Cordelia went to the bench, crouched in front of it and tugged hard on the big wooden box, expecting quite a struggle to wrestle it out. To her surprise, it rolled smoothly and abruptly towards her with a quiet, murmuring rumble. It was on casters. That was handy.

Cordelia leaned down over the box and opened it. She was wearing her gloves, of course. They were the heavy-duty work gloves and were a trifle clumsy, but they sufficed (she had a few pairs of latex gloves in her rucksack, but frankly couldn't be bothered to put them on; lazy girl).

Nevertheless, there was no problem opening the lid of the box.

Her head torch gleamed on what was inside. A mass of brown sacking of the sort you used for sandbags and, resting on top of that, a shotgun. A double-barrelled shotgun. Its barrels and stock had been sawn off to render it a portable, lethal and highly illegal weapon.

The proverbial sawn-off shotgun.

There were evidently other things under the shotgun, beneath the layer of sacking, but Cordelia decided she wasn't going to delve any further. She closed the box, leaving its contents undisturbed, and slid it back under the workbench and then conscientiously closed all the windows she'd opened.

After that, she went back outside and carefully locked the shed door behind her, reflecting that she had provided Colin Cutterham with his own personal locked room mystery.

Back through the allotments, back past the gnomes, high white moon gazing benignly down on her.

Back to the wooden door in the brick wall.

Cordelia flicked on her head-torch briefly for one final time to get sight of the doorknob, raised her right foot, stepped onto it, pressed down hard and sent her body rising upwards—rising then toppling, losing her balance, tilting suddenly backwards, *falling* backwards, out of control, dropping down again, slamming emphatically and painfully onto the ground flat on her back.

Cordelia hadn't made allowance for the additional weight of a hundred or so paperbacks in her rucksack and they'd thrown her decisively off balance. Now she was lying, the wind knocked out of her, staring up at the sky, the ironic moon gazing back at her.

She would later reflect with pride that her first fear was for the books in the rucksack under her, pressed against the ground with her full weight on them. But they were all well and truly padded with the bubble wrap and would prove to be, when finally examined back home, all in fine condition.

All *still* in fine condition.

After the books, as she lay there catching her breath and gathering her strength, Cordelia's next fear concerned her foot, her right foot, the one that had slipped off the doorknob. It was hurting a little.

The question was, how much more would it hurt once she stood up and put her full weight on it?

Not only was there the matter of climbing over the door, that diverting little pastime which still lay ahead of her, but also the long walk home.

Of course, she could get a bus.

Girl with a rucksack full of stolen books getting a bus from the place where she'd stolen the books. All duly recorded on the CCTV on the bus. What could possibly go wrong with that?

Saying a little prayer to the deities of paperback theft, Cordelia climbed gingerly to her feet and cautiously approached the door once more. Leading with her left leg this time, she stood on the knob and swiftly scrambled on top of the door.

Going in this direction, leaving as opposed to entering the allotments, she was moving out of shadow into the glare of streetlights, which required caution.

Also, she would be dropping down onto concrete pavement instead of nice friendly grass, which required a different kind of caution—and quite a lot of it, since she might already have injured at least one leg and was carrying the additional weight of all those purloined paperbacks, as she had so recently and rudely been reminded.

So she pursued the enterprise with caution.

Just as Cordelia began clambering over the door, a great roaring sound destroyed the silence of the night.

After an instant of heart-stricken terror, and the arrival of an impressive amount of sweat all over her body, Cordelia identified the sound and calmed down again.

Just a vehicle, roaring by in the street. Unnervingly close at hand, true, and very large indeed, looming over her, all thunderous noise and bright glaring lights...

But it was merely one of her old friends, a double-decker bus.

Positioned as she was, hunkered on top of the door, Cordelia was pretty much on the same level as the people on the top deck of the bus as they swept past.

There was a teenage couple avidly kissing, a fat man wearing headphones enthusiastically bobbing his bald head to whatever fearful music he was listening to, and a thin, serious-looking woman with long black hair who was staring at her phone as if her newsfeed had just apprised her of the end of the world.

Not one of them looked in Cordelia's direction.

Behind the bus there was not a single following vehicle as far as the eye could see.

Moving in the other direction, on the other side of the street, a solitary black cab went speeding past, its driver intent on nothing except the road ahead of him.

Now Cordelia was alone.

She swung around, clinging to the top of the door, lowering herself gently down until she was hanging just above the ground.

She let go and fell to a gentle landing.

Then she set off walking in a businesslike fashion.

Actually, her foot wasn't too bad at all.

22: EXONERATED

After getting home from successfully robbing the shed, Cordelia had slipped under her cosy duvet (one hundred percent New Zealand wool) and slept the sleep of the just, or at least the sleep of the successful shed robber—a sound and satisfied and seemingly bottomless slumber—until she'd abruptly woken up just as a rosy dawn glow was flooding her attic room, riveted by the conviction that the whole thing had merely been a dream, a wish fulfilment dream.

But when she climbed anxiously out of bed, she found the piles of stolen paperbacks stacked reassuringly on her table, *Kiss Me Deadly* on top of them exactly as she remembered. Just to make absolutely sure there was no dream aspect to it, she'd gone to her bookshelf to find her other copy and confirm that there really were two of them. Yes, there were.

Although the books were both in exemplary condition, each easily grading as fine, on close inspection the following morning she found that the one she'd originally nicked, from the house in Putney, was in slightly better shape. The shed-theft copy had a tiny, barely perceptible tilt to the spine and a hint, just a hint, of a dent to the lower outer corner of the bottom back cover.

Over a microwaved coffee she agonised about which one to give to Agatha. One copy was clearly superior, even if only infinitesimally. So surely she should give that one to the object of her dreams?

Or, on the other hand, surely she should keep it for herself.

She went back and forth on this decision in what began to feel like an endless loop. She was caught between the two copies of the book like the donkey in Zeno's paradox, starving to death because it couldn't decide between two identical piles of hay.

Or, wait, was it Aristotle's paradox?

Anyway, starving donkey.

In the end, with her coffee long since gone cold and the sun outside her window rising inexorably towards noon, Cordelia finally chose. In a kind of caving-in, she realised that she wanted to keep the best book for herself.

Indeed, and absurdly, she found herself getting a tad angry at Agatha.

If she wanted a perfect copy, let *her* burgle a thug!

So, Cordelia resolutely returned the better of the two books to her own shelf.

Well, there it was…

She was keeping the best for herself. As tacky and selfish as it might be, at least it was a decision. And, having made it, she proceeded to wrap Agatha's copy as quickly as possible. She'd had to replace the previous gift box because she'd torn that one apart in a heartbroken fury, or, if you prefer, tantrum.

But at least she was able to reuse the tissue paper and ribbon from last time.

Then she caught a train to Richmond, timing her arrival for about five in the afternoon, on the assumption that if Agatha was at home it was still too early for her to go out for the evening, and if she wasn't at home yet—because she'd been out for a day's work, for instance—she was likely to be returning soon.

She was at home.

Cordelia watched her come out the front door—which had been wedged open for just this purpose, using the gift box itself—to find the gift box waiting there on the step. Agatha picked up it up and then looked both ways on her street, searching for the donor. But she didn't think to look across the street, to where Cordelia was sitting on the bench.

Then Agatha went back inside the building, clutching the box, with exactly the expression of intrigued puzzlement Cordelia had been hoping to see on her face. Her face, her face. Her lovely face. Cordelia strolled all the way back to the train station as if she was walking on air. She felt like a romantic hero in the sort of book that had romantic heroes.

It was only when she was hurtling homewards on the train that she realised she'd been so distracted trying to decide which book to gift Agatha, she'd completely forgotten to put a note or business card in with it.

Oh, well.

In some ways this was even better. Even more classy.

She would simply go up to Agatha the next time they met, at some book sale or similar, and say, "How did you like the Spillane?"

Or something like that.

Sometime in the course of their situationship—Cordelia was now willing, albeit reluctantly, to acknowledge that their carnal close encounters should at least be accorded this status—she gave Tinkler her business card, because she was very proud of it, and consequently he saw her surname for the first time. (Cordelia felt it was a commendable testament to her arm's-length policy to Tinkler and their affair—my god, was it actually an affair? No, no, no, their situationship—that this moment had been delayed until now.)

And Tinkler had said, "Holy shit. *Stanmer*. You're not related to Stinky Stanmer by any chance?"

For a sickening instant Cordelia thought that Tinkler would turn out to be a fan of her brother. If so, sex with him would have immediately become unthinkable. Because there are some limits.

But fortunately, for Tinkler's sex life, and for general cosmic justice, he had not turned out to be a fan of Stinky. Quite the opposite. Very much the opposite. At first he'd been a bit guarded, a trifle reluctant—naturally enough; reluctant to belligerently badmouth the baleful brother of the beautiful babe he was belatedly banging.

Indeed, it was this (admittedly minus the alliteration) which tipped Cordelia off about his true feelings on the subject.

But she'd soon managed to draw the truth out of him. He despised Stinky almost as much as she did. Not only did good old Tinkler himself feel this way, so did his entire circle of friends, including the black-haired blue-eyed bombshell, her loser Vinyl Detective boyfriend and, best of all, *Agatha*. Just to add to her immeasurable perfection, Agatha too despised Cordelia's brother! There were no limits to the virtues of this girl.

Yes, Agatha absolutely loathed him.

Along with Tinkler and the rest of their merry company. Her brother was anathema to them all. "Long-established odious clown in our universe," were Tinkler's exact words.

Despite herself, Cordelia began to feel a certain affection towards Tinkler taking root in her bosom.

Perhaps sensing this, and trying to capitalise on it, he tried to convince her that on that exact same night some while back, at the exact same time, when a very stoned Cordelia had hallucinated strange sounds in the bathtub and strange behaviour by the water in it (it really was *strong*, that weed; she must try some more) and had suddenly found, as though the tuning mechanism in her brain had dialled in the wrong channel, that Tinkler was invading her fantasies—that, while all that was happening to her, exactly the same thing was happening to *him*.

Right down to the strange sounds in the tub and the weird water behaviour and the sex fantasy which should have been devoted to Agatha suddenly switching track and, out of nowhere, featuring Cordelia.

Cordelia didn't believe a word of it.

She knew what he was trying to do. He was trying to make out that there was some kind of profound psychic link between the two of them and they were experiencing an earthshattering romance that was written in the stars.

Cordelia knew that they were not experiencing an earthshattering romance that was written in the stars.

What they were experiencing was the aforementioned squalid, squelching third-rate sex, which, as also mentioned, with a little imagination, or rather a lot of imagination, and supplemented by sufficient drugs, had by now risen to the lofty heights of second-rate sex.

Speaking of drugs, the next time they went to score from Miss Chichester they travelled there together; it only made sense. But Cordelia made damned sure they had separate appointments, and that Mrs Chichester didn't know they were together and didn't see the two of them together, even fleetingly, because, perceptive old bat that she was, she was likely to instantly sniff out that there was a connection between them.

And Cordelia didn't want that.

But it wasn't likely to happen anyway, since Mrs Chichester always insisted on seeing her clients separately and in isolation.

However, when it was Cordelia's turn and she went in to buy her weed, Mrs Chichester did that thing again where she invited her into the parlour after the deal was done. *Oh-oh.* Cordelia went into the parlour obediently enough, however, passing through the rattling interface of the beaded curtain into the plush red room with the photograph on the wall which had, in a sense, begun everything.

"Sit down, please."

Cordelia sat down on the overstuffed red sofa.

"I owe you an apology," said Mrs Chichester. Cordelia instantly felt a warm sensation of relief. She had no idea where this was heading, but it was clearly in a direction that would be favourable to her. Mrs Chichester seemed to be searching for words. This in itself was a novelty, and something of a treat: Mrs Chichester was normally never at a loss for words.

Finally her eyes shifted to a position where Cordelia knew they were staring at the photo on the wall, and accordingly the direction of her gaze made the direction of this discussion begin to seem a little more evident, though still baffling. And a little unsettling. "Do you remember when I talked to you about my landlord?"

"Yes."

"And I mentioned that he'd been robbed?"

"Yes," said Cordelia. Monosyllables seemed much the wisest course of action at the moment.

"Well, you see…" Long pause from Mrs Chichester at this point. "You see, when he was robbed, I thought you'd done it."

Cordelia tried her best to look shocked. She apparently did a primo job because Mrs Chichester rushed on into an apology. "Because you'd commented on the books in that photo, you see? You said how much you liked them. And then those books were stolen, and I thought you'd done it."

Mrs Chichester gazed at Cordelia, apparently hoping for understanding and perhaps even forgiveness. Instead, Cordelia contrived to give her a rather fine look of astonished hurt and scandalised condemnation.

"So that is why I gave you that veiled, or rather not-so-veiled, warning," said Mrs Chichester. "About him being a dangerous man and so on."

Some kind of response from Cordelia seemed called for at this point, even though she was so astonished, hurt, scandalised, etc. at the revelation that she'd ever been considered capable of such behaviour...

"I remember," she said tersely. Icy politeness seemed the best way to go. No actual upbraiding or angry remonstration. It wouldn't do to overdo it; after all, this was her dealer.

"But now," said Mrs Chichester, "I realise that I was wrong and quite out of line."

Yes you were, thought Cordelia. (Though, of course, neither of those things was actually true, Mrs Chichester was truthfully neither wrong nor out of line.) But all she said was, "I see." More icy politeness and monosyllables.

Mrs Chichester sighed. "Because now I realise that it couldn't have been you," she said, gazing contritely at Cordelia. "Since I've just seen my landlord and it turns out he's been robbed *again*. This time someone has robbed his lockup."

Cordelia almost said, "Shed," to snottily correct Mrs Chichester, and only just caught herself in the nick of time.

Phew.

"And clearly it's the same person, or persons, who previously robbed his house. And while you did see that photograph of a room in his house, obviously there's no way you could have known anything about the lockup. So it was wrong of me to suspect you. And I wanted to apologise."

Cordelia just nodded tightly and said nothing.

"I really am sorry," said Mrs Chichester. "Clearly you had nothing to do with it."

Cordelia allowed her manner to warm marginally, and even

smiled a brave little smile despite her wounds and injuries, thereby showing that she was magnanimously overcoming her wholly justified resentment at having been so falsely accused. (Cordelia really did feel this way despite actually, as she was only too aware on a kind of parallel track in her mind, being as guilty as hell.)

"He was absolutely livid when he told me about it," said Mrs Chichester. "About this other robbery. He was absolutely wild. He really is doing his nut in. He's beside himself. He's on the warpath. He's on the rampage. I've never seen him like this, in such a state…"

She went on in this vein at considerable length but Cordelia, basking in her exoneration, wasn't really paying attention.

Which, in retrospect was something of a pity.

A bit less arrogance and a little more attention from Cordelia could have avoided what was shortly to happen…

23: COFFEE AT SADIE'S

"I need to see you as soon as possible, if you don't mind," said Toba Possner.

She was now back from France and Cordelia tried to draw her out about exactly what was on her mind, but Toba refused to be drawn. So, Cordelia arranged for them to meet for coffee at Sadie's, as requested, i.e. as soon as possible, which turned out to be the following morning.

It was a richly autumnal morning, mild and mellow with dried leaves crunching underfoot and the smudged early sun burning away the mist around the duckpond, much to the apparent approval of the ducks, and there were all manner of extraordinary pumpkins and squashes—purple, green, orange, red and yellow, and various dramatic mottled combinations of the above, several of them looking positively like alien artefacts, perhaps from a Jack Finney novel, perhaps about bodysnatching extra-terrestrial invaders in pod form—on display in the greengrocer's window.

Cordelia walked past the duckpond, the greengrocer's and the rather high-end new charity shop where she had yet to find anything very inspiring in the way of vintage paperbacks (but you never knew; one lived in hope), towards Sadie's.

Before she got there, though, she was ambushed by an all-too-familiar figure, presaged by an all-too-familiar whiff of stale beer. And this before ten in the morning—though, of course, it could be last night's beer. Hence the staleness.

"Hello Cordelia," cried Monika Dunkley. Cordelia had recently been reading some 1930s crime fiction in which the abounding bozos never "said" anything; instead they "cried" most of their dialogue at each other. Her reflection at what a stupid term this was, and how inaccurate and untrue to life, was somewhat undermined by the way Monika was now, quite literally, crying (or at least crying out) her name. "*Cordelia*."

"Yes, Monika." Businesslike exasperation seemed called for, since Cordelia, paying the price of being distracted by speculation about what might be on Toba Possner's mind, so emphatically on it as to require an immediate meeting, had not been sufficiently alert to spot Monika lurking in her path at one of the tables outside the bakery with the young mothers and dog owners, and therefore Cordelia hadn't been able to take evasive action (crossing the road and detouring past the arts centre) to avoid this rather unwelcome encounter altogether.

"Have you heard about the church?" said Monika, who had risen from her table and was now moving in step beside Cordelia, leather jacket creaking in an almost reassuringly familiar fashion and breathing beer fumes in Cordelia's face, less reassuringly but with equal familiarity. Did she eat her breakfast cereal soaked in the stuff?

"St Drogo's, you mean?"

"Yes."

Cordelia watched their shadows, cast by the bright early morning sun, bob along cheerfully on the pavement as they walked, Monika's shadow rendered the more bizarre and, to be fair, visually noteworthy, by her Mohican haircut. And Cordelia found that she was actually, *mirabile dictu*, interested in what her companion was saying.

After all, St Drogo's and the book sale there had been a highlight of Cordelia's recent activities, although somewhat eclipsed by subsequent events.

"No. I haven't heard," she said. "What's happening?"

"Well, it's the big oak in the churchyard. You know about the big old oak tree?"

Actually, Cordelia did not know about the big old oak tree, but she was willing to wait, more or less patiently, while Monika explained.

It seemed there was a huge ancient oak beside the church which was famed locally (did it reflect badly on Cordelia not to have ever noticed this arboreal luminary?) for its majestic age and beauty. Well, the big old tree, or at least one of its big old limbs, was now in danger of being a menace to St Drogo's glorious stained-glass window—*sainted* glass window in Cordelia's lexicon—with its monochrome raree-show of hideous faces. At least Cordelia had noticed that.

All it would take was a high wind from the wrong direction to send a massive tree limb smashing catastrophically through the window. The obvious solution was to give it the chop. The limb, not the window. But wait, this wasn't so simple, given the age and size and fragility, not to mention beloved nature, of the tree.

In fact, it was going to be a very expensive operation.

"So you see what I mean?" said Monika.

"Yes," said Cordelia. "They need to have another money-raising event."

"And you see what that means?"

"We could do another paperback sale."

"Right," chortled Monika. Even the repulsive beery aroma of those chortles didn't entirely put Cordelia off, lost in thought as she now was of another potentially lucrative dodge at good old St Drogo's. Of course, this was why Monika herself was so interested.

The lucrative bit. She needed cash, as ever, and had done all right from their last little caper together.

"Okay, let me have a bit of a mull," said Cordelia, although as soon as she said it she imagined Monika picturing mulled wine, hopeless boozer that she was. But Monika seemed to get the gist.

"Great. Well, keep me posted."

"I will," said Cordelia. And she kept walking, while Monika stopped and fell behind her, the creaking of her leather jacket and the aroma of her beer fumes ceasing, and their shadows separating.

Cordelia arrived at Sadie's early for their meeting but found Toba had arrived even earlier. She already had a coffee on the go, and ordered one for Cordelia as soon as she sat down. Cordelia was rather relieved that there wasn't going to be any mint tea nonsense.

There was no nonsense of any kind. Toba Possner got right down to business, and her first words made Cordelia's insides go cold.

"I'm afraid that commission with that chap you put me in touch with, Colin Cutterham, has gone rather badly wrong."

Her head whirling with the possible ways it might have gone wrong, Cordelia immediately and without waiting for any further information began to apologise. Toba cut her off, not rudely but very firmly, and proceeded to provide her with exactly that further information.

"You see, I did a bit of research about him. Unfortunately, as it turns out, I waited until after he'd commissioned me, after he had actually paid a deposit on a painting, before I did this research. The smart thing to do would have been to scrutinise him before I even approached him. But I'm afraid I slightly let my enthusiasm get the better of me."

She sipped her coffee, looking at Cordelia. "You were quite right, he was delighted at the prospect of me recreating one of my Sleuth Hound covers for him. We had a rather nice time narrowing down the list of possibilities and finally choosing the one I was going to paint for him."

Cordelia wanted to ask which cover they'd gone for, but she didn't. Her sense of dread about what might have happened was too great to allow for any such fun, relaxed chat. And the taut, methodical way Toba was telling her story certainly didn't invite any such questions.

"The *first* cover I was going to do for him. It looked like I was going to paint at least half a dozen commissions for Mr Cutterham. We were going to eventually work our way through his entire shortlist. And that was just for starters."

Again Toba's gaze met Cordelia's, then moved away as the waitress arrived with Cordelia's coffee. "As a matter of fact, it looked as if it was all going to work out exactly as you'd suggested. The cash flowing in from these paintings was going to put me well on my way to that farmhouse in Provence." The cold all-in-the-past way Toba said this made Cordelia's heart sink. Further.

"It became very clear to me," said Toba, "that our friend Mr Cutterham had plenty of money at his disposal. And at a certain point I began to grow curious about just what the source of that money might be." She sipped her coffee, never taking her eyes off Cordelia. Cordelia, for her part, hadn't touched her own coffee. Somehow she wasn't really in the mood for it, with her stomach roiling restlessly as though it might try to climb out of her body and make a run for it at any moment.

"So I started looking into Colin Cutterham. And it so happened that there was a lot to look into. And the more digging I did, the worse the picture became. There certainly was no shortage of material to dig into. Many a website is devoted to the culture, if that's the word, and the history of the London gangster."

Gangster, thought Cordelia glumly, though without much surprise.

"Of which our friend Colin is a prime example, industriously working his way up from his humble beginnings as a low-level hoodlum to where he is now, and has been for many years, a senior gang leader. Along the way he has been deeply embroiled in extortion, bank robbery, hijacking, kidnapping…" Toba drained her coffee. Cordelia's was in danger of getting cold but she still felt no inclination to touch it.

"And murder," said Toba. "Of course, these days he doesn't have a direct connection with any such dealings. He is well insulated by layers of hierarchy and doesn't need to dirty himself in person. He is the man behind the scenes. But he wasn't always the man behind the scenes. (Not that it would have excused him if he was.) He was once a foot soldier, a vicious street-level lout, a red-handed killer in his own right."

She fell silent and Cordelia decided it was high time that she started saying something herself. "I had no idea," was the first thing she said. Then, realising this wasn't entirely accurate, was in fact a reflex lie, she quickly added, "I knew he was *dodgy* but—"

Toba Possner must have accurately read the alarm on Cordelia's face because she suddenly reached across the table and seized her hand.

"Don't worry. This hasn't damaged our friendship."

If you'd asked Cordelia how she would feel about having one of her hands (she was very fond of her hands) being abruptly gripped by a random oldster's wizened claw, she would have offered a pretty accurate forecast that her reaction would be mighty disgust. But this wasn't really a wizened claw. This was the hand that had painted so many masterpieces she loved. And this wasn't a random oldster. This was the revered genius who had conceived and executed those masterpieces.

So what Cordelia felt was not mighty disgust but mighty relief.

Because that was exactly what she'd been worried about: that it might have damaged their friendship.

The waitress, a chubby, cheery blonde, came back to their table, all smiles, and presented them with some complimentary biscotti. The perks of being a regular customer, the results of bringing all her business clients here, were beginning to flow in, just as Cordelia had hoped. Her plan had begun to come together. Although right now it seemed a pretty pathetic and unimportant plan.

"So of course," said Toba, "I couldn't possibly be involved with a man like that. Couldn't do business with him. The thought of one of my paintings hanging on his wall was really too unpleasant to contemplate. I suppose it's like a dog breeder not wanting to sell one of her puppies to a bad home. I just wasn't going to do it. So, I gave him his money back."

Toba paused at this point, rather infuriatingly, and suddenly took an interest in the biscotti. "These look rather nice. I think I'll have another coffee to go with them. Would you like another one?"

"No," said Cordelia truthfully. "I haven't been able to drink this one. Would you like it?"

"Well I will, actually, if it stops it going to waste," said Toba.

"I haven't touched it," said Cordelia, gratefully pushing the cup across the table to her.

"Oh, that wouldn't matter," said Toba, and broke one of the biscotti in half and dunked it in the coffee. "Anyway, I gave him his money back and he was rather surprised. Really quite surprised. Taken aback, in fact. He wanted to know what was wrong, to know why on earth I wouldn't do the painting for him. Well, of course, I made up some malarkey about being suddenly too busy and all that. But I'm afraid he soon saw through it, saw through my malarkey. Especially after he started offering to increase my fee, to take precedence over all this other, quite imaginary, work that was getting in the way of doing his painting. He kept increasing his offer and I kept turning him down and eventually he began to smell a rat. He finally demanded to know why I wouldn't take his money, and unfortunately by that time I'd got so fed up with the whole business that I told him. I told him the truth. And I told him I wanted nothing to do with him or his money."

Toba smiled a wry little smile. "That probably wasn't an entirely clever thing to do," she said. "He is clearly a man who is used to getting his own way, and when he doesn't get his own way, he tends not to take it kindly. He tends to lash out. As l learned to my cost."

Cordelia found herself frantically scanning Toba, looking for any signs of physical injury and feeling sick with dread. "What happened?" she said. "What did he do?"

"Nothing—which is to say, nothing personally. Instead, he enlisted some confederates, reportedly in their teens or twenties. I say reportedly because they were seen leaving our estate. Sometimes it pays to have nosy neighbours." Toba smiled again, eyes gleaming. She seemed to be enjoying telling the story; certainly more than Cordelia was enjoying hearing it. The suspense was torturing her and, perhaps realising this, Toba went briskly on with her account.

"These two young comedians broke into my studio and ransacked the place and destroyed some new paintings I'd done."

"Oh Christ," said Cordelia, genuinely mortified.

Toba Possner shook her head. "Oh, it looked worse than it was. The jesters just knocked over some furniture—some very sturdy and already somewhat battered furniture that they couldn't really have harmed. I just had to pick it back up and generally give the place a tidying."

"But what about your *paintings*?"

Toba's smile acquired a certain wickedness. "This is where the jest really was on these jesters. The cretins don't seem to realise— thankfully, I suppose—that these days artists work digitally. The paintings they destroyed had been printed from digital files. I had signed them, but otherwise they were essentially the creations of a printing process, on A2 five-millimetre Foamex. I merely have to print them again, and sign them again. There's some small expense involved, of course. But I could even claim that on the insurance if I don't mind kissing my no-claims goodbye."

"Well, thank god," said Cordelia. Sincerely.

"However," said Toba Possner, and now her smile faded, "they did also steal some paperwork that was lying around in my studio, I have no idea why. Or rather, I suspect they thought there might be something of value in it. I don't know what, though. But in any event, your name and contact details were among the papers. In fact, your business card. I hope this doesn't somehow make you vulnerable. I don't see why it should. But I thought you ought to know, seeing as you specifically said not to mention you to Colin Cutterham."

Cordelia wasn't particularly worried to hear this part of the story. Cutterham's emissaries had got hold of her business card, but so what? He had no way of knowing she was the one who had robbed him. Twice.

She and Toba concluded their meeting, after the latter had convinced Cordelia that she really was all right and not too upset by the whole experience, and had also gleefully scoffed the last of the biscotti. "These really are rather good," she said.

They parted company at the bus stop near the Red Lion, Toba to ride back to Richmond and then get the tube to Sloane Square, Cordelia to walk home in the autumn sunshine, very thoughtful and more than a little shaken.

Not as shaken as she was, though, when she got back to her room and switched on her computer to find that the Paperback Sleuth had a new client.

And that it was Colin Cutterham.

24: BURNING OIL AND DETONATION

Cordelia's classy, fresh and redesigned website featured a handy booking form for new customers where they could make an appointment to meet the Paperback Sleuth in person, to have coffee and discuss their business with her. She'd even included an amusing 1950s graphic of a smiling Stepford-style housewife pouring coffee.

Nothing was very amusing about any of it now, though.

Colin Cutterham had used the form and booked to meet her at Sadie's; Cordelia had made it clear on the website that this was her preferred method of commencing business, at least with anyone who lived in London. And she was now a victim of her own policy.

Why had she insisted on meeting her clientele in person? It was fucking madness, she now realised, since it left her exposed to situations like this. Of course, she couldn't have foreseen that the very dangerous gangster whom she had robbed (twice) of the beloved artefacts belonging to his revered dead mother would be using this booking form. But still; fucking madness.

And now, to do something different with Cutterham, to duck a meeting, would be to invite suspicion.

There was no way out of it… Of course, she could close down the whole Paperback Sleuth business, shut down the website and disappear without a trace (and, presumably, have to steer clear of Sadie's for the foreseeable future) but there was no way she was going to do any of that, and even if she did, doing so would look suspicious. Very suspicious indeed. It would immediately focus Cutterham's full attention on her.

No, there was nothing else for it.

She'd have to meet him.

Cutterham had booked to see her the very next day. Cordelia could put him off, of course. Delay him. But that would only be delaying the inevitable. She'd have to see him in the end, so she decided to get it over with.

After all—and Cordelia kept going over this in her head, looking for flaws in the argument, but she couldn't find any—after all, there was no way Cutterham could know or even suspect that she was the one who had burgled him. The only person who might conceivably have blown the whistle on her, and only blown it in the sense that she could have made a tenuous and highly suppositional allegation against her, was Mrs Chichester.

And Mrs Chichester had already unequivocally declared that she no longer believed Cordelia had anything to do with the robberies. The Great Paperback Heist Parts One and Two (the sequel).

So, Cordelia was in the clear.

She didn't feel very in the clear, though.

Nevertheless, she sent through to Cutterham confirmation of the time of their meeting. Then she went about her business for the rest of the day firmly not thinking about the looming rendezvous with him. Or, indeed, thinking about him at all. Cordelia was fairly good at compartmentalising things like that. Luckily.

And that night she managed to go to sleep quite quickly and soundly, with hardly a thought about tomorrow's appointment. She did, however, just before drifting into unconsciousness, experience a hypnagogic flash of imagery—Cutterham's face, leering and looming at her, horribly close. And the thought crossed her nearly sleeping mind...

How could anyone with such bad hair be so dangerous?

The next morning Cordelia made damned sure she got to Sadie's before Cutterham. Somehow it seemed important, crucial even, that she was in place before her customer arrived.

Her customer.

It sickened her to think of Cutterham in this light. But, she told herself, if that was all he was, if that was the only reason he wanted to see her, then she was getting off lightly. In fact, if you thought about it, it was rather ironic, and indeed downright piquant, that this dangerous thug and gangland kingpin was going to hire the very woman who'd looted his paperback collection to look for the looted paperbacks.

Cordelia was assuming that was why he'd booked an appointment to see her.

Why else would you want to see someone whose profession was searching for rare paperbacks unless you wanted her to search for rare paperbacks?

Anyway, she was going to find out soon enough.

So she got to the table, her favourite table with a commanding view of the window and the front entrance of the restaurant, soon after Sadie's opened, and started drinking coffee. Cordelia actually had to force herself to slow down on the coffee consumption. She was a sufficient bundle of nerves already without adding clinical levels of caffeine to her system.

After all that, though, it turned out Cutterham was late.

So late, in fact, that Cordelia had begun to nurture the pathetic hope that he might not come at all. She tried to stifle this treacherous feeling of relief precisely because she knew it was treacherous.

And, actually, she was right since, having left it just long enough to give her false hope, Cutterham did finally turn up.

First Cordelia heard the familiar sound of his engine, initially distant yet unmistakeable, then inexorably approaching, growing closer like the herald of doom.

Then, finally and horribly, the bulbous green sports car pulled up directly outside the big front window of Sadie's. It was like a dream, or more accurately a nightmare, seeing it here in juxtaposition with one of her favourite places on the planet, a thing utterly out of keeping, a visual non sequitur, an unwanted presence. An invader.

Then Colin Cutterham climbed, or rather jumped, out of the open top of the car instead of opening the door and just stepping out, jumping in a manner that was swift and sporty and athletic and quite at odds with his stocky thug's body.

And as he jumped onto the pavement a local whom Cordelia vaguely recognised, a spindly middle-aged dog-walking man in a stripey sweater, against all odds a rather nice stripey sweater, accompanied by a skinny aging mutt (no sweater), came over and politely addressed Cutterham.

By the way he pointed at the car and then at the sign on a lamppost, Cordelia could tell he was providing a courteous and friendly caution that parking here was still restricted at this hour of the morning.

Cutterham didn't say anything to the man. He just gave him a look that actually caused the man, the man and his dog, to physically *recoil*. Then man and dog hurried away. Cutterham watched them, grinning, and then, clearly cheered by the encounter—first significant intimidation of the day—headed into the restaurant.

Cutterham came through the front door into the shady bar area, where later in the day cocktails would be served and customers could collect takeaway meals, and stood looking around. Cordelia lifted her hand to wave him over and then immediately snatched it down, appalled at how close she'd come to disaster.

She wasn't supposed to know what he looked like.

But Cutterham hadn't noticed.

Nonetheless, Cordelia cursed herself. Their meeting hadn't even begun and already she was slick with dread sweat.

Cutterham was wandering around, blinking as his eyes adjusted to the gloom, moving away from the empty bar area and looking at the various people seated in the adjoining café alcove. Cordelia forced herself into the mindset of the person she was pretending to be—a professional waiting for a customer she'd never met, but was expecting at any minute now.

So she forced herself to look towards Cutterham with that sort of noncommittal maybe, maybe-not look you adopted if you were waiting for someone and you weren't sure if this was the person in question.

Cutterham met her eyes and Cordelia repressed the horrible shock this engendered. Instead of registering any vestige of this shock, she raised her eyebrows politely and smiled a tentative, polite half-smile, and Cutterham came swiftly over—he really moved with horrible and unexpected and sinister alacrity, like a spider striking—and said, "Cordelia?"

Full disgust points for jumping straight to first names, Colin.

"Mr Cutterham?" said Cordelia politely, forcing a confirmatory smile.

She had to keep reminding herself that although she was intimately familiar with this thug, having seen him in photos and at a distance and very nearly once from concealment in his sitting room, that he in turn didn't know her from Adam or, rather, Eve.

Cordelia had also been hoping, on the basis of Cutterham's obvious bachelor status combined with his, ahem, pronounced fondness for his old mum, that he would be another in the long hideous lineage of gay London gangsters along the lines of whichever one of the Kray twins was the gay one. (Hadn't Tom Hardy been fantastic in that part, in the movie? In both those parts?)

But absolutely instantly, from the way he looked at her as he sat down, settling heavily in his seat across from her, hard grey eyes moving over her with automatic appraisal, she knew without doubt that Colin Cutterham was another in the even more horrible and lengthy lineage of hetero hoodlums.

Cordelia hadn't exactly sexed it up for this meeting. Obviously. In fact, she had dressed in her most sober and businesslike mode. But now, as Cutterham's eyes crawled over her—continuing the theme of spider imagery—she fervently wished she'd leaned even more emphatically into the frump zone. So to speak.

For his part, Cutterham had foregone the usual jeans and T-shirt and had clearly dressed up for the occasion. He was wearing tan chinos and a red, white and blue checked Ben Sherman shirt under a bright red Harrington jacket with a tartan lining that rather overdid the red, white and blue theme. It was the same sort of jacket James Dean had sported in *Rebel Without a Cause*.

Cordelia would much rather have been sitting with James Dean right now. Even a long dead and recently exhumed James Dean.

The cheerful chubby waitress came over and beamed at them. How could she not know something was wrong? thought Cordelia. How could she not even now be ringing the police?

But far from ringing the police, this untroubled grinning waitress was handing them a plate of free biscotti which Cordelia's regular customer status had begun to earn her. Chocolate coated this time. Cordelia forced herself to smile and say thank you. Unbelievable as it seemed at this moment, there would be a future in which she would have to come back to Sadie's again and continue to transact business here, and she needed to remain on good terms with the staff.

And, after all, it wasn't really the grinning waitress's fault.

How could she know what was really happening here?

After ordering his coffee—nothing fancy, black, no sugar—Cutterham said, "Sorry I'm late."

"Not at all," said Cordelia taking the high road, regal and polite.

"Traffic," said Cutterham, by way of explanation.

"Mmm," said Cordelia. The most noncommittal of monosyllables. But not sufficiently noncommittal to prevent Cutterham launching into a lengthy dissertation (even receiving his coffee didn't stem it) about the current closure of Hammersmith Bridge, highly critical in general terms about its impact on the entire road congestion situation in this part of London but also with special reference to its particular effect, not a beneficial effect, on his ability to get here on time today.

Then he fell silent and Cordelia, forced by social norms to pick up on this cue and now say something herself, to contribute her own share to the mutual small talk, opened her mouth and began to politely ask Cutterham why he would have even needed to cross Hammersmith Bridge to get here today when, after all, he lived south of the river in Putney.

She'd actually begun to ask this question, actually begun to vocalise the word "Why" when she realised—

You don't know he lives in Putney. You shouldn't know he lives in Putney. You mustn't know he lives in Putney. You only know he lives in Putney because you robbed his fucking house.

Cordelia caught herself just in time, the sweat of terror squirting out of her and flowing freely down her ribs, her heart pounding so hard that she could feel it in the back of her throat, pounding so hard that she was afraid Cutterham could *hear* it, with her mouth open.

Her mouth open and her not saying anything, having fallen silent mid-word, him looking at her, starting to look at her strangely—

Cordelia changed the "Why" to "What" and said, "What a beautiful car," looking past Cutterham to the window where his vehicle could be seen parked, illegally, outside.

It turned out this was absolutely the right thing to say, thank god, with Cutterham immediately forgetting about anything odd in the way Cordelia had frozen up, just for an instant, just for a subliminal fraction of a second, forgetting all that and twisting around in his chair to gaze fondly himself at his car.

Then he turned back to look at her, grinning, the awkward moment (let's be frank, dangerous moment; dangerous for Cordelia) quite erased by his enthusiasm as he said, "Yeah, it's the model with the four-wheel disc brakes and the twin overhead camshafts."

Cordelia was caught in a kind of whiplash now between an instant and instinctive zoning out at this dreadful boring technical car talk, and the equally instant realisation that this was exactly the sort of thing that Agatha—Agatha, Agatha, *Agatha*—would be keenly interested in, so she, Cordelia, should be keenly interested in it too (what on earth was a camshaft?) because it might be useful for chatting up her dream girl one day.

Please let that day come soon.

Please let *this* day *end* soon.

"It's a Jaguar, isn't it?" said Cordelia, naming the only British sports car she knew. And, in fairness, it did look, as she would later confirm in a stung and insulted search online when she got home, quite like a Jag.

But Colin Cutterham leaned back in his chair and relaxed into prolonged and hearty laughter which, while stinging and insulting, also clearly indicated that Cordelia had again managed to say exactly the right thing. By saying the wrong thing.

Because it now gave Cutterham the chance to mansplain to her about cars.

"No, love," he said, Cordelia inwardly shuddering at the word *love*, "it's an MGA 1500. Most of them were sold to the Yanks, but a few stayed over here, and I got one of them. It's got the low compression engine so it doesn't have any of the usual aggro with burning oil or detonation."

Cordelia swept aside the thought that burning oil and detonation were just two of a long list of things that she would have happily wished on the man sitting opposite her and said, "Well, what can I do for you, Mr Cutterham?"

"Colin. Please."

Repressing any tendency for bile to rise in her throat, Cordelia nodded and smiled and said, "Colin."

"Well, as it happens, I've got something for you, Cordelia," said Cutterham, reaching into the pocket of his jacket.

For one extraordinary moment of stupendous shock Cordelia thought he knew everything after all and was about to pull out a gun and shoot her dead right there in broad daylight in her beloved Sadie's with her free biscotti still as yet uneaten in front of her.

But, of course, he did nothing of the kind. Instead, he took from his pocket several folded sheets of paper, and placed them on the table in front of her.

"I want to hire you to look for these books."

Cordelia steeled herself to stop her hand trembling as she picked up the list. It was handwritten in pencil on lined paper in classic ransom-note block capitals. Her eyes couldn't quite focus on the titles and authors, some of them misspelled in what at another time and in a different context might have been an amusing fashion. But she didn't need to focus on them. She could have recited the list from memory.

They were the books she had stolen.

"You're pretty good at finding books, yeah?" said Cutterham, watching her.

"Yeah," said Cordelia, simply and with such conviction that this one word, this one rather slangy word, had the impressive effect of making both of them relax completely. She had uttered an emphatic truth and, strangely, he absolutely believed her.

There they sat for a moment in this oddly relaxed silence, just two strangers at a table in a restaurant in London.

Then he said, "How do you do it?" This seemed to be a question motivated by genuine curiosity about Cordelia's work methods, rather than any kind of attempt to expose her as a book burglar. "Where do you look?"

"Bookshops—second-hand bookshops, antiquarian bookshops—charity shops, antique shops, jumble sales, book sales, estate sales, house clearances, auctions, book fairs, boot fairs, small ads, classified ads…" Cordelia was breaking up one of the biscotti absent-mindedly on the plate in front of her as she enumerated this list.

"And I imagine you use the internet, right?" Cutterham was gazing steadily at her.

"Naturally."

"But I mean, make full use of it. They've got this thing called a reverse image search. You stick in a picture and it looks all over the internet. Crawls all over the web." *Continuing the arachnid vibe here*, thought Cordelia, with a not entirely rational pang of disquiet. "And the software finds it if it crops up anywhere," said Cutterham. "I don't know why they call it a reverse image search. I mean, it's just an image search, isn't it?"

"Of course," said Cordelia. "I mean, I am aware of that technique."

"So you can do that with the covers of the books we're looking for."

"Naturally," said Cordelia. Had she said "naturally" already? Was she sounding artificial? Was she sounding suspicious? Then she realised that he'd just said *we*. The books *we're* looking for. And she was simultaneously reassured and disgusted.

"I did that," said Cutterham. "The reverse image business. I had a bit of a search myself online, before I got in touch with you, using that. Quite easy once you get the hang of it. Quite handy, really. In fact, that's how I got in touch with you. I mean, that's how I found your website." He chuckled. "You had one of the Sleuth Hound covers on there."

Indeed she did, thought Cordelia, an Abe Prossont cover—she mustn't refer to it as a Toba Possner cover to this man—along with McLoughlin and a Bonfils and, what was it? A Steranko.

But that wasn't how she had come to Colin Cutterham's attention. Cordelia was convinced this was a lie and a cover-up. He had actually discovered her through the business card his goons had stolen along with the other paperwork when they'd ransacked Toba Possner's studio. A business card that had a Sleuth Hound cover printed on the other side.

She had no doubt that he really was using the reverse image search software, though, relentlessly hunting for any evidence of his stolen books turning up online.

Cordelia suddenly realised that Cutterham had stopped chuckling.

He was looking at the fragments of biscotti on the plate in front of her and Cordelia realised that it was a very strange and nervous thing to be doing, breaking up the biscuit like that and not eating it, so she made herself pick up one of the pieces and swallow it.

It immediately caught in her dry throat so she had to sluice it with coffee to force it down, and once it did go down it lay in her stomach like a piece of lead.

But relief was in sight, the end was in sight. Their interview was drawing to a close. Cutterham kept glancing towards where his car was illegally parked, and Cordelia realised that for all his dog-walker intimidation and general braggadocio, the fucker was worried about getting a ticket.

So they wrapped things up. Cordelia pocketed the list Cutterham had given her, feeling faintly unclean simply at having touched it—indeed, she felt that her brain need scrubbing after her eyes had been exposed to his primitive block-capital pencil handwriting, but she gave no sign of that. She just reassured him that she would use every method at her disposal to find the books on his list. Which, it was true, she would. Because so doing would have the welcome twin effects of getting him off the warpath he was so clearly on thanks to his old mum's books being stolen, and also getting him, hurrah, out of Cordelia's hair and out of her life forever.

Roll on that glad day.

Cutterham seemed reassured by her confidence, her candour and her professionalism.

Which was itself reassuring.

There then ensued what was rapidly becoming a standard, indeed traditional, argument about who was going to pick up the tab for the coffees. Cutterham was bullishly assertive in his insistence that he should be the one to pay, and something in his manner caused Cordelia to boil over. She'd been tormentedly tense for the entire duration of their interview and now she just snapped. He was holding the handwritten paper bill the waitress had handed him (no block capitals or pencil here; cursive script in pen) and was already reaching for his wallet.

But, with a flash of contained rage, Cordelia snatched the piece of paper from him.

"I'll pay," she said, through clenched teeth. Then, terrified that she'd gone too far and given too much away—why was this young woman so on edge?—she added, rather lamely, "Company policy."

But Cutterham was looking at her with fond approval.

"Fiery temper, eh?" he said. "Nice one. I like a girl with a bit of guts."

So much to hate here, and for so many different reasons…

Cutterham held out his hand, offering it to shake.

Cordelia was about to refuse to do so when she realised that this would have been very strange behaviour from the woman she was pretending to be. So she wiped her hand carefully on the linen napkin. Luckily this gesture seemed perfectly plausible, since her fingers were coated with traces of chocolate from the biscotti she had been busy fragmenting.

But really she was doing this because her palm was slick with treacherous give-away sweat.

So, she offered her hand and he closed it in his, like the sealing of some vile compact between them.

He held on to her hand.

For what seemed like forever.

She wished to Christ he'd let go, not just because this was horrid in and of itself, but because at any instant the telltale sweat of fear would spring out again on her palm.

Cutterham let go of her just before this happened and smiled at her, a horribly knowing smile, and walked out of the restaurant and got into his car—just as a traffic warden was approaching, as it happened—and roared off, the reverberation of the engine lingering bestially in audibility long after he was out of sight.

It was fully five minutes before Cordelia trusted her legs enough to rise from the table and walk homewards.

25: EXORCISM

Cordelia waited the absolute minimum amount of time before she sent Colin Cutterham a message saying she'd found him some Sleuth Hounds. There was categorically no chance of him thinking any of these had come from his own (or rather his mother's) collection, because they were all in considerably less than fine condition. Indeed, several had writing inside them, the previous owners' names (and in ballpoint! Ouch). Even the ones that weren't mutilated thus were pretty clearly not the pristine copies she'd looted from his house.

And Cordelia was sure that Cutterham would register this.

He wasn't stupid, or unobservant.

Unfortunately.

When she got in touch with him, Cutterham seemed very pleased with her finds. And he paid her swiftly.

In fact, he paid her a bonus.

This put Cordelia in a quandary. She wanted to reject the bonus. It made her feel unclean and compromised to accept it.

But on what grounds could she reject it?

What grounds that wouldn't make him suspicious?

So in the end, with great reluctance, she accepted it.

But as soon as the funds arrived, she made a donation of exactly the amount of the bonus to a dog charity. That way it almost felt like it had never happened.

Despite everything turning out all right—quite against the odds, she felt, and very much thanks to her own nimble footwork, and also admittedly a healthy portion of luck—Cordelia found that she was in a state of continual heightened nervous tension. She had to get out of her little attic room and go somewhere, do something.

She considered ringing Tinkler but decided she didn't want company. What she did want was food.

She booked a table at Sadie's—managing to just obtain one as they rapidly filled up for the evening service. Because it was Sadie's, she dressed up a bit before setting forth. She'd anticipated that the walk would do her good, and it did. The bite of oncoming winter was now beginning to make itself felt in the autumn air and Cordelia had made the right call in putting on her favourite coat, her Joseph black-and-white-check blanket coat, and she admired her reflection in the dark shop windows as she walked past. Soon it would be sufficiently nippy to start wearing hats.

Perhaps in response to the autumn chill, Sadie's had a roaring fire going in their modernist fireplace at the back of the restaurant. Cordelia had managed to score her favourite table, next to the one next to the fireplace. (The one next to the fireplace got a little too hot, in her experience.)

Cordelia had also lucked out in that both her beloved cheddar soufflé and the fabulous French onion soup were on the menu this evening. She immediately ordered both and pleasurably postponed the decision about dessert until she'd eaten. Then she ordered the house Rioja, a carafe of it, and set about getting happily smashed while she waited for her food to arrive.

All around her the buzz of convivial conversation seemed to form a protective cocoon. One of the genius things about Sadie's was that whatever savant had designed it had actually worked out that restaurants could be too noisy. A universal truth which seemed to have eluded all other architects of eating places. So the tiles on the floor here—red and black tiles—were rubber tiles, which cut the decibels dramatically. They also meant you could drop your wine glass (although Cordelia had no intention of doing so) and it wasn't guaranteed to break, in the traditional manner.

The walls were hung with tapestries, art deco McKnight Kauffer tapestries (good old McKnight Kauffer had done some great crime paperbacks for Pocket Books), which provided further audio mitigation, although they didn't do anything to protect wine glasses—unless, of course, someone hurled one at the wall, in which case they were fab. And the ceiling was adorned with big circular sound-absorbing discs that continued the modernist theme of the restaurant.

All of which meant that the noise surrounding Cordelia was a soft, comforting layer like the bedding in a bird's nest. She relaxed into it as she sipped her ruby-red Rioja.

One reason Cordelia had come to Sadie's tonight was that she felt the restaurant needed to be rehabilitated after the trauma of her recent meeting here with Cutterham. The place had to be exorcised, so to speak. Hence, this relaxed and lavish dinner. The fact that it was Cutterham paying for the lavish dinner seemed to make the exorcism all the more effective.

Soon Cordelia felt there was no trace of him left here at all.

And in the end, she opted for the cheese board for dessert.

Cordelia walked home feeling delightedly drunk. The waterfowl by the pond were all tucked in for the night and silent. The moon, her gleaming accomplice in her recent allotment heist, was shining benevolently down on her. Her key eventually slotted into the lock in the front door after a modest number of inebriated attempts. She clumped happily upstairs to her room, her cosy little sanctuary from the world, locked the door behind her, drank a glass of water to stave off a hangover, and undressed for bed.

Just before retiring, she decided to quickly check her emails. Then she couldn't resist also just touching base with social media. Specifically with the posts of one Agatha DuBois-Kanes.

Agatha was not an incessant updater, but she did post fairly regularly, and when she did so you could generally count on her for a good photo. High quality, stylish and characterful. Plus her captions tended to be short, witty and/or informative, always to the point and invariably providing a flavour of her personality.

All of these attributes were amply exhibited by her latest post.

The caption simply read: *Look what I've got!*

And there had never been a more beautiful photograph of Agatha herself, perhaps because never had she been captured, as in this selfie, smiling with such a joyous open smile—the pure childlike innocence of that smile was heart-breaking.

Agatha was smiling with obvious pleasure because of what she was holding up in one hand, the hand not holding her phone taking the photo, the hand held up beside her beautiful smiling face.

The hand holding the book.

The hand holding the copy of the Sleuth Hound edition of *Kiss Me Deadly* which Cordelia had given her.

Which Cordelia had given her after stealing it from Colin Cutterham.

I don't know why they call it a reverse image search. It's just an image search, isn't it?

26: COUNTERMEASURES

Cordelia took her copy of *Kiss Me Deadly* and placed it carefully on the table, standing it upright, propping it up against a pair of coffee mugs. Clean coffee mugs, of course. Scrupulously clean coffee mugs.

She adjusted the angle of the book, checking how the light from the lamp fell on its cover, then compared it with the reference photograph on the screen of her laptop. Once she had a satisfactory match, she took a photograph of the book with her phone. As she was transferring the photograph from her phone to her laptop via Bluetooth, the phone began to ring, coming to life in her hand and somewhat startling her.

When she saw who was calling, she answered instantly.

"Hey," said Tinkler. "I got your message. You said to call right away?"

"Yes," said Cordelia. "Sorry it's late."

"No problem."

"Thank you for getting back to me."

"No problem," repeated Tinkler. "You sound… serious."

"I am serious. This is a serious situation. I need to ask you a favour."

"Ah… Okay."

"And in return for this favour I am willing to do you a favour."

"Oh, really?"

"In return I am willing to indulge any sexual fantasy you have, go along with any sex prank you fancy. Anything. Within reason."

"Oh my god. Really?"

"Yes."

"Oh my god. Does that include—"

"Anything. Within reason."

"Oh my god. That is so perfect. The timing is so perfect. Sex Accessories International has got a special discount this month on—"

"Tinkler. Pay attention. You remember the bit where I said you had to do me a favour first?"

"Yes, of course."

"Without asking any questions."

"I'll do my best."

"Okay. I want you to get in touch with Agatha."

"Agatha… Okay…"

"I don't care what story you make up," said Cordelia, "or how you couch this, so long as you achieve the necessary objective. And that objective is to get her to leave town."

"Leave—"

"Don't interrupt," said Cordelia.

"Okay. Sorry."

"Get her to take a holiday. A short break. She has to leave London at the very least. But leaving the country would be better still."

"But—"

"Don't interrupt," repeated Cordelia.

"Sorry."

"This is vitally important. Agatha has to go away, because if she stays around here her life is in danger."

"Shit. Really?"

"Yes, really."

"What—"

"I told you," said Cordelia. "No questions. But believe me, her life is potentially at risk. She will be perfectly safe if she clears out for a little while. But, at least for the moment, she is in serious danger. I don't know if you should tell her that. I'll leave that up to you. If you do tell her, you will not bring me into it, is that clear? You make no mention of the fact that this information, this warning, comes from me. Is that clear?"

"Yes. Okay. Sure."

"Make up any story you like, but make sure she understands that she mustn't remain in London. That is a fact."

"How long will she have to stay away?"

Cordelia looked at the photo she'd just taken with her phone, now on the screen of her laptop side by side with the reference photo. It was an excellent match.

"If certain countermeasures are successful," said Cordelia. "Not long at all."

After she'd hung up, leaving Tinkler hearteningly motivated by the promise of forbidden sexual pleasures, Cordelia resumed the next phase of those countermeasures, using picture editing software to combine the photograph she'd just taken of her copy of *Kiss Me Deadly* with the reference photo.

She'd lucked out with the reference photo.

Cordelia had thought she would need to use a picture of her brother holding a record or CD, or, heaven help us all, some kind of award or trophy.

But she'd actually found an image of him holding a *book*. What were the odds of that? Stinky with a book. Admittedly the book was something called *Rut Me* by someone called Rut Gylling and was apparently her autobiography—she appeared on the cover in a state of bondage-freak undress, all leather and tattoos and, mostly, bare flesh. Nevertheless, it was ideal.

Stinky was gleefully holding it up, cover full and flat on to the camera for display, and altogether it couldn't have been better for Cordelia's purposes.

True, the book was a despicable modern large format paperback, but Cordelia was able to replace it with the smaller *Kiss Me Deadly* with only minimal alterations of Stinky's hand positions, and she easily cloned in the background to fill where the rest of *Rut Me* had been.

When the job was completed to her satisfaction—it really did look like Stinky was holding *Kiss Me Deadly*—Cordelia logged in to Stinky's official website as an administrator.

Cordelia had helped her brother set up this site, or rather she had done the entire job herself, and charged him considerably more than the going rate for so doing. And consequently she still possessed all the necessary passwords to access it.

Of course, anyone with a brain in his head would have promptly changed those passwords as soon as Cordelia had completed the job. Anyone with half a brain in his head.

In other words, Cordelia had been able to proceed secure in the knowledge that the passwords would be exactly the same as she had left them. And naturally she was proved correct in this assumption.

Indeed, very little had changed since she'd last visited the website. Certainly none of the functionality she'd established had been altered in the slightest and she was able to find her way around with ease. Any differences since she'd first set it up were purely cosmetic. Apparently Stinky would occasionally prevail on one of his disposable mistresses to do some work on it and freshen it up, but given the rapid turnover of these creatures very little had been achieved.

Cordelia now uploaded the photo that she'd doctored and added the caption, *I'm giving this one to my mate Agatha, but I'm keeping all the others for myself! After all, I'm the guy who got them!!*

She studied this for a while, then added some more exclamation marks to it, and a winky smiley face, and then posted it on Stinky's news feed, near the top.

Among the other recent posts was the one featuring Stinky boasting about, and posing with, his new bodyguards-cum-minders. They were a pair of massive, hulking, heavily muscled Swedes who looked like identical twins thanks not least to their shaved heads and ludicrous, elaborately braided and dyed beards—one tiger-striped, the other leopard-spotted. But they weren't twins, despite having the same first name. They were identified in the photo caption as Röd Sill and Röd Strömming and were apparently ex-Swedish special forces.

They certainly looked it. Both special forces and ex.

Stinky looked as delighted with his formidable security detail as he did with the incriminating book Cordelia had given him in the doctored photograph.

She put her computer away with the warm relaxed satisfaction of a job well done, wondering how long it would take for Colin Cutterham to find the photograph of Stinky with the book. Hopefully not long at all.

The question was, would Cordelia have unleashed a vengeful and murderous psychopath on Stinky if he hadn't just recently acquired a formidable matched pair of daunting guardian goons?

Would she still have put her brother in the path of potentially lethal jeopardy if he didn't have such protection?

She certainly liked to think so.

27: TIMBER

Two days later, Cordelia went for a meeting—that was rather a grandiose term for it—with Monika Dunkley at the Sun Inn near the pond in Barnes. While Monika enthusiastically slurped the beers which Cordelia provided, they discussed St Drogo's. As Cordelia's undercover agent at the church, she was able to provide a progress report on the proposed fundraising activities which were currently under discussion there.

Specifically, on the progress of Cordelia's proposal, presented via her envoy Monika, for another sale of paperbacks. Cordelia couldn't see why the St Drogo's people didn't just drop all the other schemes they were considering and embrace this. After all, the last one had been a roaring success.

But apparently there was one particular holdout on the committee who was reluctant to go ahead with the paperback sale. Old Vulture Face, of course.

Despite this, Cordelia remained confident that her bid would prevail. The rest of the committee, according to Monika, were all in favour of it, and Vulture Face's objection, motivated purely by her personal antipathy towards Cordelia, was really just a token manoeuvre. She couldn't let the proposal pass unchallenged, even though she knew it would likely go through in the end. So, effectively, it was no more than a face-saving gesture. A vulture-face-saving gesture.

"Anyway," said Monika, draining another substantial portion of her beer and renewing the moustache of froth on her upper lip, "they'd better do something soon or they're going to have a branch of that oak tree coming through their stained-glass window. All it would take is one strong breeze from the wrong direction and *smash*. And there's more than a strong breeze coming. Have you heard about the big storm? They reckon there's going to be a huge storm. I hope it doesn't arrive on Halloween and ruin the trick-or-treating. I love to see the little kiddies trick-or-treating. Dylis and I love to get a big bowl of sweets and dish them out to the little ones when they come trick-or-treating." Dylis being Monika's invalid flatmate-cum-landlady-cum-employer.

Cordelia politely sat through a bit more of this monologue, which alternated in violent swerves between apocalyptic meteorological prognostication about the "big storm" and saccharine reminiscences about costumed tots begging for sugary treats on All Hallows Eve. Then she purchased a final pint for Monika and took her leave.

There might be a devastating storm cell fermenting over some distant ocean, but tonight was warm and still, unseasonably warm and uncannily still, with dramatic salmon-pink ramparts of cloud banked high in the western sky over the river. Cordelia walked home through the village, past shop windows adorned with paper cut-outs of cats and witches and jack-o-lanterns. Also spiders, which made her think of Colin Cutterham, so Cordelia chose to ignore those.

Things on that front seemed to have settled down satisfactorily, however. Agatha had indeed left London as requested, for parts unknown. At least to Cordelia. Which was fine with her. If she didn't know where Agatha had gone, neither did Colin Cutterham.

Anyway, with a bit of luck he would now be targeting Stinky instead. In which case Agatha, who was blameless in this matter whichever way you looked at it, would be, quite rightly, off the hook.

Nonetheless, it was good to know that she was safe in some far-off anonymous locale.

For this, Tinkler deserved thanks. He had come through with startling speed and effectiveness when the chips were down. In fact, come to think of it, he deserved more than thanks. Cordelia made a mental note to get in touch with him and schedule whatever depraved banality he had in mind for his reward.

But tonight Cordelia was flying solo. Or rather bathing solo. Yes, it was bath night.

She checked to make sure that Edwin was securely occupied—no bath-time interruptions, please—in his quarters at the back of the house. Yes, the strains of the evening concert on Radio 3 could be distantly heard, which meant that he and Rainbottle would be engaged in listening to the wireless and resisting the urge to eat biscuits for a good hour or so. Cordelia hurried upstairs, got undressed, put her robe on, dropped her phone into the pocket of the robe, and came back down carrying her washbag and her laptop.

She set water plunging into the tub, locked the bathroom door, and got comfortable. There hadn't been time to consume any green butter tonight, but that didn't matter; it would be fun anyway.

Soaking indolently in the hot fragrant water, Cordelia watched selected adult shenanigans on her laptop for a while and then abandoned herself entirely to her own, rather vivid and powerful, imagination.

Soon, thanks to that vibrant and resourceful faculty, Cordelia was sharing this nice big bathtub with the girl of her dreams.

In this particular dream, Cordelia was wrapping the smooth warm skin of her inner thighs around the smooth warm skin of

Agatha's immaculately shaven head. Starting at the top of her skull and sliding down. Sliding to settle with the tender ticklish morsels of Cordelia's innermost inner thighs riding on Agatha's cheekbones, those beautifully sculpted, high, regal cheekbones.

Those cheekbones flexed in Cordelia's imagination, as Agatha opened her lovely mouth.

Cordelia was open too, as open as the ocean.

Quite a bit later, feeling as pleasantly warm and drained as the bathtub itself now was, Cordelia was sauntering back down the hallway, scented skin moist, perfumed hair damp, with her beloved MacBook (source of so many hours of pleasures, not to mention the backbone of her business) cradled in her arms, when she suddenly realised that she'd left her washbag in the bathroom.

So she turned around to go back to get it.

That was when she saw the man with the shotgun.

The man was just standing there in the hallway behind her. Clearly he'd been there when she'd emerged from the bathroom, but she hadn't seen him.

Until now.

The shotgun he was holding was a sawn-off shotgun, very similar to the one she'd seen in Colin Cutterham's allotment shed. Indeed, perhaps the very same one.

Similarly, the man holding it might well have been Cutterham himself. It was hard to say for sure because of the black ski mask he was wearing over his face. Besides the ski mask he wore a dark green bomber jacket, baggy blue jeans and a pair of oxblood Doc Marten boots. But the main point of interest was the shotgun.

Which he was now pointing at her.

Cordelia had quite forgotten about her washbag. She quickly reviewed the earlier part of the evening. Had she eaten dope-infested butter? Super-strong dope-infested butter? Could this be a remarkably realistic and decidedly unwelcome hallucination?

But she hadn't eaten any dope-infested butter.

But *could* she have eaten some, some so powerful that part of the ensuing hallucination was the belief that she hadn't eaten any?

No.

Unfortunately, no.

Cordelia backed fearfully away down the hallway, her damp feet leaving wet footprints on the carpet, clutching her MacBook Air, her body wet and her hair wet, wearing nothing except her green silk robe.

The thug with the shotgun followed her for a few steps then gestured brusquely with the gun, moving it abruptly up and down, and Cordelia understood that he was signalling her to stop. They were now about two thirds of the way along the hall, nearer the front door than Edwin's flat. Further out of earshot of Edwin's flat. Which was the point.

Because now the thug leaned towards her—she caught an acidic smell of cheap aftershave and sweat—and spoke, in a hoarse, low whisper.

Some distant part of Cordelia's mind analysed the man's voice and registered the fact that this wasn't Colin Cutterham. Some even more distant part registered a crazed feeling of being offended that he couldn't even be bothered to attend to this matter personally. Instead, Cutterham had sent this thug. This other thug. This more menial thug.

"Now," said the thug. "Now, listen…" and he paused thoughtfully, looking at Cordelia, looking her up and down, standing there wet and wearing nothing but her silk robe and clutching her laptop tight to her as if she could shield her entire body with it. She couldn't.

"We can do it right here and right now," said the man with the shotgun, after a moment, holding up the gun meaningfully. "Or it can happen later, a lot later, somewhere else. Entirely up to you." This last was pronounced in a hideously fair-minded and even-handed tone.

Somehow, the entire ugly meaning of what he was proposing to Cordelia was absolutely clear to her. If he didn't murder her here and now, then he would take her somewhere else and a certain length of time would pass. As far as Cordelia was concerned, an eternity would pass, and she had no doubt about exactly in what fashion that time would be passed. By the thug, and possibly by his friends. And Cordelia.

She had no illusions at all about what would happen to her between now and "a lot later" when this man took her "somewhere else".

And it was like a big invisible door had open just a fraction, allowing her a searing glimpse of hell itself.

Entirely up to you.

She was being offered a choice. But Cordelia knew that it was no choice at all. Be killed now or… Allow this other thing to happen…

But surely he wouldn't pull the trigger now? If he did, Edwin would hear and come rushing out. And then…

And then Edwin would be dead too. She found it all too easy to believe that this man could kill Edwin. Ineffectual Edwin in his corduroy trousers, probably with the *Guardian* crossword puzzle clutched in one hand, half finished, never to be finished. Edwin wouldn't stand a chance. Rainbottle might do a little better. He might growl and bare his fangs and try to attack the intruder but…

Then that just meant the dog would be killed too.

Somehow, the thought of Rainbottle being killed was the worst thing.

Cordelia was defeated, and the thug knew it. She could see just enough of his mouth in the slit in the ski mask to see that he was smiling. She could see that by the shape of his lips, what she could see of them.

He jerked the shotgun upwards, indicating the staircase, meaning that she should go upstairs and that he would go with her.

They resumed moving down the hallway.

It looked like the time they were going to pass together was going to begin here. In her attic room, in the room that had once been her retreat and sanctuary, where she had been safe from the world. Where the worst thing she'd had to worry about was dodging the rent and fixing a blatantly forged signature in a valuable paperback.

She and the thug moved slowly along the hallway, towards the foot of the stairs, him holding the shotgun pointed at her and Cordelia backing away, facing him, terrifyingly aware that the thug knew that she was naked under her robe and aware also that her robe was loose and getting looser, starting to fall open as the loosely knotted slippery silk belt on it was becoming looser still, getting ready to undo itself.

Cordelia reached to tighten the belt and fasten it more firmly, and as he watched her, the thug's mouth split open in a toothy grin (remarkably white teeth. Who would have expected good dental care in an individual such as this?) because he knew exactly what she was doing and exactly why she was doing it. Cordelia hugged her MacBook to her with one hand and with the other she reached down to try to tug the silk belt more tightly around her, to stop the robe falling open…

Later, she would decide that it was seeing the toothy white grin that did it. But she couldn't be sure.

All she knew was that then, like lightning, she changed her mind.

Instead of tightening the belt, Cordelia tugged on it the other way, *loosening* it, and the belt came unknotted and the robe fell open and Cordelia stopped moving, standing stock still, while the thug was still moving towards her. And her robe was wide open now and the thug's eyes dropped from her face to her body.

And at that moment, that moment of distraction for the thug, Cordelia took a quick step towards him, closing the distance between them just enough, and as she did so lifted her MacBook Air and swung it, swung it with all the considerable strength in her body, powerfully supplemented by the adrenaline afforded by mortal terror and—

Smashed the thin, compact metal wedge with all her might, sharp edge on, into the ski-masked skull of the thug.

It connected—*bit* in, in fact—like the blade of an axe biting into the trunk of a tree, with an oddly wooden chunking sound.

The impact was so brutal that, radiating back through her hands gripping the laptop, through the bones of her fingers, through the bones of her wrists and arms, it shook every bone in Cordelia's body and rattled the teeth in her own head.

But no doubt the impact was, it has to be admitted, even more profound for the one on the receiving end...

The thug dropped, like a tree toppling as it was felled.

What was it they shouted when a tree was falling?

Timber.

As he fell, he dropped his shotgun, which landed softly and harmlessly and undischarged, thank god, on the rug. And then the thug sort of folded into a foetal position as he himself fell to the floor with a powerful thump.

Lying there on the rug at her feet, the thug said something incoherent and indecipherable as though he was starting on a long and complex statement but had lost the power of speech. Which indeed he had. After a few nonsense syllables, he fell silent. As though pausing to rethink what he was going to say. But he wasn't going to rethink. He wasn't going to say anything.

Not least because he seemed to have stopped breathing.

Cordelia stared down at the man.

She was still clutching her MacBook. Interestingly, the impact only seemed to have left the slightest dent on one of its fashionably rounded corners.

As if for propriety's sake, she closed her robe snugly and knotted her belt again. She did it mostly one handed because she didn't want to let go of her laptop. As if she might need it again.

For the purpose she had just used it.

But she wasn't going to need it again for that purpose.

The thug was quietly lying on the floor, one of his feet twitching. It twitched briefly and then stopped, at which point Cordelia herself instantly *started* twitching, as if in response, as though they were two partners in an avant-garde dance company performing a way-out routine. Cordelia twitched from head to foot, shaking uncontrollably.

At this point she must have begun making some strange noises of her own, and apparently at considerable volume, because Edwin immediately came hurrying out of his flat at the back of the house, followed by Rainbottle.

He looked at her, and then looked at the thug on the floor, and then he crouched beside the body, examining it, while Rainbottle circled it, sniffing with interest. Then they both paused and looked at each other, like two oddly assorted, very oddly assorted, medical experts consulting over a puzzling patient.

The phone in the pocket of Cordelia's robe began to buzz.

Without thought, an automaton, Cordelia answered it. It was her brother.

"Hello Cordy. I thought I'd better ring. You see, there was this geezer who turned up, very sketchy geezer, he tried to breach the security perimeter and Röd and Röd caught him and asked him what he was up to. And it turns out that he had this photo of me with this book and it was all about the book, and when I saw the photo I saw that the book had been changed and it was, like, this old paperback. And I said it was my sister who knows all about the old paperbacks. And so it must be her who had changed the photo. As a joke. Or something. Anyway, he seemed to believe me and he left. And then Röd said, I think it was Leopard Röd—no, tell a lie, it was Tiger Röd—he said that he thought this geezer actually seemed quite dangerous, and he thought that now that he'd heard it was you, this whole business with the photo and everything was all your doing, he thought you might be in trouble and that I should check with you and make sure you're all right. Are you all right?"

"Yes," said Cordelia, forcing her voice not to tremble for the duration of that single syllable, and hung up.

Edwin and Rainbottle were both still in silent consultation over the thug on the floor. But Edwin now turned and looked up at Cordelia and said, "He's dead."

Cordelia's heart rippled and jumped in her chest. Had Edwin said what she'd thought he'd said?

"Dead?"

"Yes."

"Are you sure?"

"Absolutely," said Edwin. "Nice work."

"What?"

"Good job. Nice work. Especially if it was your first time. I assume it was your first time."

"My first time?"

"Killing someone." Edwin smiled at her.

"Yes."

"And I suppose you'd be wanting help getting rid of the body?"

"What? Yes. Yes, I would."

28: EDWIN

So anyway, it turned out that Edwin was a serial killer.

At first, when he offered to help dispose of the body, Cordelia thought this was just some kind of bizarre wish fulfilment fantasy based on his avid true crime reading.

But Edwin wasn't just a true crime fan, he was a true criminal, so to speak. And he'd disposed of bodies more than once.

Yes, a serial killer.

Not a Thomas Harris, Hannibal Lecter type, killing-for-creepy–thrills-and-trophies serial killer in the modern manner, though. More a good old-fashioned reassuring Patricia Highsmith, Tom Ripley type, killing-for-personal-gain-or-advantage serial killer.

It had all begun when a member of Edwin's cycling club, a woman, had sustained mysterious but substantial injuries, sufficient to hospitalise her, and it had gradually come out that she'd been beaten up by her boyfriend. And it wasn't the first time.

The police weren't doing anything about it, and the woman wasn't pursuing the matter, and it was clear that it was going to happen again and go on happening and that things were only going to get worse.

So Edwin had decided to do something about it. His quest to do something about it had been immeasurably aided by the fact that the boyfriend was a heavy drinker, no surprise there, who was in a habit of getting a skinful at a pub called the Dove in Hammersmith and then walking back home across the bridge late at night.

It had simply been a matter of following the drunken boyfriend, of carefully shadowing him unseen for a number of such late strolls, until the perfect conjunction of events—moonless night, no other foot traffic on the bridge, etc.—allowed Edwin to push him off the bridge and into the river below.

The Thames was a very good river for drowning in, especially around Hammersmith Bridge, as attested to by a brass plaque set in the wooden railing of the handsome old Victorian structure, which commemorated one Lieutenant Charles Campbell Wood who, on 27 December 1919, had dived into the river from this spot to save a woman, a complete stranger, from drowning. The waters of this stretch of the Thames were notoriously treacherous.

Anyway, no one had saved the drunken boyfriend who, if you thought about it, was also a complete stranger, to his assailant. Edwin. Although Edwin felt he'd come to know him quite well in the days of stalking him while getting ready to rid the world of one abusive drunken boor.

Effectively Edwin had been a knight in shining armour in this scenario, though no one knew it, at least until now, until he told Cordelia all about it over hot chocolate in his kitchen with Rainbottle at their feet, wagging his tail and appearing to also be listening with approval.

Edwin was, Cordelia believed, secretly glad to have someone to tell.

The people who didn't know about his chivalrous, indeed heroic, act included the battered and abused girlfriend.

The thing that had most surprised Edwin, and indeed the only thing that disturbed him about the whole affair, was how upset the cycle club girl had been at the loss of her life partner. The life partner who had very nearly been her death partner. She had seemed, at least at first, inconsolable that the drunken swine had gone to his watery doom.

But she'd got over it in the fullness of time, of course, and had later married someone whom Edwin believed to be a decent chap, or at least not a wife beater, and they had lived happily ever after (Edwin's interpretation) and moved to Cumbria.

Personally, Cordelia thought the woman might have been better off in London risking a beating—honestly, Cumbria?—but there was no accounting for taste.

So all in all, Edwin could consider that his first killing had been conducted as a chivalric knight in defence of a lady fair.

The second one, not so much.

This time Edwin's ire had been raised by an ignorant hoodlum, his own description, who had a habit of working on his hoodlum car, his pimped and blinged boy racer car, at all sorts of inconvenient times, but mostly Sunday mornings, with hideous pounding music, Edwin's own description, blaring out at thunderous levels as he worked on the car while Edwin was trying to listen to Radio 3.

This had been when Edwin was living in a flat on Putney Hill near Robin Hood Corner, before his parents had kicked the bucket and Edwin had inherited the house where he now lived in Barnes, with its for-rent attic room where Cordelia dwelled.

Edwin stressed that the noisy car fellow hadn't just been a colossal nuisance. He'd also been a local figure of fear. A drug dealer—a *hard* drug dealer. By which Edwin meant a purveyor of heroin and cocaine. The kind who carried a gun and terrified people. He'd certainly terrified everyone in his neighbourhood, which was why no one had dared to speak out against him or confront him. He was a ruthless criminal and, more than likely, a killer in his own right.

Cordelia had no doubt that all this was absolutely true. However, she also had the nagging suspicion that if the culprit had been, say, a blameless church bellringer, his ultimate fate might have been not entirely dissimilar.

The fate, in this case, had consisted of being killed with one of his own weapons in what apparently (and, importantly, the police had been willing to believe) was a drug gang war.

Anyway, dead hoodlum.

It turned out that you didn't want to get on the wrong side of Edwin.

As they finished their hot chocolate, he made an oblique reference to "a few other occasions" when he'd had to deal with matters that had resulted in the need for the disposal of bodies. He smiled reassuringly at Cordelia, evidently wanting her to feel, given his pedigree, that this evening's business was in safe hands.

And Cordelia did indeed feel that it was. Edwin, annoying landlord, interrupter of baths, doer of crossword puzzles and repairer of bicycles, whose only redeeming feature had up to now been his cute dog, had been transformed in Cordelia's mind.

He was suddenly interesting.

And he certainly seemed entirely competent in the way he'd bagged up the shotgun thug in large bin liners and hauled him out to the seldom used garage behind the house, loaded him into the even more seldom used silver Volvo, relic of his parents' tenure in the house but faithfully maintained for roadworthiness by Edwin, and driven him off somewhere and disposed of him.

Cordelia did not ask where or how. She was just deeply grateful to Edwin for looking after everything. She had simply stayed huddled up on his sofa with Rainbottle for company until Edwin had returned. Now, as they were finishing their hot chocolate, Tesco Finest Santo Domingo Single Origin, Edwin's favourite and fast becoming Cordelia's, he looked at her and asked the obvious question.

"Why on earth would anyone be coming after you with a shotgun?"

Cordelia told him.

When she had finished her account of the Great Paperback Heist, Parts One and Two, plus all relevant ancillary information, Edwin nodded, non-judgementally, and simply said, "I wondered about that backpack."

Then, reflecting on Colin Cutterham, he said, "He's the sort of man who delegates his vengeance. Judging by what you say, all the properties he owns and so on, he's some kind of senior crim. That would also explain why his house in Putney was so easy for you to break into. He didn't think he needed any security. He was assuming his reputation would be his security. And he would have been right, regarding the criminal fraternity. All of them would have known better than to rob a man like that, even if he left his door wide open."

Edwin looked at Cordelia. "But you weren't a member of the criminal fraternity. You don't know anything about any of that. You're a respectable law-abiding young woman." He didn't seem to have any problem squaring this description with the fact Cordelia had actually burgled the house, and later the allotment shed.

Nor, for that matter, did Cordelia.

Go figure.

"So… where are we?" said Edwin, taking their hot chocolate mugs from the table and putting them in the kitchen sink. He came back and sat down again and addressed his own rhetorical question. "The way I see it, there are two possibilities. By far the most likely one is that, having failed in their attempt to take your life—well done, by the way. Full marks for the way you dispatched that brute—they'll cut their losses and this will be the end of the matter."

"And the other possibility?" said Cordelia, rubbing Rainbottle behind the ears as he huddled close to her chair. Perceptive pup that he was, he seemed to sense that she'd had a rough evening and needed company and comfort.

"That's the one we must now prepare for," said Edwin.

"Prepare how?" Rainbottle forced his cold wet nose into the palm of Cordelia's hand.

"Well," said Edwin, "at the moment, Mr Cutterham has no idea what has happened. All he knows is that his emissary has yet to report back. He will eventually grow impatient and try to get in touch with the deceased ruffian. Who, of course, will not respond. Mr Cutterham will grow increasingly impatient, but there is very little he can do. Give him a day to wait for the ruffian to get back in touch and then finally realise he isn't going to. Then, give him a day to formulate a response; and then, on the third day, I'd say that he'll take action." Edwin looked at Cordelia. "From that point on, I'd say, you should clear out of here for a while and leave me to handle matters."

Edwin got up from the table and went to the sink, where he began to wash up their mugs while he continued talking. "They might have the common sense to send more than one emissary next time," he said.

Edwin didn't sound frightened at the prospect.

If anything, he sounded a little excited.

Cordelia hadn't seen him this animated since the Rohan sale catalogue had arrived.

29: CATH KIDSTON

Three days later was, as it happened, Halloween.

The seasonal mood was established pretty much from dawn, with the day starting and continuing utterly grey and overcast under a continual flowing ceiling of charcoal cloud which provided a mood of funereal glumness or, for the more impressionable, the approach of the apocalypse. This latter interpretation was heightened by a steadily strengthening wind that began by tentatively fondling the windows in Cordelia's room like a shy burglar, but within a few hours had escalated to lustily rattling the panes in their frames. Like an impatient burglar.

At midday it was as murky outside as the middle of the night, bringing to mind the phrase *Darkness at Noon*. (None of the paperback editions of the book of that title by Arthur Koestler were particularly collectable.) By now Cordelia was downstairs in the back of the house with Edwin.

"Listen to that wind," said Edwin. He looked a bit odd with a pair of sunglasses pushed up into his hair, ready to pull down over his eyes at a moment's notice. But he looked odd in a dashing sort of way. "I hope the bad weather doesn't put them off," he said. "I would quite like to get this sorted out tonight if possible. If for no other reason than to bring Rainbottle back home."

Edwin and Cordelia were sitting at the table in the kitchen, and Edwin was right, she thought, the place seemed oddly empty without the dog. Cordelia missed Rainbottle but she agreed with Edwin that billeting (or kennelling) him with one of Edwin's boring ex-girlfriends for a day or two was the sensible thing to do. "The poor chap might get underfoot otherwise," Edwin had said.

Now he was showing Cordelia the screen of his laptop, an unexciting PC but serviceable, which was displaying the feeds from a network of newly installed small surveillance cameras which would have done credit to Mrs Chichester.

Cordelia had offered to help defray the cost of these—after all, it was *her* the hoodlums were after. But Edwin wouldn't hear of it. "They'll come in useful in the future, I'm sure," he said. He was surprisingly cheerful. Indeed, the two of them had never got along so well, or at least not since the night of the purloined curry.

"Now look at this," he said. "This took place just before daybreak."

From a number of angles, a man—a large young white man—could be seen moving cautiously around the front garden of the house and then the back garden, inspecting doors and windows. The cameras recording him were low-light technology rather than thermal imaging, so a lot of detail was visible. For instance, the fact that he was wearing a baseball cap with, rather oddly, a floral pattern. It was quite nice—was it a Cath Kidston design?—but it looked very much out of place on this bruiser. The rest of his ensemble consisted of a three-quarter-length denim coat with a sheepskin collar and lining, and jeans and trainers.

"He's a sizable brute," said Edwin. Indeed, the Bruiser looked like a super heavyweight boxer, which apparently was the next size up from heavyweight. And was big. Really quite big.

"This was this morning?" said Cordelia.

"Just a few hours ago," said Edwin. "He's clearly casing the place, getting ready to make a move, so I'd say that our original prediction was correct. Tonight's the night." Edwin sounded positively jolly when he said this. He really did seem to be enjoying himself. Cordelia was definitely seeing another side of her landlord.

The two of them had spent the last three days getting the house ready for uninvited visitors, preparations which included stashing weapons in various places where they would be easily accessible for Edwin but were unlikely to be discovered by any intruder. Among these weapons was the sawn-off shotgun which he'd retained from the thug who'd tried to kill Cordelia. But Edwin also possessed a fairly impressive assortment of other firearms, mostly handguns, some of which, he explained, had come from the collection of the ill-fated drug-dealing car maintenance enthusiast.

These were now distributed in such a way that, wherever he was in the house, Edwin would have swift and easy access to one of them if—or, more likely, when—he was confronted by an uninvited visitor. "Much easier than carrying one around with you," said Edwin. "And also you don't tip off the crims that you've got one."

He had also splashed out on three voice-activated standing lamps, and had placed one in a corner of each downstairs room with its spotlight angled at eye level and a very high intensity LED bulb installed. All Edwin had to do was say the word, quite literally, and the lights would come on, dazzling and effectively blinding anyone in the room.

Anyone except Edwin, who, probably alone in London on this intensely gloomy day, had a pair of sunglasses perched on his head, ready to don.

Other recently acquired toys included a system of alarms which wouldn't have allowed a mouse to approach without issuing a warning. One more reason to have Rainbottle off the premises. And, soon enough, Cordelia too.

As the wind howled outside, like an increasingly hysterical banshee, Cordelia spent the rest of the afternoon helping Edwin with some final preparations, notably fixing heavy-duty decorators' polythene dust sheets on the floors and walls of all the downstairs rooms. "To keep things clean and tidy," Edwin had said. He was too tactful to mention that they would be particularly handy if he had to use the shotgun.

Once the last of the rooms had been fitted with these, Cordelia said, "Shall we put some in the hallway?"

"No," said Edwin. "Then they would see them when they entered the house and that would tend to tip them off that something was up. We want the crims to get right inside before they realise they've walked into a trap. Or, rather, the crim, singular." Edwin reasoned that due to the extraordinary size of the Bruiser who'd been snooping around their place, he was likely to be working solo.

"I can't imagine someone like that needing, or wanting, a partner."

Cordelia agreed with this logic, but Edwin was prepared for pretty much any eventuality, including a matching set of multiple Bruisers.

Outside, the wild wind now began to partner with wild rain, falling in vast sheets or whipped against the windows like waves lashing a cruiser on stormy seas. It felt cosy being indoors and there was a comfortable sense of achievement as Cordelia and Edwin ticked off the tasks on their to-do list.

Finally there was only thing left to do, and they did this as Edwin cooked them a meal, a late lunch or early dinner, with some assistance from Cordelia. While they cooked, and later dined, they recorded their conversation using an expansion microphone situated in the centre of the table and plugged into Edwin's computer.

Cordelia and Edwin played up a bit for the microphone, chatting with rather more animation and laughing more frequently than was entirely natural. At least, at first. But somehow this role-playing got them in the mood, and they soon found themselves laughing a lot and chatting happily and animatedly in an entirely natural way. By the time they finished eating and washed their plates, they had nearly fifty minutes of recording. More than enough. When it was played back on a loop, no one, even the most perceptive and alert of listeners, would realise that Cordelia and Edwin were repeating themselves after almost an hour of material.

Not least because no one was likely to eavesdrop for that long before taking action.

Cordelia and Edwin listened to the recording as he played it back through the speakers on his hi-fi system. It sounded very convincing. Anyone listening would think the two of them were having a right old party.

When, in fact, Cordelia would be nowhere in the vicinity. Only Edwin would be present and, although he might be in a party mood, it wouldn't be the sort of fiesta any intruder might have in mind. Or would welcome.

Finally, the moment arrived for Cordelia to take her leave.

She had planned to spend the night at Tinkler's, but Edwin had counselled her to go somewhere she'd never been before. "If you've never been there before, they can't guess that you'll go there again," he said, with immaculate logic.

So, Cordelia had prevailed on Monika Dunkley. She'd invented an excuse about her room being decorated and having to clear out for the night, and had asked if she could crash at the flat, the lovely big flat in Riverview Gardens which Monika shared with her friend and employer, Dylis. Monika had checked with Dylis and said this was fine. Monika was obviously quite excited about the prospect of a sleepover, no doubt with visions of pyjama party hijinks and possibly pillow fights dancing in her drink-addled brain. She'd also lined up a series of movies for the three of them to watch together, all Halloween-appropriate.

Cordelia hadn't tried to dissuade her from this madcap scheme, but she had made it clear that she didn't want to be a nuisance and was more than happy to sleep on the floor. Monika had replied that there was a spare room and spare bed and that she would be very welcome. Indeed, tonight would be trick-or-treat time, and she and Dylis would be happy of the additional help dishing out sweets to the legion of local youngsters they envisaged knocking on their door in fancy dress.

Cordelia thought this was an optimistic assessment of the situation, given the prevailing weather conditions.

Outside, the rain had now hardened and transformed into a simmering bombardment of hail which rattled against the windows and began to set off car alarms in the street.

"Filthy weather," said Edwin. As if the car alarms weren't enough, the wind had now commenced howling like an express train. An express train that was passing, but never quite passed. Eventually the hail abated and was replaced by nothing more inclement than monsoon-level rain, and Cordelia and Edwin decided it was time for her to make a move.

She put on a hooded Rohan jacket loaned her by Edwin that was rather too large but nonetheless very welcome and, it would turn out, impressively waterproof. On top of this she strapped her small rucksack with her overnight things in it. A heavy sweater, a pair of wet weather jeans (allegedly quick drying) and her most sensible footwear (the hiking boots from the Putney heist) completed Cordelia's outfit.

She and Edwin stood in the hallway, in the faint pearly rain light coming in through the glass panels in the front door, and looked at each other.

"Well…" said Edwin. Cordelia, for her part, said nothing, and he in turn fell silent. For the first time that day—in fact since the shotgun thug had invaded their home—they were at a loss for words.

Cordelia gave him a quick impulsive hug and he patted her reassuringly on the back.

"I will be pretty much incommunicado until tomorrow," he said. "I'd suggest that you can come home any time from, say, noon onwards. I will put out some kind of signal to indicate that it's safe to return. What shall I do? Let's see… I shall hang Rainbottle's lead on the handle of the front door, so when you see that you'll know it's safe to come in."

Cordelia wished him luck and told him to take care, and Edwin said he would, but she could see his mind was already elsewhere. So she said a quick goodbye and went out the front door, trying not to hear the sound of it closing behind her as possessing an odd and emphatic finality.

But having to face the frenzied wind and frenetic rain instantly obliterated any gloomy thoughts she might be entertaining. It really was dark out here, and it took a moment for her eyes to adapt sufficiently for her to see her way.

Cordelia went out the front gate into the street, where the only light came from the headlights of passing vehicles sweeping through the deepening water flowing in the road. It seemed the streetlamps around here were on a timer rather than optically activated, because they hadn't come on yet despite the day being as black as night.

It hardly mattered. Cordelia could certainly see well enough to make her way. She turned away from the river and set off. She would walk through the village to the Red Lion on Castelnau, where she might catch a bus to take her as far as the bridge, where one of the side streets led to the palatial flat in which Monika and Dylis lived. Cordelia was quite looking forward to seeing the place.

It wouldn't be a problem if she couldn't get a bus. It was only a ten-minute or so walk from the Red Lion. But she was hoping she wouldn't have to walk it; she had to square her shoulders and lean into the wind to make progress as she trudged along now. And when the wind changed direction, it spat rain right into her face with such ferocity that she had to close her eyes.

For the most part, though, the good old hood on the good old jacket that good old Edwin had loaned her was shielding her head from the worst of the weather, while providing a constant audio accompaniment which was the miniature equivalent of rain drumming on the roof, as rain drummed on her hood. She splashed through puddles, heading for the Sun Inn and the duck pond.

Cordelia was just thinking that this was a good day to be a waterfowl when the wind changed direction again, sending an onslaught of rain directly into her face. She closed her eyes but, rather foolishly, kept walking. Especially foolishly given that she had just begun to cross the road at this notoriously complicated intersection.

The intersection where Agatha had nearly run her over on that memorable occasion in her silver sports car.

And indeed, Cordelia was very nearly run over this time, too. Glaring headlights suddenly slashed across her, accompanied by the dramatic sounds of a car slewing to a sloshing halt. Just in the nick of time.

It would have been a remarkable coincidence if this had turned out to be Agatha in her silver car. But it wasn't.

This was a remarkable coincidence, too, though.

But a rather less welcome one.

Cordelia turned to see Colin Cutterham's little green sports car, not a Jaguar but an MGA 1500 featuring twin camshafts, disc brakes and a low compression engine. And with its fabric roof deployed for once in deference to this end-of-the-world weather.

Colin Cutterham stared out at her. The hood on Cordelia's coat meant that he hadn't recognised her at first. But now, judging by the expression on his face, he had rectified that omission.

30: AL FRESCO

Colin Cutterham opened the door of his car and started to get out, very clearly not in the spirit of wishing to offer Cordelia assistance or a warm greeting. He quickly abandoned this enterprise, though, both because of the ferocity of the rain hammering down on him (he was only dressed in jeans and T-shirt and his Harrington jacket) and because Cordelia nimbly scampered across the road with great speed, swiftly and decisively moving out of his reach.

Cutterham got back in his car—soaked to the bone, Cordelia hoped—and started the engine again, and pulled around in a precipitous and perilous U-turn that caused a 209 bus to lunge to a sudden and violent stop, its driver leaning blaringly on his horn in affronted rage. But Cutterham kept coming.

Cordelia was now on the village green by the duck pond. And there was very little Cutterham could do to get at her unless he proposed to drive off the road and across the pavement and through the railings at the edge of the pond. He didn't do that. Instead, he shot down Station Road, which paralleled the pond, and came to an abrupt halt about fifty metres from Cordelia, just past the GP surgery.

She could see him sitting in his car, speaking on his phone.

Cordelia wanted to start speaking on her own phone. To let Edwin know what had happened. In fact, to warn him that she was coming back to the house. That seemed like the most sensible thing to do now. Or maybe Edwin should come and meet her and escort her back. In any case, Edwin would know what to do.

Cutterham's car wasn't moving and he was still on his phone. The rain was pouring down, splashing into the pond and pebbling its surface while the baneful wind tore through the trees around the green, shaking them frenziedly. Cordelia didn't feel like standing here and making a call. Not least because her phone was secreted in her rucksack, wrapped in a towel to protect it from the blitzkrieg of this weather.

The smart thing to do was to get inside, inside somewhere with a lot of other people, where neither Cutterham nor any minion of his would be able to make a move against her.

Luckily there were at least two suitable places of refuge close at hand: the arts centre and the restaurant which abutted it. Cordelia opted for the restaurant, which was glowing with cheerful light inside its glass walls, and visibly full of customers.

Going in there would involve moving in the general direction of Cutterham, but she was confident that she could get safely inside the restaurant before he could do anything to her, or even get near her. Cordelia wandered casually around the perimeter of the duck pond so that her direction of travel wasn't immediately evident, and then quickly doubled back, making a beeline at top speed for the restaurant.

She need not have bothered with this elaborate manoeuvre because, as she watched, Cutterham stopped talking on the phone and pulled away, his car disappearing down Station Road. Cordelia came to a halt when she saw this and she stood hesitating for a moment, blasted by the wind and rain, fully expecting another U-turn from Cutterham and for the small green sports car to come roaring back.

It didn't.

So, Cordelia wiped the rain from her eyes and started for the restaurant at a leisurely and civilised pace. It really looked like Cutterham wasn't coming back, at least any time soon. Which was a tremendous relief.

Or at least it would have been, if Cordelia wasn't convinced that she'd seen a broad smile on his face before he'd disappeared.

She had almost reached the restaurant, all glass and light and promise of warmth and human companionship, when the door open and the Bruiser stepped out.

He wasn't wearing his floral baseball cap but he was wearing his denim coat with the sheepskin trim, not that there would have been any chance of mistaking him, given his size and bulk. In any case, he now took out his baseball cap and put it on, as if to prove a point. Although more likely to protect his head against the rain, which was driving down with renewed ferocity. As soon as he'd put the cap on, he put his hand back in his pocket and took out his phone. He spoke into it, staring all the while directly at Cordelia, who was now hastily backing away.

She had little doubt to whom he was speaking.

How unfortunate that the Bruiser had been eating in this particular restaurant, though it made sense given its proximity to Edwin's house, which he'd no doubt planned to visit later this evening. Cordelia deeply regretted interrupting his dining experience. In the hand that wasn't holding the phone, he was still clutching a hamburger. Now he put his phone away and began gnawing at the burger as he started towards Cordelia at a leisurely pace. He didn't look especially pleased about having to continue his meal al fresco, though.

Cordelia turned and ran, glimpsing as she did so the Bruiser throwing aside his burger—no respect for the local anti-litter ordinances—and his big legs pumping as he began running after her.

It was quite unfair that such a big man could run so fast.

Cordelia had a decent head start, but he began to eliminate that and efficiently reduce the distance between them almost immediately. Cordelia was running across the village green diagonally, heading back for the main road and assorted outposts of civilisation where she might take refuge. The sodden grass sploshed water under the impact of her dashing feet while the rain continued coming down in torrents and the ceaseless fury of the wind made it impossible to, for example, scream for help if she'd wanted to.

As Cordelia reached the edge of the green at the corner with Nassau Road, she chanced a backward glance and was struck with horror at how close the Bruiser now was. She turned back to the road and resumed running towards it with everything she had. She was running faster than she ever had in her life, and had just reached the road when a vehicle swept past through the gloom and the spray. A dirty Land Rover which looked oddly familiar. Two figures sitting in it looked even more familiar. They were massive men, each at least as large as the Bruiser, but with the added distinctive feature of bizarre beards, one tiger-striped, the other leopard-spotted. Her brain, frozen with terror, failed for a moment to process who they were.

Then she spotted her brother in the back seat of the Land Rover, hunched over a games console.

It was Stinky and his bodyguards. His massive, Swedish, special-forces-trained bodyguards. What were they doing here? It didn't matter. Salvation was at hand. If she could just catch up with them.

Cordelia hit the pavement and went pelting after the Land Rover. It was pulling away ahead of her in the gloom and the rain, but she was praying that it would have to stop for the traffic lights at the junction with the main road. Even if it was only held there for a few seconds, she stood a good chance of catching up with it. And then she would be inside the vehicle, safe and dry in the company of her brother and his coordinated pair of gigantic combat-ready bodyguards (well, two out of three wasn't bad).

Cordelia's lungs were now on fire and her heart was hammering so fast that its beating threatened to transform into one continual explosion. But she was running even faster, the wind at her back now and propelling her along at still greater speed, puddles slashed apart by her flying footsteps.

And the Land Rover was back in sight.

She was closing the gap with it as it slowed down…

And it did better than stop at the traffic lights.

It pulled up in front of Sadie's, and Cordelia saw Stinky and the two Röds get out and go into the restaurant.

Not only was salvation now at hand, she could have dinner at her favourite restaurant.

If she was ever able to eat anything again. Her stomach was just a cold cramped knot of viscera, and with good reason. The Bruiser was pounding along the pavement behind her, looming up on her like a lorry on a cyclist.

Cordelia was almost at Sadie's when she heard his feet splashing into puddles so close behind her that she actually felt the spray of water from them. Knowing he was only an arm's length away from her, Cordelia flung herself into the road, into the headlight beams of a fast-moving stream of traffic. Scream of brakes, enraged squawks of horns, but she was on the other side of the road and the traffic had resumed flowing at even greater speed towards the traffic lights, now thankfully green, and therefore keeping the Bruiser at bay on the far side.

Cordelia had been forced to run *away* from Sadie's, to the opposite side of the road. But at least she was safe. For a moment. Behind her there was a small parade of businesses. A charity shop that was closed for the day, a dry cleaners that was closed for the day, and an off licence that was not yet open. No refuge here. She could run to her left, towards Castelnau, but this would take her past a kitchen appliance shop, very much closed, and a bank, ditto. And every step in that direction led her further away from Sadie's and Stinky and his security detail.

The other direction, to her right, was more promising—a cinema and a café. Cordelia started towards it, only to find that she was cut off by the Bruiser, who had managed to get through the traffic and across the road and was now standing on the pavement on this side just ahead of her.

But…

But that meant the other side of the road was clear again. She could cross back and go into Sadie's and join Stinky and Röd and Röd, and the Bruiser could go fuck himself. Cordelia flung herself back into the road, now mercifully free of traffic, just as the door of Sadie's opened and Stinky and the two Röds came out, carrying bags of Sadie's takeaway.

She screamed at them as they climbed back into the Land Rover but they didn't hear her.

She ran across the road just as the Land Rover pulled away, sending a spray of dirty water into her face as she chased it, but they didn't see her.

The Land Rover reached the main road, moving fast, and turned south, disappearing from sight.

Cordelia heard big feet splashing through puddles, coming towards her, closing on her quickly.

31: THE EYES OF ST DROGO

As the Bruiser ran to this side of the road, Cordelia hastily cut back across to the other side. But the usefulness of this manoeuvre seemed to be at an end. With no helpful swiftly moving string of cars to hold him back, the Bruiser was instantly running after her again, across the road. Or rather, running *in* the road, the now empty, windswept, rain-lashed, flooding road, running in the middle of it, ankle deep in water, at a gradual angle bringing him towards her.

The point about this strategy was that if Cordelia tried crossing the road again herself, it would bring her closer to him.

And she was already too close. Far too close.

Cordelia realised that she'd made the fatal mistake—hopefully only *potentially* fatal—of fleeing past the café and cinema instead of directly to them. Again, any attempt to head in their direction now would bring her back nearer to the Bruiser.

And she was already too near. Much too near.

With the Bruiser in close pursuit, Cordelia was running, but she was also running out of options. The next strip of shops was close at hand, yet too far away—the Bruiser would catch her easily before she got to them. She had to seek sanctuary somewhere *now*. And her choices were a residential street running off the main road—she could get to someone's house and ring on someone's doorbell and beg them to let her in and/or immediately call the police. But she would have to get lucky on her first attempt, both in terms of finding a householder who was at home and one who was amenable, because she wouldn't get a second chance—or…

The only option besides the residential street was the churchyard.

Good old St Drogo's.

Cordelia made a split-second decision, veered towards the low brick wall on her right, jumped over it, and was in the churchyard, her boots biting deep into the muddy grass, rain pounding on her back as she resumed running. There were small spotlights in the churchyard illuminating the gravestones and flower beds and long flailing strands of black and yellow hazard warning tape which had been fastened somewhere but were now blowing loose in the ferocious wind of the storm, whipping and waving savagely, accompanied by their savagely whipping and waving shadows like the tentacles of some science-fiction beast.

A furiously lashing length of the tape slapped Cordelia in the face as she ran towards the church. But that was the least of her problems. Would the church be open? Surely churches were required to always be open, in case some poor soul needed sanctuary? Surely there would be some kind of church function afoot? Lots of lovely churchgoers and church officials in attendance. Even old Vulture Face. Cordelia would be enormously grateful to see old Vulture Face now. She would kiss her. She would kiss her *feet*. Surely the church would be chock-full of people? After all, it was Halloween, admittedly a pagan festivity, but still…

Cordelia, splashing pell-mell through puddles in a graveyard in a howling gale with a science-fiction monster's tentacles writhing around her, experienced a sudden crisis of faith. (Well, this was the place for it. Not to mention the time.)

The crisis was which door to run towards…

Which door to have faith in being unlocked…

Previously, when sneaking in and out of the church, Cordelia had used an unlocked and unguarded door around the rear. But instead of heading for that, right around the other side of the church, she was currently running hell for leather for the main entrance.

Which was nearer.

And which would be open, surely?

The problem was, if it wasn't…

No second chances.

There wouldn't be time to get around to the back of the church. Not if the Bruiser was following her into the churchyard. Cordelia didn't waste any time looking over her shoulder to check if this was the case. Of course, there was always the possibility that, like a vampire in certain schools of vampire fiction, the Bruiser couldn't operate on hallowed ground—but it wasn't much of a possibility and definitely not one Cordelia was going to stake her life on.

She reached the entrance of the church, a sheltered alcove with mosaic murals on either side and a pair of tall glass doors, each with a horizontal chrome bar in the centre and a long, elegant art deco cross engraved above. Cordelia hit one of the doors, arm extended, moving at full tilt, expecting it to fly open at her touch.

It didn't fly open at her touch.

Instead, she bounced back off it having very nearly broken her wrist.

Cordelia recovered her balance, not quite falling flat on her back in the pouring rain. Well, that fucker was locked, all right. And, in a spirit more of forlorn hope than robust confidence, she darted out of the rain back into the alcove and tried the other door.

It was unlocked, it swung open at her touch.

And Cordelia was inside the church, running through the shadowy entrance hall, past a notice board with coming events on it, no paperback sale listed yet, her boots slapping wetly on the polished wooden floor, footsteps echoing loudly as she dashed towards the big main hall where, a million years ago, she had once attended a previous paperback sale.

Into the main hall she went. The shadowy main hall.

Shadowy because no lights were on. Or rather, only a few modest security lights. Because there was no one here. There was no church function taking place. There was no Halloween service, no black mass or orgy. Sadly. The place was deserted. Cordelia was all alone in the big open hall with just a few dim electric lights and the dimmer grey storm-shrouded daylight coming in through the giant monochrome stained-glass window, the giant *sainted* glass window, rearing up several storeys tall behind her.

St Drogo and his fabulously ugly cronies gazed down at her, intermittently growing darker and then lighter as the wind, now approaching hurricane force, strengthened or eased, like an enormous beast breathing.

The huge space around Cordelia was eerily still, except for this roaring of the wind outside, the distant ceaseless rattle of the rain on the roof far above, and a strange harsh rhythmic sound, which began like a knocking and then changed to a kind of sharp high-pitched chiming—like a bell that would almost but not quite ring.

This rhythmic sound was synchronised with the brightening and darkening of the giant sainted glass window, and Cordelia, staring up at the window, realised that the cycling change in the light conditions, and the repetition of the sound, was the result of a big, shadowed mass growing closer to, and then further away from, the window.

Oh yes, the big old oak tree.

As the gusts of wind strengthened, the branches of the giant oak swayed into contact with the window, tapping at it as if to be let in. Tapping with increasing vigour and assertiveness. As Cordelia stood there, after one particularly loud and sharply ringing impact on the window, something dropped and shattered on the floor in front of her, seemingly out of nowhere.

In psychic lore, at seances and so forth, there was the term *apport* which referred to objects that appeared, or appeared to appear, out of thin air, as this one apparently had.

In a church, though, they were presumably classed as miracles.

Cordelia looked down at the thing.

Fragments of what had once been a black disc. She picked up a piece. Except at the jagged point of fracture, it was smooth and cool to the touch. And damp on one side. It neatly filled the span of her hand, cool and smooth as glass.

This realisation caused her to look up, and see that poor St Drogo was missing one of his eyes, or rather the pupil from it. There was now a hole in his pale green iris where the black disc of glass had previously been and rain was blowing in through the newly created aperture in a rather gruesome fashion.

The impact of the oak branch had knocked a hole in his eye. And that was clearly just the start. Any moment now, given the growing frenzy of the storm, the whole fucking window would go.

This realisation made Cordelia scoot hastily back. She had been standing exactly in the danger zone.

She stuck the fragment of glass in her pocket—the sharp edge of it suggested a weapon to Cordelia, though heaven help her if she ended up in close quarters combat with the Bruiser. She put the piece of glass away and forced herself to concentrate on the task at hand. Which was staying alive.

So Cordelia ran, footsteps echoing in the big empty space, to the door in the wall where once she'd snuck out of the book sale and off to an illicit rendezvous with Monika and a crate of crime paperbacks in a vestry. When she was through that door and in that warren of corridors and rooms on the other side, she would be able to find a place to hide where the Bruiser would never find her—maybe in the vestry?—and she would have time to use her phone. To call Edwin.

Of course, Cordelia recalled now that Edwin had said he would be "incommunicado" until tomorrow. Which presumably meant he wouldn't be answering the phone. Because he would be fully concentrating on preparing a welcome for the Bruiser. The Bruiser who would not be turning up now, a fact which Cordelia would be unable to notify him of if he was not answering the phone.

So perhaps she would have to swallow her pride and call the police. Which would entail a lot of explaining, but…

The door was locked.

Cordelia wrenched at it with furious futility but it didn't budge. Why the hell was it locked?

Cordelia backed away from the door, realising that she was trapped. Admittedly trapped in the big open space of the main hall of the church. Despite how big this space was—massive, actually, including the open empty shaft of air space rising towards the roof high above—Cordelia began to feel rather claustrophobic. Perhaps she shouldn't have come in here after all. Maybe she should go out again.

But what if the Bruiser was waiting for her outside?

Come to think of it, why hadn't the Bruiser followed her into the church? Perhaps there actually was something to the aversion-to-hallowed-ground theory…

This notion was instantly contradicted by a sudden flow of cold air and a sharp increase in the sound of the storm outside, both abruptly cut off as the front door of the church was closed again. And then the Bruiser came into the big hall.

He had removed his baseball cap and, perhaps out of a sense of occasion, had pulled a stocking over his face—the traditional stocking mask.

If he thought it made him look more frightening, he was right.

He saw Cordelia and he came straight towards her, not running but walking briskly. As he did so there was a loud chiming sound from the stained-glass window as the branch of the big oak tree made contact with it again and another black disc fell and shattered on the floor between Cordelia and the Bruiser. *There goes St Drogo's other pupil.*

The Bruiser didn't seem to notice. He had stopped, still a fair distance from Cordelia, and he was pulling on gloves, thin latex gloves. Whatever his reason for this, it would not be to Cordelia's benefit. She glanced up at the big window. Light was coming in through both St Drogo's eyes now, in twin sprays of rain, and then big shadows gathered across the glass as the branch bashed it again with a pealing resonance.

The whole thing was going to go any second. Which could prove a useful diversion. Even better, if the Bruiser was standing in the danger zone when it went…

Cordelia moved to one side and, as she hoped, the Bruiser moved too, matching her position to his. Excellent. Cordelia just needed to get him a little nearer the window. She kept manoeuvring and he kept adjusting his position until…

Until he *stopped*, still inconveniently far from the danger zone, too far from the danger zone, not in fact in danger at all, damn him, and reached into his coat and took out a handgun and pointed it at her. With an enormous sense of outrage, Cordelia realised that this was it. Unless she did something.

She shouted at the Bruiser, "Don't you want to know what happened to your friend?"

This seemed to give the Bruiser pause. "What friend?" At least, that's what it sounded like he said.

"The first one they sent after me," yelled Cordelia. She had to yell because, unbelievably, the wind had grown even louder outside—aided by the grotesque openings in Drogo's eyes which were *hooting* in a horrible way—and the volume of rain on the roof high above had increased, and then there was the sound of the branch colliding with the window at regular and increasingly frequent intervals, and if she could keep the Bruiser talking, even though he was out of the danger zone, the branch crashing through the window would *distract* him and give Cordelia a chance to run.

If she could keep him talking.

"Oh, him," said—or rather shouted—the Bruiser. He shrugged. "What happened?"

"I killed him," Cordelia shouted back.

This seemed to give her assassin pause. And pause was what was wanted at the moment.

"How?" he bellowed.

"With my computer," bellowed Cordelia. "I hit him in the head with my computer." Cordelia managed to get this out in a brief interval of relative quiet between the big brutal sound of the branch connecting with the window. (Surely it must give way at any second?)

So the Bruiser must have heard her.

But he just laughed. He laughed. He clearly didn't believe her. Ridiculously, Cordelia was *insulted* that he didn't believe her.

And now he lifted his gun.

Cordelia's fingers closed on something in her pocket, the slick cold fragment of glass from St Drogo's eye. A sharp-edged shard of his obsidian pupil. She pulled it out and *threw* it at the Bruiser.

He just ducked away from it easily, not even moving from where he stood, and laughed some more.

The wind outside thundered with unprecedented violence as the Bruiser took aim at Cordelia. Surely the window must give way now?

The window didn't give way.

Instead, there was a curious kind of soft toppling sound from far above them and they both looked up to see a translucent cloud descending, as St Drogo's infamously susceptible flat Bauhaus roof decisively gave way and released all the water which had gathered on it, a veritable indoor waterfall coming straight down towards the Bruiser.

Who scooted out of the way with commendable agility. But this movement took him directly under the stained-glass window.

Which didn't matter, because the window was still intact and it was all too late and the Bruiser, not a man to be easily distracted, raised his gun again and pointed it at Cordelia, who was running for the door, but the Bruiser tracked her casually, taking aim calmly and with professionalism. It would be an easy shot at this distance.

And then, what bad luck for the Bruiser, at just that moment the wind gusted again and the branch of the oak tree, a great gnarled black fist, came crashing through the glass. The Bruiser looked up in surprise, which was an unwise use of what little time was left for him. Because the colossal oak branch had splintered free of the tree. It was a vast limb as heavy as, say, a motorcycle. Or two motorcycles. And it was now in freefall.

Falling.

Falling on the Bruiser. Smiting him. Smashing him to the floor. Flattening him on the floor.

As Cordelia watched his gun went flying, landing in the water on the floor, well out of reach of his outstretched hand.

But it didn't look like he would be reaching or indeed moving any time soon, or in fact ever again. On one of the few undamaged portions of the window above, St Drogo looked down on him, bland and benign and smiling.

32: AMBER

"So I used the stocking to pick it up," said Cordelia. "I pulled the stocking off his head and I wrapped it up in it and carried it in it and brought it back here. His own stocking mask, so any DNA on it would remain his DNA."

"Very sensible," said Edwin, looking at the gun. "Why did you take it?"

"Well, I thought if they found him there with a gun on him it would suggest there was someone else there, and that there was more to the story, so to speak. But if I took it away, and also his stocking mask, then he doesn't seem like a hitman with a gun and he—"

"He just becomes some dead bloke," said Edwin.

"Right. Some dead bloke in a church."

"Tragic accident."

"Right."

"In St Drogo's."

"Right."

"Good thinking," said Edwin, examining the gun. He handled it like a man who was accustomed to handling firearms. "Plus it might come in useful."

Cordelia knew that it was called an automatic, having read Dashiell Hammett's scathing comments on the difference between

316

revolvers and automatics, and the stupidity of crime writers in frequently confusing the two kinds of gun. (Dismayingly, even John Dickson Carr, aka Carter Dickson, seemed to have made this booboo. Was it in *The Judas Window*?)

Anyway, she was familiar enough with firearms that she should have known the name of the thing that Edwin pulled back on the top of gun and examined. But she didn't. (Was it the *slide*?) But she definitely did know the name of the thing he released and removed from the handle of the gun—the magazine. Edwin examined the bullets in the magazine and then put it back inside the gun.

"Thank you," he said, looking rather happy with the weapon. "I'll put it with the others." Edwin reached out and took the stocking mask from her. "And I'll get rid of this." Cordelia handed it to him gratefully. He put it in the canister of kitchen rubbish, the one that wasn't destined for recycling, then he sat back down at the table with her again.

Since Cordelia had come home tonight, Edwin had ceased to wear his sunglasses shoved up in his hair and had put them on the kitchen table. Now he looked at them. "I suppose I'd better put these away." He sounded disappointed.

Monika was disappointed, too, when Cordelia rang to tell her she wouldn't be coming over to spend the night after all. "But I made popcorn," she said.

The only one who wasn't disappointed was Rainbottle, who was overwhelmed with excited pleasure to be back home again, after Edwin had gone to his ex-girlfriend's to collect him. Tail wagging wildly, he set about sniffing the new standing lamps which Edwin had elected to leave up, at least for the time being.

"You never know," he said. "We might have cause to use them yet."

Cordelia said goodnight to Edwin and Rainbottle and went upstairs to her room to change out of her wet things. As she did so, she found the other items she'd retained as souvenirs from her memorable evening at St Drogo's.

The fragments of the two black glass discs which had once been that eponymous holy person's pupils.

She was sure she could glue the fragments back together, and once she did she thought they'd make a rather attractive pair of drink coasters.

As it happened, they didn't have cause to use the lamps, or any of the other imaginative countermeasures they'd prepared for Halloween.

A week passed peacefully before Edwin invited her to come down for a chat in the kitchen. She was pleased to see that he'd made hot chocolate. They sipped it and Rainbottle immediately stationed himself under Cordelia's chair while they chatted.

"Over the years," said Edwin, as though embarking on a bedtime story, "I've now and then had occasion to cross paths with certain members of the local criminal fraternity. And as it happens, the other night I bumped into one of these chaps when I had dinner at Albert's."

"Albert's?" said Cordelia. "Wait, is that a gastropub?"

"Yes. They do a herbal hamburger there that is monstrously tasty. And on Monday nights these monstrously tasty herbal hamburgers are half price. Anyway, I saw this bloke that I know, and he's plugged into the local crim network, and we had a rather illuminating chat."

Cordelia forced herself out of her viciously jealous reverie— Albert the gastro pub owner was the bastard who was dating *Agatha*—and made herself pay attention. Because what Edwin was saying was important.

"For a start," he said, "it turns out that they've found the body of the shotgun thug."

"The body that you disposed of?"

"The body that I *thought* I'd disposed of," said Edwin, with a measure of chagrin. "It seems, despite the fact that I searched him carefully and took his phone and other belongings, he must have had some other kind of device on him. They can make them so small these days, that's the trouble." Edwin sounded genuinely put out. If he was going to have to take account of such things, the body disposal business had just become that bit more arduous.

"Anyway, he had some kind of GPS device on him and so they could trace him."

Cordelia found this disturbing. She had genuinely and comfortably come to think of the dead shotgun thug, and indeed the whole matter, as disposed of. Into oblivion. Once and for all. "So they found him?"

"Yes, and then they had the body examined. Properly examined. By a forensic pathologist, a bent one, who works for the crims." Edwin looked at her. There was amusement in his eyes. Highly inappropriate amusement, but there you go. "And they couldn't work out what the murder weapon was."

Murder weapon. The phrase sent a thrill through Cordelia. It wasn't an entirely welcome thrill.

"When I gave them a description of your computer..."

"*You did what?*"

"Calm down and hear me out," said Edwin. Rainbottle whined beneath Cordelia's chair, as if encouraging her to hear his master out. "I described your computer to them, and they checked a similar one against the wounds and, lo and behold, perfect match. Incidentally, they were quite impressed when they heard that your computer's still working. Everyone was quite impressed by that."

"Edwin, why did you tell them—"

"Because," Edwin interrupted her, but interrupted her patiently, "they knew that this chap had been sent to dispatch you and had turned up dead. So obviously someone had dealt with him. And they were going to know that either it was you yourself, or someone associated with you. And much better that they know it was you. Because Colin Cutterham was already in trouble in the crim community for putting out a hit on you just because of a few stupid books, arranging to kill a mere slip of a girl—I am describing this from the sexist old-school crim point of view, you understand—a mere slip of a girl who nevertheless managed in self-defence to pluckily kill the hitman with her girly computer. So, massive black marks against Cutterham in the crim community at this point. But does he back off? No, he doubles down and sends *another* hitman after you, who also ends up dead, this time by an act of god, but nevertheless he got killed while pursuing Cutterham's foolish and reckless errand. Now, the code of the crims means Cutterham has a financial obligation to the surviving family and dependants of these men he got killed. He will have to make a substantial cash settlement. On top of that, he is in very bad odour with his senior crim associates for having created this mess in the first place. All over a few silly books."

Cordelia didn't bother pointing out that there were more than a few books, and that there was nothing silly about them.

"Anyway," said Edwin, "we're lucky the crims realise where the blame lies in this matter. By which I mean with Cutterham. Who is now under immense pressure, I would say irresistible pressure, to drop the matter and let bygones be bygones."

"Let bygones be bygones?" said Cordelia.

"Yes, forgive and forget."

"And you think that is what is going to happen? That Colin Cutterham is going to forgive and forget?"

"Not for a moment. I'd say we've made an enemy for life in Cutterham." Cordelia was deeply grateful that he said *we*.

And then Edwin yawned. He actually yawned. "But I'd put the threat level at the moment at no more than amber."

"Amber?"

"If that."

33: THE DEVIL'S LIQUORICE

Autumn deepened into winter and then winter thawed into spring, the seasons passing uneventfully—at least uneventfully in the sense of there being no sign of a psychotic gangster seeking revenge.

Other things happened. Certain other things happened. Certain other things certainly happened.

On one raw, wet and blowy December night, with the wind and rain putting Cordelia, cosy in her attic room, in mind of that Halloween, although this was small beer by comparison, Edwin announced, via a text (or an "EMS message" as he tediously and tautologously insisted on referring to it) that she had a visitor. Since Edwin would already have closely vetted this visitor—he'd never taken down the surveillance cameras he'd installed—Cordelia said to send them straight up to her room.

The worst-case scenario was that it would be her brother.

But it wasn't Stinky.

Instead, it was a bedraggled but breath-taking beauty called Araminta Hodge. Araminta had a sort of pre-Raphaelite thing going on (flawless milky complexion, very long, very curly auburn hair). She was soaked to the skin and very upset. And a total stranger to Cordelia, who nevertheless immediately invited her in. Who wouldn't?

It transpired that this ludicrously lovely rain-soaked young maiden was one of Stinky's mistresses. More specifically, one of his discarded mistresses. Stinky was ghosting her and she was heartbroken. She'd found Cordelia's address and, knowing she was Stinky's sister, had come here in desperation, hoping Cordelia could help her find the little shit.

Cordelia gave Araminta a towel, made her a coffee, told her that she had no idea where the little shit might be, but said she would nevertheless try calling him. Of course, Cordelia's call proved futile, going straight to voicemail. Stinky was pretty much impossible to contact unless he was in the market for drugs.

Cordelia put her phone away. Then she read Araminta the riot act, making it absolutely clear just what a reprehensible creep Stinky was, and how unworthy of her he was, with special reference to the fact that he was always treating women like this. Women whom, in a just world, he shouldn't have been able to get within miles of.

Araminta nodded through all this, agreeing vociferously. But vociferous agreement didn't stop her from bursting into tears as soon as Cordelia stopped talking. Cordelia gave her a shoulder to cry on, helped her dry her eyes, then offered her some contraband green butter on toast, explaining carefully what it was. Araminta had enthusiastically wolfed it down.

Then they'd put on some music and talked for hours and hours.

Soon it was very late and Cordelia offered her guest her bed to spend the night, Cordelia herself saying (truthfully) that she would sleep in the armchair. But Araminta had insisted that she do no such thing, so they'd climbed into bed together, intertwined, enjoying the drugs and music and the warmth of each other and Cordelia breathing in the intoxicating scent of Araminta's still-damp hair.

And one thing led to another…

So, starting with an achingly beautiful interval that lasted most of the night, soundtracked by Arlo Parks on repeat, the two young women embarked on a scorching affair intensified for Cordelia by the knowledge that she'd decisively deprived her brother of one of his acolytes.

Tinkler's eyes had bugged out when he learned of the affair but, mercifully, he didn't make the obvious (for him) request, because Cordelia had already put him firmly in the friend zone.

Cordelia's relationship with Araminta prevailed for several weeks and then even made it to the several *months* stage before it ran out of steam. As Cole Porter might have said, but didn't, even the hottest affairs were ultimately subject to the laws of entropy.

And so the two of them drifted apart, although Cordelia insisted on ringing Araminta up at regular intervals for a friendly chat, which Araminta found rather moving. She might not have found it quite so moving if she'd known that Cordelia was mostly checking to make sure that she didn't go back to Stinky.

The attic room seemed a bit empty without Araminta bouncing around in various states of undress but, truth to tell, Cordelia was rather glad to have her own space back.

The breath-taking pre-Raphaelite Araminta had not been entirely without annoying habits. Also, her tawny silken hair, so beguiling when tousled and tumbled in passion, was rather less appealing when you kept on finding long glossy strands of it everywhere, for instance in your hairbrush and even, on one particularly deplorable occasion, in the *butter*.

Meanwhile, Cordelia found that she'd come to terms with her feelings about Agatha. That passion, once so incendiary, had now effectively burned itself out. Indeed, it had begun to end as soon as Cordelia realised that she wouldn't part with her copy of *Kiss Me Deadly* for this woman, supposedly her immortal beloved.

And when she had obtained a duplicate copy, she'd given her the *inferior one*.

At that point, the fever had broken, so to speak.

So, Cordelia took the photo of Agatha in its circular silver frame which resided on her bedside table (interestingly, Araminta had never remarked on it; in many ways she wasn't a very observant or perceptive girl) and she opened the frame and took out the photo of Agatha.

Cordelia set it aside and picked up the carefully trimmed photo of herself and Rainbottle, snapped by Edwin. It was a genuinely great photo and it cheered her up every time she looked at it.

She slotted it into the frame and began to seal it back up. Then, on impulse, she picked up the photo of Agatha and slotted it back into the frame too, tucked away behind the other image. It wouldn't do any harm to have it hidden in there, and who knows, she might find it one day, maybe when she was an old bat, and smile nostalgically.

So there they were, if you thought about it, all snuggled up in the frame together, her and Rainbottle and Agatha.

She hoped Agatha liked dogs.

Paperbacks had been conceived as a disposable medium. The idea was that people would buy them, read them, and throw them away. Indeed, that was the way some people treated them—the first thing they did was open them so ruthlessly that they broke the spine of the poor little book.

But Cordelia could read a paperback and leave it looking like it had never been touched.

Which was what she was doing now.

She was sitting in the café at Sadie's on a sunny but thunderous Friday in April with daffodils springing up all over the village green. Cordelia was holding a copy of *Cold Angel, Dead Angel* with great and scrupulous care and reading the damned thing. She couldn't quite believe that she was reading it. But it was her last copy and she'd now sold it to a buyer online, and she was going to post it off this weekend or at least no later than Monday.

She wasn't likely to have another copy of this book any time soon, because there was no way she was going to buy it at the sort of prices it was currently commanding. And there was no way she was going to *keep* it when she could sell it for the sort of prices it was currently commanding.

Cordelia felt she somehow owed it to the book's poor dead author, who had so enriched her—inadvertently, true, but nonetheless enriched her considerably through her sales of his book—to read the damned thing. And if she was ever going to read it, it had to be now.

It wasn't easy going, though. It was the sort of novel in which there was a tendency for things to take place on "a bleak ebony winter's night"—an infuriatingly repetitive tendency. But within its pages, its many pages, of relentlessly dogged and undistinguished prose, the repetitive tendency for ebony winter night bleakness was as nothing compared to the word-for-word repetition of a description of an eddy of snow as a "forlorn little dancer in the dark" as it spun around in the wind. The first time she'd read it, Cordelia wanted to vomit. The *second* time this immortal piece of prose cropped up she felt a very real inclination to kill the author.

But, of course, someone had beaten her to it.

Cordelia sighed and set the book down on the table and sipped her coffee.

As she did so, she realised that someone was standing beside her table.

She turned to see—

Agatha.

Agatha was standing there. Smiling at her. "Sorry," said Agatha. "But we couldn't help noticing what you were reading."

We? Cordelia's consciousness expanded to take in the fact that the black-haired, blue-eyed bombshell and, yes, the Vinyl Detective were standing there with Agatha. They'd evidently just dined in the restaurant part of Sadie's, and were on their way out past the café and had spotted her.

"What do you think?" said Agatha, indicating the book.

"Not great," said Cordelia. And Agatha chuckled, and so did her friends. Cordelia had clearly said exactly the right thing.

"But you are," said Cordelia. "You *are* great." And she stood up and took Agatha's hand…

No, none of that happened. Or at least, it only happened in Cordelia's head.

She just sat there while Agatha said, "Not great. A very apt description. Well, nice talking to you." And then smiled again at Cordelia as she and her friends walked out the door and were gone.

A very apt description.

Nice talking to you.

Cordelia paid the bill, as always leaving a tip for her waitress, then packed the book back in her rucksack, packed it carefully because, rubbish though it might be, it was a valuable commodity. Then she took out the little art deco enamel ladybird pill box which she'd recently acquired and opened it and, making sure no one was looking, surreptitiously licked the hash oil, also recently acquired, out of it.

The oily evil taste squirmed on her tongue, as bitter as sin, the devil's liquorice.

Mrs Chichester had really come through with this stuff. Soon her head would be going off like a box of fireworks. First, though, a leisurely walk home past St Drogo's, now well under reconstruction, with the church notice board outside announcing a grand sale of paperbacks (Vulture Face had been vanquished finally) and then across the village green and past the duck pond.

She sent Edwin a text asking him to put the hot water on.

The hash oil should be hitting just about the time the bathwater was thundering out of the taps and into the tub.

Early bath.

ACKNOWLEDGEMENTS

Special thanks to Richard Creasey for allowing me to invent *Lady Burglar* by John Creasey and thereby take his dad's name in vain, adding another title to his six hundred or so real novels. Big thanks to Ann Karas for reading early drafts of the manuscript and offering invaluable advice. And to Sarah Docker for developing concepts for the cover art.

As ever, thanks to my agents Stevie Finegan and John Berlyne, my editors George Sandison and Daniel Carpenter, and to Nick Landau and Vivian Cheung at Titan.

To Ben Aaronovitch, whose continuing support has allowed me to pursue my mad career as a writer.

To Scott Cochrane, for sous vide advice.

And to Hollie Stephenson, whose magnificent self-titled debut album provided the soundtrack for writing most of this book.

ABOUT THE AUTHOR

Andrew Cartmel is a novelist and playwright. He is the author of the bestselling Vinyl Detective series, which operates in the same fictional world as the Paperback Sleuth. He began his career with a legendary stint as script editor on the television series *Doctor Who* (the "Cartmel Masterplan"), has written graphic novels and audio dramas and toured as a stand-up comedian. His plays performed on the London Fringe include *Under the Eagle*, *Glacier Lake*, and *As Real as Anything*. He lives in London with far too many vintage paperbacks, but luckily no eccentric landlord. You can find Andrew on Twitter at @andrewcartmel and listen to his weekly radio show Vinyl Detective Radio online on Reclaimed Radio or Medway Pride.

For more fantastic fiction, author events,
exclusive excerpts, competitions, limited editions and more

VISIT OUR WEBSITE
titanbooks.com

LIKE US ON FACEBOOK
facebook.com/titanbooks

FOLLOW US ON TWITTER AND INSTAGRAM
@TitanBooks

EMAIL US
readerfeedback@titanemail.com